"Just shut up," insisted Willy. "I fire the missile, the missile locks on to the wooden spoon, here it comes" — — n unerring missile — — — — — ur — "it's two hu— — — — —d, fifty, and the— — — — — harply veered a— — —

"It mis— — — — — — —y time? You're trying to te— — — — the U.S. Air Force is equipped with missiles that *miss*? But surely they've *tested* these missiles?" Daniel protested.

"Oh, sure," Willy agreed. "And they still work now, when they're tested on the Air Force ranges. But what you have to realize is that we never test them against real Soviet airplanes. We usually use a PQM-102 RPV, which is a pilotless Delta Dagger. Now, each airplane has a different and distinct radar signature. And although our radar is obviously happy to lock onto the signature of a Delta Dagger, or any other U.S. target plane, it seems to have a widespread aversion to Soviet signatures."

"But it's *insane*," said Daniel. "How can a whole Air Force be equipped with missiles that don't work?"

"What can I say?" asked Willy, blowing flour off the table. "It's the greatest scandal in the history of the Air Force. And I mean the greatest. Heads will start rolling, believe me."

Look for these other TOR books by Graham Masterton

IKON

GRAHAM MASTERTON

TOR

A TOM DOHERTY ASSOCIATES BOOK

IKON

Copyright © 1983 by Graham Masterton

A TOR Book

Published by Tom Doherty Associates,
8-10 West 36 Street,
New York, N.Y. 10018

First TOR printing: September 1984

ISBN: 0-812-52191-9
CAN. ED.: 0-812-52192-7

Printed in the United States of America

"RINC (usually pronounced 'rink') is the acronym coined by the Joint Chiefs of Staff for the current talks between the United States and the Union of Soviet Socialist Republics aimed at an eventual mutual Reduction In Nuclear Capability."

—Joint Services Review,
No. XVII, 1981.

"We instructed our officers to dismantle (the weapons) and return them to the Soviet Union."

—Nikita Khruschev,
October, 1962.

"Others were as physically beautiful as she was, but there was obviously something more in her—a combination of wistfulness, radiance, yearning—that set her apart."

—Lee Strasberg,
1962.

ONE

He had been searching for her for so long, twenty empty and irritating years, that when at last he caught sight of her sitting in the darkness of the cocktail lounge of the Arizona Biltmore Hotel, her freckled hands cupped around a large Mimosa, he choked on his lunch, and had to walk quickly across to the men's room to spit it out, half-digested club sandwich, and stand there staring at himself in the mirror over the washbasin in both triumph and jangling alarm.

Jesus, I've found her. After all these years, I've actually found her. Jesus. But, looking down at his hands on the rim of the washbasin, hands that were twenty years older than the day he had first started trying to find her, he suddenly thought to himself: I hope it isn't her. I hope I'm hallucinating. If it's her, I'm going to have to kill her. They want me, quite literally, to bring back her head.

And apart from that, what am I going to do now, for the rest of my life? Who's going to employ a man who has done nothing for twenty years but cross and re-cross America, from rainy days in Philadelphia to snowbound Januaries in Oregon, looking for one woman?

He came out of the men's room and the door squeaked loudly behind him. She was still sitting there, alone, in one of the bulky

1920s sofas, under the tinkling art-deco chandeliers. The Arizona Biltmore had been designed in the mid-1920s by Frank Lloyd Wright, outrageously modern, a Jazz Age resort for America's rich and notorious, with pre-cast concrete bungalows in floral gardens, dining rooms with deco fountains and combed-plaster ceilings, handmade carpets in geometric motifs. And here she was, amidst all this decadent splendor—fat, as he had imagined she must be, at least 185 pounds, in a pleated lilac tent-dress, with skin as pale as milk. Her hair was gingery brown, with streaks of gray, drawn back tightly away from her face and fastened with combs. It would have been a better disguise if she had stayed platinum blonde, he thought, or dyed her hair henna red. But he had always believed that she would be brunette when he found her, and so she was.

There were no obvious signs of plastic surgery. To anyone except a man who had spent twenty years of his life studying photographs and sketches and clay simulations of her face and head from every possible angle, in every kind of light, the fat would have made surgery unnecessary. Her eyes were puffed into Mongoloid slits, and she had developed a deep double chin. She had probably believed that as soon as she reverted to her plain unglamorous self, the self she had been born with, she would be safe. Unknown, unwanted—an ugly-duckling orphan whom nobody wanted to adopt. Her lack of deviousness had betrayed her all her life. Now it had betrayed her again.

He sat down opposite her, quite close, crossing one perma-pressed leg over the other, and lit a cigarette, and watched her. If she was conscious of being watched, she didn't show it. She sipped her Mimosa, and fiddled with the single gold band on her wedding finger, and occasionally glanced towards the sliding doors which led out to the lawns and the bungalows and the brilliant afternoon sunshine; and once she smiled at a three-year-old blond-haired English boy who ran past her calling for his mommy. The sad, indulgent smile that any fifty-six-year-old woman would have given, childless after three marriages, and precluded from marrying again because she was a fugitive from vengeances far more terrible than justice.

The cocktail waitress had just come on duty. She came over and asked him what he wanted. He thought about it, and then said, "A Bud, and some nuts," mainly because it seemed appropriate to order beer on an occasion like this, a kind of dated, baseball-park drink. Maybe it was a nod to Joe DiMaggio. He wondered how she had coped with that—knowing that Joe DiMaggio had so regularly laid roses on that grave in Westwood. He rubbed his eyes, and smoked, and the past twenty years came silently crowding into the cocktail lounge like a party of unwelcome ghosts.

His name was Henry Friend, and he had started to look for her two weeks and two days after his thirty-eighth birthday. He was now fifty-eight, two years older than she was, a tall, crumpled, offhand man with eyes that were screwed up in what looked like a permanent headache. He had a bulbous nose, loose wrists, and a funny-dry way of talking that always reminded the people he met of Walter Matthau. His friends had no opinion on the matter because he had no friends. He had an older brother in Bend, Oregon, and that was his only family. He spent his life in hotels, motels, boarding-houses, trailer parks, and hostels—and (occasionally) in the arms of widows, whores, or lonely wives, behind the dim net curtains of midwestern bedrooms. He smoked Winstons, read *Playboy* and *Guns & Ammo*, and drove, as an affectation, a 1969 Ford Thunderbird Landau. He washed his shorts in hotel washbasins, with those little sachets of powder they give you, and he talked to himself in hotel mirrors.

He had been a mechanic once, which is the polite word for killer. He had probably been the best of his entire generation, but he often wondered after twenty years if he still had it in him. Jack Ruby had once told him, "You can think you're the greatest. But your talent can disappear down the goddamned toilet while you're still washing your goddamned hands."

Jack Ruby. Henry still smiled to himself when he thought what a transparent *nom-de-guerre* that had been. Jack Ruby, Ruby Red, Red Jack. After all these years, nobody had noticed. It made you wonder what the FBI were doing for a living, apart from filing their nails and going to Senate cocktail parties and jousting for offices with more than one window. Jack fucking Ruby.

She had finished her Mimosa too quickly, like a woman who needed to drink. In a moment or two, she would be trying to catch the cocktail waitress's attention for another one. Henry didn't know it, but she always came in here at five o'clock in the afternoon and drank three of them, sometimes four, always alone. Alone, after everything that had happened; after all the crowds. But she was fat now, a middle-aged Sun-Belt matron, living a life of loneliness, and beauty parlors, and failed diets, and *The Price Is Right*.

He said to her, quite loudly, "Pardon me, I couldn't help noticing. You remind me of someone."

She looked towards him and blinked. Her mind had been exclusively fixed on beckoning the cocktail waitress. She said, "What? Are you talking to me?"

"I'm sorry," he smiled. "I didn't mean to startle you. But you remind me of someone. I can't believe the resemblance."

She stared back at him with those slitty little eyes. The cocktail waitress came up to her, and said, "How're you doing, Mrs. Schneider? Can I bring you another Mimosa?"

Henry offered, "Will you have one on me?"

Mrs. Schneider said nothing, but looked from Henry to the cocktail waitress and back again, as if she were suspicious that something was going on between them, some secret joke.

Henry said, "Go ahead. Another Mimosa. And I'll have another Bud."

When the waitress had gone back to the bar, Henry picked up his beer and came over to sit beside Mrs. Schneider, not uncomfortably close, but close enough. He offered her a Winston, but she shook her head. "I gave up. My doctor insisted."

"You look well enough to me. May I say even blooming?"

She placed a hand on her chest. "I have to watch my heart, that's all. It's nothing serious. But it's better not to smoke."

"Do you mind if I do?"

"I'd rather you didn't."

He tucked the cigarettes back in the pack. "In that case, okay, I won't."

There was a difficult pause. Mrs. Schneider glanced towards the sliding door. Outside, in the heat, baize tables and bright-yellow parasols were being set up for the weekend's Easter Fair. A hotel handyman walked past with three large wooden rabbits under his arm, green and white and red.

"Are you staying through Easter?" she asked Henry.

"I don't know. It depends. I'd like to."

"You're here on business, right?"

He nodded. "That's right. Motorola."

"I guessed as much," she smiled. "If it's not Mafia, it's Motorola. The two big Ms in Phoenix. Well, I hope you're having a successful trip."

"I am now," said Henry.

Another pause. She looked across at him. "You said I reminded you of someone. Who was that?"

"I don't know. It was a long time ago now. Nineteen or twenty years, at least. None of us are getting any younger."

"But who? You really can't remember?"

"A girlfriend, maybe," said Henry. "I never married. I guess I wasn't cut out to be a husband. So, I've had girlfriends. All pretty, mind you."

"I'm a widow, myself," said Mrs. Schneider. The cocktail waitress brought them their drinks.

"I'm paying," Henry reminded her, and laid a ten-dollar bill on her tray. "Keep the change."

Mrs. Schneider took a large mouthful of champagne and orange juice. She closed her eyes as it fizzed down her throat. Then she said, "My husband used to fly from Luke Air Force Base, you know—out near Litchfield Park? A major, flying F-16s. A handsome man; and a good one, too. Do you know what they paid him? One thousand seven hundred dollars a month. A major, with twelve years' service. And one day he flew straight into the side of the White Tank Mountains, and so that was the end of that. I was left with a house, an Air Force pension, and a small collection of dirty magazines which I found in his sock drawer."

Henry finished his first beer and picked up his second. He gave Mrs. Schneider an understanding but rather distracted nod, as if he were listening to the story of her life for the third or even the fourth time. As a matter of fact, all this about an Air Force major flying straight into the White Tank Mountains was quite new to him, but then whatever biographical details she gave him, they were all bound to be fabricated, carefully rehearsed during twenty years of hiding. To Henry, they were irrelevant. She would never deflect him from the serious task he had at hand.

In truth, he quite liked the bit about the dirty magazines in the sock drawer. That gave "Major Schneider" some imaginary depth, some touch of reality. Whoever had invented *that* little detail for her had been a professional.

She said, "I never drink anything else, only Mimosas. Sometimes just orange juice. If I drink too much, I can't take my sleeping pills, and if I can't take my sleeping pills, I start to panic. Do you know what it's like when you can't get to sleep? When your mind races over and over until it feels like it's going to burn itself out? That's what it's like for me, every night—or would be, if I didn't take my sleeping pills. Over and over, like a wheel."

Henry smoked, and watched her. "You've lived here long, in Phoenix?"

"Ten years. They were going to post us to Wheeler, in Hawaii—that was before Martin had his accident. I was looking forward to that. I don't know if Martin was. Before that, we were at Myrtle Beach, in South Carolina. I didn't like it there too much, at Myrtle Beach. The wives were all too upwardly mobile. Rank was everything. A major's wife was never expected to speak to a colonel's wife unless she was spoken to; and nobody spoke to warrant officers' wives at all."

"But Luke is friendlier?"

She patted one plump white hand agitatedly on top of the other. "It *was*. I guess it still is. I don't see too much of my Air Force friends any more. You know how it is. Now that Martin's gone, there really doesn't seem to be too much point in it. What do I care if Colonel Bickerstaff thinks that Captain Willis is a cretin; or if Major Hodges is screwing Mrs. Bickerstaff every Wednesday at the Mesa Motel on Indian School Road?"

Henry made a face. "Sure, what do you care?"

There was a silence between them, but she was not at ease. She seemed so anxious and agitated that he almost expected her to change her mind and ask him for a cigarette.

"Do you have the time?" she suddenly wanted to know.

"Ten after."

"Well, still early," she said, although she didn't say in

relation to what. To dinnertime? To bedtime? To dusk? To the end of the world? "You shouldn't let me keep you," she said. "You must be a very busy man."

"You're not keeping me," he said placidly. "I don't have any more appointments until tomorrow."

"Oh? Well, there isn't too much to do here in Phoenix. We're still Westerners, you know. Eat early, go to bed early. Healthy, wealthy, and wise as all hell."

"That sounds like a good idea. Early to bed, I mean."

She frowned at him. She sipped at her Mimosa again, quickly, like somebody who is thinking about more than drinking. Henry's calmness obviously unsettled her; yet he hadn't said anything or done anything that could give her an excuse to ask him to leave. She said, after a while, "What the hell are you *doing* here?"

It was then that he was completely convinced that he had found the right woman. Nobody else would have said that; no genuine Western widow would have challenged him with such arrogance, and yet expected him not to be offended. She turned to look at him, and it was clear from the expression on her face that she didn't dislike him, not particularly, and that she hadn't intended to upset him. She was simply speaking the half-forgotten lines from some half-forgotten movie.

He said, "I'm working. I'm a salesman. I sell semiconductors."

"I don't mean that," she said impatiently. "I don't mean that at *all*. What I mean is, what are you doing *here*, talking to me?"

"I like you," said Henry, in a flat voice. Flat, but still strangely provocative.

"You *like* me?"

"I like the look of you. Do you think we could go someplace else?"

She peered at him closely. "What do you mean by someplace else?"

"It's kind of formal here. Don't you think so?"

Abruptly, she laughed out loud. "You're making a *pass* at me. Isn't that it?"

Henry pretended to be embarrassed. He lowered his eyes, and gave an offhand, high-school kind of shrug.

"Well, you *are*!" she smiled. Then she laughed again. "I don't believe it. You're actually making a pass!"

"I didn't mean to be fresh," said Henry. "It was just that you remind me strongly of—I don't know. I can't think who it is. But you look like a movie star. You have that charisma, you know? You have that kind of magnetism."

Mrs. Schneider patted her hair. "They always said that I did. No matter what."

"Who did?" asked Henry.

"Everybody. Martin. My friends. Just about everybody."

Henry nodded. "Sure," he said.

After ten minutes or so, they left the Biltmore and walked out into the sunshine. The temperature at Sky Harbor was ninety-seven degrees, according to the radio. There was a smell of heat and dust and blue paloverde. Henry unfolded his orange-lensed Ray-Bans and carefully set them on his bulbous nose. Mrs. Schneider kept her face shielded from the sun with her wide-brimmed white hat.

"Why don't we take my car?" Henry suggested. It was a dark blue Oldsmobile from Avis, parked under the trees on the far side of the parking lot. Anybody who saw the two of them climbing into it, smiling and nodding to each other, and backing slowly out of the parking lot, sedate and careful, would have assumed them to be a newly retired couple, members of the Biltmore's golf club perhaps, going home for a snooze after nine holes in the hot morning sun and a Mexican lunch at the Adobe clubhouse. They did good empanadas at the clubhouse, and good ribs, too.

She said, "Make a right at 24th Street, and then another right at Lincoln." Henry smiled, and drove with exaggerated smoothness and courtesy. The very last thing he wanted now was to be noticed, or, worse still, to be involved in a traffic accident. Tomorrow afternoon he would deliver the car in person to the Avis desk at Los Angeles International Airport, and his alibi would be simply that it would have been impossible for him to drive all the way from Arizona to Los Angeles if he had been here, in Phoenix, with Mrs. Schneider.

Mrs. Schneider asked, "You live in Los Angeles?"

"That's right. A little bachelor bungalow on Sixth Street."

"I used to live in Brentwood."

"Really? That used to be movie-star country, twenty or thirty years ago, didn't it? Was your husband posted there?"

Mrs. Schneider didn't answer. She looked out of the car window at the dusty roadsides, at the dry and distant view of Camelback Mountain. Henry touched her hand, and said, "You mustn't pay me too much mind. I'm an old Hollywood fan from way back. Greta Garbo, Bette Davis, Marilyn Monroe, Jayne Mansfield. I loved them all. Loved them."

They had reached the crest of 24th Street, where it met up with Lincoln Drive. Henry said, "You still haven't told me your name. If we're going to be friends—"

She smiled, although not at him. "Margot," she said. "Margot Schneider. Née Petty."

"Ah, *Margot*," said Henry. He waited for a Trailways bus to toil its way past him, then made a right on Lincoln towards Paradise Valley. The road curved upwards, glaring and hot and dusty. Far away to their right, the tall buildings of downtown Phoenix wavered in the late-afternoon heat: the Convention Center, the Compensation Fund Building, KOOL Radio. Henry felt as parched as a Gila lizard in a vivarium, trapped under the sun. He took out a cigarette, and pushed in the car's lighter, but when Margot Schneider gave him a reproachful sideways look, he let the lighter pop out, untouched, and patiently put the cigarette away.

She lived in a one-story ranch house on Oasis Drive, a select suburb in the eastern wrinkles of the Phoenix Mountains. Below the veranda, sprinklers sparkled on a vividly green rhomboid of lawn. Wind chimes hung along the eaves, tinkling in plaintive celebration of the first breath of wind that Oasis Drive had felt all day. Margot Schneider led Henry up to the front door, fluted glass backed by gilt and wrought-iron roses. The street number was 62, which Henry thought morbidly appropriate.

"Nice place," he remarked as she opened the door. "How are your neighbors?"

"Quiet. The Millers next door are really sweet. He runs a bathroom boutique in Scottsdale, Tub Time. Across the road, the Kargs, they're okay. He works for Mountain Bell."

"What do their wives do?"

"Oh," she shrugged. "They raise the kids, and watch *As the World Turns*."

"I'm a *Guiding Light* fan myself," smiled Henry.

She led him into the house. There was a large white-painted living-room, with an angled ceiling, and an oak fireplace. On the walls were luridly colored American Indian prints by Barrie Tinkler. The rug was off-white, shaggy, and needed cleaning. There was a mock-Louis XIV console, a pair of mock-Chippendale chairs. But it was the little spindly-legged table in the far corner of the room which interested Henry the most. A cluster of black-and-white photographs stood there, framed in silver. Mrs. Schneider at the age of 12. Major and Mrs. Schneider on their third anniversary. The family dog, Natasha. Major and Mrs. Schneider at a barbecue at Myrtle Beach. Henry picked up a photograph of Major Schneider standing confident and clean-profiled beside the nose-needle of an F-16, and marveled at the care and attention which had gone into creating Mrs. Schneider's new life.

"Your husband was a good-looking man. When did you say you met him?"

"I didn't. But, December, 1950."

"Ah, December, 1950. That was when they were shooting *As Young As You Feel*."

She was taking off her white hat and she stopped suddenly. "What?"

"I told you," Henry grinned. "I was always a movie fan. Movies, and soap operas. Did you ever see *River of No Return*?"

She squinted at him, her eyes deep in her fat-pillowed cheeks. "No," she said. "I can't say that I ever did. Was it on Midnight Movie?"

"Maybe. Yes, maybe it was."

There was another pause. In the far distance, they could hear a siren. Then Margot Schneider said, "Would you care for a drink? I don't have any beer."

"Anything will do. Whiskey, wine, you name it."

"I have some Stag's Leap Riesling, from Napa Valley."

"Okay. Stag's Leap Riesling would be fine."

They sat on the terrace and drank wine which, for Henry, was too cold and too sweet. It was very late afternoon now, and as the sun sank over Yuma County, to the west, the mountains were filled with crumpled shadows. Their faces, like Margot Schneider's face, were suddenly revealed by the light to be old.

Margot said, "I never liked the movies much myself."

"You didn't like the glamour?"

She grimaced slightly. "They were never glamorous. Not really. They *looked* that way, but a human being is only a human being, after all. You don't think when you see one of those movie stars on the screen that they ever get *sick*, or have *headaches*, or painful periods, or get frightened to death because they don't believe they're going to act a part well enough. You don't think that, do you? But it must be true."

Henry watched her closely. "Sure," he said, after a while. "I guess it must be."

"It's like my husband," Margot went on. "He never understood that anyone else could be weaker than him; that anyone else could find it impossible to cope. He *said* he understood, oh sure, but deep down he couldn't, because *he* was equipped to cope with the world and I wasn't. But, well, I *have* to cope now. Though it's lonely, most of the time." She brushed her dress straight, and then looked up at Henry and gave him an embarrassed, apologetic smile. "You don't want to hear about me, though. You didn't come all the way out here to be burdened with somebody else's troubles."

"On the contrary," said Henry. "I think you're one of the most interesting women I've ever met. I've been looking for a woman like you for a very, very long time."

"Would you care for something to eat?" she asked him, abruptly. "I have pepperoni pizzas in the freezer."

"I don't think I'm hungry," Henry told her. "All these business lunches, they build up on you. Clog your system after a while. I'll stick with the wine."

"Well, then, would you mind if I changed into something more comfortable?"

"Go ahead. I'll help myself to another drink, if that's okay."

She went inside through the patio door, turning for a moment to give him a look that she must have thought was coquettish. Henry sat by himself, carefully sipping his wine, and watched a distant Air Force jet sparkle like a needle in the dark lilac-colored sky. Then he reached into his pocket and brought out a black vinyl wallet, which he laid on the table, and a pair of surgeon's disposable plastic gloves. He whistled between his teeth, "Some Day I'll Find You."

From inside the house, he heard the sudden blurt of the television, tuned to KPHO "—*A dust storm alert between Gila Bend and Yuma on Highway S . . . if you observe dense dust blowing or approaching the highway, do not enter the area . . . pull off the road as far as possible and stop, extinguishing your lights . . .*"

He unfastened the flap of the black vinyl wallet, and drew out a portable saw—two feet of shark-toothed blue-steel wire, with black wooden handles at each end. It was like a garrotte, with a serrated edge. He flexed it, and it made a slightly musical metallic twang. He had bought it in an old-fashioned hardware store in Rumney Depot, Vermont. The proprietor had assured him that it would cut through a six-inch hickory branch like a wire through cheese.

He finished his glass of wine with a frown of absent-minded distaste. Then he carefully eased his fingers into his plastic gloves, tugging them until they were tight. He could feel his pulse beating at that regular, almost-forgotten pace, the pace it always beat when he was preparing himself for a kill. It had been twenty years, but it still felt the same. A sense of calm, controlled elation. A tremendous sense of power.

In the old days they had called him Gentleman Henry because of his self-control, few of them ever understanding what a pitiless nature it actually took to kill a human being to order. He had specialized in revenge killings—jobs in which the client required the victim to suffer in agonizing and appropriate ways. After his work had been completed, he would matter-of-factly report on what he had done, how the victim had mutely appealed to him for mercy in spite of the fact that most of his intestines were in the next room. How the victim had screamed and sobbed. And the client's eyes would never rise to meet his. The money would pass across the desk without a single look exchanged. Henry had concluded that hardly anyone has a stomach for killing, not even by proxy, and he had raised his prices, twenty years ago, to $5,000 a job. The next week he had killed a man in

Pittsburgh with a Bosch electric drill, boring five holes into his skull before he finally died. He had never heard anybody scream so much, not before, nor since. But he never had nightmares about it.

He wiped his wine glass clean with his soft white linen handkerchief. He also polished the arms of the chair, and every other surface he might have touched. There was no point in washing his glass, no point in trying to make it look as if Margot had died accidentally, or as if she had committed suicide. Nobody could do by accident what Henry was about to do to Margot; and nobody could ever do it to themselves.

He got up, and crossed to the patio doors, still flexing the saw, and stood listening for a moment. Then he stepped inside.

She had taken a quick shower, and now she was sitting in her bedroom brushing her hair and warbling happily to herself. Henry didn't find it any more difficult to kill happy people than angry or frightened or miserable people. In fact, it was more satisfying if they died happy. He was old-fashioned that way.

He walked in without knocking. The off-white carpet was soft and quiet, and so she didn't hear him. The television was showing a news report on angry parents who were picketing a school in Flagstaff. There was a queen-size bed with a white quilted satin bedspread, and white drapes; a white bedside telephone; a bottle of Nembutal. The door to the bathroom was still ajar, and inside, Henry could see Margot's clothes strewn on the floor, her tent-dress, her slip, and one discarded sandal. Margot herself was sitting in front of her white rococo dressing-table, wearing a white satin bathrobe with a large silver satin star sewn on to the back of it. She was pouting at herself as she tinted her lips with Vivid Pink.

He thought: that's a vestige from a long, long time ago. A pink like that, only a blonde would wear.

He came right up behind her, only a few inches away, and it was only then that she focused on his reflection in the mirror, and realized that he was there.

"*Well*," she said, without turning around. She replaced the cap on her lipstick and reached for her blusher. "If I'd known you were the kind of guy who likes sneaking into a girl's bedroom . . ."

"What would you have done?" he asked her. His pulse was still beating with that even, purposeful, rhythm, but his voice sounded light and amused. On the television, an angry parent was saying, "I won't have my child educated side by side with hoodlums and trouble-makers and ignorant Indians, that's all. My child has a right to the education *I* had."

"I don't know," she said. "Maybe I wouldn't have asked you home."

"I knew you were going to ask me home the moment I set eyes on you," he said.

"Oh, yes?" Her voice was a little sharper.

"No slight intended," said Henry. "I didn't think you looked cheap, or easy, or even particularly lonely. But I could see what qualities you possessed, straight away. Star qualities, you know? You're a star, in your own way."

"I wish I was."

"Oh, believe me," said Henry. He raised the flexible saw behind her back, his hands firmly grasping the two wooden handles, stretching the blade out until it was taut.

Margot Schneider applied her blusher, then pressed her lips together and stared at herself in the mirror, as if she wasn't at all pleased with the way her face looked.

"I should lose some weight, you know? But it's so difficult when you don't have anybody to lose weight *for*."

"Why don't you lose it for me? I'm as good as anyone."

"I don't suppose I'll ever *see* you again, shall I, after today? That's the way they all are. Horny, tired, sick of business. All they need is one evening of comfort. Then they go back to their wives."

While she rummaged in her dressing-table drawer, Henry raised the saw higher, until it was only a few inches above her head. "I'm so *untidy*," she said. "They used to tell me that when I was a little girl, you know? I can never find *anything*."

Henry said, "Look up. Look at yourself in the mirror. Now, what can you say about a woman who looks like that, at fifty-six?"

Margot Schneider kept on rummaging for a moment, and then froze. Henry could see the muscles in her back tense. It seemed like a whole minute before she spoke, and when she did, she sounded like someone else altogether, someone frightened and small.

"You know who I am, don't you?" she whispered.

"What do you mean? You're Margot Schneider, that's what you told me."

"You said fifty-six. How do you know I'm fifty-six?"

"You told me."

"I never told you any such thing. I always tell people I'm fifty-one."

"Well, I don't know," said Henry. He was trying hard to make his voice sound normal, praying even harder that she wouldn't turn around and see him standing right behind her with that thin steel saw held upraised in tense fists.

She said, in a haunted gush, "Haven't I given *enough*? I never had anything to start with. Haven't I given *enough*? For the love of God, all of you, you've taken everything!"

"Listen, Margot—"

"Don't lie to me," she whispered. "You've been taunting me all afternoon with it, haven't you? Hollywood, the movies, the *River of No Return*? And I was dumb enough not to understand."

He said, in a tone that was almost shocking because it sounded so sincere, "Margot, believe me, I don't think you're anyone but Margot Schneider. Why should I?"

Seconds went past. One of the parents on the television snapped, "If they want guinea pigs, then let them use guinea pigs. They're not using *my* kids."

Then, almost as if she knew what was going to happen, and had decided to accept it with the dignity of Joan of Arc, Margot raised her head and stared at herself full-face in the mirror. In that instant, and in that last instant only, she looked just the way she had always looked in all her photographs, wide-eyed, surprised, frightened by everything she knew but even more frightened by everything she didn't.

In that same instant, Henry Friend snapped the saw down past her face and pulled it tight against the flesh of her bare neck. He was so fast, he had trained for this single act for so long, that she didn't even have time to inhale enough air to scream. All she made was a high inward gasp, and then Henry had ripped the saw hard to the right and hard to the left, tearing through soft white skin, through the strong muscle at each side of the neck, through the fibrous sheath which contained the carotid artery, the jugular vein, and the vagus nerve.

He let out a loud, desperate *"Ah!"* of effort and horror, and then he gave one last rip to the right, and the wire-bladed saw pulled clear through the cartilage between her cervical vertebrae, and her head rolled off her shoulders and dropped with a hideous drumming noise onto her dressing-table among her combs and her make-up.

Blood fountained spectacularly out of her open neck, gouting all over her mirror and halfway up the wall. Her body fell heavily to the floor, still pumping pints of sticky red all over the white carpet, all over the bedspread, like some ghastly and relentless action-painting, a Jackson Pollock enacted in gore. One foot twitched and shuddered, and actually kicked off its fur-trimmed satin slipper.

It took Henry a long time to recover. He stared down at the floor because he couldn't face the severed head which was lying on the dressing-table. The head was splattered with blood, but it still looked unnervingly alive, as if Margot's eyes would suddenly roll and stare at him, as if Margot's voice would whisper from its lips.

"Jesus," he said to himself. He was shaking all over. He must be losing his nerve.

After two or three minutes, he turned away and went to the bathroom. It was still steamy and fragrant from Margot's shower. He washed the saw under the basin faucets. The mirror was too cloudy for him to see himself: all he could make out was a foggy pink face, an indeterminate monster from a past that was probably better forgotten, the ectoplasm of other people's nightmares. Blood circled the basin in whorls down the drain.

He folded up the saw with the neatness of a professional workman. Then he left the bathroom, closing the door behind him, and walked straight across the bedroom, deliberately averting his eyes from the dressing-table. He went into the kitchen and found a large green plastic trash bag under the sink. He peeled off his bloody gloves and dropped them into the bag. For a moment, he closed his eyes like a man with a migraine. But it had to be done. He returned to the bedroom, carrying the bag, and forced himself to step right up to the dressing-table and look down at Margot's head.

It wasn't the blood that disturbed him. Blood was no problem. Blood was part of the job.

Yet, Margot's head unsettled him badly. He wasn't sure why. Maybe it was because, historically, she was already dead, twenty years buried; and while he might have succeeded in murdering her body, her personality had somehow survived this execution unscathed; as if Henry had done nothing more than lop the head off a waxwork dummy. Her life-force, her legend, remained intact. That inexplicable radiance that had always made her appear to be far greater and far more glamorous then she actually was—that radiance still shone. He had killed her, but she was still alive. For Henry, this wasn't like the old days at all. It was too much like Hollywood voodoo, Sharon Tate and Jayne Mansfield and Anton LeVey. It was too much like *Helter-Skelter*. Henry looked down at her head, at the way she stared so intently and yet so blindly at her pots of cosmetics, and he knew that *he* was fated, too. Twenty years of his life, for this. Twenty years to discover what doom really was.

He gingerly picked up the head and tumbled it into the green plastic bag. His stomach turned over, but he managed to keep his wine down. He took one last look around the bedroom, deliberate and slow, making absolutely sure that he had left nothing behind which could identify him. Once, in Marion, he had left a striped necktie in a woman's closet, and that little bit of forgetfulness had cost him sixteen days in jail and $8,000 to a heavyweight Mafia lawyer. It could have cost him his life.

It was almost dark when he closed the door of the house behind him, and crossed the driveway to his car. He unlocked the trunk, and stowed the bag carefully on top of the spare tire, so that it would stay in place when he turned corners. He spread a plaid blanket over it, just in case. Then he climbed quickly into the car, started it up, and drove back down Oasis Drive without lights. In a few moments, he was speeding along Lincoln Drive, back towards 24th Street, where he would turn left for Sky Harbor airport.

The getaway contingency was simple. It had been devised years ago, when he had first started looking further afield than

California. Henry would park the Oldsmobile at Sky Harbor's long-term parking-lot, unscrew the license-plates and peel off the special decals. Then, from the terminal, he would telephone his people in Los Angeles and tell them what had happened. While he boarded his flight at Phoenix, an identical vehicle would be rented from the Avis desk at LAX, and by the time Henry arrived in Los Angeles, this new vehicle would be waiting for him, minus its license plates, in the LAX parking lot. Henry would attach to it the plates from the car he had rented in Phoenix, and check it into the Avis desk, making a point of telling the girls there how arduous the drive had been from Arizona. "And those dust storms, phew. . . !"

The accomplice who had rented the car in Los Angeles would fly to Phoenix with *his* license plates, screw them onto Henry's old car, and then drive immediately to Las Vegas, and check it in there.

The switch would remain undiscovered until one or the other of the cars was serviced; and even then the mechanics probably wouldn't bother to check the vehicle numbers.

Henry turned on the radio as he drove south on 24th Street towards the airport. The yuccas on either side of the road were silhouetted against the evening sky like black-paper cutouts. He lit a cigarette and his hands were trembling. Twenty years between killings was far too long. Twenty years between anything was far too long. He felt like a medieval mariner, hoary, bearded, hopeless, who had suddenly reached the brink of the world.

TWO

Daniel was awakened by a loud, insistent purring, like the sound of a cat eating its breakfast. He opened his eyes and blinked at the sunlit adobe ceiling above him, and wondered for nearly a minute where he was, and what century he was in. He thought: Buck Rogers must have felt like this, when he woke up from that gas-filled mine in Pittsburgh and discovered that he was in the twenty-fifth century. Where am I, and who is this woman lying next to me, and why is she snoring so loudly?

She was a coppery redhead, although her hair was all that Daniel could see of her. He seemed to remember that her name was Cara. At least, that was what she had said it was. Hitchhikers rarely told the truth, and it was a kind of unwritten law of the highway that they didn't need to. It was enough that they were entertaining, or sexy, or both. Cara from South Dakota, making her way to the Coast. Daniel had been to South Dakota himself, playing the Treble Clef Club in Rapid City, and he didn't find her story at all incredible. All that South Dakota was good for, as far as he could tell, was escaping from.

"Hey," he said, gently shaking her shoulder.

"Mmmph?" she said, stretching herself out.

"You're snoring."

She wrestled the sheet around herself. "I am not, either," she told him, without opening her eyes. "Ladies never snore."

"Oh no? Well, what's that purring noise you're making?"

"Emphatic breathing," she said. "Now, let me get some sleep, will you? It isn't even dawn, for God's sake."

Daniel leaned over and looked at her. "It's six-fifteen," he announced. "I have to be open at seven." He decided that he still had pretty good taste in women after all. She was sharp-faced, white-skinned, and big-breasted, with those wide flaring hips that always reminded him of milkmaids. It was amazing the women you could encounter on the highway between Superior and Phoenix on a hot Thursday evening, or any evening for that matter. Vassar graduates, lady truck drivers, hookers, viola players, feminist activists, gambling shills; and now Cara.

She kept on snoring, deep and low, but Daniel couldn't really complain about it. Last night, after the last of his customers had gone home, she had helped him to clean up; and then, sweet and high on good red wine and Bruce Springsteen records, she had tumbled among the sheets with him with such fun and energy and unembarrassed lust that it had taken all his self-control not to let out his famous window-vibrating rebel yell, just for the sheer joy of it. This morning, his back and thighs were scratched like Br'er Rabbit's in the brambles, and his lips felt as if they had been caught up in a catering-sized garlic press.

He climbed stiffly out of bed, and the springs squeaked. His jeans and his T-shirt were crumpled up on the bare floor in the most peculiar heap, as if he had leaped out of them last night without even undoing them. The large Mickey Mouse alarm clock on the bureau said 6:20. He yawned so hard that he almost dislocated his jaw, and sniffed.

Susie was standing just outside the door, in her long pink Mary Poppins nightdress. She watched him silently as he took out a clean shirt and dressed, and then followed him along the corridor as he went to pee and to throw water on his face. It was only when he had risen from the depths of his towel to stare at himself in the cracked bathroom mirror that she said anything.

"Who's that?" she asked. She was seven, with blond braids, and china-blue eyes in a pretty little perky face. Just like her mother. Mega-cute. And very precocious.

"That's, er, Cara. Cara from South Dakota."

"Is she staying for breakfast?"

"I guess so."

"Do you like her?"

Daniel stared down at Susie for a long time. In the end, he said, "I don't know yet. We haven't really done a whole lot of talking."

"And you don't hate yourself? And she doesn't hate *her*self?"

"I don't know. She's still asleep. It's kind of hard to assess how much you like or dislike yourself when you're still asleep."

"I can *sing* when I'm asleep."

Daniel shuffled down the narrow wooden stairs to the old-fashioned Mexican-style kitchen. Susie followed him, with all the intentness of a concerned wife. Daniel opened up the huge Amana icebox and began to take out bacon strips and eggs and hamburger patties and sausage links in preparation for the morning stampede. In addition, there would be two gallons of coffee to perk, three dozen oranges to press, twenty-five buns to be sliced, and nine tables to be laid. He drank a large gulp of grapefruit juice straight from the carton, and helped himself to a handful of stale Cheetos.

Susie said, "It's time you settled down, you know."

"Settled down?" Daniel demanded. "I *am* settled down. What could be more settled down than living here with you, doing what I'm doing?"

"I mean you could marry."

Daniel shook his head. "I tried it. You know that. I'm not the right type for marriage. I don't have the right amino-acid chains for marriage. Besides, I'm allergic to fidelity. It breaks me out in hives."

"You've been faithful to *me*."

"You're my daughter. Being faithful to your children is different."

Susie toyed with the magnetic clips stuck to the front of the icebox. "Don't you ever think about Mommy, ever?"

"You know I do. Your mommy was the prettiest lady who ever lived. And to prove it, you're the prettiest daughter who ever lived. But she wanted something else, somebody else. Not here, and not me. I couldn't do anything about it."

Susie said, "Would you take her back, if she came?"

Daniel had an armful of fresh eggs. But he stopped where he was, and looked at Susie seriously, and then set the eggs down one by one on the counter so that he could take her into his arms and hold her very, very close. She had that warm-bready smell of a young child who has just been sleeping, a hostage freshly released by the sandman.

"Susie," he said, in a hoarse, affectionate whisper, "I have all I need in you."

"You won't take her back, then?"

"No," he said. "It wouldn't be fair."

She looked at him, and there were tears in her eyes. "Who wouldn't it be fair to?" she asked.

"It wouldn't be fair to your mommy, nor to me, nor to you. We'd argue all the time, you know that. We'd shout. We'd wind up hating each other when we should love each other."

Susie pressed her forehead against his, and then said, in the smallest voice, "I miss her."

"I know," said Daniel. "So do I."

A cat-curious voice interrupted, "I hope I'm not breaking up anything meaningful here." Daniel looked up. It was Cara, sleepy-eyed but awake, with her red hair brushed into chrysanthemum curls. She was wearing one of Daniel's blue denim workshirts, unbuttoned, so that she was revealing her deep alabaster-white cleavage, her flat white stomach, and the rusty tangle of red pubic hair between her long white thighs. She was unashamed, provocative, and highway-stylish—possessed of that same vagrant elegance that had attracted him to Candii, his first-ever wife and Susie's mother. Susie recognized the breed, and kissed her father on the nose with childish promptness, and left.

"Did I drive her away?" asked Cara, not altogether without satisfaction.

Daniel stood up, and rubbed the back of his neck. "She's used to it. She's only trying to make me feel guilty. She misses her mommy."

"Understandable," said Cara. She came up close and kissed his cheek, then his mouth. "Do you want me to fix us some coffee?"

"Don't worry. I have to fix enough for the whole of Apache Junction in any case. Would you pass me that skillet?"

Cara stood beside him as he melted lard in the skillet for the hash browns. She touched his shoulder sensitively, as if she couldn't quite believe that he was real. The sun crept in between the slats of the venetian blind and suddenly illuminated the white china bowl of Spanish onions, so that they took on the charmed radiance of a detail in a Vermeer. And as he stood over the hot kitchen range in his jeans and his white short-sleeved shirt, slightly-built, dark-haired, a little used-looking but still attractive, Daniel seemed to become irradiated with the same domestic magic. Portrait of the chef as a tired but friendly angel.

"You were strange last night," she told him. "Strange and wonderful. Too gentle for a short-order cook."

"Restaurant proprietor," he corrected her. He scraped onion slices into the skillet and they began to sizzle.

"Whatever," she smiled.

"You think I'm *strange*?" he asked.

She nodded happily. He frowned at her for a moment and then shrugged. As a matter of fact, he had often thought that he must have been born into some kind of backward-facing looking-glass land. His life and his career always seemed to turn out the polar opposite of what he really wanted, and of what he was really capable of achieving. Even his thirty-six-year-old face, when he saw it in photographs, looked as if it were the wrong way around; as if the man he glimpsed in mirrors and store windows was the way he actually should have been, and the face with which he walked around all day was his awkward other-self, his klutzy doppelganger.

He should have been a famous TV entertainer, a kind of alternative Johnny Carson, a poor man's Dan Rather. Instead, he ran Daniel's Downhome Diner, in Apache Junction, Arizona, near the heat-wavering horizon of the Superstition Mountains, and the famous Lost Dutchman Mine. Daniel's Downhome Diner was popular enough, if popularity meant anything at all in a town of 2,391 and falling. There was an intermittent passing-through trade, truckers and tourists and windpump salesmen, as well as hitchhikers and assorted mysteriosos. Sometimes the customers were friendly; sometimes offensive. Sometimes they cried into their coffee, or threw chairs through the window. There were nine red gingham-covered tables, with plastic tomatoes full of ketchup, and a 1967 jukebox with *Happy Together* by the Turtles and *Penny Lane* by the Beatles, not because Daniel held any special memories of 1967, but simply because the lock was broken and nobody could get into the jukebox to change the records. On the wall there was a smeary blackboard menu: Franks & Beans, Minute Steaks & Beans, Tamales, Empanadas, Cheeseburgers. All good downhome stuff, although Daniel was actually capable of tossing together *oysters Bienville*, or *pompano en papillote*, or even *pigeonneaux royaux au sauce paradis*, with equal equanimity. His father had been a chef at Alciatore's in San Francisco in the 1950s, and had taught him to cook with all the care and patience and calculated disgust of a real professional. Daniel rarely prepared such exotica these days, mainly because he was more than seriously tired of cooking by the end of the day, and because nobody in Apache Junction would have wanted to eat anything like that anyway. Apache Junctioneers ate a lot of steak and a lot of beans and that was just about it. He could imagine the reaction he would get from Indian Bill Hargraves if he served him up tender fragments of crab and mushrooms and fish in a paper poke. "What the hell's this, a Western Airlines sickbag?"

He had never meant to run a restaurant, especially not here in Pinal County, Arizona. He had tried singing, and selling, and sucking out sewers, and collecting tolls on the Indian Nation Turnpike in Oklahoma. He had even worked as a stand-up comedian in a quasi-Victorian topless nightspot in Nevada called the Gaslight. "And Moses is standing on top of the mountain, right, and he says to Jehovah, listen, let me get this straight, you want us to cut the end of our *dicks* off?" That was where he had met and married Candii, Susie's mother, blonde curls and snub nose and Little Annie Fannie eyes, giggly and small and sexy, with breasts so big that when she jiggled down the street men used to stop and stare with their mouths wide open. A tabletop dancer supreme, a burlesque *artiste* out of her time, the rage and the love of his life. Candii had sworn filthy curses at him in the obstetric clinic in Reno, while a red neon light across the street had flashed the word DIVORCE on and off all night, and the doctor had warned vaguely that the baby would probably die. Susie hadn't died, thank God; but Candii had left them after eight months, taking her tight silk dresses and her seamed stockings. He missed her badly, even now, six years later, because she was an unassailable sexual fantasy and because she always used to laugh at his jokes and because he loved her. What was more, her name was actually Candii, on her birth certificate.

He had arrived in Apache Junction by accident. He had been heading towards Sante Fé, New Mexico, to show off Susie to Candii's mother (only 42 herself, by God, and just as busty as her daughter) and to panhandle a few hundred dollars from Candii's father to pay off some of his overdue rent. A few miles outside of Phoenix, his old green Mercury had finally collapsed and died by the glaring roadside. The Navajo mechanic, face creased with wrinkles, had stared at the Mercury's rusty green carcass, and then at last pronounced, "No point in fixing *that*, my friend. Transmission's shot." When he had looked around, the signs had said *Apache Junction*. They had also said *Thriving Diner for Sale*. The moon-faced man who was selling the diner had peered out suspiciously from his darkened porch and said, "You're not wasting my time, are you? I get more time-wasters, I can tell you."

There wasn't much in Apache Junction. A couple of gas stations, a few peeling houses, an Indian jewelry store. But it was as good or as bad as anyplace else. The weather was warm and dry, helpful to Daniel's sinus condition. The crime rate was low. The only habitual offender was a halfbreed Navajo called Ronald Reagan Kinishba, and he and Daniel were good friends. They played cards together occasionally, and got themselves drunk on Löwenbrau, and sometimes Ronald took Daniel out on the pillion seat of his Honda 749-cc Nighthawk, blaring through the night at 110 mph, oblivious to anything but speed and grit and hot wind, and lights that flashed past them like space missiles out of *Star Trek II*. Afterwards, they would sit astride the bike at some unmapped desert intersection, trembling in marvel at the rush and excitement.

It was a silent life, sometimes; a life in which a man could turn in on himself. At night, in high summer, with the sky as clear as a black lawn sprinkled with silver daisies, with Susie sleeping in her rumpled cot, and the odd aromatic smell of the desert on the breeze, Daniel would sit out on the balcony at the back of the diner listening to the small voice of KSTM inside the kitchen, and wonder if he was real or not. He would cheer himself up by remembering one of Woody Allen's characters, who hated reality but realized it was the only place to get a good steak. He often felt like a Woody Allen character these days: anxious, and just about able to cope. And the longer he lived in Apache Junction, the greater his uncertainty about coping became.

Cara said, "You feel like a vacation, maybe?"

He looked up from the onions. "A vacation? What do you mean?"

"Well, getting away from it all."

"You don't think Apache Junction *is* away from it all!?"

She reached forward and kissed him. "This is *work*," she said. "I'm talking about swimming, or surfing, or climbing up mountains and making love on the snowline."

"Oh, yes? And who's going to take care of Susie?"

"Don't you have a friendly old couple who could take her in for a week or two?"

Daniel stirred onions, and then reached for the seasoning. "I'd miss her," he said.

There was a long pause. Then Cara said, "Would you mind if I stuck around for a little while? Maybe a day or two?"

Daniel glanced at her, and smiled. "You're welcome, if that's what you want."

Cara took his wrist, and nudged back the shirt she was wearing, and held his hand firmly over her bare left breast. She stared at him challengingly, and he felt her nipple crinkle and rise against his palm. "Destiny," she said.

"What is?" he asked her.

"You and me, meeting. Destiny. Not *great* destiny. Not thunder and lightning and whole continents catching fire. But good sweet destiny; something we can both remember forever, when the mood comes over us."

He kept staring into those pale blue eyes of hers, and gently rotating the palm of his hand around her breast. "Cara," he said. "Cara from South Dakota. I don't even know your last name."

"Does it matter?"

Just then, there was a rattling knock at the kitchen window. Through the frosted glass, Daniel could see the blurry outline of a man's face. "Daniel! You there? Daniel!"

"Willy?" called Daniel. "Hold on a second. I'll let you in." He turned to Cara, and said, "It's a friend of mine. Do you want to go get dressed?"

Cara looked down at herself. "Oh, sure," she said. She blew him a kiss, and then, with a sassy twirl, turned around and pranced back upstairs.

"Holy shit," came Susie's voice from the diner, although Daniel had paddled her twice in the past week for talking like a trucker. But sometimes women knew when they could get away with it, and Susie was no exception.

THREE

Daniel lowered the gas under the onions and opened the back door. Willy Monahan came tumbling in with his usual awkwardness, brushing dust off his Air Force uniform. "Whose damn chickens are those? Are they yours? Damn things almost pecked the laces straight out of my damn shoes!"

"They're Bill's," said Daniel, mildly. "Pima Indian who lives out back there; he's peaceful enough; and gives me plenty of eggs, too. Do you want some coffee? You're early."

"I'm not early, I'm damn late," Willy retorted. He hung up his major's cap next to a huge Hungarian salami. "I've been working all night in the armory." He sniffed, and then he said, "What's that smell?"

"Onions."

"No, the other smell. The subtle, sensual, underlying smell. Do I detect woman with a capital W?"

Susie came into the kitchen, carrying a stack of clean red gingham napkins. "Hi, Uncle Willy."

"Hi yourself. Don't tell me the old man has company again."

Susie nodded. "Redhead. From South Dakota."

Daniel took down another skillet, and scraped some more lard into it. "I'm outnumbered, you know that? My daughter, my best friend, who's it going to be next? Just because a pretty young lady from Woonsocket decides to spend a little time here, helping me out—"

"Woonsocket? You're serious?" asked Willy.

"Of course I'm serious. Woonsocket is in Sanborn County, a couple of hundred miles south of Huron."

"Oh, *that* Woonsocket," teased Willy. "Well, my friend, if it's *that* Woonsocket, you don't have much to worry about. They're known for their obliging redheads. In fact, eight Woonsocket women out of ten are redheads. They're also known for the Woonsocket Jew's Harp Orchestra, and Woonsocket Pie, which is a whole gopher in a flaky pastry crust."

Susie giggled, but Daniel closed his eyes and raised his head as if he were appealing to the Lord to save him from smartass Air Force majors. "To think, Willy, that we depend on you to protect this great nation of ours in time of war."

Willy noisily pulled across one of the Mexican kitchen chairs and sat down, propping one angular leg across the other. "You don't know how damn lucky you are," he said. "The reason I spent all night in the armory was because single-handedly and unaided I have discovered a flaw in our air-to-air radar systems. Now, what do you think about that?"

"What should I think?" asked Daniel.

"What *should* you think? You should only think that you have sitting in your humble little kitchen the greatest genius in ordnance and navigation systems in the entire United States Air Force. And that's just for beginners."

"Have some coffee."

Willy was unusually disarrayed-looking for an Air Force major, particularly a major who flew regular tactical training missions in a jet airplane which could fly at 920 mph and had cost the American taxpayer something over $18 million. He was thin, Willy, with a large hatchet nose, and bright dark eyes. He had been married once, years ago, but his wife Nora had left him during Viet Nam, and he had sworn to himself that he would never try marriage again. Instead, he had devoted himself almost fanatically to the Air Force's new and sophisticated weapons systems, becoming an amateur expert in radar and guided missiles. His off-duty hours were devoted to Chivas Regal, poker, and scandalous womanizing. He was the only officer in the Air Force who had completely overhauled a Boeing B-1 defensive radar system single-handed, and the only officer in the Air Force who had actually succeeded in tugging the white nylon panties off Corporal Sherry P. Kearns, the Junoesque but notoriously inflexible secretary of General "Tailpipe" Truscott at Nellis Air Force Base.

Willy was Nebraskan by birth; rangy, funny, but also very good at what he did, an Air Force man through and through. If his wife hadn't left him, and if he had behaved himself, he could have been a major-general by now. But he had remained a major for six years, while younger men of more conventional life-styles were promoted over his head, and his latest posting to Williams AFB to train inexperienced young pilots on F-15 Eagles had been an unmistakable message from Tactical Air Command that he could expect to rise no further. He called Williams "the Graveyard of Dreams."

But he hadn't quit the Air Force. There was nothing else he could do, not happily, at least. Yet now and then, when he was drunk, his chagrin rose to the surface like the boiling bubbles from a sunken submarine, and he foully cursed all wives, and all superior officers, and most of all himself.

He sipped his coffee noisily, and helped himself to a handful of chocolate-chip cookies. "I can't wait to lay all this stuff on Colonel Kawalek's desk. I can picture his face already. 'Well, Willy, what's all this, Willy? What do you mean our radar's up shit creek? Apart from being *distasteful*, Willy, it's politically impossible.' " Willy did a particularly cruel impersonation of the blustery Kawalek.

Daniel peeled strips of bacon out of a pack and laid them in the skillet. "Is it serious, this flaw you've found?"

"Is it serious? Was Hiroshima serious? Of course it's serious."

Willy munched cookies and swallowed coffee.

"Well, are you going to tell me?" asked Daniel.

"It's very technical," said Willy. "I'm not sure I could explain it to a short-order cook."

"Restaurant proprietor, if you don't mind."

"Whatever. It isn't easy to understand, not unless you have a moderate grasp of the principles of X-band pulse-doppler radar."

"Are you kidding?" said Daniel, flipping the bacon over.

"My mother used to tell me bedtime stories about X-band pulse-doppler radar. Didn't you ever hear the one about X-band pulse-doppler radar and the seven dwarfs?"

"Seriously," said Willy, "this is one of those high-tech discoveries a man makes just once in a lifetime."

"Will you pass me the pepper? No, that one. Thanks. Go on, then, tell me what you've found out."

"Ah, shit," Willy despaired. "How do you explain anomalies in APG-63 multi-mode radar to a guy who's frying onions?"

"Try, will you? I'm listening."

Willy dragged his chair across to the table and laid a wooden spoon on one side, and a blue-and-white china butter dish on the other. "This radar is highly sophisticated, very advanced. It fits into the nose of a fighter plane, and it controls every move that the pilot is going to make in any kind of combat situation. It can track one enemy airplane, and at the same time it can keep on looking for others. It can lock from one target to another instantly. Up until now, I thought it was the best air-to-air radar in the entire world."

"In that case, I'm glad that it belongs to us, and not to the Russians."

Willy blinked at him.

"That's all I could think of to say," Daniel apologized.

Willy took the pewter flour-shaker, and carefully sprinkled a fine white coating all over the table. Susie watched him with grave interest; Daniel thought, God in Heaven, here we go again. "This table is our attack scenario, right?" said Willy.

"I thought you were making piecrust," Daniel retorted.

Willy raised a hand to silence him. "Don't make fun. This is serious. This wooden spoon is an enemy intruder, right? And this butter dish is me, okay, in my F-15. I'm protecting the homeland in the late stages of a protracted nuclear confrontation. Enemy wooden spoons are coming in from all sides."

"What do you do, Uncle Willy?" asked Susie, frowning.

"Do? I'll tell you what I do. I get up there in my F-15, fully armed with a 20mm M-61 multi-barrel gun with 960 rounds of ammunition, plus four AIM-7 Sparrow air-to-air missiles and four AIM-9 Sidewinder air-to-air missiles, and I track those wooden spoons on my radar until I've locked right on to one, and I'm ready to blow it right out of the sky, and then I fire one of my Sparrow missiles, and then what happens?''

"You're telling us," Daniel reminded him. He sneezed, twice.

"I'm glad that's not *my* breakfast," said Willy, caustically.

"Just tell us what happens," Daniel told him.

"Okay—I've fired the missile. It's really hot stuff, this missile. Radar-guided, with a PD capability and lock-in up to 10 db clutter in the look-down mode."

Daniel turned over the strips of bacon one by one, setting up a tremendous sizzling chorus. Lannie Watts from the Globe Trucking Corporation would be there in five or ten minutes, demanding his breakfast. Lannie always ate seven strips of bacon, three eggs, toast, and a heap of hash browns, but he insisted on drinking grapefruit juice with it to keep his weight down.

"Are you listening to me?" Willy demanded.

"Sure I'm listening," said Daniel. "Listen, I'm *listening*. But I'm not at all sure what the hell you're talking about. What's this 'clutter'?"

"Just shut up," insisted Willy. "I fire the missile, the missile locks on to the wooden spoon, here it comes"—he traced an unerring missile-track through the dusted flour—"it's two hundred yards away, one hundred, fifty, and then what happens?" His finger sharply veered away. "It misses. Just like that."

"It misses? You mean, every time? You're trying to tell me the U.S. Air Force is equipped with missiles that *miss*?"

"It's a one-in-a-million flaw," said Willy, with satisfaction. "If it hadn't been for the tests I was running on X-band radar, I doubt if anyone would ever have discovered it."

"But surely they've *tested* these missiles?" Daniel protested. "They worked during their tests, didn't they?"

"Oh, sure," Willy agreed. "And they still work now, when they're tested on the Air Force ranges. But what you have to realize is that we never test them against real Soviet airplanes. We usually use a PQM-102 RPV, which is a pilotless Delta Dagger. Now, each airplane has a different and distinct radar signature. And although our radar is obviously happy to lock onto the signature of a Delta Dagger, or any other U.S. target plane, it seems to have a widespread aversion to Soviet signatures."

Daniel forked out Lannie's bacon. "This is really true? This isn't just some isolated error in one particular piece of equipment?"

Willy shook his head. "I've run diagnostic programs through the armory computer on three different radar systems. Each system failed in exactly the same way, at exactly the same moment. But, of course, if a pilot didn't realize that his radar was snafu, he'd simply believe that he'd missed. Mind you, if he was in a real combat situation, he wouldn't have too damn long to worry about it, since I doubt if the Soviet air-to-air missiles have a similar aversion to hitting *our* planes."

"But it's *insane*," said Daniel. "How can a whole Air Force be equipped with missiles that don't work?"

"What can I say?" asked Willy, blowing flour off the table. "It's the greatest scandal in the history of the Air Force. And I mean the greatest. Heads will start rolling, believe me."

"Jesus," said Daniel.

"I have more tests to make," Willy added. "I want to take a look at the IR seeker nose on the Falcon; and maybe check the laser-beam proximity fuse, too."

"Don't befuddle me with technicality," said Daniel.

"I'm simply telling you that I want to check the guidance and detonation systems on other missiles, too. Every missile has its own fancy new system, and some of them are so far out you'd hardly believe them. Some of the latest ground-to-air missiles have phase-arrayed radar that's capable of surveillance, acquisition, track/engage and guidance. They can do everything except serve up lunch."

"None of which is any use if they don't hit the airplanes they're supposed to hit," said Daniel.

"Precisely," Willy agreed.

Susie sneezed in one still settling cloud of flour.

"Leave it," Daniel told Willy. "Cara will clean it up."

"Oh, Cara, that's her name? Nice name, considering she comes from South Dakota. Usually, they're called Waynette or Laurene or Trixie."

"Or Candii?" said Daniel.

Willy made a face. "Sure. Or Candii."

There was a shuddering knock at the front door of the diner. That must be Lannie Watts, wanting his breakfast. "Go let

Lannie in, will you?'' Daniel asked Susie. ''Tell him I'm just cracking his eggs.''

When Susie had gone through the plastic-strip curtain to the diner, Daniel said seriously to Willy, ''This thing you've found out. It's pretty serious, isn't it? I mean, it could be trouble.''

''Just like I said, Daniel, heads will roll.''

''You're sure it won't be *your* head? You know what Kawalek's like, all jokes apart. And Kawalek's only a colonel. There have to be plenty of generals and top brass at the Pentagon who won't particularly like being embarrassed by a know-it-all major from Williams.''

''I have to do what's right, Daniel.''

''Of course you do. But you also have to protect yourself. Whoever designed those missiles, whoever ordered them, whoever passed them as okay for active duty, all those people are going to want you out of the way. You just think to yourself how much money changes hands in a successful missile contract. Billions. Well, people get killed in the streets for pennies. So, be warned.''

''Daniel,'' insisted Willy, ''it's all a question of *fact*, that's all. The missiles don't work against Soviet radar signatures and that's it.''

Daniel wiped his hands on his jeans. ''You want some breakfast?''

''You don't want to talk about it?''

''Get yourself more information, that's all,'' Daniel told him. ''Don't go breezing into Kawalek's office with something you can't substantiate. And before you go, leave a copy of whatever it is you've been working on here with me. Or somebody else you trust.''

Willy pushed back his chair, and stood up. Susie came into the kitchen and announced, ''Lannie says please move your hindquarters with his breakfast.'' Daniel smiled, and nodded. ''Okay.''

Willy said, ''I guess I'll go catch myself a couple of hours' shuteye. Then I'll head back to the armory and run the last of those programs. I'll meet you at ten for a drink at Hank's. Is that okay?''

"That's okay. But you'll leave your findings with me before you go talk to Kawalek?"

"So that you can sell them to the Russians, and make yourself rich?" joked Willy.

"Willy," Daniel cautioned him.

Willy came over and flung an awkward arm around his shoulders. "I know, Daniel. I know. Discretion is the better part of valor. Don't fire until you see the whites of their eyes."

Daniel, one-handed, cracked two eggs. They had played racketball together, he and Willy. They had talked for hours, all night sometimes, until they knew each other like brothers, or maybe closer. Daniel had never been to Omaha, but he could have found his way to the hollow tree in Fontenelle Park where Willy used to hide his slingshot as if he had played there himself.

They were buddies, in the curiously old-fashioned sense of the word. But now Daniel had the unsettling feeling that the responsibilities of the real world were about to come between them; and although he tried to smile, he couldn't. His face was stiffening like rapidly cooling glass.

FOUR

Titus had seen Joe Jasper's Cadillac approaching through the willows, its amber lights dipping and bouncing through Beahms Grove; and so by the time Joe had awkwardly parked by the bank of the river, and picked his way in his polished Bejan shoes through the rough muddy grass that sloped down to the water's edge, Titus had been able to wade twenty or thirty yards further into midstream, still near enough to hear what Joe might shout out, in case it was anything interesting, but far enough to pretend that he was out of earshot, in case it wasn't.

It was a silent foggy afternoon in the Shenandoah Valley, old Civil War country. Titus was taking his first fishing vacation in three years, and whatever Joe Jasper had to say, it couldn't be half as absorbing to Titus as the deep swirl of the Shenandoah River, or the dripping of condensation from the overhanging trees, or the call of thrushes. Titus, after three-and-a-half years as Secretary of State, and five-and-a-half years of marriage to Nadine, was awarding himself three days and three nights of complete peace; peace that was punctuated only by the sound of a fishing-reel, or the whirr of nylon line.

"Titus!" called Joe. He was teetering on a boggy clump of grass, desperately trying to keep his $200 shoes out of the mud. But Titus kept his back to the bank, puffing at his corncob pipe even though it had died on him almost twenty minutes ago, and generally tried to look occupied with the current, and the weather, and the fish. He'd often heard that the greatest actors could communicate volumes of Shakespeare through their turned backs, although he wasn't quite sure how. What he was trying to communicate now was: get the hell out of here, Joe, unless it's something really good.

"Titus!" Joe called again. He had a thin voice, like a whippet. "Titus, can you hear me?"

Titus took two or three steps further into the stream. The water-level was uncomfortably close to the top of his waders, but he stayed where he was, deaf as a rock, occasionally turning his head upstream to make his pose look natural, whistling too for a moment but then forgetting to keep it up.

"Mr. Secretary, this is absolutely vital!" Joe yelled. "It's too sensitive to shout out to you; you'll have to come in to the riverbank and listen close!"

There was a long pause. The river gurgled and flowed. Titus stayed where he was, his pole held up numbly, his eyes closed. Of all the instincts that Joe could have appealed to, his curiosity was the most easily aroused. He could stay here, pretending to be inextricably absorbed; or he could admit that he had heard Joe calling, and wade back, and listen to what this sensitive news might be. It was too damned exasperating for words, especially since Joe would say nothing at all about his apparent deafness, but gloat silently, and make him feel angrier than ever.

He was still trying to make up his mind when he heard water splashing close by. He turned around, and to his complete astonishment, Joe was wading right up to him in his $750 Christian Dior suit, his thin triangular face fixed in the kind of expression you might expect to see on a man who has had an entire bowl of Jell-O emptied slowly into his jockey shorts.

"Mr. Secretary!" he gasped.

Titus forgot to pretend that he hadn't heard Joe calling before. "Why the hell didn't you stay on the bank? You gone crazy or something?"

"Titus, Mr. Secretary; this is urgent."

They stood facing each other, nearly waist-deep in the river.

Titus took the corncob pipe out of his mouth, then stuck it back in again, and started to wind in his line.

"I wouldn't have disturbed you for anything, Titus," said Joe. "But I think we've come up with the answer to the RINC problem; accidentally; fortuitously; and I knew you'd want to be the very first to know."

"How can I be the first to know when *you* already know?" growled Titus, reeling in his line as abruptly as his vacation, wrapped up and wound up like everything else he tried to do that wasn't connected with the State Department, or Nadine, or Nadine's hideous children.

"What I mean is, you're the first VIP to know," Joe corrected himself. "And, well, what we decide to *do* about it depends entirely on you."

"Do you realize you're soaking?" Titus asked Joe. "I mean, do you realize that you're absolutely fucking soaking wet?"

"Yes, sir," said Joe. Then, more sheepish, "I have another suit in the car."

Titus fastened his hook and then began to make his way slowly back to the bank of the river in deep, rhythmical strides. "That's typical of you, Joe. Do you know that? Heroism without inconvenience. You're always prepared to get your hands dirty, provided there's a handy pack of Wet Ones around."

Joe sloshed after him. He reached the edge of the river and stood in the mud with water streaming from his suit in a noisy cascade. Titus opened up his fishing bag to put away his fly and his hook, and dismantled his expensive carbon-fiber pole. Nadine had given him the pole when they were married. This was the first time he had taken it out. The walls of his library were crowded with trophies from his younger days, stuffed and mounted, but he hadn't added a single decent fish to his collection since he had left the Army and sought greater glory in politics.

Joe said, "It was one of those real breaks. One of those real one-in-a-million breaks."

"Why don't you change your suit before you tell me?" Titus snarled at him. "You might as well be comfortable."

"Well," said Joe, trying to be self-deprecating.

Titus walked across to the Cadillac and climbed into the passenger seat unbidden, tossing his fishing bag on to the back seat. The leather upholstery was virgin white, and his waders were very muddy, thick with that black silty Shenandoah bottom-mud; but he figured it would do Joe good, to have to sit there and watch helplessly as his pristine custom-upholstered car was gratuitously besmirched. Good for the soul.

Joe changed into his fresh suit behind the upraised trunk. Titus put down his window and called, "Don't be too long about it. Any man without pants is considered fair game in West Virginia." Joe reappeared in less than a minute, tucking in his shirttails, tightening his tie, sweating and discomfited.

"I was only joking," said Titus, as Joe climbed in behind the wheel.

"Well, it's not a thing to joke about," said Joe. His substitute suit was considerably less expensive than his first suit, a rather nasty knit in light blue, but Titus felt that it probably suited the occasion better. "Do you have any of those rotten cheap cigars you smoke?" he asked.

Joe opened the glove compartment and passed over a cigar-case containing four first-quality Havana coronas. Titus selected one, and Joe clipped it, then produced a box of British Swan Vesta matches, which were his ultimate snobbery. Titus could tell that he felt very uncomfortable in his blue knit suit, and made a point of rubbing his lapel between finger and thumb as Joe lit his cigar for him. "Nice stuff," he said, as he puffed. "You ought to have it remodeled into a Batman suit."

Joe, his face lit by the flickering match, said calmly, "We've found a hooker who spent the night with Roberts during the 1979 primaries. She's prepared to say publicly that he asked her to perform some very unnatural acts. She has a friend who may be prepared to be a witness. All her facts and dates and times add up. And, most stunning of all, she has Polaroids."

Titus examined the tip of his cigar. It was burning evenly. "You've seen the Polaroids yourself?"

"I've got copies of them here." Joe reached under the driver's seat and produced a small buff envelope. He handed it to Titus and watched him closely for his reaction. Titus didn't open the envelope at first, but tapped it against Joe's sleeve.

"You've tape recorded the girl's evidence?"

"Better. Video recorded it. *And* the evidence given by her friend."

"Her friend's a hooker too?"

"No. A chambermaid at the Las Vegas Futura."

Titus opened the envelope and took out the Polaroids. "Anything known?"

"On the chambermaid, no. Clean as a whistle. First-class witness."

"Better and better," said Titus. He held the Polaroids up to the Cadillac's dome light, and squinted at them narrowly.

"You want your eyeglasses?" asked Joe Jasper.

Titus shook his head. "I can see what's going on. Or am I mistaken? Maybe I've got it upside down."

"It's the correct way up," said Joe, tightly.

"Well," said Titus, rubbing his eyes. "This is pretty bad news for our glorious President, wouldn't you say so? I mean, it's obviously him."

Joe nodded.

Titus examined another Polaroid, then another. "I don't know what the hell turns anybody on about doing that," he remarked, turning one of the pictures around to show it to Joe. Joe shrugged, noncommittal. Titus demanded: "*You* don't get turned on by doing that, do you?"

"No, sir."

"Good," said Titus, shuffling the pictures and then tucking them back in their envelope. "Good." Then, after a long silence, "Wouldn't want to have anybody on my staff capable of enjoying something that I don't."

"Right," said Joe.

Titus wiped the side of his filthy wader on Joe's off-white rugs. Joe watched him in a kind of martyred fascination, while the names of several auto upholstery cleaners went through his mind. Delco made a good one, he remembered.

"Question is," said Titus, "what are we going to do about this lady? What's the best way to handle her?"

Joe smiled, but then he realized that Titus hadn't meant any *double entendre*, and quickly looked grave instead. "First off, we have to protect her," he said. "The minute the media get a sniff of what's going on, they're going to be after her like hounds. And if I know anything at all about Uncle Roberts, the Unfortunate Accident Squad isn't going to be far behind.''

Titus nodded seriously. "You're right, Joe. See to it. Fix her up in some dinky suburb just outside of Washington. Rockville, some place like that. Keep her guarded, and make sure that she's available when we want her. Keep her happy. Give her good food, and lots of booze. Give her a couple of well-hung guys if that's what she wants. Dope, anything. But keep her secret and keep her ready. Better still, I might persuade Nadine to take care of her.''

"Yes, sir," said Joe.

"Where is she now?" asked Titus.

"Philadelphia, seeing her sister. But Nielsen's with her.''

Titus was about to say something vicious, but held his tongue. Just because he personally hated the sight of his own family, that didn't mean that other people shouldn't go to visit theirs. It was one of those human aberrations that couldn't be avoided.

"We'd better get back to the hotel," said Titus. "I want to talk to Senator Rodney.''

"There's a phone right here," offered Joe, picking up the car telephone, and switching it on.

"You think I want to talk to Senator Rodney in my waders?" demanded Titus.

"No, well, I guess not," said Joe.

"Right, then," said Titus, folding his arms. "Let's go.''

It took them only ten minutes to reach the Elkswood Hotel, a white timber-lapped building overlooking a foggy curve of the Shenandoah River. Joe carried Titus' tackle for him as Titus walked with loudly wobbling waders through the lobby, and up to his two-bedroom suite. A Secret Service agent was sitting outside on a folding chair, deep in *The Playboy Advisor*. He stood uncomfortably to attention when Titus came past, but Titus absent-mindedly squeezed his shoulder, and said, "Don't worry about it. Thanks for letting me get away for a couple of hours.''

Joe raised an interrogative eyebrow at the agent as he followed Titus into the room, and it was clear from the agent's slight inclination of his head that Titus had never been really alone. Another Secret Service agent would have been waiting patiently in the woods by the river, with a pair of binoculars and a high-powered rifle. Titus was too unpopular with too many nuts and oddballs to let him go off on his own, unprotected. Somebody had taken two shots at him in Cleveland; and in Fort Worth he had been hit on the side of the head with a can of chickpeas. His office received at least a dozen threatening letters a day, including a recurring promise of "fiery execution" from somebody who called himself "the Great Blast."

"Fix me a drink, will you?" Titus told Joe, as he struggled out of his waders and unbuttoned his shirt. "No, it's over there, inside that thing that looks like a desk."

Joe opened the front of the desk, and found a bottle of Johnnie Walker Black Label, and lead-crystal glasses. He poured out a large splash of whiskey, and carried the glass to where Titus was now wrapping a royal-blue bathrobe tight around his hard, gray-pelted body. Titus took his cigar out of his mouth just long enough to swallow a mouthful, and then coughed, "Get me Rodney on the phone."

Joe opened Titus' black security briefcase. It contained anti-bugging alarms, infra-red detection equipment, and a scrambler telephone which could be plugged straight into the wall socket like a normal telephone. He punched out the 414 number and waited for the call tone to disturb Senator Rodney in his large split-level house in Kenosha, Wisconsin. Senator Rodney was a keen fisherman, too, and most of the time he was able to spend back in his home state he devoted to the lake and his twenty-three-foot boat *Spirit of Southport*.

Titus stood by the window looking out across the hotel driveway. It had been foggy all day, and now that evening was drawing in, it was almost impossible to see as far as the river. A time of ghosts, he thought to himself. A time for cold visitations, and prophesies to come true. He believed in destiny.

Titus had been in Korea and Viet Nam. He had been the last general to leave Saigon; and he had always privately sworn to himself that he would be the first general back in again. At fifty-two, he was fit, muscular, and handsome as Mount Rushmore. He exercised every morning, one hundred push-ups, fifty sit-ups, twenty back stretches. He could punch a hole through a plywood door with his fist, and he had once laid a nuclear disarmament demonstrator out cold. He wasn't from a rich family, but he had been a tough and uncompromising soldier, and he made his way in politics with the help of powerful friends in the Pentagon, and in defense-related industries anxious that America's foreign policy remain hotly belligerent.

Titus had once said, "I would rather see America *melt* than fall into Soviet hands." *Newsweek* had dryly remarked that when Israel Zangwill had referred to America as "the Great Melting-Pot," that wasn't exactly what he had had in mind.

Joe suddenly said, "Senator Rodney? Good evening. Yes, sir. I'm sorry to disturb you at home. It's Joe Jasper. I have Mr. Alexander for you. No, from the Shenandoah Valley."

Titus took the phone, wiping it first on his robe as if Joe might have left some slime on it. "Ken? It's Titus. How are you doing? Yes. Sure. Did you hear the latest on RINC?"

Senator Rodney was suffering from a summer cold, and he wheezed a little. "I heard that Marshall is already talking about mothballing a third of our cruise missiles. Provided, of course, he gets some reasonable guarantees from Moscow."

"Yes, well, that's partly correct," said Titus. He snapped his fingers at Joe to bring him over his drink. "He's expecting some wider Soviet cutbacks in Europe as well; but still nothing that could possibly justify reducing our cruise missile complement by one-third."

Senator Rodney sniffed, and coughed. "There was an NBC editorial last night saying that he was going soft on the Soviets. And considering the way he *used* to talk, before he was inaugurated . . . He used to make the hair stand up on the back of *my* neck, and you know what *I* feel about arms limitation."

Titus swallowed more whiskey, and then said, "We may have a way of stiffening him up again."

"Is this why you're calling?" asked Senator Rodney, cautiously.

"That's right. Joe Jasper has just stumbled across some very interesting visual and recorded material which shows President Marshall Roberts in a position which you might euphemistically call compromising."

"Witnesses?"

"The very best. The lady herself, and also another lady of spotless character who happened to see them go to his suite together, and who had the unenviable task of cleaning up when they'd finished.''

"Cleaning up? What kind of cleaning up?''

"I always said you were prurient, Ken. Let's just say that our beloved President asked the lady to give him a little shower.''

There was a digestive silence. On the other side of the room, Joe thrust his hands into his pockets and gave a funny little shiver of satisfaction. Then Senator Rodney said, "What are you going to do? This is pretty hot stuff.''

"What I'm *not* going to do is rush around to the Oval Office waving a fistful of Polaroids and tell Marshall that he's got to call off the talks on Reduction In Nuclear Capability right away, or else.''

"But you don't want RINC to go very much further, do you? Nor do any of us. The further we go, the more promises Marshall makes, the more difficult it's going to be to extract ourselves with any kind of credibility. The worst thing you can do in politics is look as if you're always changing your mind. It's worse than being wrong.''

"I'm not going to put any kind of a squeeze on Marshall until I'm sure of my strategy. Let's be realistic. There's always the possibility that next week's RINC talks may break down of their own accord. Jesus, Ken, it took them three months to decide how long each delegate could spend in the men's room. And the point is that I don't want to waste the nastiest, smelliest piece of information I've ever had against Marshall, not if it isn't really necessary. This stuff could be even *more* useful at election time.''

"Still got your eye on the Lincoln Sitting Room?'' asked Senator Rodney, with noticeable sharpness. Titus had often visited President Nixon in the Lincoln Sitting Room when the President was working there after dinner, and it was obvious he had always coveted it.

"When destiny calls, destiny calls,'' said Titus, unruffled. "Meanwhile, I'm going to install our principal witness in a house just outside of Washington, where we have easy access in case we need her; and I'm going to make sure that she's guarded day and night. Joe tells me the other lady is probably safer where she is, at home in Las Vegas. If we start putting pressure on

Marshall because of what he did at the Las Vegas Futura, and one of their chambermaids disappears, then Marshall's men are going to know who to look for. The woman has a husband and children, and the last thing we want is to have her chickening out because Marshall has threatened to incinerate the family home.''

Senator Rodney said, "This is going to be dangerous, you know. Marshall isn't going to like it one little bit.''

"I'm not frightened of Marshall.''

"Well, maybe not. But he won't take it lying down.''

"These days, I'm not so sure," said Titus. "All the guts seem to have dropped out of him. Don't you remember that speech he made at the San Francisco Cow Palace, during the primaries? All that talk about 'the light of liberty'? All that rhetoric about 'containing Communism'? Well, what happened to *that* when he promised the Soviets that America would keep hunter-killer satellites out of space? What happened to *that* when he pardoned that Soviet spy, what was his name, Nevsky? Let me tell you, Ken—Marshall used to be the backbone of American political conservatism. Now he's a goddamned jellyfish.''

"I agree with you, Titus, you know that," said Senator Rodney. "The only problem is, he's strong, very strong. And paranoid. He's got water-tight security, and the best intelligence network since Eisenhower. It's going to be hard to get to him, I warn you, and even when you do, you won't be safe.''

"Safety," Titus retorted, "is not my primary consideration. I was at Changjin Reservoir, remember? I was at Khe Sanh. I didn't care about my safety then, and I don't care about it now. All I care about is putting a stop to these goddamned disastrous RINC agreements.''

"Well, I hope you won't be sorry," said Senator Rodney. "Keep me in touch, will you? When are you going back to Washington?''

"I'm going to drive back now. I have a few traps to set.''

"How was the fishing?''

"Good enough. A fair catch of trout. Not what it used to be, though. Maybe I've lost my touch.''

"There are bigger fish in Washington, Titus. Whales, and swordfish, and sharks, too. Plenty of sharks.''

Titus grunted in amusement, and then put the phone down.

Joe Jasper said, "You don't have to go back right away; the girl won't be arriving in Washington until the day after tomorrow. You could have yourself one more day's fishing, if you wanted to."

Titus finished his drink, and held out his glass for another one. "Joe," he said, "fishing requires calm, and concentration. Right now, I'm not in the mood for it. I smell blood, thanks to you, Joe. I smell blood!"

"You're flattering me, Mr. Secretary."

Titus stared at him. Joe Jasper was such a weasel, such a sharp, nibbling, chiseling kind of a creature, that Titus found him compelling company. Joe would accept any insult, and perform any task, no matter how menial or degrading. He had first come to Washington with Nixon's West Coast *cosa nostra*— John Ehrlichman and Hank Haldeman and John Dean; but he had survived Watergate by attaching himself ("like a leech," Titus often thought) to the caretaker administration which followed. Joe Jasper, despite his pale, unappealing face, despite his fastidious clothing and his ostentatious gold rings, could worm his way in anywhere in Washington and get the goods on anyone. "Pay the check," said Titus. "I want to leave for Washington right away."

"What about your luggage?"

"Send Wilkins down to collect it in the morning."

Joe closed the communications briefcase, and gathered up the papers and notebooks which Titus had left around his suite. A thorough search would be made of the entire room tomorrow, to make sure that not even the slightest scrap of classified documentation had been left behind. Other, personal objects would be removed, too. It wouldn't do for the left-wing media to discover that the Secretary of State regularly ate Ex-Lax, nor that he used Chestnut-7 hair colorant.

Titus showered, and dressed in a gray mohair business suit, with a 2nd Infantry Division necktie, and a pocket handkerchief of exact isosceles sharpness. Meanwhile, the Secret Service man arranged for Titus' official black Cadillac to be driven around to the front of the hotel, ready for the drive back to the capital. It was almost 6:30 p.m., a grainy Shenandoah evening, and because of the fog it was practically dark.

"We're all set to go, Mr. Secretary," said Joe as Titus came out of the bedroom smelling of Jules aftershave, the last of his cigar still clenched between his teeth.

"Did you put in that call to my wife?"

"Yes, sir. She's decided to stay in Philadelphia one more night, but she's expected back by Thursday afternoon. Your stepchilden are both at home."

"Shit," said Titus, tugging at his left cuff, and giving himself a last inspection in the mirror. "That's all I need. Carl and Samantha, unlovability incarnate."

Joe picked a wiry gray hair from Titus' shoulder. "There was a call from Mr. Nott, in Britain, but apparently it wasn't urgent. And Mr. Yusef called, about the pipeline arrangement."

"Any word from Schmidt?"

Joe shook his head. "None. He seems to be playing this one really close to the chest."

"Hm," said Titus. Then, "Let's go. We got everything?"

They left the suite and walked down the corridor. From inside one of the rooms they passed, there was the buzzing of some-body shaving, and from inside the next room, the muted burble of the *Mary Tyler Moore Show*. The Secret Service agent walked a pace or two behind them, whistling between his teeth. His colleague was waiting in the lobby.

"Mr. Secretary," nodded the second agent, as Titus came down the staircase to the lobby. "Everything's ready. I'm real sorry you had to cut short your fishing."

"Well, can't be helped," smiled Titus, wryly. Over the hotel's reception desk there was a large stuffed pike, illuminated with a spotlight. The Front Royal Towers had always advertised itself as "The Compleat Resort for Anglers."

They descended the wet stone steps outside. Titus' official black limousine was parked just beside the wall that surrounded the sun patio. This evening, the sun patio was barely visible, puddled and mossy, with a solitary sundial dripping in the twilight like a forgotten tombstone.

"I think I'll travel with Joe," Titus told his Secret Servicemen. "Joe? I want to go over some of this RINC business with you. Maybe we can work out some angles."

"Mr. Jasper's car isn't bulletproof, sir," one of the agents pointed out. "If there should be any kind of irregularity . . ."

"Don't you love it?" said Titus, cracking into a grin. "They call an assassination attempt an 'irregularity.' Well, I can tell you, son, the only irregularity that's going on around here concerns my bowels, and that's only because of those damned stepchildren of mine occupying both damned bathrooms for hours on end, making-up and shaving and using acne scrub while I have to get myself off to the State Department. I was so damned regular in Viet Nam that the USS *New Jersey* used to fire off its morning salvo as soon as their lookouts saw my toilet door open. Better than a goddamn naval chronometer."

The Secret Servicemen shrugged, and walked across to the official limousine with that arms-swinging round-shouldered gait exclusive to bodyguards. Titus climbed into Joe Jasper's car, and said, "How about another one of those cheap cigars of yours, Joe?" The car's windshield was beaded with moisture, so Joe switched on the wipers, and cleared it away.

"I've got to tell you, this is the first time I've gladly cut a fishing-trip short," said Titus. "You've got to tell me how you managed to lay your hands on that stuff. That was a stroke of genius. You heard that? I'm paying you a compliment."

Joe started the engine. "The whole thing came to light when I was talking to a man called Iacono in Atlantic City. He simply said that he'd met a girl who was boasting that she'd once—"

With a shattering crash, like the bow of an icebreaker cleaving its way into a glacier, the car's windshield imploded, and dumped a slushy pile of sparkling broken glass into their laps. A nanosecond later, the car rose and bucked and dipped on its suspension.

Then they heard the explosion, so loud that it deafened them, and their ears sang as they saw Titus' huge black polished limousine rise into the air, its doors flapping open as if it were desperately trying to fly, turning over on its back twenty feet above them, and then rolling over and over onto the sun patio, crushed and still rolling as it hit the sundial and broke through the stone balustrade which overlooked the garden.

There was a second explosion, and Titus said tightly, "Gas tank." A ball of flame licked up into the fog, and then the

Cadillac was blazing fiercely from end to end, with a soft and hungry roar which Titus hadn't heard since Nam.

He climbed out of the car, brushing showers of glass off his suit. Joe said, "Titus—Mr. Secretary—we ought to get the hell out of here. They may have marksmen."

But Titus ignored him, and walked across to the ten-foot-wide hole in the brick-paved driveway where the explosives had gone off. The device had probably been slipped under the Cadillac while it was parked there a few minutes ago, and been detonated by remote control. Titus looked narrowly up at the hotel windows, checking one after the other, but they were all blank, giving nothing away.

He climbed the low stone wall on to the sun patio and walked across the scoured, battered flagstones. The car was still burning, although its bodywork was already blackened and blistered, and there was more smoke now than flame. Hanging from the passenger window he saw a human hand, charred, with the tips of its fingers still spouting little flames like a menorah. There was something ominously supernatural about it, and Titus bit his lip and turned away, disturbed.

Joe came hurrying over with his gun held high in his left hand. It was a gigantic .357 revolver, and if he had ever fired it, the recoil would probably have knocked him flat. When he saw the burning car, he stopped where he was. "Holy Christ."

People were running down the steps of the hotel, and opening up their windows. Lights were being switched on everywhere. Somebody said, "Call an ambulance. There's been an accident."

An accident? thought Titus. He started to walk back to the car, and he was trembling like an old man of 80. No, not an accident. An *irregularity*; that's what it was. And he dearly and deeply wanted to know who was responsible.

FIVE

Chief of Police Walter Ruse considered himself to be a true Westerner, in the sense that he believed in justice being fair, prompt, and memorable. He was known to deal with traffic offenders by giving them a swift hard kick in the pants, rather than writing them a ticket.

He was a big, huge-bellied man, with a fat, tanned face, and two small closely-set eyes the color of cold steel. Kathy Forbes always said that his eyes reminded her of two nails sticking in a pig's behind. Chief Ruse always said that Kathy Forbes reminded *him* of a medium-class madame. There was little love lost between the press and the police department in Phoenix; particularly that summer.

Because of his direct approach to justice, Chief Ruse was not at all happy with the obvious complexities of the homicide on Oasis Drive. Here was a woman found with her head sawn off, one of the most brutal attacks he'd ever seen. Yet there was no apparent motive, no robbery, no rape, no vandalism, not even "Death to Pigs" scrawled in blood on the wall. Just her head sawn off; and, worse, her head was missing. Police dogs had searched the area all morning and all they had come up with so far was an unpleasantly dead coyote. Chief Ruse hoped very much that this wasn't going to be the beginning of one of those random and inexplicable waves of violence of some terrorist group. He had enough to contend with right now, keeping the husbands and wives of Phoenix from blowing themselves away with their own handguns. It always happened in the summer, when the temperature hit the high 80s. Chief Ruse took off his large Western hat and wiped the inside of the brim with his handkerchief, and sniffed.

The headless body had just been taken away. Chief Ruse heard the ambulance siren warbling away down 36th Street. He stood with his hands on his bulging hips, and contemplated with absent-minded seriousness the hysterical splashes of blood on the walls and bedspread, and the dark tide of coagulated gore which spread out over the white carpet like a monstrous scab. He heard the front door of the house close behind him, but he didn't turn around. He knew who it was.

Lieutenant Berridge, humming to himself. Berridge was perhaps the best homicide detective that Phoenix had seen in fifteen years—young, fit, intelligent, well-trained and experienced. Chief Ruse found him unbearable, not only because he was so damned *good*, but because he looked like one of those toothy California tennis-players, all flashing incisors and tanned chest, and because he was only thirty-one years old, and because he had thick sun-blond hair and sharp blue eyes, and because his wife Stella was exactly the same, virtually a twin—blond, athletic and wholesome; and because he was such a conceited paralyzing pain in the ass. *And* because he would never keep still, but was always hopping or jumping or shuffling around as if he were warming up for a basketball contest.

"You want to tell me *your* opinion, chief?" asked Berridge, lacing his fingers together and popping all his knuckles, one after the other, in a controlled salvo. Chief Ruse closed his eyes. He hated people who made noises with their bodies. He said without opening his eyes, "Whatever opinion *I* happen to have, I know that *you've* got yourself an opinion which is a hundred times more dynamic, so why don't you tell me what it is now and get it over with?"

"Right, okay," said Berridge, raising his finger to make point one. "There isn't any question that we have some unusual difficulties here, particularly as far as identification is concerned.

But I *do* think that we can safely assume that the dead woman is in fact Mrs. Margot Schneider, widow of the late Major Rudolph Schneider, of the United States Air Force. Everything we have here supports that assumption. We have no ID. No Social Security card. In fact, we have nothing with a picture. But we do have her pension papers, and when I checked with Luke Air Force Base, they confirmed her age and her general appearance—and they tally. Her doctor confirmed her blood group, which is another plus. What's more, there are letters in her writing-table from old girlfriends in the service, going right back to 1951.''

Chief Ruse opened his eyes, and turned around to stare at Berridge as if the young lieutenant were babbling complete nonsense. But Berridge was too arrogant to allow Ruse's famous death-ray stare to put him off. He raised a second finger, and said, ''As far as I'm concerned, the most important question is not *who* she is, or *why* she was murdered, but *why would anybody want to take her head?* Don't you agree? And, personally, I think there are three possible answers to that. One, her killers may have wanted to remove all traces of some unusual and incriminating head-wound. Perhaps she was killed with something incredibly specialized, like a glazier's hammer, or a carpet-fitter's tool—which is possible, but not particularly likely. Second, they may have taken it for kicks.''

''You mean they wanted to play soccer with it?''

This time, Berridge was genuinely startled. But he managed to say, tersely, ''They may have taken it for some kind of *ritual*, that's what I mean. Sexual, or magical. *Those* sort of kicks.''

''And the third possibility?''

''The third possibility is that they may have taken her head as proof to some third party that they'd actually killed her.''

''In other words, our poor Air Force widow was killed by contract? '*Bring Me The Head Of Alfredo Garcia*,' that kind of stuff?''

''That's the inference, yes.''

''Well, now,'' Chief Ruse drawled slowly, ''those are all possibilities. But they still don't get us any nearer to finding out who killed her, and why.''

''On the contrary, chief,'' argued Berridge. ''The first thing we should do is run a computer make on any violent crimes which have involved blows to the head with unusual weapons. Then run a second make on any sex or black magic cults which hold the human head or skull to be particularly significant. And finally a make on any contract killings on which the head or other parts of the body were taken as proof of death."

There was a chime at the front door. Berridge said, "I'll get it. It's probably the food I ordered."

"You ordered *food*?"

Berridge looked surprised. "I'll probably be working on this thing for the rest of the night. Besides, it's only a diet burger."

"God help us," breathed Chief Ruse, hitching up his pants. "A diet burger."

There was talking by the front door. After a while, Chief Ruse went out into the corridor, and said, "Berridge? What's going on?"

"Ah, chief, there you are," said a girl's voice. "I've been looking for you everywhere. They told me you went downtown with the coroner."

"I never ride with stiffs," said Chief Ruse. "Now get your tail out of here, Miss Forbes. This is a police-restricted area."

The officer at the door said, "I'm sorry, chief, she just pushed past me."

Berridge said, "It's okay, chief. We can let in the star reporter from *The Arizona Flag,* can't we? Maybe she can give us some assistance."

"Another damned Californian," grumbled Chief Ruse.

"I'm not, as a matter of accuracy," said Kathy, unbuckling her black shoulder-bag so that she could check her tape-recorder. She gave Chief Ruse a wide, toothy grin. "I was born in Tucson, near Randolph Park. I was raised in Phoenix, and I only went to Los Angeles when I was fourteen years old."

"Thanks for the c.v.," said Chief Ruse. "Now, what can you possibly want to know that you haven't already been told? The body's gone, the photographers have gone, the forensic team have made their initial studies and they're going to be back tomorrow to do a little more. Everything's running routinely."

"Do you have any theories?" asked Kathy.

"Yes," said Chief Ruse flatly. "I suspect that Mrs. Schneider was murdered."

Kathy didn't blink. "How about you, lieutenant? Any ideas?"

"Don't ask him," Chief Ruse interrupted. "According to him, Mrs. Schneider was decapitated either by someone who didn't want us to know that they'd hit her over the head with some kind of weird object, like a piano; or some kind of sex-magic lunatics who get off on severed heads; or a hit-man who needed a souvenir to prove that he'd done what he was paid for."

"Is that right?" Kathy asked Lieutenant Berridge.

Berridge drummed his fingers in a complicated tempo on the doorframe. "Not exactly. But I guess you could say that it's close enough."

"So I can say that you're looking for a piano-wielding sex-magic madman with a neurosis about being believed by his employers?"

"Miss Forbes—" burst out Chief Ruse. But Berridge raised his hand to quiet him down, and laughed. "Come on, chief, she's deliberately goading you. You should know that. Miss Forbes, I have to congratulate you on your technique."

"Lieutenant Berridge is married, by the way," said Chief Ruse, hitching up his belt again, and sniffing.

"Maybe we'd better go through to the kitchen," suggested Berridge. "It's kind of gory right here."

He took Kathy's arm and guided her through to Margot Schneider's neat wood-paneled kitchen. "You won't touch anything, will you?" he told her. "The forensic boys have finished in the murder room, but they have to go over the whole house."

On the kitchen wall, next to the icebox, was a memo pad with the legend, "*Don't forget brocc! also bank I's check!*" A half-finished cup of coffee had been left on the worktop, still impressed with the pink lipstick of a woman who now had no head. Lieutenant Berridge thrust his hands in his pockets and looked around, and said, "Pretty strange, isn't it? The last person who came into this kitchen is dead."

Chief Ruse followed them in, and folded his arms over his belly. "I don't want to rush you, Miss Forbes, but I'm going to rush you. Three questions and then that's it. I have a duty to *all* of the Phoenix media, not just to *The Flag*."

"Oh, sure, I understand," said Kathy. "Tell me—do you happen to have any photographs of the victim—anything that we could publish?"

Chief Ruse glanced at Lieutenant Berridge uneasily. The question of photographs was one which he would have preferred to delay. The truth of the matter was that they had found no photographs of the murdered woman at all, not even amongst the framed pictures of her family on the sitting-room table. Even when they had sent a sergeant around to Luke Air Force Base this afternoon to check on any photographs on file of social gatherings and parties, they had found no identifiable picture of Margot Schneider in any of them. Plenty of Major Martin Schneider, smiling and holding up glasses of champagne. Even one tantalizing picture showing him waltzing with Mrs. Schneider— she with her back to the camera. But that was the only one, and it was impossible to make a positive identification from that. It seemed, oddly, as if Margot Schneider had never in her life been photographed. Even her Social Security card was missing.

"Er, we have *some* pictures, but we have to show them to her next-of-kin first," Lieutenant Berridge extemporized. "You understand how it is."

"May I see one?"

Chief Ruse shook his head. "Not at this time. And not ahead of any of the other media."

"Well, suit yourself," said Kathy. "But I have to tell you that Mrs. Margot Schneider seems to have been the world's least-photographed human being. None of her neighbors have pictures of her. The Arizona Biltmore doesn't have any pictures of her, despite the fact she often used to go to dinners and social functions there. And, of course, we can't even photograph her dead."

"Right," nodded Lieutenant Berridge. "No head." It sounded like a comic one-liner.

Kathy said, "Hasn't it occurred to you that the murderer might have cut her head off simply to prevent you from finding out who she was?"

"She was Margot Schneider," said Lieutenant Berridge. "All the papers prove it. She has pension papers, letters from friends. She was wearing one slipper when she died and that slipper was bought from the Scottsdale Shopping Mall nine weeks ago by

Margot Schneider. She used her American Express card. Listen, there are theories in homicide cases and there are wild guesses. Sometimes, very rarely, the wild guesses pay off. But if we begin to doubt the overwhelming circumstantial and documentary evidence that the murder victim was Margot Schneider, then we're going to complicate ourselves right out of business. Chief Ruse and I don't usually see eye-to-eye on very much when it comes to detective work, but I think we're in agreement about that. The fundamental undeniable fact is that a woman called Margot Schneider has been murdered by decapitation. Now we have to work on the probable theories about *why*. That's what we're doing, and that's all. All I can say in our favor is that we're very good at what we do. We're the best.''

Kathy Forbes was silent for a moment. Berridge looked at her with patronizing interest and thought for the first time how pretty she was. She had dark shoulder-length hair, tightly tied-back with a scarlet-and-yellow silk scarf. She had a square face with high cheekbones and wide hazel-brown eyes, one of those nice short, straight noses he had always admired, and a wide mouth that looked as if it could smile a lot and talk a lot and kiss a lot. Her figure wasn't anything to complain about, either, in spite of her severe gray linen suit and her sheer gray stockings (seamed, too—he liked that). He categorized her: 25 years old, married once and probably divorced, no children, a small-time career girl, Christopher Cross fan and aerobics enthusiast. A feminist until she can find a man who can really take care of her. One hundred percent wholesome American girl, no dental fillings, closely shaved underarms, breasts just a little too large to hold in one hand. A genuine article of American womanhood, Ms. Kathy Forbes, no doubt about it.

"If you want to discuss the theories in more detail, I can at least do *that* with you," suggested Berridge. His voice dropped almost an octave. "I don't think I really want to do it here, though. Maybe a restaurant? I haven't eaten all day."

"Didn't you order a diet burger?" asked Chief Ruse, sarcastically.

"A diet burger?" asked Berridge, with an uncomfortable, laugh. "What the hell would I need with a diet burger?"

"Maybe you could slim down your head," said Chief Ruse.

There was another chime at the door and Chief Ruse went to answer it. It was Jackson Dawes from the mayor's office, wanting to talk about the political side of this murder. "We don't want Phoenix to look like the kind of place where . . ." murmur, murmur. "Well, you understand what I'm saying, I'm not trying to put a lid on it, but . . ."

Kathy Forbes said to Berridge, "You're really married?"

"Separated. Considering divorce. Mary never liked the idea of police work. It's the hours, mainly. She's a very systematic kind of a lady, doesn't like her life to be full of surprises."

"Are you really sure this was Margot Schneider?"

"You want to see the evidence? There's no question."

"Then why did they do it? Why did they cut her head off? And why did they kill her, if she was nobody more important than a plain old Air Force widow? All the neighbors said she was sweet. Why should anybody want to kill a woman like that?"

Berridge folded a stick of gum into his mouth, and shrugged. Then, remembering his manners, he offered Kathy a piece. "Juicy Fruit?"

"No, thanks. I think I'd better be getting back to the office. I want to file my story by ten."

"You don't want dinner? We could go to Mother Tucker's, it's on the way back to town. They have a terrific salad cart."

"Well . . . maybe."

But at that moment Chief Ruse came back into the kitchen, and slapped Berridge on the back. "There isn't any need for you to stay any later, lieutenant. I'm sure Stella will be missing you—as much as anybody can."

"Stella?" asked Kathy.

"The delectable Mrs. Berridge, Ms. Forbes. Our ace detective here has one of the tastiest wives on the force. It makes you sick, doesn't it?" Sick to your stomach.

Kathy smiled at Berridge tartly. Berridge, in spite of his bravado, couldn't help blushing. "Yes, chief," said Kathy. "It does make you sick."

"Do you need a ride back to town?" Berridge asked her. "*Without* stopping anywhere to eat."

"No, thank you. I have my own car."

"In that case, you can give me a ride. Just wait a couple of minutes while I make sure I've got everything. Chief, do you want to meet for breakfast tomorrow morning—say seven o'clock? I really want to run over this computer thing.''

Kathy waited in the kitchen while Chief Ruse and Lieutenant Berridge arranged meetings for the following day. She felt tired now; she had been up at six, as soon as news of Margot Schneider's murder had broken. She wanted a cigarette, but it was nine weeks since she had smoked her last, and she was determined to keep up her record. This time, it was going to be for keeps. She didn't want to be a slave to anything or anyone.

Lieutenant Berridge had been wrong about her age—she was 29—but right about her divorce. In Los Angeles, six years ago, she had married an incandescently brilliant young actor, David Forbes, and for four years they had lived a life of fun and laughter and beach-parties and dancing at dawn. Then she had come home from a trip to Arizona to find David in bed with two wide-eyed girls of 13 and 14, and the world had split open like a broken alabaster egg.

Maybe she should have been more sophisticated about it, more Hollywood. After all, men needed their fun. But every single reaction inside her had been negative. She had married David for ever, however old-fashioned that seemed to be, and if it wasn't going to be for ever, then it wasn't going to be for one more minute. She had walked out.

She hadn't asked him for anything, not even a half-share in their Westwood apartment. But he had given her his Mirada, probably on the advice of his lawyer, and his complete collection of Miró lithographs. That had been the first thing he had ever said to her, ''Come up and see my lithographs.''

While she waited, a police officer came into the kitchen with a large folder. He was slightly-built, round-shouldered, with a mustache, one of those police officers who always seemed to be called Rizzo or Wuschinsky, and who always seem to be apologizing, even as they busted you. He put down a messy collection of magazines, photographs and papers on the kitchen table and said, ''You seen Lieutenant Berridge? I was supposed to hand over all this stuff to him.''

''He'll be back directly,'' said Kathy. ''He's talking to Chief Ruse.''

"Oh, right. Well, can I leave these here? You'll make sure that Lieutenant Berridge gets them? I have to get home. It's my birthday, would you believe, and my wife's been planning this surprise party for weeks. They'll all be hiding in the closet bursting their goddamned bladders if I don't get back there and act like I don't know what's going on."

"Okay," smiled Kathy. She took the file and shuffled it straight. "What shall I say your name was?"

"Russo. Officer Russo. They'll know who you mean."

"Not Rizzo?"

The policeman looked at her strangely. "*Rizzo*?" he asked.

"It's a private joke," said Kathy. "I'm sorry. I'll give these papers to Lieutenant Berridge for you."

"It's the stuff from Mrs. Schneider's attic," said Russo/Rizzo. "There was nothing else up there, only clothes."

"All right." said Kathy.

Officer Russo left and Kathy was alone in the kitchen with Mrs. Schneider's papers. There was no question that she wasn't going to look at them: the *Flag*'s ace girl reporter? She leafed through them hurriedly, her eyes flicking across insurance policies, invoices, lawyer's bills, garage estimates, a small assembly of news-cuttings about Clark Gable, of all people, fastened together with a rusty paper-clip; a torn review of *The Misfits* (why *The Misfits*, of all movies?); and then something which stopped her cold. A Polaroid photograph, an *old* Polaroid photograph, because it was yellowed and blotchy and black-and-white, of a man who was smiling into the sunshine and just about to push back his thick shock of hair, a man whose face she had seen a thousand times before in news and magazine photographs, and yet never quite in this pose, never quite from this particular angle. It was John F. Kennedy, no doubt about it: smiling, alive, and wearing a white short-sleeved tennis shirt. So alive, in fact, that he had signed the Polaroid in ballpen: "For N, special memories, P."

"P"? she thought to herself. It was certainly John F. Kennedy, nobody else. Maybe "P" stood for "President," or some other pet name. But who was "N"? Maybe he had been writing "M" for "Margot." She frowned at the Polaroid for almost two or three minutes before she heard Chief Ruse and Lieutenant Berridge come out of the murder room, and Lieutenant Berridge saying, ". . . the blood tests tomorrow and then we can check with her doctor. Well, sure."

She tucked the Polaroid into her suit pocket, and propped her mouth into an innocent smile. Lieutenant Berridge came into the kitchen and said, "How're you doing? You still going to give me that ride?"

"If you want," she smiled. "By the way, some officer called Rizzo left these papers for you."

"Rizzo?"

"Russo. Same difference."

Lieutenant Berridge pulled a face. "No wonder they never spell my name right in the goddamned newspapers. What did the *Star* call me last week? 'Burberry.' "

Kathy's car was parked outside on the curb. It was almost dark now on Oasis Drive, except for a single gleam of sunset over the Phoenix Mountains. Under the evening clouds, the lights of Paradise Valley and Phoenix twinkled and shimmered, hope and desperation and struggle and ease each represented by a single white sparkling light. Lieutenant Berridge opened the Mirada's passenger door, got in, and said, "Nice night. Mind if I smoke?"

Kathy started the engine, and pulled away from the curb. "You really think you're going to catch this joker?" she asked him, as he snapped his lighter and noisily sucked in smoke.

"We'll get him."

"And you really think that the woman who got killed was Margot Schneider?"

"What other woman could it possibly be?" Lieutenant Berridge demanded. "Is there another woman who wears your slippers and your nightwear and your make-up, and lives in your house?"

Kathy made a left into 24th Street without replying. Then, "It's a pretty heavy murder, all the same," she said. "Can you imagine how much strength that guy must have had? To cut her head off like that?"

Lieutenant Berridge shrugged.

"And what does Chief Ruse think about it?" asked Kathy. "He seems pretty upset."

"Well, sure he is. Three streets to the east, and the whole

thing would have been out of his jurisdiction, and dumped in the laps of Paradise Valley. But, don't you worry, we'll find out who did it. Crimes like this one have a way of solving themselves when you least expect it.''

"They solve *themselves*? Isn't that going to put you out of a job?"

They were passing the King of Beef restaurant, on the corner of Campbell Avenue. "You're sure I can't interest you in a steak?"

Kathy patted his knee, and smiled indulgently. "I should go home to Stella, lieutenant, if I were you. She'll be wondering where you are, even if Mary isn't."

Lieutenant Berridge flipped open the car's ashtray and stubbed out his cigarette. "Screw you, Lois Lane," he told her.

SIX

Unlike most Western drinking establishments, the bar they called "Hank's" was not one of those concrete bunkers with freezing cold air conditioning, plastic venetian blinds and a men's room that looked like a combat zone. It didn't even have one of those blue-and-red neon signs in the window saying "Coors" or "Bud" or "Eats."

It was an old-fashioned parlor, in the only elegant house in the whole of Apache Junction, a gingerbread creation that had been built in the days of the Lost Dutchman Mine by an enterprising but ill-starred madame called Regina Smibbs. "Hank" was a bald-headed one-time piano salesman called Rufus McNeice, whose wife had never held with drinking. Rufus had lived a double life for thirty years, preaching temperance in public but privately sneaking snorts from a flask which he attached to the underside of his car with magnets. When his wife died in 1972, Hank had applied for a liquor license, and opened up a bar where he wanted a bar the most, in his own front parlor.

Daniel was sitting there with Cara when Ronald Reagan Kinishba came in, fully dressed in black motorcycling leathers, swinging his black crash-helmet. He was tall, with a handsome pock-marked face and a nose modeled on the beak of a golden eagle. He raised his hand in greeting to Hank, behind the bar, and then came over and put down his helmet on the table in front of Daniel.

"Hi, Ronald," said Daniel. "How are you doing?"

Ronald unzipped about ten different zippers, and took off his jacket, hanging it over the back of the chair. Underneath he wore a turquoise T-shirt that was emblazoned with the legend "Remember Ah-jon-jon."

"Well, I'm fine," he said, in his husky voice. "Are you going to buy me a beer?"

"This is Cara," said Daniel. Cara nodded, and said, "Hi." Ronald planted his elbow on the table and examined her with some interest. She was wearing a tight pink T-shirt, through which her nipples showed as dark and provocative smudges; and an even tighter pair of pink Bermuda shorts.

"Daniel been treating you good?" asked Ronald.

Cara laid her hand on top of Daniel's and smiled. "As good as any man could, thank you."

"Cara's from South Dakota," said Daniel. "What do you want? Coors Lite?"

"That'll do," said Ronald. Then, to Cara, "Are you passing through, honey, or staying?"

"A little of each," said Cara.

"You be careful of this guy," Ronald warned her. "He has a very weird effect on women. In fact, he has a weird effect on everybody. The Indians have a word for guys like him."

"Oh, yes?" said Cara.

"Sure. They call them 'moksois.' "

"What does that mean?" giggled Cara.

Ronald looked at her with great mock-seriousness. "Potbelly," he said. Then he laughed out loud.

"Don't pay him any mind," said Daniel.

Hank brought them over two Lites, and a pina colada for Cara. "Willy coming in tonight?" he wanted to know.

"He was supposed to be here by ten," said Daniel. "But, well, you know what he's like. Gets himself involved."

"Not just with work, either," grinned Ronald, dragging his chair six inches nearer to Cara, and staring at her with undisguised appreciation.

"You keep your distance," Daniel warned him.

"Be very careful," Ronald murmured to Cara. "He's very possessive, as well as being crazy. If he catches you even *glancing* at another guy, he'll kill you. You don't have any idea what you've let yourself in for."

Cara giggled again, and said to Daniel, "He's cute. Don't you think so?"

"Cute? Is a sidewinder cute?"

"Oh, come on," said Cara.

They talked and teased and drank for another hour, until well past eleven o'clock. Then Daniel checked his watch again. "This isn't like Willy, you know. He's never on time, but he's never as late as this. Particularly when there's drinking time a-wasting."

"Maybe they gave him extra duty," suggested Ronald.

"Why *did* your parents call you Ronald Reagan?" asked Cara.

Ronald shrugged. "They weren't too bright, either of them. Well, they were quite *bright,* but they weren't educated. They thought that if they named me after a famous white hero, I'd find it easier to get on in the white man's world. The only famous white hero they knew was Ronald Reagan."

"At least they didn't call you Mickey Rooney," said Cara.

Daniel fidgeted for a while, and then said, "I think I'll call the base. Maybe he's been held up."

"Well, why don't you just go do that," said Ronald, inching even closer to Cara. "And—please—take as long as you like."

Pete Burns the deputy sheriff came in, and gave them a wave of acknowledgment. He was a placid, big-bellied man, but he had booked Ronald eight times in two years for speeding, and he had always made it quite clear that he would happily run any citizen of Apache Junction straight into the pokey at no notice flat if he or she even *looked* as if they were doing anything illegal. "Laws don't get passed to get mocked," he used to say, too often for it to be interesting. Ronald, just as often, had accused him of "legislative flatulence."

Daniel went out into the hall. Hank had fixed a pay-phone by the front door, next to the elephant's-foot umbrella stand. Daniel thumbed in a dime and dialed the number of Williams Air Force Base.

Inside the parlor, Ronald was saying to Cara, "What's a

foxy-looking lady doing with a nice tame guy like Daniel? Did
you ever ride on the back of a motorcycle? Pillion? The wind in
your hair, the stars in your eyes, and 749 cc of throbbing engine
clutched between your thighs?''

Cara replied, "Daniel's *cute*."

"Listen, nobody said he wasn't. But I'm talking about four
transverse-mounted cylinders, double overhead cams, transistor-
ized pointless ignition and Pentroof heads."

Cara said, "You're talking about *what?*"

Just then, Daniel came back in again looking perplexed. He
sat down and said, "He's not there. They say he hasn't been
there all day."

"Well, maybe he hasn't."

"No, he specifically told me he was going to go back to the
armory to run some tests."

"Maybe he changed his mind."

"It wasn't the kind of thing he was going to change his mind
about. It was something urgent."

Ronald pulled a face. "I don't know what to say. If he isn't
there, he isn't there."

Daniel finished his beer. Maybe Ronald was right, and maybe
he was just being ridiculous. But he couldn't help remembering
what Willy had been telling him so earnestly this morning: all
that stuff about missiles that wouldn't work against Soviet radar
signatures. All that stuff about "heads will roll." And now, he
wasn't there.

Cara said, "You don't have to worry. He's a grown-up. He's
a major in the Air Force, for Christ's sake. I'm sure he can look
after himself. Well, I hope to God he can look after himself,
when you think that he's supposed to be looking after *us*."

Ronald suggested, "How about another beer? Especially if
you're buying."

Daniel bit at his thumbnail. "Listen," he said, "how about a
quick ride down to the base, just to make *sure* he's not there?"

"Are you kidding?"

"I'm just worried, that's all. Willy positively and definitely
said that he was going to be working in the armory for most of
the day, and that he was going to be round here at ten."

Ronald leaned back in his chair in exasperation. "You know

what this is, don't you? A cheap way of getting me out of here, so that I won't be able to impress your girlfriend any more with my obviously superior intelligence and clearly superior looks.''

"You're nuts," said Daniel. "Do you want to take me down there or not?''

"Okay," agreed Ronald, reluctantly. "I guess I wanted to try out my new tune job anyway.''

"And what am I supposed to do, while you're speeding like the Seventh Cavalry to Williams Air Force Base?'' Cara demanded.

Daniel leaned over and kissed her cheek. "You can go back to the diner and tell Mrs. Koperwas that she can go home and give Mr. Koperwas his Hungry Man dinner. And if Susie's still awake, you can switch off her television and paddle her fanny.''

"Isn't it true about history?'' said Cara, finishing her pina colada. "The men get the fun and the women get to sit around and wait for them to come home.''

But outside the bar, in the darkness, as Ronald went to get his motorcycle, Cara slid her arm around Daniel's waist, and pressed her breasts against him, and kissed him once, twice, three times, with a passion he wouldn't easily forget. "You won't be long, will you?'' she breathed in his ear. "I'll be waiting for you, when you come back. And I mean, waiting.''

Daniel kissed her back and cupped the firm rounded cheeks of her bottom in his hands. "You know something?'' he whispered back at her. "You have the finest ass since the Sabine women.''

"All right, cut the groping," said Ronald, wheeling up his shiny black Nighthawk. "If there's one thing I dislike more than petty meanness, like not buying me a second beer, it's smugness, like feeling up this delicious red-headed young lady right in front of me.''

"You've got your bike to love, what more do you want?'' asked Daniel.

Ronald shrugged. "It's okay, I guess. It's just that it leaves oil on the sheets.''

Cara blew Daniel a last kiss, and walked back along the side of the highway to the diner. Under the fluorescent lights, she cast four shadows, one to each point of the compass. "That's some girl," said Ronald, straddling his motorcycle and fastening his helmet. "Just your type, too. Travel-stained, worldly-wise, with a used but pretty face and huge but shapely knockers."

Daniel climbed on to the high black-leather pillion seat and grasped Ronald tightly around the waist. "Did anyone ever tell you that Indians were only supposed to grunt, and yodel, and refer to everyone they met as 'kemo sabay'?"

Ronald turned around and frowned at him. " 'Kemo sabay'? What's that? Some kind of wine?"

"Just move your ass," said Daniel, impatiently.

Ronald kicked the Nighthawk into life. It blared and burbled as Ronald revved it up; and then they were away, bouncing across the dusty roadside, overtaking Cara and giving her a last berrp-berrp on the horn before roaring away westwards on Route 60 towards Mesa.

As far as Ronald was concerned, there were only two speeds on a motorcycle: flat-out and Geronimo. Daniel clung desperately on to his leather jacket as Ronald hurtled into the darkness, insects pattering on his helmet like soft shrapnel. The motorcycle weaved and angled from one side of the road to the other, overtaking trucks, cars, and a vast tractor-trailer carrying livestock. "Tomorrow's cheeseburgers!" shouted Ronald, as he accelerated past the truck and topped 110 mph. Daniel closed his eyes and tried not to think what would happen if they hit a stone or a stray animal or a vehicle without lights.

They made a left on South Lindsay and Ronald opened up the throttle again as they headed southwards towards Williams Air Force Base. A Hercules transport plane was landing from the south-east, its lights winking as it descended over the desert like a huge black Roc. At last they were slowing down and turning into the main gates of Williams, where an Air Force sentry came forward and said, "Identification, please?" His face under his white steel helmet was as bland as hominy, but there was a tensile twang in his voice which made it clear that nobody was going to get past here without all the proper passes, especially an Indian in black leather.

"I came to see Major William Monahan," said Daniel. "He told me this morning he was going to be working in the armory. Maybe you could call him up and tell him I'm here."

The sentry said, "What's your name, please? Do you have any identification?"

Daniel reached into his back pants pocket and handed the sentry his Social Security card. The sentry peered at it from beneath his helmet, and said, "Daniel F. Korvitz?"

"That's right."

"Okay, then, hold on for just one moment." The sentry went back to his brightly-lit office and picked up the telephone. He seemed to be talking to someone for almost five minutes, and meanwhile Daniel and Ronald waited for him, still astride the motorcycle, under the dazzling floods which illuminated the air base gates.

"I've been meaning to ask you something," said Daniel, as they waited.

"What's that?"

"Who's this Ah-jon-jon? The guy you've got on your T-shirt?"

"You never heard of Ah-jon-jon? He was an Assinboin Indian who went to Washington and met President Andrew Jackson. He was so impressed by the white man's ways that he abandoned his buckskins and his feathers and dressed himself up like a dandy. Then one day he beat another Indian with his cane because this other Indian doubted his word. It was the kind of thing that he had seen white men doing. The only trouble was, the Indian came back, quite unlike a white man, and shot him dead."

"There's a moral in that?"

"I don't know. Maybe. Be yourself, that could be it. Or, don't try to play the game if nobody else knows the rules."

Daniel cleared his throat. "That's worth wearing a special T-shirt for?"

"Maybe."

The sentry finally put down the telephone, and came back out. He handed Daniel back his Social Security card, and stood looking at him as if he couldn't quite decide what to say.

"Well?" asked Daniel. "Is Major Monahan there or isn't he?"

"He's there, but he's not."

"What the hell is that supposed to mean?"

The sentry lowered his head so that all Daniel could see below the curved rim of his helmet was his pale-lipped mouth, which said, "I'm sorry to have to tell you that Major Monahan is dead."

Daniel felt as if he touched an exposed electric wire—a freezing, tingling sensation, not quite real. "Dead? What are you talking about? I saw him this morning. They told me on the phone that he hadn't been around the base all day."

"Well, I'm sorry, but there must have been a misunderstanding. He has been here all day. But shortly after 1430 hours, there was an accident, involving Major Monahan and a Hughes helicopter."

"He was flying?"

"No, sir, it was a ground accident. But I'm afraid that's all I've been authorized to tell you. If you leave me your address, somebody from the base will write to you and give you the full details in due course."

Daniel climbed off the motorcycle. He could hardly stand up. Ronald said to him, "Daniel, *moksois*, easy now."

"Easy? This guy's telling me that Willy's dead. For Christ's sake, what happened?"

The bloodless mouth below the rim of the helmet said, "I regret that I haven't been authorized to tell you that, sir. But if you leave me your address—"

"Fuck my address, *what happened*?"

There was a long and terrible silence—almost too long, as if it had been written into a bad Monday-afternoon soap opera. A moth whirred and shone in the air between them, and somewhere on the air-base a jet engine suddenly rumbled into life and then died away again.

The sentry said, in a dry voice, "He didn't see it. He backed into it. The rotors took off his head."

Daniel stared at the man without saying a word. Then he turned to Ronald and whispered, "You'd better take me home."

Ronald's face was strained; eyes glittered with sudden tears—tears of shock and frustration and sadness. He said, softly, "Okay."

They rode back slowly through the night. Even when they reached Apache Junction, they said nothing; but after Daniel had dismounted he took hold of Ronald's wrist and squeezed it tight.

"Remember Ah-jon-jon," he said, so quietly that Ronald

could hardly hear him. "Don't try to play the game if nobody else knows the rules."

"You're talking about Willy?"

"I don't know," said Daniel. He had to purse his mouth together to hold back the grief, and the lump in his throat was so constricting that he couldn't answer at first. "I'll talk to you tomorrow, okay? Thanks for the ride."

Ronald stayed on his motorcycle and watched Daniel walk across to the diner, fish out his keys, and open the door. Upstairs, in Daniel's apartments, a light went on.

SEVEN

Chief Ruse was sitting in front of his huge colonial-style television set, his trousers comfortably open, the clips on his red suspenders unfastened, his boots propped up on a stool. He was watching a late-night movie called *They Saved Hitler's Brain* and drinking warm milk from a mug with Pig-in-Chief printed on it. In spite of the rattling air-conditioning unit under the window, the living room was still oppressively hot, and now and again Chief Ruse tugged out a handkerchief the size of a small bedsheet and dabbed at his perspiring face.

His wife Ingrid was upstairs in front of her taffeta-frilled dressing-table, wearing an oatmeal face-pack, her hair tightly wrapped in rollers. His daughter Maisie-Ann was lying on her pink quilted bedspread in her pink quilted bathrobe eating a large bag of M&Ms and reading *The 3-Day Diet Book*.

The door chimes played *The Bluebells of Scotland*. Ingrid's grandfather had been a Scottish engineer on the Union railroad, and she always liked to think that she had true Scottish blood in her. Chief Ruse tolerated her plaid rugs and her plaid tablecloths, just to humor her, but he had drawn the line at wearing a kilt. "I'm not wearing a dress for anybody," he had told his deputy. "Maisie-Ann, you want to get that door?" he yelled out.

There was no reply, and the door chimed again.

"Maisie-Ann!"

Ingrid called, "She's dressed for bed already! You go!"

Exasperated, Chief Ruse hauled himself out of his armchair, buttoned up his fly, and shambled out to the hallway. "Women," he grumbled under his breath. The door chimes rang again, and he shouted, "I'm coming, for Christ's sake!"

He opened the door. Outside, under the moth-encrusted light, stood a thin tall man in a pale-blue suit, and a silver-tipped bolus necktie. His face was hidden by the brim of his Western hat. "Chief Ruse?" he asked. "I'm sorry to disturb you so late. My name's Skellett."

"What's your business, Mr. Skellett? Isn't it something that could wait until the morning?"

"It won't take very long, Chief Ruse." The man reached into his suit and produced a black leather wallet, which he handed over without any explanation at all. Chief Ruse flipped it open and read, "James T. Skellett, National Security Agency."

Chief Ruse dragged out his handkerchief again and patted the back of his neck. "National Security Agency? You want to tell me what's wrong?"

Skellett took his wallet back, and tucked it into his pocket. "I'd prefer it if I could come in. This isn't something I want to discuss on the doorstep."

"All right, then, step inside," said Chief Ruse, and stood back against the wall while Skellett squeezed past his stomach. "I just hope it's not too complicated. I've had a day of it, I can tell you. Appropriations committee all morning, the highways department all afternoon, and one pretty damned hair-raising homicide for most of the evening. Came home and my dinner was all dried up. Not that I had too much taste for it."

They went into the chintzy living-room. Chief Ruse switched off the sound on the television, and then offered Skellett a chair. "You want a beer?" he asked.

"No, thank you," said Skellett. "I don't want to take up too much of your time. The fact is, it's that same hair-raising homicide that I've come to talk to you about. The Schneider case."

Chief Ruse sat down. "Oh, yes?" he said, looking at Skellett narrowly. "What about it? You know something that we don't?"

Skellett took off his hat. He had thin, wavy blond hair, combed across from one side of his narrow skull to the other to cover his widening bald spot. "You'll be gratified to know that the FBI discovered the whereabouts of Mrs. Schneider's killer at a little after one this afternoon."

"Why didn't anybody tell me?"

"Nobody told you because until now it had to be kept under total wraps. But I'm authorized to brief you now because you have a right to know, and also because you have a duty to take all the appropriate action to make sure that it remains confidential."

"You want to explain yourself, Mr. Skellett?"

Skellett leaned forward, and said in a conspiratorial murmur, "The fact of the matter is that Mrs. Schneider was involved in a little business involving Air Force security. Passing information to folks who had no right to have that information. You get my drift? But—it appears that she failed to do what the folks to whom she was passing this information instructed her to do, or else she passed them some bum information, but in any case they decided to do away with her. They took off her head because they didn't want anybody to recognize that she was actually a Communist agent called Olga Voroshilov, who came to this country in 1948 with the express intention of meeting and marrying an Air Force officer. She was what we call a 'sleeper.' You've heard of that? An agent who stays dormant for ten, maybe twenty years, building up a respectable background. Then, when they're given the signal, they start passing information."

"I've heard of that," said Chief Ruse. "And she was one of those?"

"That's what she was," nodded Skellett. "And that's why you have to keep so much of this secret. Olga Voroshilov was part of a whole ring of Communist spies, many of whom are still in business, and if we make too much of a fuss about her death, they're all going to get nervous, and go under cover. Instead—we want to track them down, and bring them to justice."

"You say the FBI got the guy who killed her?"

Skellett smirked. "They didn't get him. They *found* him. He was down at the bottom of a ravine in Deming, New Mexico, in a burned-out pick-up truck. Looks like he probably fell asleep while he was driving."

"How did they know it was him? I mean, how could they be sure?"

"They found a flexible saw in the truck. She was murdered with a flexible saw, wasn't she? And they also found her head."

"They found the head?"

Skellett nodded, almost smugly. "Roasted right down to the bone, but there was no mistake."

"Well, can I see it?" asked Chief Ruse. "I'd sure like my medical examiners to make a check on it, make sure that it's the *right* head."

"Chief Ruse," said Skellett, "how many men do you think were within driving distance of Phoenix today with a flexible saw and a severed human head in their vehicles?"

"No more than one, I'm sure," Chief Ruse agreed. "But I still want to have my M.E. check it out."

"I'm not sure that's going to be possible, chief. In fact, I have a warrant from the National Security Agency for the handing-over of Margot Schneider's body. We'll have a meatwagon around to collect it first thing in the morning."

Chief Ruse sniffed, and shifted heavily in his armchair. "You just hold on a minute, Mr. Skellett. This was a *prima facie* homicide within the city limits of Phoenix, and as such it's under my jurisdiction, in my territory. Before that cadaver leaves my turf, I'm going to have to be satisfied that it's been properly examined and identified by my medical people, and that all the required paperwork is in order. You got me? This woman didn't just lose her purse, she lost her *head*, and I'm not leaving any openings for anyone saying that I didn't follow the correct and proper procedure. Not with a case like this one, no sir."

"Chief Ruse," said Mr. Skellett, testy now. "You have to understand that you're being outgunned here. This is a matter of national security. Far more important than any local investigation."

"Mr. Skellett, I can't ignore proper procedure."

"The National Security Agency warrant will cover your ass."

"I have a big ass, Mr. Skellett."

"It's a powerful warrant."

Chief Ruse was silent. He peered into his Pig-in-Chief mug at the wrinkled skin which had formed on the surface of his warm milk. Skellett got to his feet, and tugged his coat straight.

"That's settled then, chief?" he asked.

"Not on your life. No sir."

"You intend to defy a warrant that was issued in the interests of national security?"

"I intend to do my job. My job is to identify that dead woman and to carry out a proper post-mortem examination. Anyone who tries to hinder or obstruct me is going to find their ass in a cell. That's all."

"You want me to call a judge right now?"

"Not on my telephone, you don't."

"You want to appear in next week's *Time* magazine as the local yahoo police chief who obstructed the biggest spy operation ever carried out in the United States?"

Chief Ruse stood up, and hitched up his pants. "I want to tell you something, Mr. Skellett. I don't care how I look in the media just so long as I've been doing the job the people of Phoenix pay me to do. And I want to tell you something else. If you had the authority you claim to have, and the legal clout you're trying to pretend you've got, then you wouldn't have to make insulting threats to a local officer of the law who is simply and clearly doing his duty. What's more, if you really *were* engaged in the biggest spy operation ever carried out in the United States, you certainly wouldn't be telling *me* about it. I think it's time you left."

Skellett picked up his hat. "I have to warn you that we'll be round for the body in the morning, whatever."

"Just try it," said Chief Ruse, still smiling. "You'll find an armed guard around the mortuary, and all the TV and newspaper reporters you can handle. You want to drag a headless body out into the street, and try to abduct it? Well, try, that's all I have to say. You just try."

"You're making a mistake, chief," said Skellett.

"No, Mr. Skellett. *You're* the one who's making the mistake. You don't come around to a police chief's private residence in the middle of the night unless you're trying to pull some kind of a number. So, let me tell you something. Nobody pulls numbers in Phoenix; especially not junior agents for government agencies. Now, get out of here before I try out my boots on your ass."

Skellett sighed, and positioned his hat on his head with resigned precision. "You know something," he said, as he went to the front door, and opened it. "I really wonder sometimes which side people are actually *on*. You know that? You probably did more to help the USSR in one night tonight than Julius and Ethel Rosenberg did in a year."

He nodded goodnight, and turned, and at that moment Chief Ruse swung back his Western-booted leg and kicked him so hard in the backside that his feet actually left the doorstep. He tumbled over, tried to stand up, and then fell over the low chain-link fence which bordered Chief Ruse's front path.

"Are you crazy?" he screamed. "Are you completely out of your fucking mind?"

Chief Ruse stood in the doorway and folded his arms over his enormous stomach. "You were an intruder, Mr. Skellett, and in this state a householder can't be held liable for shooting an intruder, even if he kills him dead. You're lucky you're just sitting on your butt in the front yard, yelling at me. You could be dog meat. Now, get out of here, and don't come back."

Skellett stood up and angrily brushed down his suit. "Have to get the damned thing dry-cleaned now," he muttered. "Goddamned $250 mohair."

Chief Ruse closed the door on him, and locked it. Then he walked through to the kitchen, opened up the icebox, and took out a large cold can of Coors.

"Walter, you're not drinking beer, are you?" demanded Ingrid, from upstairs.

Chief Ruse said nothing, but sucked thoughtfully on the can, leaving the wet impression of his lips on the frosted aluminum top. He thought of the pink lipstick which Margot Schneider had left on her coffee-cup.

"Walter?" Ingrid called again. "You're not drinking beer, are you? You know how it makes your breath smell."

"Jesus," Chief Ruse whispered to himself. "Women."

He carried the can into the sitting-room, and picked up the phone. He tried two numbers before he located Lieutenant Berridge. Unhurriedly, he explained what had happened. Berridge, who was obviously in bed with Stella, judging from the rustling and the seductive giggling that was going on in the background, said, "They want the body? They can't do that! But they've actually found the head."

"They *say* they have. I haven't seen it. It's been burned, too, according to Skellett. No flesh on it."

"Still no problem making a firm identification, chief. Teeth, jawbone, no problem at all. And besides, the sawn-through neck should exactly match the body we've got down on West Washington."

Chief Ruse swallowed beer and belched. "Listen, I'll see you down at headquarters at seven o'clock tomorrow morning. Meanwhile, I'm going to call up Kearney and make sure the whole block is sealed off. I'm going to put people on the roof, too. Nobody is going to take anything out of this town until I'm good and ready, and especially not the remains of Mrs. Margot Schneider."

"You bet, chief. I'll see you tomorrow."

"You bet," said Chief Ruse. He put down the phone, and then stood in the middle of the room, one hand in his pocket, occasionally swallowing mouthfuls of cold beer, and wondering if maybe he ought to have handled Skellett a little less precipitously. If he really was an agent from the National Security Agency, and if he really did have a warrant for possession of Margot Schneider's body . . .

"Shit," he said to the pink-tinged reflection of himself in the mirror over the fireplace. A big hefty man framed in gilt, in a room crowded with green glass Bambis, and reproductions of snowy mountains in Vermont, and doilies, and chintz, and ugly varnished "traditional" armchairs. Anything that didn't have a frill or a fringe on it was decorated in plaid. Chief Ruse sometimes felt like bringing home an Ingram sub-machine gun from the police armory and blowing the hell out of the whole lot.

But that, of course, would break Ingrid's heart.

EIGHT

The news finally broke at 11:30 p.m. A State department limousine had been blown up at the Elkswood Hotel, in West Virginia, killing two Secret Service agents. The Secretary of State, Titus Alexander, had missed assassination by seconds by deciding to travel in an alternative vehicle. First theories were that the bomb had been planted either by the PLO or by a lone maniac called "the Great Blast," who had frequently threatened Mr. Alexander's life.

Nadine had flown back from Philadelphia at once, to be seen close to her husband's side. She was filmed at Dulles in large dark glasses which made her look like a very tall owl. She said she was "shocked, and outraged, but thankful to God." She forgot to say she was sorry about the two dead bodyguards.

She arrived back in Georgetown, to their elegant ivy-grown colonial house, to find that Titus was in the library with Joe Jasper, and that the library was thick with smoke. Before asking Titus if he was all right, she stalked across the room and threw open the sash window. Titus said dryly, "Hello, Nadine. I thought you were seeing your sister."

"I *was*, my dear, until three hours ago. Three hours ago I had just finished my soup, and was just picking up my knife and fork to eat a plateful of roast duck."

"Your sister always makes you eat too much. With your height, you should stay thin."

Joe Jasper glanced uneasily at Nadine, and then back to Titus. "I can always take a walk," he suggested.

"Stay," Titus told him.

Nadine, striking a pose, said, "Are you all right, Titus, darling? You weren't hurt?"

"Do I *look* hurt?" asked Titus. Then, realizing that he was being too hard on her, he stood up, and held out his arms to her, and said, "I'm fine, thank you. I was lucky and those two poor bastards weren't. Thank you for coming down."

He held her elbows, and kissed her on the cheek. She looked as disinterested as she could manage. "Aunt Betty said I should give you her love."

"That's unexpectedly cordial of her."

"Well," said Nadine breathily. "She's seventy-two. She's growing senile."

Joe said, to divert the course of the conversation, "Would you like me to fix you a drink, Mrs. Alexander? There's a jug of martinis in the icebox."

"A dry sherry, if you don't mind," said Nadine. She unwrapped the white mink stole around her shoulders, and sat down opposite Titus in one of the big red-leather armchairs, angling her perfect legs with exasperating elegance. The damn woman was still as attractive as all hell.

"How's Penelope?" asked Titus.

"Oh, Penelope's all right. Dowdier than ever."

"She can't be any dowdier than the last time I saw her."

Nadine let out a little, annoyed breath. "That's it. As soon as I'm home, you're criticizing my family again."

"Nadine, it was *you* who said she was dowdier than ever."

"Well, I've a right to. She's my sister. What do *you* know about sisterly love?"

"Not a lot, except that it seems to be a small-scale version of the Punic Wars, acted out by two female siblings every July Fourth and Labor Day weekend, Thanksgiving, and Christmas."

Joe Jasper uneasily handed Nadine a glass of dry sherry. She sipped it, grimaced faintly, and commented, "The usual piss. Why don't you ever buy Croft Original?"

"Because when I *did* buy Croft Original, you made the same face and said, 'The usual piss. Why don't you buy Croft Original?' "

"You're lying as usual," said Nadine, opening her purse and taking out a cigarette. "No wonder they made you Secretary of State."

"Nadine, some people tried to kill me tonight."

Nadine looked at him, her eyes a fraction wider, freeze-framed in the act of taking out a Raleigh. Then she gave a careless, one-shouldered shrug, and crossed her legs, and waited for Joe to come over and light her up. "I'm sorry," she said. "I can't really help the effect that you and I have on each other."

Titus sat down again, and steepled his stubby fingers. His voice sounded very harsh and very serious. "It may be a coincidence, but only a few hours before this happened, Joe came up with some pretty spectacular material on Marshall. *Leverage*. Something which we could use to affect his entire defense policy, and put RINC on ice."

Nadine blew smoke. "Don't tell me that Marshall ever misbehaved himself."

Joe put in, "He's like all human beings, Mrs. Alexander. He has certain, you know, appetites and vulnerabilities. Certain, well—"

"Perversions?" asked Nadine.

Titus' face remained hard. "That's right," he told her. "Perversions."

"And you mean to use whatever this 'pretty spectacular material' is to break down the RINC talks?"

"Only if Marshall fails to see sense."

"What's sense to you? That we go on stockpiling nuclear weapons at massive expense and for no reason? You know that I'm not a pacifist, Titus, for God's sake. But we already have enough bombs and missiles to wipe out the world a hundred times over. What's the *point* of it?"

Titus cleared his throat. "The point, Nadine, is to prevent imbalance. That's the point."

"*Imbalance*?" mocked Nadine. "Is that all you're worried about, imbalance?"

"There's also the global obliteration quotient," put in Joe.

"Ah, yes, that's my favorite," said Nadine. "General Housman calls it GOB for short. The number of times that the United States is capable of totally obliterating the world, versus the number of times that the Soviet Union is capable of totally obliterating the world. Poor General Housman was *so* worried about it, the last time I spoke to him. We can only obliterate the world forty-one times over, while the Soviets are capable of obliterating it sixty-three times over."

"Nadine," said Titus. "Please. Save it."

"Ah, yes, I forgot," said Nadine. "As the loyal and devoted wife of the Secretary of State, I'm not really supposed to say things like that. When you're married to a hawk, you have to behave like one."

Titus said, "However cynical you are, Nadine—"

"Cynical!" she burst out. She held up her half-empty sherry glass to Joe and said, "This is terrible. Get me a martini." Then, to Titus again, "I'm not cynical, Titus darling. I'm just realistic. And adult."

"What I was going to say was that I know that I can trust you, cynical or not."

She looked at him sharply. "What are you getting at?"

"I'm simply saying that I know that I can trust you."

"Well, of course you can trust me. I don't propose to give up the chance to be First Lady next year, just for the dubious pleasure of passing around the tedious little details of your grubby little plots. God, Titus, you haven't ever said or done anything worth gossiping about."

Titus said, "I want you to do something for me. I can't do it myself, not now. Because of what happened at the Elkswood Hotel, I've got Secret Service men standing three deep all around me."

"I did notice rather a lot of men with short haircuts and dark suits milling around in the garden."

Titus finished his martini and flicked the rim of the glass with his fingernail so that it rang. "Nadine, I want you to take care of our principal witness. The girl with whom Marshall was involved, the one who can help us stop the RINC talks. I want you to meet her, set her up in a safe location, and then keep her happy until we need her."

"What do I have to do? Read her *The Lives of the Presidents* and feed her on Pepperidge Farm gingernuts?"

"*Nadine*," cautioned Titus, quietly. Joe Jasper tried to smile, but found it difficult.

The truth was that the marriage between Titus and Nadine Alexander was one of the spectacles of Washington, to be ranked beside the Lincoln Memorial and the Smithsonian. They were fiercely attracted to each other sexually, and yet their politics and their personalities were at complete odds. All they shared, besides their hunger for each other in bed, was ambition. Nadine was a natural-born Southern Democrat (her father had been a warm friend of Herman Talmadge and B. Everett Jordan) while Titus was a bullet-headed Yankee from Illinois, whose father had known nobody but the local tax-collector and a cop called Cummings with whom he had played Saturday-night poker.

Titus and Nadine had met at a cocktail party at the Nixon White House. They had both been drinking too much. Afterwards, they had gone to the Madison Hotel, "Washington's Correct Address," and made ferocious love all night and all the following morning. They had married because Titus wanted to be President and Nadine wanted to be First Lady. She still browsed through *Architectural Digest*, selecting furniture and tableware and hand-embroidered sheets for the White House. Their marriage, according to Joe Jasper, was straight As—acid, amour, and ambition.

Nadine often thought she should have been a movie star, or a model. She was 5 feet 10, with thick wavy brunette hair, shoulders like Arnold Schwarzenegger and a magnificent thirty-eight-inch bust. Somebody had once said that she would have looked better as the figurehead for a ship. But she wanted the White House more than anything. She had once told her mother that she wanted the White House more than happiness. Her father had died when she was ten. He'd had a coronary, tumbling from the top of a flight of stairs at a birthday party. Since then, birthday cakes had always reminded Nadine of death.

"This girl, she's a hooker I suppose?"

"Not so much a hooker," said Joe. "More of a hostess."

"You realize that what you're asking me to do is completely against my ethical and moral principles?"

"Possibly," agreed Titus. "But not against your personal interests. If Marshall Roberts fails to pull off the RINC talks, then there's no question that he's going to be badly hurt politically. He may well have to resign before next year's primaries."

Nadine sipped her martini and stared at Titus thoughtfully. "It has occurred to you, of course, that Marshall Roberts may have been responsible for the bomb himself?"

"It did cross my mind."

"He knows how hungry you are for the White House; and he knows that you've promised to do everything possible to break down his détente with the Soviet Union."

"That's right. I'm not denying it. He's very high up on my list of possible suspects."

Joe Jasper put in, "I can't believe it was the PLO. Not after the discussions we've been having with Arafat. It could have been a lone banana, or a fringe group. Some of these '60s underground groups like Yippies and Black Panthers are starting to get pretty restless again."

"That's because they want a last fling before they get too old," said Titus, caustically. "No—my money's on Marshall's unfortunate accident squad, or one of these lone assassins. Don't you realize that it's very *fashionable* these days to knock off a controversial politician or a legendary rock star; it's the growth profession of the eighties. Well—thanks to Marshall's economic policy, the population doesn't have much else to do, do they?"

Nadine turned to Joe. "Tell me about this hooker. This *hostess*."

Joe perched on the arm of a library chair. "Her name's Colleen Petley, also known as Rita Haze, twenty-five years old, from Forth Worth, Texas. She left home at the age of 19 after becoming pregnant. She lost the baby, but she didn't go back. She went to Las Vegas with the idea of becoming a croupier. It wasn't long before she was picked up by a man called Denny DiMarco, a very heavyweight Las Vegas pimp. He groomed her, trained her, and set her up as a high-class thousand-dollar-a-night hostess. She's the kind of girl who will do absolutely anything a man wants. She's classy enough for him to take out to dinner and pretend that she's his steady date, or even his wife; and yet when it comes to bedtime she'll perform in any way that you can imagine, and in a few ways you can't."

Nadine edgily tapped the ash off her cigarette. "And what do you expect *me* to do for this doyenne of the horizontal?"

"It's vital to keep her feeling *important*," said Titus. "We're going to fix her up with every creature-comfort she could possibly need; men, dope, you name it. But we can't pay her any money, because that will look too much like bribery, and if she has to go in front of a Congressional committee, I want her to be as clean as possible—at least as far as the reliability of her information is concerned."

Nadine said nothing. Joe Jasper leaned towards her, and asked, "Another martini?" but she shook her head.

"You're a well-known, well-publicized, well-admired woman," Titus told her. "Colleen Petley, when she sees you, will begin to realize just how serious and how important her testimony is going to be, not only to herself, not only to me, but to the whole of America. If not the world."

"You really think she's aware of her duties to the United States?" asked Nadine. "A Las Vegas hooker?"

"That's your job, to make her aware," said Titus. "Make her believe that she's going to be famous, and honored. And, above all, make her believe that she's going to be *respectable*. If there's one thing that hookers crave, it's respect."

"I suppose you have that from first-hand conversations," Nadine commented, sharply.

"Oh, sure," said Titus. "I have enough time and energy to take care of the State Department, argue with the President, act as chairman of the American Legion, be married to you, take care of your snotty kids, fish, exercise, and fuck two or three hookers every night. As well as *talk* to them, by God."

Nadine crushed out her cigarette. Then she looked across at Titus and her expression had softened. "I'm sorry," she said. "I don't know how many times I've told you I'm sorry—probably just as many times as you've told me the same thing. But I still love you, you know; and I'm glad that you're safe."

Joe let out a quiet breath of relief. Tonight wasn't going to be so combative after all. And, with any luck, Nadine would help to keep Colleen Petley smiling and cooperative until they were ready to twist Marshall Roberts' arm.

There was a roaring noise outside the window. Titus glanced

up alertly, but Joe was already holding the curtains back to see what was happening.

"Relax," he said. "It's only Samantha, with her latest boyfriend. You didn't know there were any Hell's Angels in Georgetown, did you? Well, Samantha found one. Hold on, it looks like the Secret Service guys are giving him a hard time."

"*Titus*," appealed Nadine.

Titus pulled a face, but when Nadine tilted her head to one side, coaxingly, he knew that this was going to be part of the price of having her take care of Colleen Petley. He picked up the antique-style telephone next to him, and said, "Wallis?"

"Yes, sir."

"That simian being who brought my stepdaughter home on the back of his motorcycle. He's allowed to escort her into the house."

"He's tattooed, sir. He has 'Fuck The World' inscribed on his left bicep."

"Wallis, just let him in, will you? You can hear language like that every day in the Oval Office. There doesn't seem to be any valid reason for excluding it from the State Department. What's good enough for the President is good enough for us."

"Okay, sir, if you say so."

"I say so, Wallis."

Titus put down the phone. "Those children of yours are totally out of control," he told Nadine. "Do you know that? They're like wild animals. Maybe we should install a cage."

"Titus, darling," smiled Nadine. "I'll do anything you want. But right now, I'm very tired."

Titus flicked a quick look at Joe Jasper, but he had already picked up the message loud and clear. He straightened his note-book and his file, bowed to Nadine, nodded to Titus, and made for the door. "We'll talk early tomorrow," said Titus.

"Yes, sir," said Joe. Then, with a heavy-lidded smile, "Sweet dreams, Mr. Secretary. If possible."

NINE

Nadine had been away from him for five days, and she was feeling an urgent need for sex. When he came out of the bathroom into the richly-furnished colonial bedroom, with its mahogany four-poster bed and its deep wine-colored drapes, she was lying on the bedspread naked except for a tiny but expensive pair of handmade French-silk panties, with an insert of Alencon lace through which her glossy dark pubic hair curled temptingly.

He stood at the end of the bed in his pale-blue pajama bottoms, his towel around his neck. He couldn't help admiring her. Even at forty she had a magnificent figure: large, rounded, wide-nippled breasts, a narrow waist, flaring hips, and legs so long that she could lock her ankles together behind his back when they were making love. And her brunette hair was spread out on the white lace-embroidered pillow like the beautiful, mysterious and doomed Lady of Shallott.

He sat down on the edge of the bed, and placed his hand on her thigh. His chest was muscular and ridged, with a small diagonal scar under his left nipple. In the light from the white-glass lamp, he looked tired but more handsome than usual; and there was a gentleness about his expression which Nadine hadn't seen on his face for a long time. He had come close to being killed, not by North Koreans or V.C.s but by his own countrymen.

His penis, already erect, protruded from his open pajamas, the obvious evidence of how much this particular wife attracted this particular husband. Nadine reached down, and opened his trousers wider, and embraced his erection with her long fingernails.

"Did you miss me?" she said, breathily.

"What do you think?"

"Don't ask me what I think. Tell me."

He nodded, not smiling. "I missed you."

"You really think you have the goods on Marshall this time?"

He nodded. "We really do. I've seen the pictures for myself."

"What was he doing?"

Titus didn't answer at first, so Nadine clutched his penis and squeezed it tight. "What was he *doing*?"

"Well, you've heard of golden showers."

Nadine's eyes widened. "Marshall Roberts was doing *that*?"

Titus said, "You wouldn't believe it, would you, to look at him? You wouldn't think that the same lips which have been coming out with all of those holier-than-thou speeches about arms reduction and détente with the Soviets and how we can help the poor . . ."

Nadine leaned forward a little, so that she could reach his pajama cord with her left hand. She gave it a tug, and it came free. "Don't want to talk about Marshall," she said. "Come here . . ."

Titus said, "Nadine, I really don't think that I'm up to too much tonight. I have to warn you."

"Come here," she encouraged him.

He pulled down his pajama trousers, and then climbed onto the bed naked and straddled her waist. His erection lay between her breasts, and she lifted and squeezed them together with her hands so that he was deeply massaged by their soft, warm flesh. He bent forward and kissed her forehead, her cheeks, her mouth with increasing passion, but now she coaxed him upward, until he was kneeling astride her chest. She opened her mouth and took him between her lips.

Titus closed his eyes, and softly groaned. But Nadine swallowed him deeper, sucking him gently, and licking the underside of his erection with the tip of her tongue, probing the narrow opening which was already slick with juices. She worked at him with increasing speed and urgency, until he felt as if a volcano were rising up between his thighs.

"Nadine—" he whispered, a stage whisper by an actor who has long forgotten his lines.

She drew his saliva-glistening organ out of her mouth, and caressed it against her face, against her cheeks, kissing it and nipping at it with her teeth. She even caressed it with butterfly-flutters of her eyelashes. It was then that Titus shuddered, and ejaculated, and three spurts of thick white semen crowned her forehead, formed pearls in her hair, and clustered in her lashes.

He kissed her, again and again, and then reached up with his hand to wipe the semen from her face; but she held his wrist. "I want this," she said. "And I want more."

She reached down, and drew aside the thin triangle of silk and lace that covered her. "Fuck me," she insisted.

It was difficult at first. Titus kept softening, and having to thrust himself into her faster and faster to regain his stiffness. But after fifteen minutes, when he was breathing harshly, and his muscles were glistening with sweat, he felt the irresistible sensation of a second climax. Beneath him, Nadine moved with a fierce undulating rhythm, gasping with every thrust, her nipples crinkled and stiff, her breasts swaying, her eyes squeezed tight in concentration on her rising orgasm.

She suddenly gasped, and began to shake, and Titus ejaculated deep inside her. It took almost a minute before she was able to stop shuddering, and then open her eyes. For a moment, he saw in her eyes something that was approaching affection. It couldn't be, of course. They had been through too many bitter arguments, and staked their tents too firmly on opposite hills. But Nadine lay where she was, all the same, crowned and anointed with Titus' semen, until the flush began to fade from between her breasts, and her nipples softened, and she sighed and sat up at last. "I suppose I ought to take a bath."

There was a brisk knock at their bedroom door. Titus found his pajama trousers and dragged them on. "Who is it?"

"Titus? It's Carl. I just got back."

"Fine," said Titus. "Maybe we can talk in the morning."

"Are you okay?" asked Carl, through the door. "I heard what happened on the news."

"I'm okay, thanks. A little shaken. But I guess that's only to be expected."

"I hope you don't mind," said Carl. "I borrowed the Porsche."

Titus looked meaningfully at Nadine, but all Nadine could do was throw her hands up in imitation of a Jewish momma. He's a grown boy now, what can I do?

"I did make it clear that I'd rather you *didn't* use the Porsche, didn't I?" said Titus. "And you do have the Zephyr."

"Oh, Titus. Have a heart. I can hardly pull girls in a Zephyr."

"When I was your age, all I had was a beaten-up Nash 600."

There was a pause. Then Carl said faintly, "The Porsche is a little beaten-up, too."

"You damaged the Porsche?" snapped Titus. The veins in his neck swelled, and he clenched his fists. "What happened? How bad is it?"

"Well," said Carl, carefully, "the front end doesn't look too good. I left it down at the H Street garage."

Titus stared at the door and decided that for the sake of everything he wanted to do to bring down Marshall Roberts, he had better not open it. Because Jesus Christ, if he opened it, and saw Carl, then he'd beat the living crap out of that boy, and that would be the end of him and Nadine. He tried to think to himself: it's only a car. Cars can be fixed. But he knew without being told that it was totally ruined. He was a perfectionist: the slightest scratch was enough to put him off a car completely.

"Okay, Carl," he said, in a voice like a manhole cover being dragged across a city street. "We'll forget it this time. Get the car fixed and then we'll talk about it some more."

Nadine, tall and naked, taller than he was, came across and laid her hands on his shoulders.

"You're a fascinating man," she said. "I only wish sometimes that I could really like you."

He momentarily closed his eyes, then nodded. "The feeling's mutual," he said. "Extremely mutual."

TEN

Susie came into the room and stood in a sloping triangle of sunshine watching him solemnly.

"Daddy?" she asked. "What's wrong?"

He eased himself around in the creaking basketwork chair. His hair was ruffled and he looked tired. Somewhere outside, a tinny radio was playing *La Cucaracha*. It was 101 degrees at Sky Harbor, one of those relentless Arizona days when even the saguaro appears to throw no shadow, and the horizon ripples with glassy mirages.

He held out his hand for Susie and she came and leaned close to him. She had been eating a Mounds bar and she smelled of candy. He kissed the fine blonde down on her forehead, and said, "I'll get over it. But I did love him, you know. He was a good friend. A funny, nice person."

"Will they bury him?"

"I guess so. It depends what his family wants. He came from Omaha; they'll probably fly him back there."

Susie was silent for a while, stroking the back of Daniel's hand. Then she said, in a small voice, "I'm sorry. I said a prayer for him this morning."

"Me, too," said Daniel. "Do you remember that old rhyme I

used to sing to you, when you were very small, when Mommy was still here?

> *My daddy is dead, but I can't tell you how;*
> *He left me six horses to follow the plow:*
> *With my whim-wham waddle-ho!*
> *Strim stram straddle ho!*
> *Bubble-ho! pretty boy, over the brow.*"

Susie sang it with him; an old tune from long ago. On this very hot day, they sang it together for Willy Monahan. Daniel thought: even today, there is still *some* sentiment left, of ours—still *some* room for genuine grief and sadness in a jaded, tired world.

Cara came into the room and stood listening to them. Neither of them had slept. They had tried to talk, tried to get drunk, tried to make love. But it had been a relentlessly hot night and Willy's sudden death had been too overwhelming for both of them. Daniel had dozed off for five or ten minutes in his bedroom chair, but he had dreamed of Willy's smiling head, flying through the air, and had awakened with a jolt, sweating, trembling, wondering whether Willy's death was real, or just another nightmare. Cara had knelt beside him, naked and soft, and soothed him, but at that moment the night had seemed longer and darker than any other night in the history of mankind.

"Are you opening for lunch?" Cara asked him.

Daniel shook his head. "You put the card in the window?"

"Sure. But you have to carry on sometime."

"Yes. I know."

"Ronald was around this morning," Cara said. "He asked if there was anything he could do. He's cute, don't you think?"

"Assuredly. The cutest Indian traffic offender this side of the Continental Divide."

"Dan, Daniel," said Cara. "Don't be bitter. It was an accident."

"Sure," he said. But there was a phrase which kept turning over and over in the back of his mind, *Just like I said, Daniel, heads will roll.* And he remembered what he had said to Willy in reply. *You're sure it won't be your head? You're sure it won't be your head?*

Susie said, "Can I go play with Lucy, down at the gas station?"

"She's off school too?"

"She's always off school. Her daddy says he doesn't mind if she goes or not."

"Okay, then, honey. But make sure you're back by three. And don't go near the vehicles. And *don't* go across the highway. You stay on this side, you hear?"

Susie ran off, and Daniel stayed where he was, in the creaking basketwork chair. Cara stayed by the door for a while, watching him, and then went to the window, and looked out at the dusty front lot, at the blacktop highway, at the distant brown ridge of the mountains.

"Did you call the base?" she asked him.

"I called twice. They told me they can't release any details until they've informed his next-of-kin."

"I'm sorry," she said.

"Sorry? You don't have to be. Everybody has to die sooner or later. Five hundred years ago, this part of Arizona was populated by the Hohokam Indians. They built canals branching out of the Salt River, they had a whole civilization. But then they disappeared without trace. Who knows what happened to them? Maybe they displeased the gods."

"Willy didn't displease the gods."

"I'm not so sure."

Cara turned around. "What does that mean?"

"When he came around yesterday morning, he said he was going to spend the day in the armory, checking out missiles. He had some theory that missiles fitted to U.S. fighter planes are incapable of destroying Soviet aircraft. Something to do with radar signatures. He said it was going to turn out to be the biggest scandal the Air Force had ever known."

Cara came across the room, and knelt down beside him. She reminded him so much of Candii: brash, world-weary, yet innocently erotic, a heroine out of a country-and-western song. Greece may have had its hetaerae; Rome its delicatae; France its lorettes. But America had its Candiis and its Caras, its brassy Western girls with their beauty parlor hair and their white high-heeled boots and their waggling buckskin-clad bottoms. When Cara knelt down to soothe him, she revealed a freckled cleavage as deep as the Grand Canyon, and her skirt was raised just high enough to tease but not quite high enough to reveal that she wasn't wearing any underwear, because girls like Candii and Cara never wore any underwear, they dressed to excite their menfolk.

"What are you going to do?" she asked him.

"Do?" he frowned at her.

"Well, if you think that somebody did him harm—if you think that somebody might have arranged for him to walk into that helicopter propeller on *purpose* . . . I mean, shouldn't you *do* something?"

"I've called twice."

"I know. But what have you *done*?"

"I've called! What else can I do? They keep telling me that Willy was involved in an accident, and that he's dead, and that's it. They won't even confirm what the sentry told me—that he'd lost his head. They keep saying that they're trying to contact his next-of-kin, and that until they do, they're not at liberty to release any details."

"Did you see the *Flag* this morning?"

"The newspaper? No. What's that got to do with it?"

Cara stood up, and walked across to the cheap bamboo table. She unfolded the *Arizona Flag* and showed him the second-lead headline: HEADLESS WIDOW PUZZLE, Police Seek Skull Cult. Daniel said, "I heard that on the news last night. So what?"

"Did they say on the news that the woman who was killed in Phoenix was an Air Force widow?"

"I don't think so. Is that what she was?"

"Umh-humh. Mrs. Margot Schneider, fifty-two, widow of Major Martin Schneider, who was killed several years ago on a proving flight from Luke Air Force Base, outside of Phoenix. Daniel—she was beheaded, just like Willy. The only difference is that *her* head they took off with a saw, not a helicopter."

Daniel looked at Cara thoughtfully. "You know something," he said, "You're definitely more intelligent than you look."

"I don't know whether that's a compliment or an insult."

"It's a compliment. You look pretty and dumb. In fact, you've turned out to be pretty and intelligent."

"If that's a compliment, I think I'll ask somebody to cut off *my* head as well."

Daniel stood up and snapped, "Don't joke about it."

"I'm sorry. I didn't want to upset you. But don't you think it might be an idea to go take a *look* at your friend Willy? Just to make sure that he died the way they say he did."

Daniel paced tensely, five or six circuits around the room. "They killed him, you know. That's what I've been thinking all night. He found out about the missiles and they killed him."

"Maybe they killed Mrs. Schneider for the same reason."

"Yeah," Daniel nodded. Then he looked up at Cara and said, "Get me some coffee, will you? I'm going to make a phone call."

He brought the telephone over from the windowsill and placed the call. After a long wait, a voice said, "Williams Air Force Base. How can I help you?"

"This is Mr. Korvitz here. I called earlier. Can I speak to Colonel Kawalek?"

"I'm sorry, Colonel Kawalek is away from the base today. Would you like to speak to his assistant?"

"Okay, if that's the best you can do."

There was an interminable pause, while wires sang and telephones clicked and distant voices said, "Hello? George? Hello? I can't hear you too well." At last a crisp-sounding lady said, "Mr. Korvitz? I'm sorry but Colonel Kawalek is away from the base today."

"They told me that. I just wanted to know how I could get to see the body of Major Monahan. He was a friend of mine, you see, and—"

"I'm sorry, Mr. Korvitz. It won't be possible for anyone to see Major Monahan's remains before his next-of-kin have been informed."

"Haven't they been told yet?"

"I'm afraid that's impossible for me to say."

"Well, *somebody* must know."

"I regret that the only officer who might know about it is also off the base today. He won't be reachable until tomorrow at the earliest.''

"Well, can you at least tell me his name?"

"I'm sorry. I'm not at liberty to do that."

"Who is?"

"Nobody, I'm afraid. Not until Colonel Kawalek returns."

"Jesus, doesn't anybody know anything?"

"There isn't any need to use harsh language, Mr. Korvitz. I'm simply trying to be helpful."

Daniel held the receiver as if he were going to throttle it. Then, without saying any more, he hung up. "I get the same answer all the time," he told Cara. "Colonel Kawalek's away, nobody else can help me, and no, I certainly can't be allowed to see Willy's body."

Cara said, "Where did Willy live? Do you think it might be a good idea to go round to his house? I mean, if he was working on some theory about missiles or something, maybe he left something at home. Notes, or a diary, maybe."

"Well," said Daniel, "it's worth a try. I'll just give Levon a call at the gas station, and tell him we're going to be away for a while."

Willy had lived on Indigo Street, in Mesa, which is halfway between Phoenix and Apache Junction. His house had always been maddening to find, because there are five Indigo Streets, all in a roughly straight line, but disconnected from each other by thousands of yards of open ground, and the Consolidated Canal. Willy had lived on the Indigo Street which was closest to the Mesa City Cemetery.

Daniel and Cara drove out there in Daniel's grubby, lopsided Electra. There was a neat row of ochre-painted one-story houses with shingled roofs and parched lawns. Daniel parked outside Willy's house and put on his sunglasses. He slammed the Electra's door and walked slowly up the concrete driveway, followed by Cara. Above them, the sky was almost navy blue, and the heat was dry and suffocating.

They peered in through Willy's picture windows. It was difficult to see clearly, but it looked as if the house was completely empty of furniture. Even the rugs had gone: there was nothing but shiny woodblock floors.

"Are you sure this was the house?" asked Cara.

"Are you kidding? I came out here once a week for poker and beer. I can't understand it."

A woman appeared from the house next door in upswept spectacles and a lime-green nylon headscarf. She was wearing a beige double-knit jump suit and a profusion of gold charm bracelets. She said, "Are you looking for anyone?"

"Major Monahan. I'm a friend of his."

"He was posted. To Langley, I think they said."

"Who said?"

"Why, the men who came around to clear his house. They said he'd been urgently posted to Langley, and that they'd come to collect his belongings for him. They said that his furniture would probably arrive at Langley before he did."

"You can bet it will," said Daniel. "The truth is that he's dead."

"*Dead*? Are you *sure*? The men were quite clear that he'd been posted to Langley. They were smiling and joking and everything. I don't think they would have behaved that way if Major Monahan had been *dead*."

"Lady, Willy Monahan was my best friend. I can tell you for certain that he's dead."

"Well, I hope he enjoys himself at Langley," the woman replied. "He's a warm, considerate man. We liked him the moment we first met him."

Cara took Daniel's arm. "Come on," she said, gently. "Let's go. We're not going to find anything here."

Daniel reluctantly followed her down the driveway to the car. Cara mused, "They've really gotten rid of him, haven't they? I mean, they've made him *vanish*, like he never existed. And if they've told his next-door neighbors that he's going to Langley, maybe that's what they've told his next-of-kin, too."

"Maybe he's not dead at all," said Daniel. "Maybe they've just spirited him away so that he can't make a nuisance of himself any longer."

"There's only one way to tell."

"I know," said Daniel, glancing behind him as he rejoined Route 60, heading east. "I'm going to have to see his body for myself—if there is a body."

Cara laid a hand on his thigh, and then leaned over and kissed his cheek.

"What was that for?" he asked her.

"I don't know. Comfort, I guess."

He kissed her back, on the lips. "They don't make itinerants like you any more," he told her. "You're the last of a fine but dying breed."

"Don't you believe it," smiled Cara. "You just take a look around any city in the West, and you'll be amazed at all those budding 15- and 16-year-olds in high school; they're into double-D cups before they know what an isosceles triangle is."

"Do *you* know what an isosceles triangle is?"

Cara pursed her lips in amusement, and shook her head. Daniel kissed her, and said, "Let's go talk to Ronald. Maybe he can figure a way to get us into that air base. He's a professional lawbreaker, you know that?"

Ronald was around at Levon's gas station, two blocks away from Daniel's Downhome Diner, sitting crosslegged on the tailgate of a battered pickup truck, drinking 7-Up out of the can and discussing with Levon the finer points of torque-reactive anti-dive control. Through the picket fence at the back of the gas station, Daniel could hear Susie giggling and screaming as she played with Lucy. He left his sagging Electra by the side of the workshop, and walked across the sunbaked forecourt with his hands jammed into the back pockets of his jeans. Cara followed, a few paces behind, but not subserviently.

"Levon," said Daniel, shaking his hand. "How're you doing?"

Levon Wisby was one of Daniel's favorite characters in Apache Junction. He was rake-thin and laconic as a turkey vulture. He always wore Oshkosh dungarees and, for some reason he would never explain, a Seattle Mariners baseball cap.

"Your little girl and mine been getting on good," said Levon. "Would've been a peaceful afternoon save for this jawbreaker here, and all his talk about that motor-sickle of his'n."

"Ronald could bore the ass off a Hell's Angel when it comes to motorcycles," grinned Daniel.

"*Salut!* to you too," said Ronald, and raised his 7-Up can.

"Listen, Ronald," Daniel told him, "we just came back from Willy Monahan's place on Indigo Street."

"His house?"

Daniel nodded. "The place is empty, cleaned out. The woman next door said that some men had been around to move all his furniture and all his belongings. But—here's the weird bit—they told her that Willy was still alive, and that he'd been posted to Langley Air Force Base."

"That's ridiculous. They never post anyone as quick as that. And in any case, why didn't Willy tell you anything about it? Send you a note, or call you?"

"If he isn't dead, and he's really been posted, he certainly hasn't been posted in the normal way," said Daniel. "Maybe the Air Force put him under some kind of arrest, and moved him out of the state so that they can keep him incommunicado."

"You really believe he found out something he shouldn't have?"

"I don't know," said Daniel. "But I mean to find out if he's dead or alive, because if he's dead, then someone's murdered him, and if he's alive, then he needs help."

"Either way, this is sure going to stir up one whole lot of shit," said Ronald, philosophically.

"Ronald, I have to see Willy's body for myself. That's the only way that I'm going to be convinced that he's been killed. Or, if he hasn't been killed, I want to know where he is, and why he was whisked away. There are laws in this country; *habeas corpus* and all that kind of stuff. They can't just lock somebody up and throw away the key."

"Daniel tried to call Kawalek again," put in Cara, "but it wasn't any good. It's a cover-up, I'm sure of it."

Ronald raised his eyebrows at Levon, but Levon could only shrug and say, "Those Air Force characters, they're always screwy, least as far as I'm concerned. Either mad, or drunk, or both, and the way they fly them jets through the mountains, shoot."

Ronald said, "What we need to do is get onto the base."

"Oh yes? And how do you propose we do that? Williams is a tactical base, as well as a training center. You don't just stroll in through the front gate."

"You could dress up as Air Force pilots or something," Cara suggested. "I saw somebody do that in a Gregory Peck movie.

Well, not pilots, but sailors. Anyway, that was how they got onto a ship when they weren't supposed to."

"Where the hell are we going to find two Air Force uniforms?" demanded Ronald. "And, besides, they'd still want to see our identification before they'd let us through the gate."

"Now, hold on a minute," said Levon. "I've got three of them coveralls they wear when they're technician-ing them jets. They was give to me by one of the engineers used to work at Luke. I did him a lube job once for free, and he give me five or six pairs, surplus I guess they were, but they still got the Air Force insignias sewn on them."

"Well, that's a start," said Daniel. "If we could just get into the base, nobody would take very much notice of two stray technicians."

"Well, you could get *in* there pretty easy," said Levon. "That's always provided you could find your own way out again. Jim Pryor goes down there two or three times a week with fresh beef and milk and a whole lot of that frozen Mexican food. Owes me a favor, Jim. He'll take you in, provided you say he didn't know nothing about you stowing away in the back of his truck if you're catched, and always provided you find your own way out again."

Daniel glanced at Ronald and he couldn't help smiling. He had always felt that Levon was one of these extraordinary Western characters who could fix anything not working; who always knew where you could find that outlandish spare part; in short, someone who could help you out of whatever bizarre spot you've gotten yourself into. And now he knew it was true.

Cara said, "What will you do?"

"It's easy," said Ronald. "We'll get into the base, find the sick-bay, or the morgue, or wherever Willy's body is likely to be; then take a look at him if he's there, and satisfy ourselves that he's dead, and how he died."

"Then how do we get *out*?" asked Daniel.

"We'll bluff. Go to the front gate and run like hell."

"And supposing they catch us, and arrest us?"

"It won't matter by then, will it? We'll already know the truth about what happened to Willy."

"Oh yes? And what possible good is that going to do *us*, if we're jailed for trespassing on restricted property, and for impersonating U.S. Air Force personnel?''

"Relax," said Ronald. "I'm beginning to hatch a *plan*."

"You and your goddamned plans," complained Daniel. "It was *your* plan that we picked up those two guys in that broken-down Cadillac and played poker with them. Sitting targets, you said. They were two goddamned professional gamblers on their way back to Nevada! I'd have myself a new icebox now if it wasn't for you and your goddamned plans.''

"You're talking like Willy," said Ronald.

Daniel turned away and looked across the highway towards the mountains. The day was so hot that the store across the street was dancing in the heat waves. He said, "I miss him, that's why. And I'm worried about him.''

Ronald flipped his empty 7-Up can into the air; then knocked it with his elbow so that it described a perfect parabola and clattered into the gas-station trashbucket. "Everything's going to be fine. How many times have I told you, Daniel Korvitz, that I'm a *genius?*''

"About a thousand. But how many times have you *proved* it?''

Susie came out of Levon's back yard, carrying her Sindy doll. She held it up to Daniel and there were tears smudging her cheeks. "She's busted,'' she said.

"What's happened?'' Daniel asked her, holding out his hands.

Into one of his hands, Susie laid the Sindy doll's naked body. Into the other hand, she laid the doll's detached head.

ELEVEN

From the moment he had opened his eyes at five o'clock that morning, Chief Ruse had been nursing the suspicion that he had underestimated James T. Skellett. He was unusually edgy as he took his place outside the Phoenix city morgue, a few minutes after the sun had risen over the top of the forty-story Valley National Bank; and when Lieutenant Berridge came across and asked him if he'd heard anything about a Diamond I jet going down last night in the Dead Horse National Park with millionaire Clinton Charles on board, he gave nothing but a disinterested hmmph, as if men like Charles deserved to drop out of the sky from 12,000 feet and be pulverized among the cactus and the copper-dust.

There were thirty armed police around the morgue, as well as ten patrol cars, eight motorcyclists, and six sharpshooters up on surrounding rooftops, on KOOL radio and the Grace Court School. There were roadblocks on the Maricopa Freeway going south-east and the Canyon Freeway going north, as well as ambushes on West Indian School Road and Van Buren at 24th Street. It was all a little theatrical, but then Chief Ruse had always preferred a little theatricality to any kind of violence. "Better to ham it up than shoot it out," he had told his deputy more times than his deputy had cared to count.

Lieutenant Berridge came up and said, "You really think we're going to have trouble?"

Chief Ruse shook his chins. "I'm putting on a show, that's all."

A girl came strutting across the street in indecently tight denim hot-pants and a Hawaiian-style top, tied in a knot at the front. "Some show," remarked Lieutenant Berridge, as she wiggled her way around the parked police cars. "I think you deserve an Emmy for that."

A young black man was scrabbling on the road in front of Chief Ruse's car, picking up parcels. Chief Ruse grunted in amusement. "One look at that ass and he dropped everything."

Skellett arrived on Washington Street alone, a few minutes before seven o'clock, in a shiny white '80 Eldorado. He climbed out of the car, closed the door carefully and almost noiselessly behind him, and then walked across the sidewalk with his hat tugged low over his forehead, and his white city shoes clicking on the sidewalk. A small crowd of onlookers watched him from behind a police barrier with curiosity.

"Chief Ruse," he said, politely.

"Mr. Skellett," responded Chief Ruse.

"Chief Ruse, I have here a warrant issued by the Chief Judge of the State of Arizona requiring you to release the remains of Mrs. Margot Schneider into the custody of the National Security Agency. I also have papers from the National Security Agency requiring you to do the same. I have to tell you that unless you comply with these warrants, you will be in serious breach of the law, and in contempt of the Arizona District Court."

Chief Ruse sniffed and noisily cleared his throat. "I have to tell *you*, Mr. Skellett, that Mrs. Schneider's body is not going to leave the Phoenix city morgue until I am personally satisfied that her body has been properly identified and that the cause of death has been established by a full autopsy carried out by *my* medical examiners."

"Chief Ruse, these warrants—"

"Mr. Skellett, you can roll up those warrants and stuff them up your ass."

Skellett was silent for a moment, his lips pursed. He looked a little white around the eyes. Then at last he adjusted his hat, and said, "Okay. You're adamant?"

Chief Ruse nodded. "You bet."

Skellett looked at his heavy gold Rolex wristwatch. "I'll come back here in exactly one hour. I'll bring an ambulance with me. If you're prepared to release Mrs. Schneider's remains by then, we'll say nothing more about it, and I won't take the matter any further. If you're *not,* however, I'll have to take steps. You understand that, don't you?"

Just then, Kathy Forbes pushed herself forward, holding up the microphone of her Sony tape-recorder. "Sir?" she asked. "Can you tell me why you're so anxious to remove the remains of Mrs. Margot Schneider from the Phoenix city morgue? Is there some kind of threat to national security involved?"

Skellett gave her a tight, impatient grimace. "I don't have any comment to make to the press at this time."

"But this *is* a matter of national security?" Kathy persisted.

"We do have to evaluate certain possible infractions of U.S. military integrity, yes."

"What does that mean in English? You're trying to tell me that Margot Schneider's death may have had something to do with a military security leak?"

"I can't make any further comment on that right now."

"When *will* you be able to comment?"

Skellett turned and stalked briskly away across the sidewalk, but Kathy came after him, closely followed by two other newspaper reporters and a cameraman from KPHO television. Skellett raised his hand in front of his face to prevent the cameraman from focusing on that pale vinegary scowl of his, but the cameraman ducked and weaved around him and caught on videotape an expression which the KPHO anchorman later described as "noticeably less than jolly."

"Did Margot Schneider have anything to do with Cuba?" asked Kathy.

Skellett, already halfway into his Cadillac, froze and stared at Kathy as if she had cursed out loud. "Cuba?" he demanded. "What made you say Cuba?"

"*You're* supposed to be answering the questions, not me," Kathy told him.

"I want to know why you said Cuba."

Kathy said, "I don't have to tell you that. You're the public servant. I represent the people."

"Get in the car," said Skellett.

"Not a hope."

"You want to hear the truth about this? Get in the car."

Kathy glanced anxiously behind her. Chief Ruse was talking loudly to Lieutenant Berridge, and by now the other reporters had turned back to hear what he was saying. "Absolutely no way that Mrs. Schneider's remains are going to be released until—" She hesitated for a moment, but then she walked around the front of Skellett's Cadillac, and climbed into the passenger seat. Skellett slammed his door, started up the engine, and swung the car westwards with a sharp squeal of tires.

"Now then," said Skellett, "what's this about Cuba?"

Kathy turned around in her seat. A beige Pontiac was following them, only twenty yards behind. "They're tailing you," she said. "You know that, don't you?"

"Of course I do. They've been tailing me ever since I left my hotel this morning. They're just trying to intimidate me, that's all."

"Chief Ruse is a hard nut. He won't budge unless he really has to."

Skellett shrugged, and turned on the car radio, twanging country-and-western music. "*Don't forget me when the sun goes down . . .*" He made a right at 11th Avenue, and headed northwards in the direction of University Park. Kathy said, "I can't honestly remember when I ever saw Chief Ruse so upset."

"I'm treading on his favorite bunion, that's all."

Kathy was silent for a while. Then she said, "There's something very important happening here, isn't there?"

"Important?"

"Well, they wouldn't have sent anyone from the National Security Agency if it hadn't been important."

"No," said Skellett. "They wouldn't."

"So what's going on? The whole of downtown Phoenix is bristling with armed police. Chief Ruse is blowing a gasket. Tell me what's going down here."

Skellett glanced up at his rearview mirror. The beige Pontiac was still there, cruising steadily through the morning traffic. The sky above the buildings was a light, dry blue. The temperature was already up to 71 degrees and the radio was forecasting another hot one.

"You're a pretty girl," said Skellett. "I know that you're also a reporter, and that ever since Watergate, every reporter has been trying to break the national scandal to end all national scandals. But, let me tell you, this isn't any Watergate. This is straightforward, routine security, a simple operation to make sure that the military technology at Luke Air Force Base remains confidential."

"You're trying to tell me that Mrs. Schneider was passing out secret Air Force information?"

"I'm not trying to tell you anything, except that you'd be making a mistake if you tried to blow this story up into anything special. So, Chief Ruse lost his temper? How much of a story is that? I have warrants for the remains of Mrs. Margot Schneider to be turned over to the National Security Agency. Chief Ruse will have to give in eventually."

Kathy felt oddly prickly and frightened sitting next to Skellett. He drove with one long-fingered hand that was reminiscent of that of a menacing extraterrestrial. There was something casual but alarming about him; as if he would be just as happy strangling a dog as he would be cooking up spaghetti bolognese for his friends. A man with no perceivable conscience.

"You got upset when I mentioned Cuba."

"Upset? No, I wouldn't call it upset. But interested to know why you said it."

"It was a guess, that's all. Can you believe a guess?"

Skellett flicked his eyes up towards his rearview mirror again. "Unusual kind of a guess," he commented.

"Not unusual at all. Phoenix has some pretty heavy Cuban exiles these days. Antonio Matanzas, Juan Casilda. Ever since Marshall Roberts was elected, they've been talking about having another crack at overthrowing Castro. I thought maybe that Margot Schneider had gotten herself involved. You know—lonely widow, nothing else to do."

"Are you serious?" asked Skellett.

"Of course I'm serious. We had a case just two months ago,

an old lady from El Mirage joined up with a gang of bank robbers. She helped them turn over two banks before she was arrested. Said she was bored.''

Skellett said, ''You're bullshitting me, young lady.''

''Would I bullshit you? I'm trying to get a story out of you.''

''No, you're bullshitting me. No question. I know when someone's trying to bullshit me, and that's what you're doing. Cuba wasn't any guess. You know something, or else you've deduced something, and I want to know what.''

Kathy said, ''Well, you're out of luck.''

Skellett looked at her for the first time. His eyes were peculiarly vacant, as if he were staring right through her, and across the street somewhere. ''Are you going to tell me the truth or what?'' he wanted to know.

''Is that a threat?'' Kathy demanded. ''If that's a threat, you can stop this car right now and let me out.''

''I'm not stopping this car, young lady, and you're going to tell me why you mentioned Cuba.''

''I'm getting *out*—'' snapped Kathy, and wrenched at the door-handle, but Skellett calmly touched the central locking switch, and the door refused to budge.

''Will you stop this car and let me out of here?'' Kathy insisted. She was genuinely scared now. Skellett was so calm and inhuman, still piloting his car with one hand on the steering-wheel as if he were cruising along Main Street Mesa on a Saturday afternoon looking at used Oldsmobiles. He smiled at her, and when he smiled, she had no doubt at all that he would kill her, if he had to.

She twisted around in her seat again and the beige Pontiac was only a block behind. ''The cops are still tailing us,'' she said. ''You want me to attract their attention? Tell them you tried to rape me?''

Skellett shrugged. ''You can do what you like. I'm in charge of this situation and you're not. I just want to know what led you to mention Cuba. Or *who*.''

''I'm an accredited journalist!'' Kathy shouted at him. ''It doesn't matter who you are or what government agency you're from, you can't do this! My paper will have your head!''

"Scripps-Howard, isn't it, the *Arizona Flag*?" asked Skellett, matter-of-factly.

"No. It's still independent. The Rosner family."

"Ah, that's right. The Rosners. Nice old folk who wouldn't like to do anything to upset the President. I shouldn't think the Rosners will stir up too much of a fuss, even when one of their girl reporters goes missing."

"Are you *crazy*?" asked Kathy.

Skellett shook his head. "Just doing my job."

He had reached Woodland Avenue, opposite University Park and the Arizona Museum. He flicked down his traffic signal to turn left, but when the lights changed he gunned the Eldorado's engine and swerved right, provoking a hostile chorus of car-horns, and an upraised finger from a cab driver. The beige Pontiac was momentarily snarled up behind them, but then it bounced over the corner of the sidewalk, and came in fast pursuit.

Kathy shouted, "Stop! For God's sake, *stop*!"

But Skellett took no notice, and deftly swerved the Eldorado left, on squittering tires, and roared north-westwards on Grand Avenue, which followed the line of the Aitchison, Topeka and Santa Fé Railroad, and which was the only diagonal street in the whole of Phoenix. Kathy wrenched at Skellett's right shoulder, making him swerve, but he pushed her away flat-handed, and snarled, "Don't make me hit you, because I will. You stupid bitch."

He streaked up Grand Avenue, past West Roosevelt Street and the Arizona State Fair Grounds, running one stop light after another, with the Pontiac close behind him. Kathy gripped the edge of her seat as they bounced at seventy-five mph across the intersection with Encanto Boulevard, and set up another flurry of horns. "You're out of your *mind*!" she told him. "You're going to kill us!"

Skellett said nothing, but kept his foot flat against the Cadillac's floor. He swerved around a bus, narrowly missing its rear bumper, and then zig-zagged between a string of cars. Kathy heard a siren behind them, and turned around to see that the Pontiac which had previously been trailing them incognito was now sporting a red flashing light, and was officially in hot pursuit.

She thought for a moment that Skellett was going to turn north on to the Canyon Freeway, where he would be bound to be stopped by one of Chief Ruse's roadblocks. But he sped straight over the freeway, and kept going north-west on Grand Avenue, crossing Indian School Road on a green light at nearly eighty miles an hour.

Kathy turned around again, and she was just in time to see a huge unmarked tractor-trailer pull out of the side of the road, and begin to crawl diagonally in front of the police Pontiac that was chasing them. What followed was a slow-motion movie, and she stared in horror as every movement unfolded in front of her at half-speed, tragic and unstoppable.

The Pontiac collided with the tractor's offside front wheel, and rolled over sideways in a shower of glass and hubcaps. Kathy could see the driver rise through his shattered side window like a bloody Aphrodite rising from the waves, and cartwheel across the road. Then the car skidded and rolled again, and crashed straight into the window of a liquor store on the opposite side of the street, bringing down shelves of whiskey and wine and champagne, and thrusting a middle-aged woman customer straight through the glass front of the cooler, cutting off half of her face. Her nose and her forehead were blood soaked and grotesquely detached.

Kathy didn't see any more: Skellett immediately took a right on Camelback, then a second right on 35th Street, and began to speed due southwards.

"You had that arranged," she said, in a white and shaky voice.

"I'm a professional," said Skellett. "And meanwhile you know more about Mrs. Margot Schneider than you've been telling me."

"What are you going to do?"

"I'm going to take you back to a safe house, outside of town, and I'm going to ask you a few searching questions. Do you mind? Or would you rather answer them here and now?"

"What about Chief Ruse? He'll be wanting to know where I am."

"Don't you worry about Chief Ruse. I've taken care of him, too."

"What do you mean?"

Skellett took another swerving turn on Thomas Road, and began to head east. "I told you. I'm a professional. I do things thoroughly and properly."

"You're out of your mind. You've just killed people. Did you see that woman's face—?"

"I wasn't looking."

"*You're out of your mind!*" screamed Kathy.

Skellett stared at her coldly. "Listen," he told her, "I'm an agent for the United States government. I have the highest authority to do whatever I find it expedient to do. That accident back there was a failsafe, in case I needed it, which I did. If Ruse's men had kept well away, and let me do my job unhindered, it wouldn't have been necessary. I didn't want to hurt anybody, policemen or bystanders. But there are some government affairs which have to be dealt with secretly and quickly and conclusively. Don't think that what you saw back there was unusual."

"This is a *nightmare*," said Kathy. "I don't know anything about Margot Schneider at all. Why is she so important?"

"I didn't say she was. In any case, all that's important about her as far as *you're* concerned is why you connected her with Cuba."

"I told you, it was a guess. I was fishing."

"Too many people are fishing these days," said Skellett, cryptically. "A little less fishing, a bit more happy cooperation, we'd all get along with each other a darn sight better."

"I didn't know government agents were permitted to philosophize," said Kathy, regaining some of her confidence and sharpness, especially now that Skellett had slowed down.

Skellett gave an offhand smile. "To apply a philosophy, you have to understand it. Blind obedience isn't enough."

"Will you let me out of the car, please?" asked Kathy.

Skellett looked ahead, looked in his rearview mirror, and then looked across at Kathy. "No," he said, quietly but quite emphatically, and she knew that it wouldn't do her any good to ask again.

TWELVE

Chief Ruse was just leaving to find himself some breakfast when the mayor's official limousine drew up by the curb, and the window was rolled down. Chief Ruse said, "Wait a minute," to Lieutenant Berridge, and walked across to bid good morning to Mayor Gardens.

"Good morning, Walter," said the mayor. He was a thin, sun-wrinkled man with hair as crisp as shredded wheat. "Harris tells me you've been having some difficulty with the NSA."

"Nothing we can't handle," said Chief Ruse, leaning on the Cadillac's black vinyl roof, and affording the mayor a close-up view of his enormous belly. "A little difference in judicial focus, that's all."

"I never thought I'd see the day when *you* started talking that bureaucratic jargon, Walter," complained the mayor. "What the hell's 'judicial focus'?"

"It's the way you look at the law, Andrew. The NSA looks at it one way, and I happen to look at it another way."

The mayor drew back his lips over his clenched teeth in a grimace. He always did that when he had to say something awkward. "The problem is, Walter, that Judge Fredericks happens to share the NSA's way of looking at it, and so do I, and that kind of leaves you way out on a limb."

Chief Ruse took out his handkerchief and dabbed at his sweaty face. "I hope you're not trying to say what I think you're trying to say."

Mayor Gardens grimaced again, and looked embarrassed. "How long did he give you? Skellett?"

"An hour," said Chief Ruse, placidly. "More like forty-five minutes now."

"Well, in forty-five minutes I want you to release that cadaver. Do you hear me? I want you to do it because it's legal and because it's right and because I don't want Phoenix to get a reputation with the National Security Agency for being uncooperative and negative. We're going to need them some day, Walter, need their help, and this isn't the way to go about getting it."

"Andrew," said Chief Ruse, "I am not letting that body go. Now, do you mind if I go get some breakfast?"

Chief Ruse walked away. Mayor Gardens watched him in building frustration, then yelled after him, "Walter! You meathead!"

When Chief Ruse got back to his car, Lieutenant Berridge was taking a radio report from police headquarters. "The chief's right here," he said. "I'll tell him. Okay. Over and out."

"What's going on?" asked Chief Ruse.

"It's Skellett. Wilson and McKenzie tailed him uptown, up Grand Avenue. Apparently he took that girl reporter with him, what's her name, from the *Flag*."

"Kathy Forbes," said Chief Ruse. "You spent half of yesterday evening trying to get into her pants, and you didn't even find out what her name is?"

"Wilson and McKenzie had an accident," said Lieutenant Berridge seriously. "Hit a truck at eighty, and rolled over. Wilson's down at the County General right now, broken legs, badly concussed. McKenzie died."

"Shit," said Chief Ruse. He was silent for a moment, standing with his hands on his hips, looking down at the ground. Then he rubbed his face, and said again, "Shit."

"Skellett got clear," added Lieutenant Berridge. "Da Vito and Haskins thought they saw him driving south on 35th, but after that nothing."

"He went north and then he went south?"

"Seems like it. Probably hung a right on Camelback or Bethany."

"Hmm," said Chief Ruse. "He's got to be back in a half-hour or so, in any case, to pick up Margot Schneider's body. Or to *try* to pick up Margot Schneider's body."

"There's nothing we can actually pin on him," said Lieutenant Berridge. "Speeding, maybe, but that's all."

"What about the truckdriver?"

"What truckdriver?"

"The truckdriver in the accident with Wilson and McKenzie. Somebody took the trouble to ask him one or two questions, I hope?"

"Oh, sure," said Lieutenant Berridge. "But it doesn't seem like he was tied in with Skellett in any way." He licked his thumb and turned back two or three pages of his notebook. "His name's Gordon Farito, from Tucson. Clean record, apart from a couple of minor trucking offenses, insecure loads, that kind of thing."

"Insecure loads," said Chief Ruse, reflectively. "Insecure fucking loads."

Lieutenant Berridge didn't quite know what to say. He closed up his notebook and tucked it back into his inside pocket. "It just reminds me of something the Ziff brothers used to do. You remember the Ziff brothers, used to run stuff across the border at Nogales? They'd always have an ambush set up someplace, in case of pursuit. A van or a truck that would just accidentally happen to pull out in front of the police after the Ziffs had gone by. *This* reminds me of them."

Chief Ruse said, "Make sure we know where we can find Mr. Farito, in case we want to talk to him some more. Meanwhile, let's go eat. I don't relish the idea of losing my job on an empty stomach."

He climbed into the passenger seat of his car, and told his young police driver, "Rita's, okay? And make it fast. I have exactly twenty-eight minutes to eat a plateful of corned-beef hash and eggs and get right back."

"Very good, sir," said the driver, and twisted the key in the ignition.

Chief Ruse knew what had happened at once. It was the

slamming sensation against his ears, the way the entire world shrank into a pressurized pinprick, right in front of his eyes. And then came the unrelenting blast of fire and grit and glass and twisted fragments of metal, and the car doors flew off and tumbled away across the road.

He actually thought to himself: they've blown me up. This is what it's like to be blown up. And out of the shattered windshield he saw something resembling a bloody carcass of beef turning over and over in the air, and realized it was his driver's torso, and that his driver's legs were still beside him in their wrecked and tattered seat, still poised for a journey to nowhere at all.

He heard the bang, or the echo of it, from the surrounding buildings. He heard a pattering sound, and thought at first it was rain, but it was the sound of running feet. He thought for one ridiculous moment: I'm unhurt. I've been blown up, and I'm completely unhurt.

He heard the breathy roaring of a fire-extinguisher, as someone put out the flames. He heard someone else saying, "Don't touch him, don't move him. He's still alive," and he thought to himself, that's quite correct, I *am* still alive. Still alive, and what's more, unhurt.

"Lieutenant Berridge," he tried to say, but he could only speak inside his mind. This is absurd, he thought to himself. I can articulate the words inside me, but I can't say them. It must be the shock. That's it. I'm unhurt, but I must be suffering from shock. I've seen it happen in road accidents. Nothing that a strong cup of coffee won't cure.

He thought it would be a good idea to close his eyes for a while. Rest was another excellent cure for shock. But he was surprised to find that he couldn't do that, either. It was almost as if he didn't have any eyelids. It was irritating, because his eyes were beginning to feel very sore.

He looked up, towards the sky. It must have been some hefty explosion: there was no roof on the car any more, only a blackened framework, hung with red ribbons. He lowered his head again. He had no way of realizing that the red ribbons were all that remained of his face. His cheekbones were exposed, and his eyes were bulging in their sockets like those of a gruesome doll. He looked so ghastly that at first nobody would step near him: they couldn't believe that he was still alive.

Mayor Gardens was the first. He came forward, brisk and quick, and stripped off his coat. "Walter," he said. He knelt beside the police car's twisted chassis. "Walter, you're going to be fine."

Chief Ruse tried to focus on him, and emitted a bloody rattle from his lipless mouth.

"You hear me, Walter? Everything's going to be fine. The medics are right here."

"Skellett," Chief Ruse tried to say, but he couldn't manage anything more than a thick choking noise. He tried to lift his arm, and take hold of Andrew's hand, but even an action as elementary as that seemed to be quite impossible. Damned stupid shock, he thought, I never felt so helpless in my whole life. His arm, still wearing his broken wristwatch, lay in the gutter more than fifty feet away.

He began to feel cold. His head began to droop. He looked down and saw that someone had been inconsiderate enough to leave yards of fire-extinguisher hose in his lap. Yards and yards of it, glistening and wet. You would have thought that they might have treated a shocked man with more care than that.

Andrew Gardens covered him with his coat. "Walter? Do you hear me? Everything's going to be fine. You want me to say a prayer for you? Would you like a prayer?"

Chief Ruse could hear the mayor, remote as a faint telephone voice. Why was Andrew telephoning him? It seemed quite absurd, enough to make a man laugh. He knew that he was perfectly all right, but he felt very cold, very distant.

Andrew Gardens said, "God be merciful to us, and bless us: and show us the light of his countenance, and be merciful unto us."

The camerman from KPHO videotaped the mayor's tears, but kept his lens away from Chief Ruse. Chief Ruse died unphotographed, a few minutes later, still believing that he had escaped the explosion unhurt.

THIRTEEN

High above the street, the black smoke from the bomb still hung in the windless sky like the ghost of Walter Ruse's nemesis, the hooded reaper of the terrorist age. And only thirty yards away, in distinct profile, wearing a crumpled tan safari-suit, his hands in his pockets, stood Henry Friend. A woman standing close to Henry with a white poodle in her arms was saying, "Oh my good Lord. I never saw anything like that before, not ever. That poor *man*. Blown to pieces. I never saw anything like that before."

Henry lit a cigarette. He didn't look toward the wreck at all: not because he was squeamish, but because he didn't need to. He hadn't personally planted the explosives himself; he never touched explosives unless he had to. Henry wanted to die peacefully. That was why he had done nothing more than supervise this particular hit: the timing and the logistics and the supply of equipment.

He rubbed his eyes, and stung them with the nicotine on his fingers. He was very tired, and he needed a bath. Two days ago, only six hours after he had arrived back in Los Angeles from Phoenix, and had triumphantly deposited Margot Schneider's head in a locker at Santa Monica Municipal Airport at Clover Field, they had instructed him to return immediately to Arizona.

He had been sitting in the Black Whale restaurant in Marina del Rey, the first time that he had sat in a restaurant to do nothing more than eat and relax in twenty years; the first time that he had been able to concentrate on his own drink and food, instead of having to furtively check the identity of his fellow diners. He had ordered a giant-sized Bloody Mary and a heaping plateful of Alaskan King Crab, the Black Whale's specialty. And just as he had sipped his drink and closed his eyes in exhaustion and peace, a hand had tugged at his sleeve. The same, familiar tug.

"You have to go back," a young, half-broken voice had whispered. A voice like an adolescent numbers-runner.

"Go back?" he had said, without opening his eyes. "Go back *where?*"

"Phoenix. There's trouble."

"They've found out who she is?"

"Nope. It's something else altogether. Don't ask me what."

Henry had at last opened his eyes and stared at the young man in the checkered linen suit and the mirrored sunglasses, and thought to himself, a creep. Why did they always pick creeps? Well, maybe the kid was purposely trying to look that way. You never knew what the style was these days.

"I'm not sure I haven't had enough of Arizona," he had replied, as carefully as if the words he chose could really make the difference between going back and not going back. He had already caught sight of the waiter bringing over his pink-and-white mountain of iced crab.

"Nonetheless," the young man had said.

Henry had thought: *Nonetheless?* Who says *nonetheless?* But nonetheless, he had caught the next plane from LAX to Phoenix, without even telephoning his brother or his bookie, or unlatching his Gucci valise. He had stared out of the airplane window as the dry beige western desert of Arizona reappeared beneath him. It never ended, this job. You killed one, and you always had to kill more, as if every human life was part of an intricate chain which trembled whenever one of the links was deliberately extinguished. "Sweeping-up," the Mafia had always called these extra killings. "You sweep up for me, gumba, hah?" "For sure, Piretti, for you I sweep up." Five or six killings for the price of one.

An ambulance came whooping and warbling across Washington Street, and blocked Henry's view of the smoking wreck. He waited for a minute or two, and then worked his way out of the crowd, and began to walk southwards on 6th, where he had parked his rented car. He felt unexpectedly depressed. Not because of the carnage he had created, not because of the violent loss of two human beings, but because this whole job seemed to have become unnecessarily messy and complicated. To a man who had spent so long in motel rooms, living out of suitcases, untidiness and disarray were anathema. He had lived systematically and unobtrusively, a real professional: and that had been his pride. It had worked, too: after twenty years of self-effacement, he had found the woman who called herself Margot Schneider and killed her. The trouble was, her death seemed to have stirred up some kind of psychic vibration—some dark ripple of memory and consciousness that meant bad news.

He reached his green Mercury, opened the driver's door, and awkwardly climbed in. The young black man was already waiting for him, calm, unexcited, his peacock-blue shirt collar neatly folded over the lapels of his cream-weave sport coat.

"Worked like a dream, huh?" the young man asked, as Henry settled himself into his seat, and started the engine.

"You didn't expect it to? You're working with a lifetime professional now, young Boyd."

"*Lloyd,* Mr. Friend, not Boyd."

Henry pulled carefully out into the traffic. He sniffed. "Perhaps we can all go home now."

"I don't know, Mr. Friend. Mr. Skellett didn't say."

Henry testily drummed his fingertips on the wheel. "*Skellett,*" he said to himself, in the tone of a man who has suddenly remembered that he has left his wallet at home. "Was that a good job or was that a good job?"

"Perfect, Mr. Friend. Timing, perfect. Charge, perfect. Total effect, perfect."

"Better than that damned mess they made in Virginia," said Henry, concentrating on making a left into Jackson, past the Union Railroad Station.

Lloyd didn't say anything, but propped his elbow on the

windowsill and stared out at the street. Henry glanced at him, and said, "Were *you* involved in that one?"

"You're not supposed to know that."

"I see," said Henry. "And it never occurred to you that Mr. Alexander might possibly change cars? You didn't have a contingency plan?"

"I can't discuss it."

Henry gave a soft, unamused chuckle. "Skellett," he said again, acidly. "Skellett couldn't pour piss out of a shoe if the instructions were written on the sole. I think Skellett always wanted to be a cowboy. Clint Eastwood. Did you see that song and dance today? The way he riled up those local badges so that they came pouring out onto the street with guns, and sharpshooters, and TV cameras and press? This whole business was *supposed* to be kept completely secret."

He paused for a while, driving with care through the morning traffic. "If you ask me, Skellett's going to be lucky if he lasts the month," he reflected, as they made another left towards the Greyhound Bus Terminal.

Lloyd said, "Who knows? I don't get into discussions. I just plant the packages."

"You did well today. That took a little nerve, planting that one."

"It was nothing, man. The timing was perfect."

Henry smiled to himself in satisfaction. There had been no way of discovering in advance where the Chief of Police would be parked, or even which vehicle he would use. That was why he had chosen a 7½-lb high-explosive charge in a vinyl briefcase. He had learned years ago how easily people's attention could be distracted, and the big-breasted brunette in the tight denim hotpants had certainly earned her hundred dollars by turning every head in the street—just at the moment that a young black office-worker with too many packages in his arms had crossed the road in front of Chief Ruse's parked car. Henry supposed that he could have waited until later to eliminate Chief Ruse. Tomorrow evening perhaps, when everything had settled down. He could also have done it much more quietly. But if Skellett could grandstand, then *he* could, too; and Skellett had explicitly told him to do the job right away, without delay. He didn't like Skellett and he had sorely wanted to show him just how frighteningly efficient he could be.

There was something else, something that Henry couldn't quite pin down. A feeling that some very heavy power maneuvering was going on, a vital shift in the organization's structure. Maybe that was the reason why Skellett had taken such a risk in confronting Chief Ruse direct, to get himself noticed. Henry had been briefed and debriefed by enough NSA agents to understand that there was a constant struggle within the agency for political influence, especially now that Ikon was growing so old and infirm. Henry didn't know very much about the NSA, but he knew much more than he was supposed to. If they had discovered just how much, they would have killed him. Instantly.

He dropped Lloyd off at the bus terminal. Before he left, Lloyd said, "Maybe we'll work together again some day; how about it?"

Henry shook his head.

"Just have a drink, then, maybe?"

"Maybe," said Henry. Lloyd watched him drive away and picked his teeth with the edge of his thumbnail. There was something scary about Henry Friend.

On the way back to downtown Phoenix, Henry was passed by a howling ambulance and a keening chorus of police motorcycles, speeding in the opposite direction, towards the county hospital. Chief Ruse, on his second-to-last ride.

Back at Chief Ruse's house, Ingrid opened the front door and was surprised to see Lieutenant Berridge standing there. She stared directly at him. Then she stared *past* him, at the police-car parked by the curb, its red lights revolving.

In a voice of quiet dignity her husband rarely heard, she said, "There's been an accident, hasn't there? It's Walter."

"Yes," nodded Lieutenant Berridge. "It's Walter."

FOURTEEN

Joe Jasper drove Nadine to Dulles Airport that afternoon in Titus' freshly-dented Porsche. Titus had inspected the damage before he left for the State Department, and had said nothing at all. But Joe had been able to tell from the flinching muscles in his cheeks that he would never want to drive the car again.

Nadine was silent for most of the drive across the Potomac. It was a gray, humid day. The eastern seaboard was overcast from Boston down to Norfolk, and thundershowers were forecast for the rest of the afternoon and most of the evening. Nadine wore a yellow silk headscarf and most of her face was concealed behind large mirror-lensed sunglasses. Even Titus would probably have walked past her in a crowd.

She felt tired, but she wasn't unhappy. Apart from a night of lovemaking with Titus, which always relaxed her, she had actually achieved that most subtle of successes: to have given Titus enough confidence in her that he had finally involved her in one of his clandestine plots.

It hadn't been easy. It had taken years to make him believe in her sincerity. Not her sexual sincerity: she found him as erotically stimulating and as necessary to her daily happiness as a narcotic and he knew it. What was more, the addiction was probably mutual. There wasn't any part of each other's bodies that they hadn't explored, both with tenderness and fierce excitement.

No, the difficult part had been building up the friendship, and the trust. She had been obliged to argue with him and fight with him just to make him treat her as something more than a Washington wife. It had taken five and a half exhausting years, but now it had paid off. Nadine couldn't help smiling to herself as Joe turned into the airport entrance, and made his way toward the short-term parking-lot.

"Something funny, Mrs. Alexander?" asked Joe.

"I don't think so. It's just this heavy disguise."

Joe found a parking-space, and wrestled the Porsche into it; although he finished up so close to the car parked next to him that he couldn't open his own door, and had to struggle across to Nadine's side. "I'm not very good with manuals, you know? I'm too busy worrying about the shift."

They walked towards the terminal. Joe took his sunglasses out of his coat pocket and put them on, feeling very undercover and clandestine. Nadine said to him, "You'll recognize this hooker when you see her?"

"Sure. But you shouldn't call her a hooker, Mrs. Alexander. At the very worst, hostess."

Nadine ignored him. "What is she like, as a person?" she asked. "You've met her, haven't you, and talked to her?"

"I liked her, as matter of fact," said Joe. "Mind you, I like most people. I'm not what you might call socially discriminating."

"Oh. Thanks a lot."

"I didn't mean *you*, Mrs. Alexander," Joe apologized. "I didn't mean to suggest that—"

"Oh, for Christ's sake, stop cringing," Nadine snapped at him. "And take off those ridiculous sunglasses. They make you look like an albino."

Joe took the sunglasses off and pushed them back in his pocket. He had to skip a little to keep up with her. "Colleen Petley is class, as hostesses go. Nice background, and it shows. And of course she's pretty well off these days. A thousand a night for three hundred nights of the year, plus gratuities and other assorted goodies."

The flight from Dallas-Fort Worth was already in; and Colleen

Petley was waiting for them outside the terminal by the cab-stand, silently escorted by one of Joe Jasper's helpers, a taciturn ex-pugilist called Crack Nielsen. The meeting between Nadine Alexander, tall and svelte and supercilious, and Colleen Petley, small and pouting and obvious, was one of the classic encounters of modern politics: but, like the death of Chief Ruse, it went unphotographed. It did, however, turn heads.

Colleen Petley aka Rita Haze was blond, busty, and stunningly pretty, with wide blue eyes and a mouth like smashed strawberries. She wore an off-the-shoulder Mexican-style blouse in frilly blue, a wide white PVC belt, and pale-blue satin pedal-pushers that looked as if they had been sprayed onto her naked body. Crack Nielsen, short and heavy, his face as immovable as a heap of concrete that had been allowed to dry unshoveled on a sidewalk, carried her white airline bags and her white fun fur.

Joe Jasper took Colleen's arm and leaned towards her ear. "This is Mrs. Alexander, Colleen. The wife of the Secretary of State. Now, all you have to do is quietly shake her hand and say hi—this isn't a performance—and then we'll be on our way."

"Hallo, Colleen," said Nadine. "Welcome to Washington."

"Well, delighted," replied Colleen, in a high Texas accent. Then, to Nadine's complete amazement, she curtseyed. Her enormous breasts bulged dangerously from the elastic of her Mexican blouse.

"The car's in the parking-lot," said Joe. "I just hope we can squeeze everybody in."

They drove northwest along the Washington Memorial Parkway in awkward intimacy. Nadine said to Joe, "I don't know why the hell Titus ever buys these ridiculous foreign imports. Sixty thousand dollars for a car that wouldn't even pass the federal housing regulations on overcrowding."

Colleen chipped in, "I knew a guy in Vegas who owned this amazing stretched Lincoln. He had television, brocade seats, and a real wolfskin rug. It was just amazing."

"Very nice," replied Nadine. Then, to Joe, out of the corner of her mouth, "I thought you said *class.*"

Joe gave an embarrassed shrug. "It's a question of comparisons. It *seemed* like class in Vegas."

"Have you been to Washington before, dear?" Nadine asked Colleen.

"No, never. Is that the Lincoln Memorial?"

"That's right. Maybe in a day or two you'll have a chance to see the sights."

"I've got to tell you," said Colleen, "I'm very nervous. I mean, I'm not at all sure that I'm doing the right thing. I mean, he is the President, and all."

Nadine smiled at her, and reached around to pat her comfortingly on the hand. "Don't you worry. You're doing the most honorable and courageous thing that anybody possibly could. You realize that your name will probably go down in history?"

Colleen gave an uncertain smile. "I know. Mr. Jasper told me that. But, you know, I'm kind of concerned. Flattered, for sure. But, you know, concerned."

"That's why we're all so proud of you," said Nadine. "Because you're *concerned*."

They arrived at last in Rockville, Maryland; in a quiet tree-lined back street where the most vicious enemy was crab-grass on the lawn, and where status was measured not in political power but in late-model Oldsmobiles and push-button garage doors. There was a humid wind blowing as they climbed out of the car, and Joe went up to the single-story house that he had rented under the name of "Smithson," and opened the front door. Nadine turned to Colleen. "Go ahead. Step inside. It's your home."

Inside, the house was bland but comfortable. Thick shag-pile rugs, leather-upholstered furniture, televisions in the living-room, kitchen and dining-room. On the cream-painted walls, the kind of noncommittal abstract prints usually found in hotels. A glass-fronted bar, a breakfast den, and a patio door with a view of a small, untidy back yard, with a rusty wire leaf-burner.

"No jacuzzi?" asked Colleen, disappointed. "I always spend *hours* in the jacuzzi."

"You want a hot tub?" asked Joe, before Nadine could say anything at all. "We'll have one fitted in. No problem."

"Well," said Colleen, walking from room to room, her tight pedal-pushers rippling like freshly-caught bluefish, "I guess it isn't *too* bad, for a hideout."

"You mustn't think of it as a hideout," insisted Joe, writing down "hot tub" on the back of an envelope. "It's a temporary refuge, that's all. As soon as all of this is over, we'll be getting you someplace far better. Hot tubs in every room, if that's what you want."

"I could use a drink," said Nadine. "I don't suppose you happen to have mixed up any of those martinis of yours, Joe?"

Joe tucked away his pencil. "I do believe we have a jug or two in the icebox. I came up here last night, just to check that Colleen would have everything she needed."

"If you once taste Joe's martinis, you'll never need anything else again," smiled Nadine.

Joe poured drinks, then went to the phone to sort out arrangements for tomorrow's press conference. Crack Nielsen, stolid as ever, was keeping watch out of the window. Colleen said, "I think I'll take a bath. I feel like I've been traveling forever. Do you want to come and talk, Mrs. Alexander?"

"Call me Nadine, for God's sake," said Nadine, following her into the bedroom suite.

Colleen covered her face with her hands, so that only her wide cornflower eyes were showing. "You know something, I've been trying not to show it, but when Joe Jasper called me last night and told me that you were going to take care of me *personally* . . . well, I couldn't believe it. I promised myself I was going to be so *blahsay,* you know? But I've read so much about you in the magazines; and I saw you with Johnny Carson. Wasn't that just hilarious when he asked you to show him how a man should seduce a really tall woman?"

"Hilarious," agreed Nadine, sitting on the end of the bed and crossing her legs.

"I have to say it, I really admire you," said Colleen. "All the things that you've been doing for women's rights; and everything you've been saying about nuclear weapons. That was very courageous of you, you know, considering who your husband is."

"Everybody has to take a moral stand somewhere," Nadine told her.

"Well, for sure, and that's why I said that I'd come along to Washington. When you consider that he's supposed to be the *President* . . . Well, a man like that, a man with those sex habits, you wouldn't even ask him to run a stag party, let alone a country, you know?''

Nadine spread her hand and made a show of inspecting her long red fingernails. "How did Joe Jasper find you?" she asked.

"I'm not really sure. But I told a guy I know called Jackie Opa all about the President, you know, what he did during the primaries, and I guess Jackie Opa must've sold the information for whatever he could get for it. I mean, you can't *blame* Jackie.''

"No, sure. I can't blame him," said Nadine.

Colleen tugged off her Mexican-style blouse, revealing big soft breasts that were cradled in a Frederick's-of-Hollywood quarter-cup bra. Nadine had always considered that her own figure was Valkyrie-like; but Colleen's was center-spread quality, golden and curvy, a living breathing Little Annie Fannie. Nadine watched her as she stood in front of the looking-glass and unfastened her tight satin pedal-pushers, and thought to herself that, in spite of Nadine's sexual brashness, in spite of her own elegance and fame, they were sisters of a kind, sisters both of fate and of political expedience.

"I didn't bring too many clothes with me," said Colleen, sliding her pants down her bare hips. "I have a *huge* wardrobe back in Vegas; so many dresses I have a card-index. And *shoes*.''

"We'll find you some clothes," said Nadine. "I'll take you out shopping if you like. Now you're in Washington, maybe we'll be able to find you something more chic. A tailored suit, maybe; and some formal evening gowns.''

"You're really kind," said Colleen. "I just know that we're going to be friends.''

"I hope so," said Nadine. She was being polite when she said it, but then Colleen turned around and stood in front of her wearing nothing but her uplift bra and a cute smashed-strawberry smile, and Nadine felt an upsurge within her that she hadn't felt for years, not since she had been at boarding school and she and Tania had wrestled under bedsheets naked and—

She looked away. She found herself guiltily trying to remember whether the bedroom door was locked. Colleen sat down perkily beside her and began to file at her nails. Close up, she

was even more unreal: her skin was flawless except for a Southern Cross of moles on her left shoulder, her little nipples were
sugar-pink. Everything about her was shiny and bright and larger
than life. No wonder she made a thousand dollars a night.

Nadine said, "You won't be making much money while
you're here."

"Oh, I don't care about *that*," smiled Colleen, wiggling her
fingers. "I haven't taken a day off in two years. Can you believe
that? Two years. Then it was only a weekend at Lake Tahoe, and
that was with four guys. Four! Mind you, only one was a real
tiger. The rest were, you know, eager but easily tired."

"Do you really enjoy it?" asked Nadine. It was one of the
questions she had promised herself that she wouldn't ask. But
now that she had met Colleen, she couldn't resist it. She would
never be able to form any kind of relationship with Colleen, as
friend or helper or protector, until she understood what could
possibly motivate a girl to do anything a man wanted. Especially
a girl as pretty and vivacious as this.

Colleen blinked her big blue eyes. "Enjoy it? What do you
mean?"

"Do you enjoy doing what you do? Being a hostess?"

Colleen thought about it with obvious seriousness. Then she
said, "Yes. I guess I do."

"Even when you have to do the kind of thing that Marshall
Roberts made you do?"

Colleen shrugged, and went on filing her nails. "It's all a
question of what your tolerance threshold is, I guess. I mean
some girls get upset if their husband says he wants to wear their
dirty panties to work. They think he's a pervert or something.
Then again some girls want to do things themselves but don't
know how to tell their boyfriends or husbands without feeling
like they're whores or something. The only reason I'm in business is because ordinary people don't relate to each other, you
know? If a wife wants to tinkle all over her husband, and he
doesn't mind, then what difference does it make? Anyway,
Marshall Roberts didn't *make* me do anything. Nobody does.
They ask for what they want, and I tell them the price."

Nadine didn't know what to answer to that. She sat staring at

Colleen for a while; and Colleen stared back. It was a strange, decisive moment.

"I'd better take that bath now," said Colleen.

"And I'd better get back to Georgetown," said Nadine, looking at her watch.

Colleen stood up. She reached behind her back and unhooked her bra. Her breasts swayed a little as she took it off. She had fine blonde pubic hair, closely trimmed, and the candy-pink lips of her vulva pouted through it like some wholesome but forbidden sweetmeat. Nadine looked up at her, and attempted a dismissive smile, but somehow her face seemed frozen. She kept thinking of Tania and that warm shared bed. . . .

"You know something," she said, "when I was at school . . ."

Colleen held out her hand. Nadine, feeling foolish, but unable to refuse, accepted it. Colleen knelt down on the rug in front of her. Her nipples were pink and tight.

"Every woman feels it," Colleen said, gently. "I've had women too, you know. They pay me just like the men do. There's nothing wrong with it. And, most of the time, do you know what they want to do?" She released Nadine's hand, and squeezed her breasts so that the soft flesh bulged through her fingers. "They want to feel another woman's breasts. Kiss another woman's nipples. It's not the way that men think it is at all—like one of those lesbian porno movies. It's soft, and it's gentle, and most of the time it's beautiful."

Nadine leaned forward, only a fraction. Colleen ran her fingers into Nadine's thick brunette hair, and kissed her. It was an open-mouthed kiss, but the tips of their tongues explored each other only gently, nerves touching nerves.

"Lie back," coaxed Colleen, in a voice so soft that Nadine could almost have imagined that she had heard it inside her head. She hesitated, but then Colleen murmured again, "Lie back," and she lay back on the bed and looked up at the ceiling and made a deliberate decision to let herself go.

She felt the zipper of her Italian slacks being opened; then they were pulled down from her hips. She rarely wore underwear under trousers, and she immediately felt the coolness of the air against the moistness of her sex. I'm excited, she thought. It's madness, but I'm actually excited. I don't even know if either of us remembered to lock the door, and both Joe Jasper and Crack Nielsen are sitting in the next room, separated from the most hair-raising scandal in Washington for five years by nothing more than an inch and a half of pine.

She felt Colleen's fingers running up the inside of her thighs, and she shivered. Then she felt Colleen's curly blonde hair against her skin, and the electric feeling of Colleen's tongue between her legs.

Colleen teased her, her tongue-tip parting her flesh, arousing her clitoris with an expert efficiency that made Nadine blush; then probing into the opening of her urethra, teasing, tingling, and at last plunging suddenly and deeply into the slippery well of her vagina.

Nobody had ever aroused Nadine like this before, not even Titus. Colleen's tongue flew over her sex like a wet and fluttering butterfly, making her shiver and bite at her knuckles in ecstasy. Now she didn't care whether the door opened or not. She stretched her legs wide apart, so that Colleen could reach every crevice of her, and twisted the bedcover around herself as if in deadly struggle.

Very near to the end, Colleen moistened one finger, and slid it promptly into Nadine's anus as far as it would go, and when that happened, Nadine felt as if the ceiling were collapsing on top of her, as if the world were a dynamited kaleidoscope, flying with fragments of colored glass.

When she opened her eyes it seemed as if it were hours later, although it was only minutes. Colleen was in the bathroom, running a tubful of hot water, and scenting it with the Chanel bath oil which Joe Jasper had left for her. Nadine slowly pulled up her pants, fastened the belt, and got up from the bed. She ran her hands through her hair to fluff it up.

"I hope you realize that you've just committed a very indecent act with the woman who could be America's next First Lady?" she asked.

Colleen said, "It had occurred to me, I have to admit." Her tone seemed different now. Harder.

Nadine leaned against the bathroom door, watching Colleen swish the bath with her hand. "Are you saying that you seduced me on purpose?"

"You're worried?" smiled Colleen.

"I don't know. *Should* I be worried?"

"I'm not going to take advantage of you, if that's what you mean. But a girl always needs some insurance. Like Marshall Roberts. I asked Denny if I could service Marshall Roberts; and don't you think it's paid off?"

Nadine said nothing while Colleen stepped into the bath, and sat down. "Would you pass me that backbrush?" asked Colleen. "That's right. The one with the swan's neck. Don't you think that's *cute?*"

With the studied gestures of a drama-school student, Nadine sat down on the edge of the tub and watched Colleen while she soaped herself. "I suppose I was a fool, then, to let you do what you did."

"Not particularly. There weren't any witnesses."

There was a silence between them, punctuated only by the sounds of bathing. Then Colleen smiled and said, "You've got me all wrong, you know that? And you've got *yourself* wrong, too. You should have more confidence in yourself as a woman. I made love to you because I *wanted* to make love to you, not because I wanted to blackmail you, or bring you down, or demand money."

Nadine looked uncertain, but Colleen reached out of the water and took her hand. "I was just trying to show you that I could have blackmailed you if I'd wanted to. But I didn't, and I won't. I respect you, and the only way that I know how to show somebody that I respect them is to make love to them."

"Well, it won't happen again," said Nadine, in a brittle voice.

"It might," Colleen ventured.

"It won't. I'll make sure of that."

"But you're supposed to look after me. Satisfy my every need, with the sole exception of money. Isn't that it?"

"Yes, that is it."

"Well, that's what I want. That's my every need."

"What are you talking about?"

"*You,* Mrs. Alexander. *You're* my every need. You're beautiful and you're famous and you have the quickest climaxes I ever came across."

Nadine thought: what the hell have I gotten myself into? If this is another of Titus' nasty double-plots . . . But it didn't seem possible. It seemed far more likely that this Vegas-trained young hostess had simply discovered the secret of becoming wealthy. Fucking the famous, and then coming out with the true, unexpurgated inside story, weekly fodder for the *Star* and *National Enquirer*. The trouble was, games like that could quickly and easily become dangerous. Nobody likes to be taken for a sucker, and nobody likes to be robbed. Even more, nobody likes to be ridiculed.

"Colleen," Nadine asked, "what do you actually want?"

"I told you. I want *you*. That's for as long as I decide to stay here in Washington. I also need some money, and I want some fun. I know what Joe Jasper said about keeping me locked up here, but who needs it? I'll be good. I even promise to come home by midnight."

"Have you any idea how risky it's going to be for you to dance around in the open? You're the only girl in the world who can bring down the President of the United States simply by opening her mouth."

"So?"

"So what you don't seem to understand is that this particular President of the United States is quite likely to have you badly hurt if you try to unseat him. And when I say badly hurt, I mean badly hurt. Do you value your eyesight? Your breasts?"

Colleen rose from the bath, and reached for a towel. She wrapped it tightly around herself, staring at Nadine suspiciously. "I wasn't trying to hustle you," she said. "I was only showing off."

Nadine took her in her arms, and held her. Then she kissed her on the forehead, and on the nose, and on the lips. "Let's keep this our secret, shall we?" she whispered. She slipped her hand inside Colleen's towel, and massaged her big slippery breast, until the nipple tightened between her fingers. Colleen kissed her cheek, and then her mouth, hungrily.

Unknown to both of them, a silent camera was squeezing its

eye at them at intervals of exactly 8.3 seconds; and Joe Jasper was already on the phone to an address on Pennsylvania Avenue, speaking quickly and pointedly, and occasionally glancing towards the closed door of Colleen's new bedroom.

FIFTEEN

Just after 11 o'clock in the morning, the remains of Mrs. Margot Schneider were removed from the Phoenix city morgue in a black plastic body bag and handed over formally to James T. Skellett of the National Security Agency. Skellett refused to make any comments to the press. The mayor of Phoenix, Andrew Gardens, said that the city was simply obeying a directive from a higher authority, in the interests of national defense.

"I'd prefer to think about Chief Ruse today, rather than Mrs. Margot Schneider," he remarked. "Wouldn't you?"

SIXTEEN

Daniel was wiping up the tables after lunch when Ronald Reagan Kinishba came in with an untidy parcel under his arm, and beckoned him over to the table on the far side of the diner. Pete Burns, the deputy, was sitting at the counter, finishing off a lemon Danish, and Ronald was anxious that they shouldn't be overheard. These days, Ronald would only have to wear a loud suit and Pete Burns would run him in.

Cara, who was wiping up the counter and stacking away the dirty dishes, looked across and saw what was going on; so she turned to Pete Burns with a smile and a bounce and said, "How about some more coffee, deputy? Another Danish?"

Pete Burns turned majestically on his counter-stool and remarked to Daniel, "The help's improved around here, Daniel. Must say I like your taste. Always had a pen-chant for redheads."

Ronald gave him a quick wave and a wink. Burns was obviously about to say something cutting in reply, but Cara said, "Sweet'n'Lo, deputy?" and distracted him.

"What's happening?" Daniel asked Ronald. "Are those the coveralls?"

Ronald nodded. "Jim Pryor's coming by in an hour's time. Levon said he wasn't altogether too happy about smuggling us into the base, but he'll do it."

"I wish to hell you'd tell me what fancy plan you've cooked up for getting us out."

"You really want to know?" asked Ronald.

"It's that bad, is it?"

"It's bad, and I mean ba-a-ad."

Daniel drew back a chair and sat down. "You'd better tell me. If I'm not going to live to see sundown, I think I'd prefer to know about it in advance."

Ronald leaned his head forward, and in a conspiratorial murmur said, "It's like this. Jim Pryor's truck is large enough to take my motorcycle, hidden under a few sacks and boxes. Now, I rode around the perimeter of the base early this morning, and found just what I was looking for. There's a rocky outcrop, quite close to the perimeter fence, on the Higley side. So what we do is—once we've checked out Willy's body—we cross the base on the motorcycle, speed up when we reach the outcrop, and literally fly right over the fence. Evel Knievel can eat shit: we're going to do it pillion."

Daniel slowly rubbed the side of his cheek. He was silent for so long that even Deputy Burns turned around again to see what had caused such a lull in the conversation.

"That's bad," Daniel commented, at last. "That's *bad*."

"I told you. But what a way to make an exit. The ground's level and hard, the fence is only ten feet high. That outcrop makes a natural ramp. We'll clear the top wire by two, three feet. And if anybody's chasing us, they won't be able to follow because the nearest gate in the fence is more than a half-mile away. We'll be home free."

"That's if we're still alive."

Ronald puffed out his cheeks, and shrugged. "You want to take a look at Willy. You got to take some risks."

Daniel stood up. "You know something?" he said. "I now have a clear understanding of how and why the Indians lost the West. If they'd have had motorcycles, instead of horses, they would have lost it even quicker."

"Then you'll do it?" grinned Ronald.

"Do I have a choice?"

When Pete Burns had finished his third Danish and left, Daniel followed Cara into the kitchen, where Susie was helping

Mrs. Koperwas stack the dishwasher. Mrs. Koperwas was a fussy, motherly old biddy who had helped Daniel with the cleaning and the housework ever since he had first opened up the diner for business. She had immediately won over Susie because she could remember the last gunfight at Apache Junction, in 1907, when Robert "Chicken" McTeague had shot and killed Edward Bailey right in front of the dry goods store. "I can see Mr. Bailey's one boot standing up by itself in the street, clear as if it happened this morning."

Cara said, "You're going *now?*"

"As soon as Jim Pryor comes by."

She grasped his hands, and kissed him. "I know it was my idea, dressing up as Air Force people and everything . . . but you're sure you want to do it? I mean you're sure you ought to?"

"I don't think there's anything else I can do."

She held him close. "You keep yourself safe then, you hear?"

"I'm not usually known for my suicidal nature. Not like this Navajo kamikaze biker here."

Ronald grunted with amusement.

"There's just one precaution you can take," Daniel told Cara. "If we're not out of the base in two hours, then call Pete Burns and tell him everything that's happened. If we're okay, he'll probably throw our tails in prison; but if we're not, then somebody in authority needs to know."

They went upstairs and changed into the USAF technicians' coveralls that Levon had lent them. "They don't smell too good, do they?" commented Ronald. "You don't think that Levon sews himself into them for the winter, do you?"

Levon had also managed to dig out a couple of blue peaked drill caps, and a battered USAF tool box. Daniel prized the box open and saw that it contained three rusty octagonal spanners, the metal clips from a pair of OshKosh dungarees, and a torn copy of the Seattle *Post-Intelligencer*. "I always knew there was something funny about Levon and Seattle," Ronald remarked.

They shared a cold Coors, which they drank too quickly and too nervously. Then, at five after two, they heard the bullfrog croak of Jim Pryor's truck horn. Daniel tugged on his cap and asked Cara, "How do I look?"

"Scared," she said.

Jim Pryor was waiting for them impatiently, in his tall sweat-stained Stetson hat and his red-checkered shirt, chewing a massive mouthful of gum. His blue Ford panel truck was parked on the highway nearby, its doors wide open and its tailgate down.

"I can tell you straight, I wouldn't be taking you guys at all if it wasn't for Levon," he said, and spat into the dust. "I always thunk you two were a couple of weirdos."

Ronald slapped him cheerily on the back. "There's something else, as a matter of fact. I was wondering if you could be kind enough to take my bike along, too." He nodded his head towards the Nighthawk, and smiled.

"The bike?" asked Jim Pryor, incredulously.

"Come on, Mr. Pryor. Levon told us you owe him one."

"Jesus wept," said Jim Pryor.

Between them, while Susie watched solemnly from her upstairs window, the three of them manhandled the motorcycle into the back of Jim Pryor's truck, wedging it in between a stack of canned beets and a side of bacon wrapped in muslin. Then they locked up the tailgate, climbed into the cab, and drove off. Susie knelt on her chair watching the empty highway for almost five minutes before Cara came in, and laid a gentle hand on her shoulder.

"Daddy's going to be all right, isn't he?"

"Oh, for sure."

"You're not lying to me?"

"Why would I lie?"

"Because *you're* worried, too."

Cara sat down on the bed. "Your daddy is quite capable of taking care of himself, if only he'd realize it."

"I don't know what you mean," said Susie.

Cara smiled. "I don't believe that I know myself. But he's a strong man, much stronger than he thinks he is. He still loves your mommy, you know that?"

"He says that if Mommy came back, they'd only argue."

"Maybe he's right."

Susie looked at Cara with big round eyes, and her mouth was pursed in distress. Cara touched her cheeks, and two large tears rolled down.

In the truck, meanwhile, Ronald was determinedly singing *O Sole Mio*. Daniel was sitting with his feet up on the dash, and Jim Pryor was driving as if he had a permanent migraine. There were six or seven air fresheners dangling from the knobs of the truck's radio, every scent from mountain pine to huckleberry; and on the inside of the cab roof, there was a large picture of Chesty Morgan, the lady with the 72″ bust.

Jim Pryor said, "You guys are going to have to get your carcasses out of this cab in a minute or two, and hide in the back."

"Ten-four," said Ronald.

"Don't know why the hell you want to sneak yourselves into an air base anyway. You're not set on stealing one of them swing-wing fighters, are you? Flying it to Moscow?" He pronounced it "swang-wang farter," a real Apache Junction accent.

"No," said Ronald. "Something better than that. We're going on a panty raid. Stealing the officers' thermal underwear."

"I always thunk you was weirdos," said Jim Pryor.

They pulled up by the side of the road. It was a hot, clear afternoon, no traffic in sight for miles, except for a lone Indian driving a diesel earth-mover about a quarter of a mile away, in a nearby field. Ronald and Daniel heaved themselves up into the back of Jim Pryor's truck, and wormed their way in between the supplies until they found a stuffy niche behind a case of canned peaches. Jim Pryor locked the tailgate again, and climbed back into the cab.

"I just hope he doesn't decide to get smart," said Daniel, as the truck pulled away. "Try to tip off the sentry, anything like that."

"Well," said Ronald, philosophically, "there's always that risk. But Levon wouldn't like it too much; and I don't think Jim Pryor's going to go out of his way to upset Levon. Not if he wants spare parts, and gas, and good service."

"I don't know," said Daniel. "I'll trust him when we're inside the base; not before."

It seemed to take a whole afternoon of jostling and bumping before the truck pulled up in front of Williams AFB. Daniel and Ronald sat crouched and sweating in the darkness and listened to the sentry approaching the cab and asking Jim Pryor to produce his pass documents.

"Bacon, canned fruit, canned vegetables, potatoes, broccoli, cooking oil," recited the sentry, from Jim Pryor's docket. "Anything else? Any liquor? Beer? Perfumeries?"

"What you read on that docket is what there is," said Jim Pryor.

"Well, that's what *you* say," replied the sentry. "But the way *I* hear it, you've been bringing in some of them videos, *Debbie Does Dallas* and such-like, and some of them magazines, *Fifteen* and *Anal Fun* and *Private*."

"Young man, you certainly hear some weird stuff," said Jim Pryor. "Now, give me that docket back, and let me get on with my deliv'ry."

"I'm entitled to search your vehicle," said the sentry. "I'd be obliged if you'd step down from the cab, and open the tailgate. Then maybe we can take a look, see what you're hiding in there."

"I'm behind time as it is," Jim Pryor complained.

"That's too bad," said the sentry. "Because it's my duty to make sure that nothing gets on to this base that shouldn't; like firearms, or dope, or cameras, or questionable movies."

"This is crazy," said Jim Pryor. "You ain't never searched me before."

"I ain't never heard that you were bringing in unsavory movies and magazines before."

This is it, thought Daniel. He's going to sell us to the Air Force, to save his own neck. But then he heard Jim Pryor say, "Listen, okay, we can be reasonable, can't we?"

"What's your definition of *reasonable?*" the sentry wanted to know.

"Look here. Couple of good video movies. Let's say they're a private arrangement, kind of a commission."

There was another pause, longer. Daniel wiped the sweat from his forehead with the back of his sleeve. Ronald whispered, "Take them. For Christ's sake. Take them."

Jim Pryor and the sentry walked out of earshot, although Daniel and Ronald could still indistinctly hear them discussing the merits of *Busy Bodies* and *World of Pleasure Part III*. An

F-15 Eagle thundered overhead, blotting out all conversation and all sensible thought; but when it had gone, there was complete silence. Ronald said, "What's happening out there?" but Daniel could only shake his head.

The next thing they knew, Jim Pryor had climbed back into his cab and started up the truck's engine. They heard him say, "Have a good evening. Don't overdo it. There's plenty more where that came from." Then the truck was jouncing through the gates, and swinging around towards the stores, where Jim Pryor would unload his supplies. As he shifted gear, Daniel could hear him cursing the sentry out loud.

The truck jolted to a halt, and Jim Pryor came around and lowered the tailgate. "It's all right, you can come on out," he grumbled. "But don't ask me for no more favors because I'm not in the goddamned mood. That punk of a sentry. If I hadn't had you two guys stashed in the back, I would've told him to go shove his dick up some airplane's tailpipe. Goddamned twenty dollars apiece, those videos cost me. And now I've got to give a couple every time I go through the goddamned gate, less'n he gets suspicious."

They hefted the cycle over the tailgate and set it on the ground. Daniel said to Jim Pryor, "That's it, okay? You're no longer responsible. You never smuggled us in through the gates, and we never saw you before in our lives."

Jim Pryor took off his Stetson, and raked his thinning hair across the scalp. "That Levon, he's some goddamned smartass, I can tell you. You tell him I don't owe him no more favors."

"Double negative," Ronald commented.

"Kiss off," Jim Pryor retorted.

Daniel and Ronald left the disgruntled Jim Pryor to unload his supplies, and went in search of the base hospital. Ronald wheeled the motorcycle a hundred yards along to the shade of a stunted foothill paloverde; and parked it there ready for their eventual getaway. A flight of three F-15s screeched low behind the rows of huts, and for a moment it was impossible for them to hear each other speak. At last, as the jets began to climb towards Chandler and the Gila River Indian Reservation, Ronald took Daniel's arm and said, "You go that way, okay? That looks the most promising direction, all those concrete buildings. I'll check out the huts along here. We'll meet back here in five minutes, unless you find what you're looking for. But in any case I'll be here waiting for you, whatever.''

"Take care," said Daniel.

Ronald said, "You too, okay?"

Swinging Levon's bashed-up old USAF toolbox as casually as he could, Daniel walked towards the main administration buildings and the control tower. He had forgotten his sunglasses and so he had to half-close his eyes against the glare of the white-painted concrete blocks, and the dazzling glass of the control-tower windows. There was a heady, heated smell of aviation fuel in the air, mingled with that dry desert aroma which is always Arizona's. It was a baking hot afternoon, and there was hardly anyone around, except for a tall black airman in fatigues, painting the air base flagstaff.

Daniel walked around the main administration block, pretending to whistle through lips that were too parched to make a sound. A door suddenly opened, and a young Air Force captain came hurrying out, so abruptly that Daniel didn't have time to do anything but snap what he thought was a reasonably authentic salute. The captain flapped a dismissive hand at him, and then disappeared around the corner. Daniel stopped, and took a breath. His lungs and his heart felt as if they all had twisted up together in an impossible knot.

Locating the base hospital turned out to be ridiculously easy. As he walked around the last block, he saw a clearly-stenciled array of signposts. The hospital block was right across the road in front of him, surrounded by a white-painted chain-link fence.

He glanced quickly from right to left. Apart from a couple of technicians working on the nose radar of a distant F-15, the area was deserted. He began to walk across the road, his head lowered so that his face would be shadowed by the peak of his cap.

He was almost across when he heard the whine of an approaching Jeep. He tried to walk faster, but he was still five or six paces from the hospital block driveway when the Jeep squealed to a stop beside him. A harsh voice said, "Hey, you!"

He stopped, and looked around. Sitting in the driver's seat of the Jeep was an Air Force master sergeant, with an I.D. badge reading "Wells, H.B." He stared at Daniel out of impenetrable sunglasses, and chewed gum between his back molars as regularly as if there was an Air Force ordinance on the exact rate of correct mastication.

"What's your name, airman?" he demanded.

"Korvitz, sir."

"Well, Korvitz, what the hell do you think you're wearing?"

Daniel said, "Huh?" and then looked down at his filthy coveralls as if he had never seen them before in his life. "These, sergeant?"

"That's right, Korvitz. Those."

Daniel opened his mouth but no words seemed to feel like coming out. The master scrgeant stared at him and chewed, and stared at him and chewed.

Suddenly, Daniel found himself speaking. "It's the hospital, sergeant. The head's backed up. I've got to clear it out. They told me to wear something that they could burn afterwards."

The master sergeant chewed thoughtfully for almost a minute. Then, with considerable relish, he said, "You're going to get smothered in shit, is that what they meant?"

Daniel nodded, trying to look as unhappy as possible.

"Ha!" barked the sergeant. Then, "Ha! ha! ha! ha!" And then he thrust the Jeep into gear and drove off, still laughing. Daniel watched him go, and felt the sweat trickling down the sides of his body. Thank the Lord for the small-minded cruelty of the military sense of humor.

He walked up the driveway to the hospital block, up the steps, and pushed open the door. Inside, the hospital smelled of fresh paint and formaldehyde, and it was shadowy and cool. There was a desk near the entrance, but nobody was sitting there. A poster on the wall extolled the virtues of a daily diet with plenty of bran. "Moral Fiber Is Not Enough."

Cautiously, he walked along the corridor, peeking into the porthole windows in every door. At the end of the corridor was a closed windowless door marked *Private*. He hesitated in front of it; then turned the handle and found that it was unlocked. Beyond it was another corridor, running at right-angles, painted a particularly unpleasant shade of pea-green. Daniel closed the door behind him, and walked quietly along this second corridor, until he reached another door marked *No Admittance to Unauthorized Personnel*. He opened that, too, and found himself in the morgue.

It wasn't much of a morgue. Twelve feet square, with nothing more than two medical trolleys, parked side by side as casually as if they had been left there by a supermarket attendant; a dripping sink; a shelf crowded with bottles of antiseptic, sodium chloride, arsenic, and surgical alcohol; a *House & Garden* calendar for two years ago; and a rattling, growling refrigeration unit.

On one of the trolleys rested a U.S. Air Force body bag, which obviously contained a body. Daniel stared at it for a very long time before he stepped any further into the morgue. His pulse-rate seemed to have dropped to a slow, thunderous drumbeat, and the sweat chilled on his forehead and under his arms as if he himself were close to death. He stepped up to the trolley and stood beside it. He began to think of every horror movie he had ever seen: movies in which corpses suddenly sat upright and clutched at your throat. Knowing that this particular body might be Willy didn't make it any less alarming; in fact it made it worse. People in zombie movies were always being attacked by their erstwhile friends.

There was a label tied to the zipper of the body bag. Daniel picked it up and looked at it, but all it bore was a penciled number 755368. He knew that he was going to have to open the bag and examine the body. He reached for the zipper tag, and began to tug it down.

It took forever just to draw the zipper down to chest level. It kept sticking, and he had to ease it back up again, and then try opening it a little further. But at last the corpse inside the bag was exposed to the light, and Daniel could see for himself what had really happened to Willy Monahan.

There was no head, but he knew it was Willy. He recognized on the corpse's right collarbone the L-shaped scar which Willy had always boasted had been sustained in a rapier-duel with a Prussian count. It was nonsense, of course—he had fallen off a motorcycle when he was a cadet, and jabbed himself with the brake lever. But it was Willy's scar; and the chest and shoulders were Willy's chest and shoulders; and in Daniel's mind there was no doubt at all. Willy was dead.

What was really horrifying, though, was that Willy had quite obviously not been decapitated by a helicopter rotor. Even the thinnest rotor left a bruised, mangled neck stump. But Willy's neck had been cut off cleanly just above the larynx; and although it was thick with crusts of congealed blood, it had been as neatly severed as if he had been executed by a surgeon. Even more chilling: there was no sign of his head. Whoever had killed him had taken his head as a souvenir.

Numbly, Daniel recited the *Kaddish* for Willy. It was all he could do. He and Willy had shared such a closeness of character that they had never spoken to each other as much as they should have. They had drunk a lot, played cards, laughed, watched television. But Daniel would have done anything now for one last serious conversation with Willy, just to find out who Willy Monahan had actually been.

He zippered up the body bag again, so hastily that he caught his fingers. Then he backed towards the door with the unbalanced, firmly-planted steps of a drunk leaving a New York bar. He closed the door loudly behind him. Bang. And then the real world again.

"Lord God," he said to himself, and tasted bile in his mouth.

He made his way back along the pea-green corridor, and pushed his way through the door marked *Private*. He was beginning to feel the extraordinary coldness of shock, and a panicky need to escape from the hospital block, and get out into the sunshine again. As he walked back into the entrance area, however, he was confronted by a woman corporal, sitting behind the reception desk with a tightly-waved hairstyle and a frigid expression.

"*Airman!*" she rapped, at the very instant he raised his hand to push open the hospital door.

"Yes, ma'am!" Daniel responded. But he stayed where he was, his hand still pressed against the glass. Outside he could see blue sky and hot concrete and freedom. Inside, there was nothing but nausea and death.

"Who gave you permission to enter the hospital block dressed in that disgusting coverall?"

"Master Sergeant Wells, ma'am."

"What have you been doing here? I didn't see you come in."

"You were temporarily absent from your desk, ma'am. I did wait. But they told me it was urgent. The head was blocked."

"The head, airman, is *that* way."

"Yes, ma'am. But I was just checking the outfall. I like to do the maintenance thorough, you know?"

"Just a minute," the corporal told him, and picked up her telephone. Daniel stayed where he was, an inch away from escape. He heard the corporal say, "Get me Sergeant Wells, please. Corporal Knobla." Then she clamped one hand over the receiver and said to Daniel, "You stay there. You stay right where you are."

Daniel didn't move. Another F-15 flew over the base, making the doors rattle and vibrate in their frame, but all he could think about was Willy's sawn-off neck, the nerves and the blood vessels and the white protruding spine; the sweat slid down his back like chilled blood.

"Sergeant Wells? This is Corporal Knobla, sergeant, over at the hospital block. Yes, sergeant, I'm sorry; but I have an airman here who *claims* that he's been cleaning out the head. A blockage of some kind. Well, he says that *you* sent him. Yes, sergeant. You personally. I *know* he's wearing disgusting fatigues. I know that. Well, that's why I stopped him. Yes. But I think we ought to check his identity, don't you?"

There was a long silence, punctuated only by the voice of Master Sergeant Wells speaking from the sergeants' mess. Daniel sweated and waited and prayed. But then Corporal Knobla suddenly said, "You'll send over the SPs? Very well, I'll keep him here."

Without a word, Daniel pushed open the hospital door. The warm air flowed around him like an opened-up bread-oven. Then his vision was jiggling in *cinema vérité* as he ran down the hospital driveway, past the chain-link fence across the wide roadway, and around the corner of the administration block. His sneakers flapped on the baking concrete. His breath roared inside his head as if it were the breath of someone close behind him.

He almost collided with Ronald coming the other way. He panted, "They called the SPs! For God's sake let's get out of here!"

Ronald said, "You found the hospital?"

"I saw Willy's body. Now, let's go."

They ran heavily back towards the tree where Ronald had parked his bike. There was no alarm, and no sign of anybody chasing after them, but Daniel didn't want to take any chances. He wanted to be back in his own bed tonight, with Cara lying next to him, and Susie sleeping down the hall. He certainly didn't want to be locked up in an Air Force cell, answering questions about Willy Monahan and guided missiles that wouldn't work and headless corpses that obviously hadn't been decapitated by helicopter rotors, and most certainly hadn't been posted to Langley AFB.

They reached the Nighthawk, and climbed astride it. It took Ronald two or three kicks before he could get it started, because it had been lying on its side in Jim Pryor's truck, and flooded. But at last it burped and burbled and roared into life, and a cloud of blue smoke rose up through the branches of the paloverde, and they were away.

"You're sure this jump stunt is going to work?" yelled Daniel, as they swerved between two PX buildings, and out into the open beside the airfield perimeter.

"You want to be sure of everything, you should never take any risks!" Ronald shouted back.

They jolted and blurred past a row of firetrucks, two huts, a long wire fence, and a parked collection of partially dismembered airplanes. Out to their right, two or three F-15 Eagles were taxiing for take-off, their gleaming outlines wavering in the heat-haze which rose from the runway. Then, above the roar of jet engines, Daniel heard the *whip-whip-whip* of a siren. He twisted around and saw two Jeeps speeding towards them with flashing red lights, quickly joined by a third Jeep.

"They're chasing us!" he shouted, close to Ronald's neck.

Ronald leaned his head back. "They don't have a fucking chance! Watch this!" He twisted the throttle wide open, and the Nighthawk blared at nearly 110 mph along the edge of the runway apron, jolting so much that Daniel felt as if all his teeth were being shaken out of their roots. He turned around again, and the Jeeps were almost a quarter of a mile away, but still coming.

"If you can't get over that fence, you know what's going to

happen, don't you? Bread and water for ten years, if you're lucky."

Ronald shouted, "What the hell are you worried about? Trust me!"

Suddenly, they heard a crackling noise. Daniel looked around to their left. Another Jeep had joined the pursuit, and an Air Force security policeman was standing up in the back seat with a rifle resting against the rollbar.

"Get this goddamned bike moving!" he screamed at Ronald. "They're shooting at us!"

A bullet hit the mudguard just behind Daniel's protruding backside, and moaned off into the dust. Another one whizzed hotly through the air an inch or two beside his face. He suddenly understood that this was serious, and that they could die.

Ronald yelled, "This is it! Look! The fence!"

Daniel bobbed his head up over Ronald's shoulder and saw ahead of them an ocher-colored outcrop of rock. Beyond that was the airbase's ten-foot-high perimeter fence, double mesh with barbed wire on top.

They were committed: there was no time to stop and consider if it was a good idea to leap ten feet in the air over a high-gauge wire security fence, or how the hell they were going to land when they reached the other side. Ronald twisted the accelerator to give himself the very last ounce of power, and Daniel hugged Ronald's waist and crouched down on the pillion seat and clenched his teeth so tight that he broke one of his porcelain crowns. Then they were streaking up the flat table of rock with the Nighthawk's engine screaming at top pitch, an A-natural that could have brought down the windows of half a dozen cathedrals.

Ronald let out a war-whoop that made Daniel's hair prickle up, and he knew as they flew up into the air that they could never make it, that the Nighthawk was too heavy with two people astride it, that the natural ramp of rock wasn't angled up high enough, and that Ronald had probably never even meant to escape at all, not seriously. Ronald was more of a Navajo than Daniel had given him credit for: fiercer, and more suicidal; and this assault on Williams Air Force Base had given him the justification he had always been looking for to go out in a thunder of glory. Daniel thought of all the times they had slammed along Route 60 together at a hundred miles an hour, and realized that he was probably fortunate to have lived as long as this.

The front wheel dropped in mid-air; and then the whole bike was somersaulting. Daniel tried to hang on to Ronald but his grip was torn away, and the next thing he knew he was being hurtled over the 10-foot fence as if he had been tossed by a bull, tearing his hand open on the barbed wire. He was slammed on to the hard ground on the other side, and rolled over and over with his arms and legs flailing, breathless, his ribs pummeled by rocks, his face lacerated by dry branches.

Ronald was not as lucky, but then perhaps he hadn't wanted to be. As the bike nosedived he was thrown head-first into the wire fence, at nearly ninety miles per hour, and his face was mashed instantly into a bloody purée. He collapsed to the ground, on the base side of the fence, and it took him only thirty seconds to die, blinded and shocked, silent, and paralyzed, his hands raised in the air as if he were still grasping the controls of an invisible motorbike.

The four Air Force Jeeps skidded to a halt by the fence, raising a high cloud of dust. Two of the SPs ran right up to the wire and looked intently for Daniel, while the rest of the detail stood around Ronald's wrecked Nighthawk as if they had discovered a pterodactyl which had suddenly dropped out of the sky. Daniel, winded and bruised amongst the desert brush, stayed motionless. Almost unconsciously, he said a prayer to thank God that he was still alive; and a prayer for Ronald Reagan Kinishba, who was now dead.

He heard a voice say, "He must've run off. I don't see him there."

"There's enough damn brush around here to hide an elephant."

"Find the nearest access gate and go get him. You don't bring that guy back to Colonel Kawalek, dead or alive, he's going to have your balls."

A quick rifle shot snapped into the dry ground only twelve feet away, and the bullet sang into the afternoon air, but the SPs didn't fire again. Daniel slithered backwards through the brush, down into a gully, and then ran and hopped until he reached a deeper gully fifty yards to the west, one of the old Indian canal-beds. He was gasping so loudly that he was sure that everybody could hear him for miles around. His ankle was twisted, and he could only jump and hobble and roll. He wished to God that he hadn't come. He wished to God that it was all a nightmare, and that Ronald was still alive. He wished to God that the sight of Willy's headless neck wasn't so deeply imprinted on his mind. He sat down for a minute or two beside a giant saguaro and wiped sweat and grit from his face, and caught his breath.

There was scarcely any sound now, in the scrub. Only the distant rumbling of jets, and the chirruping of crickets. The Air Force police must have given up the search, or gone the wrong way. He thought he heard someone shouting, but it soon faded. He lay back and closed his eyes.

SEVENTEEN

It was dark when Kathy Forbes opened her eyes. An illuminated digital alarm-clock beside the bed told her it was 23:17. She felt stunned and drowsy, and for a long moment she wondered if she might have been involved in a traffic accident, and been anesthetized. She reached instinctively downwards to feel if her legs were still there.

She turned over, and then she tried to sit up. Her head was pounding, and she found it difficult to focus her eyes. She sat there for more than five minutes; but her dizziness and nausea were too overwhelming, and at last she fell back on the pillow again.

She remembered James Skellett asking her questions. She remembered a thickly-carpeted living-room, with sunshine illuminating the tightly-drawn calico blinds. She remembered a rocking-chair that creaked with every movement, and a reproduction of Picasso's *Guernica*. She remembered somebody else, too, a man in a white shirt with an expensive wristwatch. He had sat well back, smoking a cigarette that had a strange aroma to it. Now and then, he had made a remark to James Skellett in an accent she failed to recognize.

"Do you think she really has any understanding about what happened?"

"I don't know. But it is necessary to find out."

"Necessary for what reason? You could kill her immediately; or ask your loathsome Mr. Friend to do it for you. Then you would have no problem whatsoever."

"You don't think so? Supposing she has already told someone else? Supposing Mrs. Schneider confided in her before she died? She could be the most dangerous woman on this planet."

"You always over-dramatize. You should have gone into the theater, Skellett, not the security services. That nonsense today in Phoenix. Couldn't you find a more discreet way of removing that police chief than *dynamiting* him? Ikon was furious."

"Ikon wasn't here. He didn't know the difficulties. Besides, I didn't really plan it that way. I simply asked Friend to get rid of him, as promptly as possible."

"I hope that Friend wasn't overstepping his task."

"I can handle Friend."

"Can you? I didn't see much evidence of it today."

A silence; calculated rather than hostile. Then: "Friend is no problem. A little exhibitionistic, perhaps. But then, he is a genius at what he does. He found Margot Schneider, didn't he? He eliminated her, and kept her elimination a complete mystery."

"A mystery which you have done very little to *keep* a mystery."

"I don't have any duty to justify my action to you."

There had been more conversations; different men. Then somebody who had lifted her arm, swabbed it with surgical alcohol, and injected her with something that had put her to sleep within seconds. Her dreams had been populated with distorted faces, and echoing laughter, and a feeling that she wasn't here at all, but living years and years ago, speaking, talking, on a Saturday afternoon in 1962. A voice had said, "Jack? Jack Kennedy? Jack Kennedy? Jack Kennedy?" and another voice had joined in to say, "Yes! Ford Galaxie wagons for 1962, featuring walnut-grained steel panels and Cruise-O-Matic drive!"

Now she was awake; alert; and frightened. The bed was a reasonably comfortable divan, with clean sheets. There were maroon velveteen drapes over the windows; through which street-light shone; and even in the darkness she could make out the shapes of white-painted furniture. There was a hint of cigar-smoke in the air, but otherwise the room smelled clean. She could hear the mutter of a television somewhere in the house, and someone coughing.

She tried to sit up again. She was dressed in nothing but bra, panties, garter belt and stockings, and all her jewelry had gone, even the ring that Ken had given her at Lake Tahoe. Her head felt as if it were floating, and there was the taste of something bitter in her mouth. From the next room she heard more coughing, and then a woman's voice saying, "It won't be possible until tomorrow. No, of course not. I won't be able to get one until daylight."

She reached out towards the bedside table to help herself climb out of bed. But the bed suddenly rose and tipped beneath her, and she fell heavily sideways, knocking the digital clock and the bedside lamp and a glass of water on to the rug. She lay back, panting. Whatever they had used to put her to sleep, it had completely unbalanced her inner ear.

The bedroom door opened, and a man stood silhouetted against the light from the next room, watching her. She couldn't focus her eyes properly but she was sure that it was Skellett. After a while he came forward and stood right beside her. He made no attempt to pick up the clock or the lamp.

She said, hoarsely, "How long have I been asleep?"

"Two or three hours, that's all. You were supposed to sleep until morning."

She said, "I'd like some water, please."

"In a moment."

She turned her head away, and squeezed her eyes tight shut in an effort to clear her mind. She wished she didn't feel so sick or so fuzzy. She had never been seriously ill in her life, and she hated to depend on anyone for anything. Just like her father. Stubborn and independent to the point of self-destruction. It formed the central part of her character, this hardness; and any caring or kindness she showed was achieved in spite of it. Skellett stayed where he was, watching her.

She said, "You can't keep me here for very much longer. Chief Ruse—"

"Chief Ruse is dead."

She opened her eyes and stared at him. "What do you mean Chief Ruse is dead?"

"Exactly that. A bomb was planted in his car, only about ten minutes after you last spoke to him. There wasn't enough left of him to feed to your family pooch."

Kathy pressed her hand against her mouth. "Oh, God," she said. She felt as if the whole world had suddenly revealed itself to be an utterly different and nightmarish place; as if everything she had believed about people since she was a child had turned out to be a hideous misapprehension.

Skellett said, "If it's any consolation, that wasn't the way I wanted it. But Chief Ruse was being obstructive; unnecessarily and ignorantly obstructive; and when it comes down to a question of national security . . ."

"What question of national security can possibly justify you killing Chief Ruse?" Kathy demanded.

Skellett clucked mildly. "Come on now, Miss Forbes. Don't over-excite yourself. You've had a heavy shot of chloral hydrate."

Kathy took a deep breath to steady herself, and to restore her sense of equilibrium. Skellett walked across to the window and parted the drapes slightly, looking out over the street with absent-minded satisfaction. He said, "Chief Ruse deliberately ignored a warrant issued by the National Security Agency and an order made by Arizona's Chief Judge. It was urgent that the remains of Mrs. Schneider should be removed from Phoenix and taken to Washington for special examination; before any further deterioration could take place. Chief Ruse was adamant that he was not going to release the body, and therefore the only possible course of action was to remove him. I have to tell you that it was quite likely that Chief Ruse was part of a large and influential Communist espionage ring."

"Chief Ruse? You're joking. He was the biggest redneck I've ever met."

Skellett smiled wanly. "*Red*neck may be the right expression."

"But did you have to kill him? Couldn't you just have had him arrested?"

"That would have meant charging him, and at the moment we're not ready to alert the entire espionage ring by making formal detentions. Besides, we wouldn't have been able to hold him for very long. We have very little watertight evidence. We could have set our whole counter-espionage operation back by five years; and risked some of our own people's lives."

Kathy said, "Why are you holding me? What have I got to do with it?"

"That's exactly what I intend to find out."

"But I don't know anything about spy rings or Communist agents. If your intelligence is any good at all, surely you must realize that."

Skellett let the drapes fall back into place, and came across to stand by Kathy's bedside again. "I've never been so arrogant that I've claimed my intelligence setup is one hundred percent efficient. For all I know, you could be a Soviet sleeper. I'm having your background checked out now. Didn't you once belong to the Socialist Discussion Group of Palo Alto, California?"

"You're being absurd. That was at college."

"Absurd? Well, maybe. I'm not a witch-hunter. Not unless there are any real witches to be hunted."

"What do you want me to say? I've told you everything I know, and that's precisely nothing."

"You still haven't explained why you asked me about Cuba."

"I've explained. It was an odd shot, that's all."

"I don't believe you. Something made you connect Mrs. Margot Schneider with Cuba and I want to know what it was. You went up to her house, didn't you, after she was murdered?"

"Of course I did. It was my job."

"Did you find anything there; or see anything there; or did anybody mention anything there that might have led you to assume that Mrs. Margot Schneider had any connection with Cuba?"

Kathy shook her head. "Nothing."

"Maybe Chief Ruse suggested it to you."

"What does it matter?" she said, acidly. "He's dead now."

"*He's* dead but *you're* not."

"So what are you going to do about that? Kill me, too? I'm being just as obstructive as Chief Ruse. At least, you seem to think so."

Skellett paced around the bed thoughtfully. Then he said, "You mentioned Jack Kennedy in your sleep."

"Who?"

"You heard me. Now, why would you talk about Jack Kennedy, unless he were somehow on your mind? And why would Jack Kennedy be on your mind? Can you answer me that?"

Kathy frowned at him. "Why are you so concerned about Cuba and Jack Kennedy? That all happened twenty years ago. What on earth is so important about Cuba and Jack Kennedy that makes you want to keep me here? It's ancient history."

"History can be ancient but still relevant."

"I wish you'd stop this cheap philosophizing. Where are my clothes? I want to get dressed."

Skellett said, "That won't be possible."

"It had better be possible."

"I want to know why you said Cuba. Then maybe we can talk about getting dressed."

"Mr. Skellett, I don't *know* what made me say Cuba. I simply don't know. It was a silly idea, I admit. But there have been so many stories about Cuban exiles trying to persuade the President to—"

Skellett swung his arm and slapped her face, so hard that she let out a sharp cry of pain and surprise. She tried to get up, but he slapped her again, even harder, and drew blood from the side of her mouth. Her cheek felt as if someone had clamped a hot steam-iron against it. Her eyes were filled with tears.

"Don't you mention Cuban exiles to me again," he said. His voice was as cold and as even as before. "All this talk about Cuban exiles is shit. You know as well as I do that Margot Schneider had nothing to do with any Cuban exiles. What I want to know is, what connection do you believe she *did* have with Cuba?"

Kathy didn't answer, but wiped the tears away from her face with the corner of the pillowcase. Skellett waited a minute or two longer, and then said, "You're not going to tell me? Very well."

He walked back into the next room and half-closed the door. Kathy heard him talking; and then the door opened again and he returned. With him now were the man in the white shirt she had seen earlier, and another taller man whom she didn't recognize. The man in the white shirt rolled up his sleeves, a cigarette dangling from between his lips. He looked like a corrupt twin of

Alain Delon. The taller man had high Slavic cheekbones, small glittering eyes, and a large strawberry-mark across the left side of his face.

Skellett said to Kathy, "I'm going to explain something to you. It is necessary to the security and safety of the United States that you tell me what it is that led you to connect Mrs. Margot Schneider with Cuba; and why it was that you mentioned Jack Kennedy in your sleep. There are 226-and-a-half million people in the United States. You are only one. I am authorized to do to you whatever I feel necessary in order to safeguard the rest of those human lives. I can torture you and I can kill you. It is entirely my decision, and if you leave me with no choice, then I will."

Kathy said, in a choked voice, "That's murder. You can't murder me."

"You don't understand. I *can* murder you, if the security situation warrants it. We call it D.E.5, in the NSA. Disencumbrance, on a scale of five. D.E.1 is simply arranging for a change of location within the continental United States. D.E.2 is forcible expulsion from the country. D.E.3 is imprisonment, for as long as necessary. D.E.4 is injury or physical persuasion forcible enough to guarantee complete cooperation. D.E.5 is disencumbrance in the last resort."

Kathy stared at him. She had never in her whole life felt so vulnerable and so helpless. But that Forbes hardness made her even more determined to resist. As long as she refused to tell Skellett anything about Mrs. Schneider and Cuba, then she was reasonably safe. It was obviously vital to him that he knew, otherwise he wouldn't have gone to all the trouble of detaining her here. He might try to hurt her, but as long as she kept her mouth shut, he wouldn't kill her.

She didn't imagine that he might terrify her so much that she would beg him to kill her.

"This is one last chance," said Skellett. "Tell me what you know, and we won't touch you."

Kathy said, "I don't know anything."

Skellett made a mock-disappointed face. Then, without any hesitation, he said, "Walsh, let's get her tied down."

"If you even try—" snapped Kathy. But Skellett slapped her

face again, and then again, stunning her into silence. The big strawberry-marked man called Walsh came forward with a handful of scarves and tea-towels, and lashed her wrists and ankles to the head and the foot of the bed, so that she was spreadeagled.

"This is *primitive*," Kathy wept. She was furious at herself for crying. "You're supposed to be taking care of American civilization, and yet you're behaving like medieval torturers."

"It's your own fault," said Skellett. "The information that you're holding back from us is vital. Don't you see how unpatriotic you're being? We don't *want* to do this to you. But what alternative do we have?"

The man came forward again, and this time he was carrying a ten-inch carving knife. Kathy's stomach tightened in terror, but he did nothing more than lean over her, seize her bra, and slice it open with a single upward cut. Skellett looked at her bare breasts appreciatively, and smiled. The man who looked like Alain Delon said nothing, but stayed in the corner, smoking, and watching.

"You're perverted," said Kathy. "You're perverted and sick."

Skellett said, "I've no choice. I'm sorry, but that's the way it is."

Now Walsh slid the carving-knife under the elastic of her panties, and separated them with another upward slice. He didn't bother to cut her garter-belt or her stockings. It was enough that she was naked and exposed, enough that her legs were lashed wide apart and that all three of them could sit staring at her as pruriently and as intently as they liked.

Skellett said, "Walsh, bring me one of those needles. That's right, the hypodermic needles. Thanks."

He sat down on the bed beside Kathy and smiled down at her as benevolently as a family doctor. "I'm not going to ask you any more questions," he said. "I'm simply going to start working on you, and when you decide you've had enough, you tell me. All right?"

Kathy shivered, "You're crazy. You're completely out of your mind."

"I'm practical, that's all," said Skellett.

Without any further discussion, he picked up the hypodermic needle, grasped her left breast, and pushed the needle straight into her nipple. She screamed and tried to writhe and twist against the bonds which held her to the bed, but Skellett kept the needle where it was, and kept smiling at her as calmly as if he were doing nothing more than taking her temperature.

He was true to his word: he didn't ask her any more questions. But he continued with deadly cruelty to stick the needle into her breasts and nipples, until she felt that they were ablaze. If she cried out too much, he slapped her face again and again. If she was silent, with her teeth clenched against the pain, he would coax her out of her silence by pushing the needle right through a nipple from one side to the other, and twisting it around as if he were winding a clock.

She had never known anything so agonizing. She prayed for him to stop, but she knew that Skellett wouldn't until she told him what she knew about Mrs. Margot Schneider, and she also knew that if she did tell him, he would probably kill her. The thought of that was all that kept her from giving in.

Some time in the early hours of the morning, Skellett got up from the bed and left the room. Walsh stayed there, and so did the man in the white shirt, but they didn't make any attempt to touch her. She kept her eyes closed and tried to imagine that she was somebody else, and that she wasn't here at all. It occurred to her that she didn't even know where "here" was. It was probably close to Phoenix: she was sure they hadn't driven too far. But they may have moved her to another address when she was asleep. This didn't feel like the first house to which Skellett had brought her: this house seemed more permanent, better furnished, as if it were permanently occupied.

She nearly managed to sleep, in spite of the pain in her breasts. The effects of the chloral hydrate had not completely worn off, and she went into a shallow dreamless doze. When she woke up, it was light, although the drapes were still closely drawn, and Walsh and the man in the white shirt were still there, watching her. She looked down at her breasts and saw that they were mottled red and swollen.

Skellett came back in again, eating a sandwich. He said to Walsh, "There's some coffee in the kitchen. Help yourself." Walsh went out, and after a moment or two, the man in the white shirt followed him.

"Well," said Skellett, "any change of mind?"

She turned her head away. She didn't even want to look at him. Skellett sat on the end of the bed, chewing his sandwich, and said, "None of this self-sacrifice is worth it, you know. You're going to suffer like hell, and in the end you're going to tell me what I want to find out."

He finished his crust, and took out his handkerchief to wipe his hands. "You should have heard Chief Ruse, how heroic *he* was. Full of fire. Full of determination. But fire and determination don't help when you're fundamentally wrong, when you're fighting for the wrong cause. In the end, you always have to admit your mistakes, and give in. I can tell you, Miss Forbes, you're not helping anybody by being so stubborn, especially not yourself."

Kathy kept her head turned away. "Why don't you go *fuck* yourself?" she told him.

Skellett pursed his lips and thought that over. Then he said, "You're still not understanding me. What I'm going to do to you next is going to drive you half out of your mind. I'm trying to avoid the necessity of having to do it. I'm not a cruel man, by nature; but this is cruel."

"You can't do any worse than you've done already."

"You want to bet?"

"Oh, do whatever you damned well like, if it turns you on."

Skellett said wistfully, "I only wish it did."

Walsh came into the room, carrying a small cardboard box. The man in the white shirt followed closely behind, smoking a fresh cigarette. The cigarettes had an odd foreign pungency; and Kathy realized somewhere in the back of her mind that it must be the smell that she had previously mistaken for cigars. *Eastern European,* she thought, for some inexplicable reason.

Skellett took the small cardboard box and set it down on his lap, holding the lid closed with his thumbs. "Have you ever heard of *Heloderma suspectum?*" he asked Kathy.

"I imagine you're going to tell me."

"Of course. Even the ugliest of guests deserves a proper introduction. *Heloderma suspectum* is the scientific name for the lizard known as the Gila Monster, the only poisonous lizard which frequents the deserts of Texas, New Mexico, and Arizona.

But, of course, being a native of Arizona, you are quite well acquainted with him already.''

"The Gila Monster only attacks birds and small animals.''

"Of course. You couldn't call him much of a danger to humans. Except, of course, under special circumstances. For instance, if a man were to swallow a live Gila Monster whole, and it went down into his stomach. Or, if a Gila Monster were to penetrate the human body in any other way.''

For the first time, Skellett glanced down between Kathy's thighs, and drummed his fingers against the side of the cardboard box.

Kathy breathed, "You *can't.*''

"I beg your pardon?'' said Skellett. "You forget that I can do anything I want. You forget that I have official sanction to cut you into tiny pieces, if I think that it's required.''

Something shifted inside the box, making a scratching noise. Kathy couldn't keep her eyes off it. She said, breathlessly, "It's nothing to do with official sanctions. It's to do with human decency.''

"Human decency? You want to debate the subject of human decency? Well, I'm very good at that. I know quite a lot about human decency; yes, and human *in*decency, too. I would say that for you to withhold what you know about Mrs. Margot Schneider is pretty indecent, and I would say that what I am going to do to you now is justifiable in the interests of the security of this great nation of ours.''

"You're out of your mind. You can't possibly—''

Skellett jerked his head as a signal to Walsh that he should untie one of Kathy's legs. Kathy gasped and struggled and arched her back, but Walsh was too strong for her.

"Bastards!'' shrieked Kathy. "Bastards! Let me go! Bastards! Let me go!''

With an amused smile, Skellett opened the cardboard box. With a scuffling sound, a blunt, snakelike head appeared, and this was followed by one slowly-flailing claw. Skellett reached inside, and lifted out a seven-inch Gila lizard, only a young one, its scales speckled with black and orange. Its long tail thrashed from side to side, and its tongue flickered out of its black lips like a whip.

Walsh gripped Kathy's thigh so tight that his fingers dug into her flesh. She screamed at a shrill, unending pitch, but Skellett ignored her, and slowly presented the Gila Monster's head to the parted pink opening of her sex.

"Do you still refuse to talk about Margot Schneider?" Skellett asked her.

Kathy was too hysterical to do anything but twist her body around, and scream in horror. Skellett parted her vulva with his fingers and held the Gila lizard so close that its flickering black tongue touched her flesh.

"This is your last chance," he told her, his voice as chilly as ever. "If you don't tell me what you know, I'm going to push this lizard right up inside you, and then I'm going to bind your legs together so that it can't get out."

Kathy let out a moan of absolute defeat. "I found a photograph," she wept. "I found a photograph of President Kennedy. It was dedicated to N. I couldn't think why at first . . . but there were a whole lot of press cuttings about *The Misfits* with it . . . I wasn't even sure that I was right."

Skellett kept the Gila Monster where it was for more than twenty seconds. Then he lifted it in his right hand, and squeezed it until its bones crackled like breaking twigs and its tail slashed furiously from side to side. He did nothing to put the creature out of its agony, but held it up while it shuddered and squirmed, and blood ran darkly out of its mouth.

"You guessed then," he said. "Or, you *thought* you guessed."

Kathy looked away. She couldn't bear to watch Skellett crushing the Gila Monster with such terrible deliberation. She felt the tears pool against the side of her nose as she haltingly whimpered out everything she had discovered and everything she had guessed about Margot Schneider's murder. In the corner of the room, the man in the white shirt lit another cigarette with a Zippo lighter, and regarded her impassively: her tearstained face, her straggled hair, her sex wide open as if it were a symbol of her complete submission and surrender. Walsh, now that the tension of extracting a confession was over, thrust his hands into his pockets and almost inaudibly hummed the old Groucho Marx song *"Everyone says I love you . . ."*

"The photograph of President Kennedy was a Polaroid. Not

official. A snapshot taken by somebody's pool. You couldn't have worked out where it was, not unless you'd known the place, or come across it by accident. But I just had a feeling . . . and I went through the picture morgue at the office; and then through half a dozen books which my roommate owns. And there it was. The same pool. The same cabaña. It was Marilyn Monroe's pool at Brentwood.''

Skellett stood up, and walked across to the far side of the room. He dropped the dead Gila Monster into the metal wastebasket with a scaly clang. Then he said, "You still haven't explained Cuba.''

"I was telling you the truth," said Kathy. She closed her legs now, suddenly aware of her vivid nakedness. "Cuba was a guess. There were so many theories about Marilyn Monroe, why she was supposed to have died. Norman Mailer said that the FBI might have gotten rid of her, to protect the Kennedys' reputation. Other people said she was killed by the Mafia. But nobody ever suggested that she might not have died at all; that she might still be alive.''

Skellett waited for a while, and then said, "Go on. I want to hear it all.''

"There isn't very much more to tell," said Kathy. "Most of it was supposition. I guessed that N was Norma; and that P was President. I guessed that if Marilyn Monroe really *were* alive and well and living in Phoenix, Arizona, under an assumed name, then out of all the photographs she'd ever possessed, she would try and hold on to that one. Except maybe a picture of Bobby, but I didn't see any of those.''

"So you thought that Margot Schneider wasn't Margot Schneider at all, but Marilyn Monroe? You thought this dark-haired frowzy widow was the greatest screen goddess of all time?''

"Yes," said Kathy, "I did. And how do *you* know that Mrs. Margot Schneider was dark-haired? Have you ever seen any pictures of her? Because *I* haven't. Maybe you've seen her *head?*''

Skellett said nothing, but stared at her frigidly, his hands held in front of him like a male ballet dancer waiting for his cue in *Daphnis et Chloë*.

Kathy said, hesitantly, "There are so many theories about

what happened to Marilyn Monroe, whether she was murdered or committed suicide, or whether she simply took too many Nembutals. There were two or three people who could have saved her, that night that she was supposed to have died; and I began to wonder if maybe somebody did. Maybe she *did* have a row with Bobby Kennedy that night; maybe she *did* take too many pills. But maybe somebody actually answered one of her telephone calls, and came around to help her. She had a lot of friends, as well as a lot of enemies. Maybe somebody realized what trouble she was in, and spirited her away, to save her.''

"This is fantasy," said Skellett.

"I told you it was only guesswork. There was a body, after all. But there were several strange things about the body, like the odd way it was lying, and the fact that her stomach was completely empty, as if it had been pumped. One witness said that when she was dead, Marilyn looked 'remarkably young,' but if you look at Bert Stern's nude pictures of her, taken that same year, she looks lined and old; even her hands look old. It occurred to me that somebody who was influential enough to have her spirited away could also have been influential enough to substitute a look-alike body."

Skellett was silent for a long time. Then he said to Walsh, "Cut her loose. Get her a robe. Then bring her into the living-room."

It was five minutes before Kathy was ushered into the living-room, wrapped in a grubby beige robe. Walsh pushed her towards one of the armchairs. In the opposite armchair, Skellett was clipping his fingernails. It was bright morning now, and the room was patterned with sunlight. The furniture was uncompromisingly 1960s—black plastic chairs, circular shaggy rugs, coffee tables with black-painted metal legs. There was even a spindly LP rack, with red wooden balls for feet.

Skellett said, "You have to understand that you're wrong. You've been doing what every young reporter tries to do these days, trying to dig up a sensational political scandal where none exists. Well, you're wrong. I should know. I've been working for the National Security Agency for eight years, and I've seen all the files. There's no scandal."

"Then why were you so worried about my connecting Margot

Schneider with Cuba?'' Kathy demanded. ''Why did it mean so much to you that you were prepared to kill me?''

Skellett ignored her questions, and said, ''Did you tell anyone else what you thought?''

''No,'' said Kathy. ''I didn't tell anybody else. I wanted to gather some more evidence before I discussed it with anybody. All I had was that one Polaroid of President Kennedy.''

''Tell me why, exactly, you thought that Mrs. Margot Schneider had anything to do with Cuba,'' Skellett insisted.

Kathy said, ''You hurt me. You know that? You hurt me so badly.''

''You don't think you deserved it?''

''Deserved it! You bastard!''

Skellett shrugged. ''There are plenty more Gila Monsters out in the desert.''

She was silent. Then she said, ''You would, too, wouldn't you? You'd do it?''

''Of course. My only priority is national security.''

Kathy hugged her arms over her breasts. They were so sore that she could have cried, but she was determined not to. She had already shed too many tears for Skellett. She said slowly, ''I thought that Margot Schneider was Marilyn Monroe, or could have been. If she *was* Marilyn Monroe, then she was in hiding, with a false identity, and there could only be one reason for doing that—because she was afraid. So what was she afraid of? I asked myself.''

Kathy paused, and then she said quietly, ''She could have been afraid of the scandal which would have followed the public revelation of her affairs with Bobby and Jack Kennedy. But then I thought, no, she wasn't the kind of woman who worried about things like that. She was worried about her public image, and about her identity, but not her reputation. The only thing that really would have worried her would have been the threat of mutilation or murder; and in those days the only people who would have been likely to threaten her would have been the people who really wanted to get at the President. Right-wing activists who were afraid that the Kennedys were going to let in a tide of left-wing legislation. Hardline Southern Democrats, racialists, or Ku Klux Klan. Maybe Lyndon Johnson, who knows.

Or Cuban exiles, who felt that they'd been let down at the Bay of Pigs. Maybe the Kennedys wanted to get rid of her themselves. Maybe she knew too much about what they were doing; how badly they'd failed when everybody thought they were heroes. You can't hide much from a woman when you're in bed with her. Maybe Jack and Bobby told her just a little too much.''

Skellett said, "You didn't tell me this to begin with.''

"No, because I thought that it might be true. And the angrier you became, the more convinced I was that it *was* true, or partly true. Margot Schneider was Marilyn Monroe, wasn't she? However she got to live in Phoenix, however she managed to change her identity, she *was* Marilyn Monroe, wasn't she?''

Skellett shook his head. "No, she wasn't. I'm sorry to disappoint you. It sounds like the scoop of the millennium, doesn't it? But Margot Schneider was nobody more than Margot Schneider, and the truth was that she was selling off technical data about U.S. planar-array radar to a Soviet espionage ring. Nothing spectacular; nothing that would seriously threaten national security. But enough to be treasonous.''

He carefully clipped off his long left thumbnail. "The way I see it, she tried to press for a little more money. Tried to get clever. Or maybe she passed some dud information. Whatever happened, she was assassinated by a KGB hit man. That was why we had to rush her body back to Washington, to check for prints, and to compare the *modus operandi* with other Soviet hits. It was urgent. Chief Ruse tried to get in our way; and that's why he had to go. Then *you* started asking awkward questions; and that's why I had to find out exactly what you knew.''

"She wasn't Marilyn Monroe?" asked Kathy. "She really wasn't?''

"No," said Skellett.

"Well, where did she get that photograph of Kennedy? Why did she keep so many reviews of *The Misfits*, and pictures of Clark Gable?''

"We'll be looking into it, don't you worry," Skellett assured her. "But remember that thousands of people took photographs of Kennedy; and that thousands of people own the same kind of cabaña that Marilyn Monroe owned at Brentwood. A Criterion. You can buy them anywhere.''

"How do *you* know what kind she owned?"

"We've been to your apartment, Miss Forbes; and checked the Polaroid for ourselves. We're very thorough. We have to be. By the way, that wasn't a bad hiding-place, inside the coffee-jar. But not particularly original."

Kathy stared at him blankly. "You knew all the time? You tortured me like that and you knew all the time?"

Skellett grinned. "We may be cruel, Miss Forbes, but we're not dumb."

EIGHTEEN

Few people would have recognized Titus in his horn-rimmed spectacles as he sat in the back of his chauffeur-driven limousine that morning, heading south on 23rd Street from Washington Circle towards the Department of State, through sunlight and shadow and reflected light. He was trying without much success to read a sheaf of reports on Israel and Lebanon, while Smetana's *Die Moldau* played with suppressed grandeur on his car stereo. He flicked his eyes up now and again to check which street they had reached: I Street, H Street, G Street, so that he knew to the second how much time he had left to digest all this jargon-riddled nonsense which his staff had prepared for him on the latest struggles between the Phalangists and the Moslems.

Religion, God damn it, he thought. Religion was nothing but trouble. The only faith worth believing in was holy pragmatism.

Somewhere between "the re-divisionalization of West Beirut" and "socio-religious interfaces," his mind wandered to thoughts of Nadine. Last night she had come home with her breath smelling of whiskey, laughing, alight, and insisted on taking him straight to bed—even though Carl and Samantha had both been there, lounging unlovably on his antique sofa in their dirty sneakers and drinking his best brandy, watching their mother drag their stepfather upstairs with blank eyes.

Nadine had been ravenous for sex. She had torn the buttons off his shirt, and pulled out his penis before he could even take down his pants. She had sat astride him with her pink silk cocktail-dress bunched up around her waist, and ridden him with almost insatiable ferocity. As she reached orgasm, she had lifted from him, and rolled him furiously against her pubic hair, until he had shouted out loud and spattered her dress and her stomach and her tautened thighs.

During the night, she had reached out for him again and again; and it was dawn before she had slept. He had quietly eased himself out of bed and tiptoed downstairs to his library to make telephone calls to London and Bonn. For the first time in almost two years he had lit a cigar before breakfast, and smoked it thoughtfully.

"I'll pick you up at ten, Mr. Secretary," his chauffeur said, as the limousine drew up outside the Department of State, and the door was whipped open by one of Titus' Security Guards.

"Thanks, John. How's your boy? Recovered yet?"

"Much better, thank you, sir. Thank you for asking."

"Umh-humh."

Joe Jasper was waiting for Titus in his office. So was a tray of hot black coffee and a plate of Titus' favorite pecan cookies. Also, two roses boxed in cellophane, one white and one red.

"The flowers are from Nadine," said Joe, with a sly smile.

Titus picked them up and examined them. "One white, one red. The symbol of lost virginity."

"Is that appropriate?" asked Joe.

Titus glanced at him, and then tossed the box onto the desk. "It's none of your goddamned business, that's what it is."

Joe said, "Colleen Petley seems to be settling in quite well. She's relaxed, and ready, and not complaining too much, although she did ask for a hot tub. She's very flattered that Nadine is looking after her personally. That was an excellent idea of yours, sir. Excellent."

Titus poured himself some coffee, and dipped one of his cookies into it. He wasn't particularly hungry, but it was a ritual from his Army days, when he had insisted on making surprise breakfast inspections, and sharing coffee and cookies with his leathernecks. One of his many Army nicknames had been "Dunker."

"What's the news on RINC?" he asked Joe. "I called Senator Rodney this morning and he seemed to think that Marshall may be trying to outflank us by calling in support from Droxard and Smith." Hugh Droxard was the chairman of the Armed Services Commission; Nestor Smith was the deputy chairman of the Finance Commission. Both were heavyweight Southern Democrats whose views could substantially affect Congress when it come to voting on nuclear reduction.

Both would be happy to see Titus lynched from the flagpole outside the Department of State, slowly turning in the wind.

Their sudden enlistment to Marshall Roberts' cause was a clue that Marshall was thinking of resuming the RINC talks sooner than Titus had expected. An unexpected chess-move.

Joe said, "My guess is that the President's going to announce this morning that RINC II is all ready to start; and that RINC I had better be ratified as soon as the summer recess is over."

Titus reached for another cookie, and dipped it. "He's pushing it, isn't he? Faster than I thought he would. Well, maybe we're going to have to show him our hand right now. I didn't particularly want to use Colleen before we saw which way the RINC talks were going to go; but if Marshall's going to start hustling them through like a junior-league football-game . . . maybe it's time we blocked him."

"He's never going to forgive you, you know," said Joe, with detectable relish.

"I've survived one of his hits; I can survive another. Besides—if he tries anything like that again, I can make it absolutely crystal clear that I'm going to release those videos, those pictures, everything. I'll release them posthumously if that's the way he wants to play it, but I'll bring him down, one way or another, dead or alive."

Joe's face went through twenty different subservient expressions, from simple respect to complicated kow-towing. "You're a tough man, Mr. Secretary. Nobody can say that you're not."

Titus sat down at his desk. "What else?" he wanted to know. "I was reading all that shit on Lebanon this morning. Why the hell can't Gemayel keep a hold on that situation? He's like a goddamned child.''

"Fejahl is coming in later this morning, around eleven.''

"And what about Sköping? Is he coming in?''

"I don't think so.''

"Well, *demand* it. Goddamned Swedes. I want this submarine business knocked on the head as soon as possible. Did you hear from the Office of the Joint Chiefs of Staff about it?''

"There's an OJCS memo on your desk.''

Titus was still sorting through his paperwork when his intercom made a flatulent noise. His secretary said, "It's Senator Rodney, sir. He asked if you could possibly spare him two or three minutes.''

"All right,'' said Titus; then, when it was apparent that the line was still open, "Send him in.''

Senator Rodney entered the office blowing his nose. He was a short, white-haired man, with flappy trousers and a gold pocket-watch chain hung across his dark houndstooth vest. In appearance, although not in politics, he always reminded Titus of John L. Lewis, the 1930s' labor leader. The same bushy eyebrows, the same deeply-cleft chin.

"Ken,'' Titus greeted him. "Take a seat. We were just discussing this morning's Presidential talk-in.''

Senator Rodney pulled over a chair. "You've got the woman?''

"Safe and secure,'' Titus assured him. "Have some coffee.''

"I will, thanks. Do you have some whiskey? This damned summer cold's been killing me. Listen, from what I hear, you're going to have to put the squeeze on Marshall pretty damned soon. Never mind the niceties. He's been disconcertingly busy during the past couple of days; bribing, threatening, gathering up enough support to ratify the final clauses of RINC I and start the preliminary discussions of RINC II. He's going to push for some early results, too: that cute little number in his publicity office called up Jerry Rosen late last night and said that she'd already seen some brochures for Marshall's 1984 electoral campaign.''

"Can she be trusted?'' asked Titus.

"Jerry trusts her. Sexually, if not politically. She said the heading on the brochure was *America: Roberts Country*. I guess that's convincing enough, don't you? Nobody else could possibly be that corny.''

Titus said harshly, ''That was one goddamned promise that Marshall always used to make. You remember that? In Denver he made it; in Seattle he made it; in New York he made it. 'I'm in this race for one term and one term only. I'm too old for repeat performances.' The lying bastard.''

''What are you going to do?'' asked Joe.

''I'm going to sic him,'' said Titus. ''I'm going to stop him in his tracks. I wanted to save Colleen Petley for later—use her to block his tax budget, maybe. But it doesn't look like he's left me any choice.''

''All I can say is, be careful,'' Senator Rodney warned him.

''Are you kidding? After that last little Fourth of July display?''

Senator Rodney said, ''Marshall Roberts has a mean streak so deep that you couldn't touch bottom with a bathysphere. You thwart him, Titus, and he's going to do everything and anything he can to have you ousted; and when you're ousted, killed. There's no question about it, as far as I'm concerned: Marshall Roberts is a sore loser.''

Titus stood up. ''Marshall Roberts is going to be thrown out of the White House faster than any President ever was; including Nixon. And I'm going to be the man who makes sure that he is. I know he's vindictive, but he's also vain. The Proud President, he called himself once. You remember that? But pride cometh before a fucking great fall.''

Titus and Senator Rodney talked for nearly fifty minutes about the upcoming RINC meeting; and about the way in which Titus was going to start building up his political presence as a likely runner for next year's Presidential primaries. They agreed that he would have to keep himself as far away as possible from Marshall Roberts' decline and fall—in case he was implicated either as a political conspirator or as a man who had known all along about the President's sexual tastes, and for his own political ends had chosen to ignore them. No midwestern voter was going to support a Secretary of State who could turn a blind eye to a blatant sexual perversion.

Joe Jasper drank a last cold mouthful of coffee out of Titus' dirty cup, and said, "Whatever happens, Mr. Secretary, you always have to look as if your hands are clean."

"And your ass," put in Ken Rodney, with characteristic crudity.

At ten o'clock, Titus left the Department of State for the White House. Marshall Roberts had convened the RINC meeting in Titus' favorite room, the Lincoln Sitting Room, partly for its quiet comfort, and partly because he enjoyed flaunting in Titus' face that *he* was the power-in-residence. There was no doubt in anybody's mind that today there would be a tense confrontation between a once-hawkish President who had inexplicably gone soft on disarmament, and a military commander who had made his reputation as the hardest and least compromising politician since John Foster Dulles. But Marshall was deliberately late, and kept his Cabinet twitchily chattering to each other for almost fifteen minutes before he made his entrance. Only Titus appeared calm.

Marshall Roberts had always been imposing. Today he looked grander than ever. Tall, suntanned after a week's vacation near Big Sur, with a strong forehead that overhung his deep-set determined eyes, and a sculptured wave of steel-gray hair. He wore a dark plaid sport coat and gray slacks, and a crimson silk handkerchief that spilled out of his breast pocket (in Senator Rodney's words) "like fake blood from an artificial heart."

"Good morning, gentlemen," he said, easily, and went directly to his chair. "We'll be having some coffee shortly."

The doors were closed and everybody settled down. As if by natural selection, the military men and nuclear hard-liners had grouped themselves on the right-hand side of the room, an assembly of close-cropped haircuts and relentlessly shiny shoes; while the more liberal representatives had scattered themselves around on the left, in their unkempt bow-ties and scuffed suedes. Marshall Roberts waited for the shuffling and throat-clearing and document-rustling to die away, and then he began in that distinctive voice of his, chocolaty but completely self-assured.

"I'm not going to beat around the bush this morning. I'm going to inform you straight away that I intend to re-open the talks that we've been having with the Soviet Union for the reduction of nuclear weapons as soon as Congress has reconvened after the summer. Now, as you're aware, we cannot continue with these talks until the House ratifies the last two clauses of RINC I, relating to the withdrawal from British bases of cruise-type missiles. These two clauses have become a snag far out of proportion to their real political or strategic implications.''

Marshall cast his eyes slowly around the members of his Cabinet and the officers from the Joint Chiefs of Staff. Several of them grinned uneasily.

"There are some among you who have opposed the ratification of RINC I right from the beginning, either covertly or openly. Well, I'm going to tell you gentlemen here and now that those agreements are going to be approved whether you like it or not; with you or without you. My Presidency is going to be recorded in history as an administration that was strong, but also intelligent. Powerful, but also humane. I have always been the first to advocate military integrity in the face of Communist expansionism; but we stand for life as well as for liberty, and it is my considered opinion that if we continue seeking the *measured* reduction of nuclear weaponry, particularly in the European theater, then we will be doing the world the sanest and most responsible service that any administration has done in over two hundred years.''

John Gibbons, the bald-headed Secretary of Defense, raised his pencil and said sharply, "Mr. President, we all appreciate your humanity. But some of the outline proposals you've been circulating for RINC II come dangerously close, in my view, to unilateral disarmament. They certainly don't constitute mutual and balanced nuclear reduction.''

Marshall cleared his throat. "John,'' he said, in a soft voice which carried a clear threat of later retribution, "there is no such concept as complete mathematical mutuality when it comes to nuclear disarmament. Our weapons systems are quite different from the Soviet weapons systems. So is our view of nuclear strategy. An installation which *we* consider relatively unimportant can appear to the Soviets as a grave threat to their national integrity. So to strive for a one-for-one reduction in nuclear weapons is not only misguided but unnecessary. The notion of complete mutuality has been standing in the way of nuclear reduction for decades. It's up to us, in ratifying RINC I, and in proceeding as expeditiously as we can with RINC II, to break the logjam.''

''Pardon me, Mr. President,'' interjected General Paul D. Immerman, one-time Army Chief of Staff and now chairman of the Joint Chiefs, ''the JCS are very sensitive to your viewpoint. But we've already had our strategic study group run the proposals for RINC II through the computer, and there isn't any doubt at all that if even the least contentious of them are agreed and ratified, the United States will be put irreversibly into a nuclear no-win situation. If we pull back as few as half of our ALCMS from Britain, and limit the deployment of the neutron bomb by as little as a third, the Soviet Union will have a 63.9 percent chance of occupying the whole of Europe within five days. I agree with you about an obsessive concern with mutuality standing in the way of sensible reduction. But I can't go along with you when you suggest national suicide.''

Titus shifted in his high-backed antique chair, and Marshall turned towards him and asked, ''Titus? What's your view?''

There were tense glances around the room. Everybody knew that Titus was irreconcilably set against any nuclear disarmament whatsoever; and that the moment had now come for him to face up to the President toe-to-toe, or compromise everything that he had ever said about ''letting America melt.''

Titus neatly collated the papers on his lap, and smiled. ''Mr. President,'' he said, ''it appears to me that before we go chasing after nuclear rainbows, we should seriously appraise whether this is the same defense policy which this administration was elected in 1980 to carry out. The same, or even *remotely* similar.''

Marshall leaned forward angrily. It was obvious that he was furious at Titus yet was holding himself under control. He wanted Titus to say everything that he had come here to say, and wind himself tightly in the shroud of his own sarcasm; and then he wanted to bury Titus alive, in full view of the entire Cabinet, and later in front of the media. If only Titus had half a glimmer of the agony which Marshall had been going through since his inauguration: and in spite of his recent vacation Marshall felt like a man more than a decade older than his 66 years. If only that smug-faced bastard knew. If only he had the humanity to *sense* it. But he didn't, and he wouldn't, and that was why Marshall wanted him entombed.

With deliberate long-windedness, Titus went on, "It seems to me, Mr. President, that you have been overly concerning yourself with your lustrous international image as a peacemaker, and forgetting the price which your country is going to have to pay to keep your halo shiny."

"Titus—" Marshall started to interrupt him, but Titus smiled and raised a hand.

"Please, I'd like to finish. A great deal hangs in the balance today. Not just our own political ambitions; not just the defense of America; but the safety of the entire planet. And while you have obviously considered the Geneva principles in considerable detail, Mr. President, have you perhaps forgotten the Nevada protocols?"

Marshall Roberts frowned at Titus darkly. "The *what?*" he growled. He knew that Titus never said anything irrational or frivolous; every word was as lethal as one of those damned ingenious anti-personnel devices that blew up if you touched them and then blew up if you didn't.

"I think you'd better explain what the Nevada protocols actually *are*, Mr. Secretary," said General Immerman.

"Oh, my apologies," smiled Titus. "The Nevada protocols were based on a purely informal political meeting at the Futura hotel in Las Vegas, Nevada, shortly before President Roberts was nominated by the GOP."

"Can we know who was there?" asked John Gibbons. "*I* certainly wasn't." He didn't have the faintest idea what Titus was talking about, but he was beginning to sense in Titus' voice and in Titus' posture that the old killer hunter had scented blood. He could also see that Marshall Roberts had been unexpectedly silenced, and that his usually bullet-hard eyes were betraying some interesting suggestions of genuine anxiety.

Titus said, "President Roberts was present at these discussions; as were certain personnel especially chosen for their *refreshing* political views. It was generally agreed that if President Roberts were to be elected, we would soon be entering a new golden age."

Now Marshall Roberts knew for sure. His face was fixed

tightly and his eyes wavered away from Titus' face to Titus' casually-crossed knees, and then down to the yellow-patterned carpet. Titus monotonously swung his foot, and kept on smiling. His polished black shoe swung in and out of Marshall's line of vision.

I can even remember her name, he thought. Titus resumed, with undisguised triumph in his voice, "The President will recall that the Nevada protocols clearly expressed the GOP's determination to give the Joint Chiefs of Staff all the support they would need within the scope of the available Federal budget to implement as fully as possible the recommendations of JSOP II. In other words, to provide the United States with the optimum defense capability as envisaged by the military services themselves."

There was a very long silence. Marshall Roberts was still staring at the carpet. Titus added, in the gentlest of tones, "I was only suggesting that the President, in his zeal, might have forgotten how his own party feels that international peace might be more readily and more safely achieved." He bowed his head towards Marshall with unmistakable sarcasm. "I *do* hope that I have been of real assistance."

Marshall Roberts looked up at last. "Well," he said, and his deep voice sounded suddenly tired, "it appears that the Secretary of State has raised some very fundamental policy matters which require my further attention."

"Mr. President, with respect, Mr. Alexander still hasn't made it quite clear what the Nevada—" began General Immerman, but Marshall Roberts gave a quick, displeased shake of his head that silenced the chairman of the JCS instantly. General Immerman turned to Admiral Carstairs and gave him a baffled shrug.

"This meeting is adjourned," said Marshall Roberts. He stood immediately and left the room. Everybody else gathered up their papers and their briefcases in complete confusion; all except Titus, who remained where he was, still smiling his saintly smile. John Gibbons came over and said, "You really got your teeth into him that time."

Titus nodded. "It seems like it, doesn't it?"

"Don't suppose there's any chance you might give me some slight inkling what these Nevada protocols actually are?"

"Use your brains, John. There are only two commodities in Las Vegas, ~~money~~ and sex. So it's either one or the other."

John Gibbons' eyebrows rose up his bald forehead. "Well, now," he said. *"You're* playing with fire, aren't you?"

"You need fire to fight fire."

"Let me buy you lunch," said John Gibbons. "Let's talk about this some more."

"Not yet, John. In any case, I'm dieting."

Just as John Gibbons turned away, the far door of the Lincoln Sitting Room opened and Rosemary Wuppers, the President's personal secretary, gave Titus a discreet beckoning wave. Titus stood up, brushed down his suit, and then followed her into the small book-lined room next door which Marshall Roberts had turned into his private den. Marshall was standing by the window, his hands in his pockets, silhouetted like an aging lion against the blurry summer sunshine. He said, "Come on in, Titus. Close the door."

Titus came in, and laid his papers down on Marshall's leather-topped desk.

"You want a cigar?" asked Marshall.

Titus said, "No, thank you, Mr. President. I'm trying to be a little more ascetic these days."

Marshall was silent for a while. Titus watched him, standing smartly and confidently, with the bearing of a soldier. Then Marshall said, "It's difficult for me to explain to you, Titus, just what a serious mistake you're making."

"Oh?"

"You've gotten hold of some photographs, I expect?"

Titus looked quickly around. "This room wired?"

Marshall shook his head. "It wouldn't matter if it were, would it? If you've gotten hold of some photographs, I'd hardly want to advertise the fact, would I?"

"Well, there're more than photographs," said Titus. "There are video-taped confessions, pictures, and, of course, live witnesses."

"The girl herself?"

"It's conceivable."

Marshall came away from the window and stood very close to Titus, so close that Titus could feel the President's warm, even breath against his cheek. "I have to advise you of something, Titus; it will not be a good idea to attempt to interfere with the RINC talks."

"What are you talking about, Marshall? The RINC talks are giving away so many strategic concessions to the Soviets that they practically constitute a crime against the Republic."

"Believe me, they're the lesser of two evils. At least they're gradual."

Titus stared at him. "What the hell do you mean, *gradual*? What's gotten into you, Marshall? You and I, we used to be the closest of friends. The closest of allies, too. You don't believe in this strategic arms reduction any more than I do. You would have nuked the Soviets over Afghanistan, if you'd had the chance. So how can you stand in front of me now and tell me you want to pull our cruise missiles out of Britain, and still seriously believe that you're capable of continuing your administration with any kind of honor at all?"

"Honor?" asked Marshall, as if he scarcely knew what the word meant. He turned away from Titus and sat down heavily at his desk. "Honor is a rare bird these days, Titus. Especially when you start looking for it on the top of the mountain."

Titus said, "I didn't want to have to do this, you know. This Nevada business. Playing dirty isn't something I particularly enjoy. But RINC is too much of a national risk, Marshall, and you're becoming unstable and let's face it, just plain weird."

"Weird?"

"You don't think it's weird for a President to double back on one of his strongest election promises? You don't think it's weird for a President to take part in peculiar and perverted sex acts? You don't think it's weird for a President to attempt to waste his own Secretary of State?"

Marshall raised his head. "You think that I had anything at all to do with that bombing? You actually believe that I intended to have you killed?"

"Someone did, Marshall, and you're my prime suspect. I know what happened to Fred Coggins back in '76, when he tried to squeeze you out of that Asquehanna Power Project. And I *still* believe you had a hand in that Sybil Coles affair."

"You're crazy, Titus, you know that? I may be weird, but *you're* crazy."

Titus smiled. "Nevertheless, Marshall, you're going to do what you're told. You're going to put RINC I right on the back burner, and you're going to forget about RINC II for good. Do you understand me loud and clear? Otherwise, the videotapes will be handed out wherever they'll do you the most harm; and the girl will be fanfared to the media. Can you imagine facing Margaret Thatcher again, after you've been publicly accused of urolangia?"

"I'm, uh, obviously going to have to consider this for a day or so," said Marshall. He sounded blurry. "You must give me a little time."

"No time, Marshall. The answer is yes or the answer is no; and I want it right now."

Marshall drummed his fingers on the desk. "It wasn't me who tried to kill you, you know. I want you to believe that."

"Marshall, I want an answer."

Marshall suddenly banged both hands flat on his blotter. His forehead was crimson with rage and frustration. "I can't *give* you an answer, for Christ's sake! I can't postpone those RINC talks for anyone or anything! They're way behind time already! For the love of God, Titus, don't you see what I'm trying to tell you? I'm not *allowed* to!"

Titus felt an extraordinary prickle of uncertainty, right up his spine to the nape of his neck. The last time he had felt anything as unpleasant as that was in Nam. He frowned at Marshall and said hoarsely, "You're not allowed to? Am I hearing you straight? You're the *President*."

Marshall sat wearily back in his seat. "I can't tell you anything else, Titus. I've told you far too much already. But, believe me, if you try to delay or upset these talks, you're going to be digging many more graves than just your own."

"Are you under some kind of threat? Blackmail?"

"Only the blackmail threat that *you're* making against me. And of course the daily threat of seeing the entire United States collapse like a house of cards."

"I don't know what you mean. What do you mean, collapse like a house of cards? For Christ's sake, Marshall, talk sense!"

Marshall shook his head. "You're just going to have to take what I'm telling you on trust, Titus. You know that I've never been a man to beg favors, and I hope you can understand that I'm not telling you to back off just to save my own skin. I'm quite prepared to take full responsibility for everything I've done, political and sexual, when the time comes. But not now, Titus. Please not now. If you stop RINC II, or if you force me to resign from the Presidency on moral grounds, then believe me, a burden is going to fall upon your shoulders greater than you will ever be able to bear."

Titus was silent. He had never seen Marshall like this before. He had seen him threaten, cajole, bully, and flatter. He had seen him bargain. But he had never seen him *plead*. Not in such bursts of anger and fear; not with his eyes darting about under his eyebrows like trapped and frightened fish. He didn't know what to say: whether to insist that Marshall should put a stop to RINC II regardless, or whether to give him a little more time, in the hope that he might explain himself more fully. The trouble was, there were high practical risks in giving a man like Marshall Roberts more time. In a day or so, Marshall could track down Colleen Petley, and make sure that she was in no position to speak out against him. In a day or so, Marshall could stage a politically embarrassing incident anywhere in the world, like revealing that Titus was secretly sending military supplies to Ecuador, and drastically undermine Titus' power-base. In a day or so, Marshall could ensure that the bombing attempt which had failed in West Virginia was restaged, this time successfully.

At last, Titus said, "You've got an hour. That's all I'm prepared to give you. Call me at the State Department and let me know what you've decided. I might be prepared to do some kind of a deal which would leave you with the minimum of egg on your face. Say, pretending to delay RINC II for a year or so. But if you don't call, or if you call and say no, then I'm going to bring you down. Do you hear me? By the time I'm through with you, Warren Harding is going to be remembered as a saint, by comparison. And I mean it."

Marshall said nothing. But as Titus buttoned up his coat and turned to leave the den, he saw Marshall's clenched fist quivering as if it were a human hand-grenade that was just about to explode.

NINETEEN

Lieutenant Berridge was sitting at his desk eating a grapefruit yogurt when Sergeant Corso came in to tell him that Skellett's car had been identified outside a house on Palmcroft Drive, in Tempe.

"Who identified it?" Berridge asked. "Shit." He had reached for his jacket and knocked yogurt all over his paperwork.

"The Tempe fire department. They were called to a fire there about an hour ago, suspicious circumstances. Somebody set light to the bedroom drapes."

"Let's get out there. Where the hell's Norris?"

"At the hospital. His old lady's having twins."

"Well, get Pulaski then. I want somebody who can *drive*."

Within four minutes, Lieutenant Berridge and Detective Pulaski were screeching out of the police garage in their bronze Chevrolet, siren whooping and red light flashing on the roof. Pulaski drove with hair-raising precision, sliding the car around the corner of 7th Street towards the Maricopa Freeway as if it were on rails. He overtook a huge refrigerated truck on the inside, stood on the brakes, and spun the car neatly in front of the truck's huge oncoming bumper and across the street.

"I suppose that's one way of crossing an intersection," remarked Lieutenant Berridge, trying to sound casual. His feet were pressed so hard against the floor that his legs were cramping.

"There's another way?" asked Pulaski.

Pulaski may have been a hot-rod driver, but his knowledge of Phoenix's maze of suburban streets was decidedly patchy. He managed to get them on to Palm Road, but then he lost five vital minutes roaring around Loma Vista Road, Broadmor Drive, El Parque Drive, and Del Rio Terrace, passing the same smart little houses over and over, and leaving the smell of burned rubber in the summer heat. At last he found Palmcroft Drive, and howled to a dramatic halt beside three firetrucks and four patrol cars from the Tempe police department. Lieutenant Berridge stiffly climbed out, and walked across the street like a man who has narrowly avoided a fatal accident.

"Lieutenant," said Bill Hagerty, Tempe's police chief, by way of greeting. "That's where they've holed themselves up, number 1226."

1226 Palmcroft was one of the larger properties in the area, a shingle-roofed one-story building on a low landscaped hill, closely surrounded by dense bushes. On the sloping driveway was parked Skellett's Cadillac, one tire flat. Around to the side was an open bedroom window, its drapes hanging in burned tatters, its glass blackened with soot, and a dark smudge above it on the gray stucco.

"They're still *in* there?" asked Berridge.

"Sure. Three of them, a girl and two men."

"The girl's probably Kathy Forbes, from the *Flag*."

"We've tried talking to them," said Hagerty. "So far they haven't answered. The phone's off the hook, and they've ignored the bullhorn."

"What do you think about the fire?"

"If the girl *is* Kathy Forbes, then she probably started it herself, to attract some attention. She was lucky the fire department was able to put it out from outside the house. She could've been roasted in there. *All* of them could've been roasted."

"Have you met them yet?"

"Not me, but the firemen did. When they broke down the front door, trying to get in to tackle the blaze, the two men were waiting in the hall. A big guy and a medium-sized guy, both armed. They fired three shots, all .45 caliber. The fire chief told his men to back off and stay off, and I can't say that I blame him.''

"Who saw the girl?''

"That fireman right over there. He saw her briefly at the bedroom window before the smoke got too thick.''

"Nobody's seen her since then?''

"Unh-hunh.''

"So she may be dead?''

"It's possible, yes. We've got no way of telling.''

An officer came up and said, "Chief Hagerty, sir? We've been questioning the old couple directly opposite. They swear they saw three men going into number 1226 last night, three men and two girls. They were kind of ashamed to admit it at first, but they spend most of their time by the front window, spying out over the neighborhood. The wife's in a wheelchair. Last night they positively saw three men, and two girls. They believe that one of the girls left the house earlier on this morning and as far as they know she hasn't come back.''

"Thank the Lord for nosy neighbors,'' Chief Hagerty intoned.

"The third guy is probably Skellett,'' said Lieutenant Berridge. "Has anybody called the National Security Agency, and asked what the hell he thinks he's playing at?''

"I've had a call in for a half-hour,'' said Chief Hagerty. "So far the response has been underwhelming, to say the least. They keep quoting 'special prerogatives' to me. This country is going to choke itself on jargon one day.''

"What do you intend to do?'' asked Berridge.

Chief Hagerty gave a quick, barking cough. "Play it cool, that's what. There's no particular need to rush in there like the Seventh Cavalry. We've no immediate indication that the girl is in mortal danger, that's if she's still alive. I'd rather wait it out, let them sweat. They know they can't escape.''

"You don't mind if I stick around?''

"Be my guest. I've sent for hotdogs, if you're hungry.''

For the rest of the afternoon, while the sun slowly burned its way westwards, they filled the hours with coffee-drinking and smoking and leaning against hot glaring police cars and talking about baseball. Lieutenant Berridge talked a lot about Chief

Ruse, but he said nothing about his conviction that the chief's murder had been nothing more than a quick and callous way to extinguish his opposition to the removal of Margot Schneider's remains from the Phoenix morgue. The official line, as put out by Mayor Gardens, was that Chief Ruse had been conducting an in-depth investigation into Mafia corruption in Arizona, and that his execution had borne "all the hallmarks of a quasi-Sicilian revenge killing."

Chief Hagerty kept directional microphones pointed at 1266 Palmcroft, and police marksmen concealed all around the perimeter of the grounds; but if there was any conversation going on inside the house, it was being conducted in very low whispers, and none of the occupants made any attempt to poke their nose out. The house might just as well have been empty.

"I want generators, okay, and floods," instructed Chief Hagerty, as darkness began to fall. He came up to Lieutenant Berridge and said, "This could be a long one. You want to go home, come back later?"

"I'll stick it out for another hour."

"Suit yourself."

It was at one minute after sunset, at 6:42, that the broken front door of the house was suddenly pushed half-open, and a man's voice yelled out, "I'm coming out! You hear me? I'm coming out and my hands are way up! I'm unarmed!"

Immediately, there was scurry in the street, as officers ducked and dived behind their cars, and raised their weapons. Chief Hagerty shouted for the floodlights to be directed at the front door, and almost immediately the blue-white halogen beams picked out the figure of a man in a white shirt with rolled-up sleeves, his hands stretched up over his head.

"Is that Skellett?" Chief Hagerty asked Berridge.

Berridge shook his head. "That one I've never seen before in my life."

The man came halfway down the front path of the house, and stood blinking at the floodlights as if he had emerged from a week trapped in a pothole. Lieutenant Berridge said, "What's the matter with him? Why is he just standing there?" Chief Hagerty picked up his bullhorn and demanded, *"Walk forward another ten steps. Then lie down on the road, face downwards, with your arms and legs spread. Do you understand me?''*

Hesitantly, awkwardly, the man did what he was told. As soon as he had lowered himself on to the road-surface, his left ankle was seized by two police officers who were crouched behind a parked car, and he was roughly and speedily dragged into cover. One of the officers kept a Python revolver pressed to the man's head while the other searched him for weapons.

"Looks like he's clean, sir."

"Okay. Handcuff him."

The man's arms were twisted around behind his back and locked with handcuffs. Then he was hoisted on to his feet and hurried at a knee's-bent run across the road, behind a police panel-van.

Chief Hagerty left his own position behind his car, and joined the officers in the cover of the van. Lieutenant Berridge followed him, but kept a foot or two behind. He was very conscious that this was Chief Hagerty's territory, and that a small gesture of police etiquette would win him more cooperation than all the big-city assertiveness in the world. Chief Ruse always used to say to him, "Policemen are more damned territorial than coyotes."

The man was pushed up against the van and both his arms were held. Chief Hagerty approached him closely, and stood with his hands on his hips staring at him. The man was sweaty, unshaven, and smelled of foreign cigarettes. The pupils of his eyes were dilated, as if he was high on narcotics.

"Are you going to talk to me?" Chief Hagerty asked him.

"There's no use," the man told him, in a thickly accented voice.

"Oh, you don't think so? Three or four of you are holed up in that house there, and you let fly at a detail of perfectly innocent firemen with .45 automatics, and you don't think there's any use in talking? What's your name?"

"Andrej."

"Andrej? What kind of name is that? You foreign, or what?"

"Czech."

"I shall, don't you worry."

Lieutenant Berridge put in, gently, "Chief, I think he said 'Czech.' You know, like Czechoslovakian."

Chief Hagerty looked briefly annoyed. "Is that right?" he demanded. "You're a Czechoslovakian?"

The man nodded.

"Naturalized American, or what?"

"I don't have to tell you anything."

"You fucking do, buddy. There's two of your friends in that house, along with a kidnapped girl, and if you don't start talking and talking quick, you're going to wind up with telephone numbers."

The man looked completely baffled.

"You know what telephone numbers are?" asked Lieutenant Berridge, as diplomatically as he could. The man shook his head.

"Jail, buddy," explained Chief Hagerty. "Jail for the rest of your natural life."

At that moment, there was the sudden snap of automatic fire from the house. A large-caliber bullet shattered the panel van's windshield, and groaned into the bushes nearby. The floodlights swung and flickered, and there was a heavy rattle of shooting from the police marksmen crouched behind their cars. Somebody shouted, "They're making a run for it!"

What happened next would return to Lieutenant Berridge for years to come in nightmares. The man in the white shirt suddenly twisted away from the two policemen who were holding him, and butted Chief Hagerty straight in the forehead. Chief Hagerty went down flat, like a man hit by a baseball bat. Then the man dodged and shouldered his way past Lieutenant Berridge and ran around the front of the van with his hands still securely handcuffed behind his back. One of the patrolmen had already drawn his gun, but Lieutenant Berridge shouted at him, *"Don't shoot!"*

The man timed his run perfectly. Just as Skellett and Walsh appeared in the front door of the house, both of them waving Colt automatics towards the police, the man crossed Palmcroft Drive at a long diagonal, straight across the police marksmen's line of fire, and exploded.

Lieutenant Berridge stared in total horror as the man's head leapt ten feet in the air. His arms flew away in opposite directions, and then his entrails spiraled around in a grisly splattering corkscrew. Blood and fragments of tissue showered the police-men like rain, and then there was nothing but smoke and fire, and a sound like a wet thunderclap.

In the confusion, Skellett and Walsh ran into the next-door yard, clambered over the fence, and disappeared. None of the policemen even bothered to fire at them; they were too busy staring in horror at the sickening remains of the man in the white shirt, which had splattered their faces and uniforms.

Chief Hagerty, still lying on the ground, stared up at Lieutenant Berridge wide-eyed. "The guy blew up," he said. "The guy just *blew up*."

Lieutenant Berridge sat down on the curb, took out his handkerchief, and smeared blood away from his face and hands. He was so shocked that he could hardly speak. Chief Hagerty humped himself over to where he was sitting, and propped himself up beside him, nursing the bruise on his head.

"He must've been a walking bomb. Jesus. A walking bomb. We searched him, but he was still packed full of explosives. Up his ass, it must have been. Who'd have thought of that?"

"Can you imagine what a *fanatic* he must have been?" Lieutenant Berridge replied. "His whole goddamned rectum must have been chock full of gelignite; and a timing device, too."

"Jesus," said Chief Hagerty.

One of the officers came over, looking distinctly pale in the light from the halogen lamps, his shirt jigsawed with blood. "I'm sorry, sir. We lost the other two. They went over the fence and along the culvert, as far as we can make out. Nyman thought he saw them, but we can't be too sure."

Chief Hagerty managed to stand up, swaying on his feet. "I think you're forgiven this time," he said. Then he suddenly retched, and held his hand over his mouth.

"You all right?" Lieutenant Berridge asked him.

"Sure. Just that knock on the head. Spanier, find a hose, will you, and sluice this crap out of the street."

"Yes, sir. Sir?"

"What is it?"

"Do I really have to, sir?"

"Yes, Spanier, you do. Ask Montez to help you. He used to work in a processed-meat factory. He won't mind."

"There's still the girl," said Lieutenant Berridge. "We'd better go in and take a look."

"Supposing the girl's booby-trapped, too?"

"Are you kidding?"

"Look at that mess on the street and tell me this is all a joke."

"This is all a joke. Now, let's go in and see what's happened to the girl."

They found Kathy Forbes bound and gagged in the living-room, wearing nothing but a garter-belt and stockings. She was bruised, and her breasts were mottled with scarlet wounds, but otherwise she was unhurt. Lieutenant Berridge knelt down beside her as one of the officers cut her free, and said, "It was Skellett, wasn't it? He got away."

"He got away?" whispered Kathy. "I heard the gunfire; I thought you'd killed him."

Lieutenant Berridge shook his head. "They used a decoy. The guy in the white shirt. You heard that bang, a few minutes ago? That was him. Blew himself up."

"He was Czech," said Kathy, as if that made any difference. "He told me this morning he came from Pradubice. He said he missed his brothers. Isn't that ridiculous?"

"It is now. They're washing him away with a garden hose."

One of the officers brought Kathy a blanket from the bedroom, and she shakily wrapped herself up. When they brought her out into the night, there was a dazzle of TV and newspaper lights, and Lieutenant Berridge had to jostle her across the road towards the ambulance. "No questions now," Berridge insisted. "Just keep back, will you? The lady's hurt. How badly? I'll tell you tomorrow. Now keep back."

Kathy lay back in the ambulance, listening to the shouting and the arguing and the scribbling sound of sirens, and shivered like someone who has seen his own tombstone. Lieutenant Berridge squeezed himself in beside her, and said, "I'll come to the hospital with you, okay? I have to ask you some questions."

"All right," she said dully. She realized that she was nearly asleep. Shock, she supposed. Shock always sends you to sleep. "What do you want to ask me?"

"It was you who set fire to the bedroom drapes, right?"

"That's right. I was desperate. I thought they were going to torture me again."

"They tortured you?"

She nodded. The ambulance had started off now, and she felt the unreal swaying of the suspension as it turned out of Palmcroft Drive into Terrace Road, and then into Loma Vista. "They stuck needles in my breasts. I mean Skellett stuck needles in my breasts. They wanted to know about Margot Schneider."

"You know they killed Chief Ruse. At least, I believe they did."

Kathy nodded. She could hardly keep her eyes open. "They were worried, you know. They were worried that I'd discovered their secret. They were going to push a Gila Monster up inside me. Can you believe that? They had a Gila Monster, and they were going to push it up inside me."

"Listen," said Lieutenant Berridge. "What secret?"

"That's why they killed Chief Ruse, don't you see? They were frightened that he was going to find out. They were frightened that he was going to guess the truth."

"And what *is* the truth? What were they so frightened about?"

Kathy stared at him through slitted eyes. "I don't know. I can't remember it."

"Miss Forbes, you've got to tell me."

"I can't think. Lieutenant, I can't *remember*."

"For Christ's sake, this is a homicide investigation. A *double* homicide investigation, plus whatever you call someone who packs his backend with gelignite and paints the town red."

"Recticide," said Kathy, with a wan smile. Then she fell deeply asleep.

TWENTY

At five o'clock in the morning, just as the moon rose, Daniel abruptly sat up in bed and said, "What the hell's that? Did you hear that noise?"

Cara muzzily snuggled in closer to him, and said, "What noise? I didn't hear any noise."

"There was a noise. Like somebody prowling around outside."

"It's probably dogs. Or coyotes. Go back to sleep."

Daniel swung out of bed, and walked across to the window. Outside, in the moon-blanched parking-lot, he saw two stray hounds scavenging in the garbage-can which old man Tremlett next door had left out for the trash collectors. He watched them for a while as they snapped and fought over the remains of a TV-dinner tray, then came back to bed and eased himself between the sheets.

"Dogs?" asked Cara, putting her arm around him, and pressing her bare breasts against his side.

"Dogs. I guess I shouldn't be so goddamned jumpy."

"Do you want some coffee? Or a soda maybe?"

He turned towards her and kissed her on the forehead. "Just a little comfort, thank you. I've got to get up in an hour anyway."

"Are you opening the diner today?"

"Why not? Either they know who I am, or they *don't*. I'm not

195

going to run. I can't afford to. You have to be wealthy to be a fugitive these days, especially when you've got a child and a girlfriend to take with you.''

Cara was quiet for a moment, stroking his shoulder. Then she said, "They killed Willy. They might kill you."

"They killed Willy because he was just about to blow the whistle on the biggest armaments scandal in ten years. That's what I think, anyway. Somebody got a contract to build missiles and missile guidance systems and the damned things don't even work properly. Do you know what the finance for those contracts runs into? Billions. Hundreds of billions. And we're not even being protected from enemy attack.''

"Daniel, they must know that you were Willy's friend. And they're only going to have to identify Ronald to realize who was with him. Pete Burns could easily tell them, without even understanding that he's putting you at risk."

"What do you expect me to do? Pack my bags and jump on the first bus? Drive west? Drive east? I didn't manage to salvage very much of my existence when my marriage broke up; what I've got here is all that's left. I'm not leaving this behind, too.''

Cara propped herself up on her elbow and looked at him closely. The moonlight illuminated the soft curve of her back, the roundness of her bottom. She had bought some Indian perfume yesterday at the Navajo store on the way to Tortilla Flat, and she smelled like fresh cactus and spice. She kissed him, again and again and again, and whispered, "You've found it, you see. Your courage."

"Courage? Well, maybe. I don't think I actually know what courage feels like, even when you've found it. But I'm staying, if that's anything to do with courage; and I'm going to find out how Willy was killed, and who did it, and why.''

"Make love to me," she said.

They made love simply and slowly, while the moon appeared through the upper left-hand quarter of the bedroom window. He thrust rhythmically into the coppery curls of her pubic hair, and caressed her breasts in his hands until the nipples stiffened between his fingers like buttons. She shuddered in orgasm a moment before he did, and her shuddering brought him to his climax, too; and then they both lay side by side in silence, staring at each other with fondness and friendship and the warm accomplishment of a plain but almost perfect act of love.

"Do you want me to leave?" she asked, after a long interval.

"Leave? What makes you think I want you to leave?"

"Sometimes the time arrives, whether you want it to or not."

He laid his hand flat on her stomach, the way he had laid his hand on Candii's stomach when she had first told him that she was pregnant with Susie. "I don't want you to leave. Not now. Maybe not ever."

"I'll never marry you."

"I don't want you to marry me. But, for now, I want you to stay."

Cara came close to him, and ran her fingers into his hair. "You're a good man, Daniel."

Later, he went downstairs to the kitchen to make coffee. Susie came down and said she was hungry, and he gave her a bowl of cereal and a glass of orange juice. Daniel switched on the FM radio to KSTM, and whistled along with "Joleen."

In a small voice, Susie said, "Cara told me that Ronald was dead. Is that true?"

Daniel swallowed. He was still trying to keep back his own grief about what had happened yesterday. "Yes," he told her. "Yes, that's right. Ronald's dead."

"Is he going to have a funeral?"

"I guess so."

"Are we going to go? To the funeral, I mean?"

"I don't know, honey, it all depends."

"It all depends on what?"

"I don't know. Don't ask me. It all depends on . . . I don't know, fate."

"What's *fate*?"

"Ask Cara, will you? I don't know what fate is. Fate is what jumps out of the closet at you when you're expecting nothing but jeans and T-shirts."

Susie frowned at him, but didn't ask him any more questions about Ronald. She had lived alone with her father for long enough to understand when he was upset. He finished making the coffee, and then he leaned over and kissed the parting of her hair. "Finish your cereal, okay?"

The radio announcer said, ". . . right now, at the top of the hour . . . first we have more news of the dramatic siege yesterday evening in Tempe, when a terrorist deliberately blew himself up in full view of police officers and horrified local residents in order to provide a grisly and spectacular diversion to two escaping colleagues in crime . . . Rescued from the siege was *Arizona Flag* reporter Kathy Forbes, who was working on an equally grisly news story . . . the mystery of the Air Force widow Mrs. Margot Schneider who earlier this week was beheaded by an unknown intruder at her North Phoenix home . . . Miss Forbes was captured by the terrorists the day before yesterday, and held captive in a plush Palmcroft Drive home, where she was tortured and threatened before her rescue. . . . Miss Forbes says she has no idea what the terrorists wanted from her, or what information they hoped to extract . . ."

Daniel turned up the volume, but the news story was finished, and the announcer started reading out dust-storm forecasts. Susie looked up at him and said, "Blew himself up? Like a balloon?"

Daniel shook his head. "No, honey. Like a bomb. Bang, splat. You know?"

"Yuk," said Susie, and enthusiastically scooped up the last of her cereal.

Daniel took the coffee upstairs and sat down on the end of the bed. Cara was buried in the sheets at first; but soon she raised her tangled head and said, "What is it? What's the matter?"

"I just heard a news story on the radio. *Half*-heard it. You remember we were talking about that woman who had her head cut off?"

"Well, of course, that was the whole reason you—"

"Right. But the girl reporter who wrote the story was kidnapped by terrorists or something, and apparently they were torturing her to try to get information out of her. It was on the news just now."

"Where was this?"

"In Tempe, that's all. Just a couple of miles away. They said that some guy blew himself up so that his friends could escape."

Cara stared at him. "It was the same reporter?"

"That's what they said. She was working on the Margot

Schneider story and they kidnapped her. I don't know how she got away.''

"And somebody blew himself up?"

"That's what they said."

"Daniel," said Cara, in an unsettled voice. "What's going on?"

Daniel sipped his coffee. It was growing light outside now, and the moon was fading behind the peaked facade of Apache Junction's main hotel. "I don't know," he said. "But that woman had her head cut off with a wire saw, and there's no question that Willy's head *wasn't* cut off by any helicopter. A helicopter would have—Jesus, *smashed* him. The top of his neck, it looked just like it was *cut*, or *sawn*.''

"Don't," said Cara.

"But that's two people in the Phoenix area in just a few days . . . Willy and Margot Schneider. And now the reporter gets kidnapped by terrorists. I don't know what the hell goes on here, but it all sounds too damned interconnected. You know? I got the feeling that one thing happened because of some other thing, and Willy died because he shouldn't have known what he knew, and maybe this Margot Schneider did too. I don't know.''

"Well, why don't you ask this girl reporter?" suggested Cara.

"What's the use of that? She's not going to tell me anything, is she?"

"They do deals, don't they, in the movies? You know the real truth about Willy and she doesn't, so offer to trade."

"You run your whole life according to what you see in the movies?"

"In South Dakota, what else can you do?"

Later that morning, Daniel opened up the diner as usual, and Pete Burns came in for his breakfast and sat perched on his stool and said nothing to Daniel except that it looked like another hot one. Two Air Force cars had driven past, one of them from Luke and the other from Davis-Monthan, and an Air Force truck had parked outside for almost ten minutes, but there was no sign of the military police.

"Seen Ronald today?" asked Pete Burns, as he put on his cap to leave.

"Ronald? Can't say that I have."

"When you do, tell him his hearing's been fixed for the 23rd of next month."

"Oh, sure. What's the charge?"

"Driving like a frigging lunatic."

Daniel stood in the doorway wiping his hands on his striped apron and watching Pete Burns climb into his police car. "Hey, Pete," he called. "Did you hear about that siege last night, over at Tempe?"

"You bet. We had to put up roadblocks for most of the night."

"What do you know about that?"

Pete Burns put on his sunglasses, and started up his engine. "What's it to you?"

"I don't know. Just curious."

"Well, don't ask me. Read the what's-its-name, the *Flag*. The very determined lady reporter declined to answer any questions from the police, and instead is going to publish the full story in her lousy newspaper, in *episodes,* would you believe, for the next three days."

"Can she do that? Isn't that obstructing justice or something?"

"Her lawyers don't seem to think so. The Phoenix police department is going up the wall. Chief Ruse, and then this. But she's determined, this lady. Chief Hagerty at Tempe said she was lace on the outside and barbed wire on the inside."

Daniel said, "Okay, Pete. Thanks for your custom. See you tomorrow."

"You bet."

Pete Burns drove off and Daniel went back into the diner. Cara was pouring coffee for two tired-looking truckdrivers with her right hand and wiping the counter with her left.

"He tell you anything?" she asked.

"He didn't know much. The *Flag* girl refused to talk to the police; instead she's going to print her story in the newspaper."

"I *told* you to call her," said Cara. "Call her, and see if she'll make a deal."

"Well, okay."

Daniel went upstairs to the bedroom and eased himself back on the unmade bed. He propped the telephone on to his chest and

dialed the offices of the *Arizona Flag* on East Van Buren Street.
The newspaper had a computerized answering system, and it
seemed as if today they were more than just busy. It took five
minutes of schmaltzy music before a girl's nasal voice said,
"Flag."

"Oh, good morning. Listen, my name's Daniel Korvitz. I
want to speak to the girl who did that Margot Schneider story.
You know, the woman who had her head cut off?"

"Ms. Kathy Forbes? I'm sorry, Ms. Forbes isn't taking any
calls right now."

"Will you tell her this is important? I have some important
information to discuss."

"I'm sorry, you'll have to call back later."

"Will you tell her I know about another one? Another
beheading?"

"Another what?"

"Beheading, you know what beheading is?"

"You mean *beheading?* Another *beheading?"*

"That's what I said."

"Will you hold on please?"

There was another lengthy wait. Daniel was almost tempted to
hang up, to forget about the whole frightening and ridiculous
business, to pack up his case and take Cara and Susie and spend
the rest of his life in Chicago or Denver or New Orleans, grow a
beard, wear dark glasses, and never speak about missiles or
Willy or headless bodies ever again; but then the schmaltzy
music abruptly stopped and a woman's sharp voice said, "Mr.
Konvitz?"

"Korvitz."

"This is Kathy Forbes. My secretary tells me you know
something about another homicide."

"That's right."

"Have you told the police?"

"No. And I don't think I'm going to, either."

"Why not? Is this some kind of a hoax? I'm a little tired of
hoaxers this morning, thank you."

"No hoax, Ms. Forbes," said Daniel. "Just listen to me for
one minute and one minute only, and hear what I have to say;
and if you think it's a hoax you can hang up and never worry

about it again. But I don't think you're going to. Because
nobody could invent anything like this, Ms. Forbes. Any more
than anybody could invent what happened to you.''

He didn't actually know what had happened to Kathy Forbes,
except that her captors had tortured her. But it was enough of a
line to keep her attention while he told her all about Willy and
his radar-signature theories, and all about Ronald Reagan Kinishba
and what had happened at Williams Air Force Base. She believed him. He could hear it in the tone of her voice.

"You think there's some sort of a conspiracy, Mr. Korvitz?"

"I don't know. What do you think?"

"Meet me, we'll talk about it."

"At your office?"

"No, that would be too conspicuous. You're out at Apache
Junction, right?"

"That's right. But if you came out here, somebody would be
bound to notice. We notice strangers around here."

"There's a movie ranch out there, isn't there? Apacheland?
Why not meet me there . . . say, at three o'clock. Carry a copy
of the *Flag* or something, so I'll know you."

"Okay," agreed Daniel. "Three o'clock. Under the gallows."

He hung up the phone and went downstairs again. Susie was
buckling up her school sandals, and Cara was helping Mrs.
Koperwas with the morning's dishes.

"Why are you being so good to me?" Daniel asked Cara,
with false jollity, patting her tight-bottomed shorts and kissing
her ear.

"You should have a *wife* like this," said Mrs. Koperwas,
pointedly.

"I did once," said Daniel. He poured himself another cup of
coffee and stood drinking it and staring out of the window. Then
he turned to see Cara looking at him, hurt, and he said, "I'm
sorry. That was a rotten thing to say. I'm worried, that's all."

"You called her?"

He nodded. "I'm meeting her at three, out at Apacheland."

"What does she want to do, play cowboys and Indians?"

Daniel put down his coffee cup and shrugged. "I'm beginning
to think that cowboys and Indians is what this is all about.
Except that *we're* the ones who stand to get scalped."

Susie said, "Can I come? It's *ages* since I went to Apacheland."

"*You've* got to get yourself to school," Daniel insisted. "You think I want some kind of half-educated moroness for a daughter?"

"What's a moroness?"

"You don't know? Then that's what you are."

It was a busy day at the diner, with a constant traffic of travelers and truckdrivers stopping in for beer and shakes and Daniel's special three-deck Downhome Burger with mushroom sauce. Daniel was edgy and didn't feel like talking too much: but Cara made up for his reticence by bouncing around in one of her tightest T-shirts and flirting with every truckdriver who stopped by.

"Nice place you've got here," remarked a tattooed gas-truck driver from Idaho. "The help sure looks good. Tastier'n the burgers."

In the kitchen, Daniel hissed at Cara, "Will you stop jiggling your jugs so much? You'll get us closed down for indecency."

"Jealous?" grinned Cara.

Daniel shrugged, and pouted. Cara reached over and kissed him, first on the cheek and then on the mouth. "Don't be," she said. "As long as I'm with you, I'm with you."

"That sounds like a bad country'n'western song," Daniel complained, and then squeezed her close, and laughed. He didn't feel like laughing. He kept seeing the red pulp that had been Ronald's face against that chicken-wire fence like some Salvador Dali nightmare.

At a quarter of three, Daniel left Cara in charge of the diner and drove off eastwards in his beaten-up car towards Apacheland. The heat was so intense now that the Superstition Mountains rippled and wavered in the distance, and the car's air-conditioning spluttered unhappily. Two U.S. Air Force jets thundered and scratched their way across the sky, and Daniel thought of Willy, too, as well as Ronald, and the feeling of dark unexplained coincidence began to disturb him even more deeply than before.

"*It's a one-in-a-million flaw,*" Willy had said. "*A one-in-a-million flaw. And I discovered it.*"

God, Willy, if only you hadn't.

Apacheland was at the end of a half-mile track between Highway 60 and the foothills of the Superstition Mountains. Daniel's car stirred up a high trail of ochre dust as he drove between the brush and the stunted saguaro, and his suspension jolted in every pothole. Then he turned into the parking-lot and there it was: an old-style Western town with a fortlike entrance, the background for scores of cowboy movies, and now a tourist attraction for anyone who wanted to remember what an American community was like before indoor plumbing and freeze-dried coffee.

The main street sloped upwards, towards the Marshall's Office and the livery stables. Outside the saloon, two actors dressed as old-time prospectors were staging a mock gunfight for the benefit of a small crowd of tourists, and the afternoon popped with blanks. There was laughter and applause as one of the actors fell back in the dust with his legs sticking up in the air. I live in a country that finds death hilariously funny, thought Daniel.

She was waiting for him, as she had promised, under the gallows. She was sitting on the sun-warped steps, and the shadow from the noose swung slowly from side to side, across her face. She was wearing large rose-tinted sunglasses and a seersucker dress with puffed sleeves, the pale color of arrowroot. In case there was any mistake, she carried a freshly-printed copy of the *Flag*.

"Mr. Korvitz?" she said, as he approached.

"Hi," said Daniel, and shook her hand.

"Just in case you aren't *quite* what you claim you are, I brought a friend along," said Kathy. She nodded towards the livery stable, where a heavily-built man in a loud plaid coat was waiting, his hands in his pockets, steadfastly chewing gum. "My editor insisted."

Daniel made a face. "That's understandable."

"You want to tell me who you are, and what you know?"

"Well, I'm not anybody, in particular. I mean, I'm no one involved with murders or criminal syndicates or terrorists. I run a diner at Apache Junction. It's a living, and the big terrible world usually leaves me alone. At least, it did until now."

He told her everything that had happened over again, trying to remember as much of the technical detail that Willy had explained to him as he could, standing with his arms folded, his left eye screwed up against the glare of the sun, his sneaker tracing semi-circles in the dust. She listened without interrupting him, without taking notes. When he had finished, she glanced toward the bodyguard she had brought with her, and then looked back at Daniel with an expression that he was unable to read.

"Do you know why I refused to answer all the questions the police put to me?" she asked.

Daniel shook his head. "Our local deputy thinks it's because you wanted to keep the story exclusive to the *Flag*. But if that wasn't the reason, then, no, I don't know."

"I didn't answer their questions because I was scared to. If an agent of the National Security Agency was all mixed up in this, why not the police? And, if I were to tell them what I knew, or at least what I'd *guessed* . . ."

"What did you guess? What are you trying to tell me?"

Kathy took off her sunglasses and folded them up. There was a slight reddish bruise under one of her eyes. "Maybe I'm going off my head," she said. "Maybe that kidnap got to my psyche. You know? They always say that kidnap victims begin to have delusions after a while. It's something to do with having to rely on somebody else for everything—food, water, communication with the outside world, life itself."

"I wouldn't have thought you were kidnapped for long enough."

"No," said Kathy, "nor would I. Maybe I'm suffering from plain old paranoia instead. Maybe I'm getting to be like one of these old ladies who always keeps the plugs in the washbasin because she thinks that the utility company is spying on her through the drainpipe."

Daniel said, "What are you trying to tell me? You're trying to tell me that you think some kind of *conspiracy* is going on? That the National Security Agency and the police and the Air Force are all mixed up in it? Is that it? And you don't want to tell anybody in case they start thinking you've lost your marbles?"

Kathy looked up at Daniel and took a deep breath, as if she were desperately anxious to say yes, but couldn't quite manage it.

Daniel wiped sweat from his chin with his sleeve. "If it's any consolation, I feel exactly the same way," he told her. "First there was Willy and his missiles; then there was Ronald; then Margot Schneider and and—what was his name, Skellett?—and that police chief who got killed in Phoenix, and the guy who blew himself up in Tempe. Normally you'd think they were separate, unconnected incidents, right? One of those weird runs of violence you sometimes get in the summer, when it gets too hot and everybody goes bananas. But somehow it's different, all of this. It seems to have a peculiar kind of logic behind it. It seems to have a *meaning*."

Kathy said, "Thank God."

"Thank God for what?" asked Daniel.

"Thank God that somebody else believes that there's a conspiracy. Mr. Korvitz, you've made me feel sane for the first time in days."

"Wait a minute. You may not be. Maybe *I'm* crazy too."

"Crazy people very seldom agree. Besides, look. Sit down, and see what you think of this." Daniel sat down beside her on the edge of the gallows platform, and she opened her buff leather pocketbook and took out a dark Xeroxed copy of a Polaroid photograph. "It's kind of blurry," she said. "I wanted to make some proper photographic copies but Skellett's people broke into my apartment and stole the original before I could get them done. All the same, you can see who it is."

"For sure. This is a picture of President Kennedy. Why should they want to steal a picture of President Kennedy? They could get one anywhere."

"Not *this* picture of President Kennedy. This is the only one there is. This shows President Kennedy sitting beside Marilyn Monroe's swimming-pool in Brentwood, Los Angeles. Late summer of '61, I'd guess, or maybe spring of '62."

"Well, come on, everybody knows that Jack and Bobby Kennedy were both seeing her. I mean, that's common knowledge, isn't it?"

"Oh, yes. But where do you think I *found* this picture? Tucked in amongst Margot Schneider's possessions, the day after she was murdered, before the police had a chance to go through them. I'm still not sure why I took it. Maybe it struck me as kind of peculiar. You know, that an Air Force widow living in Phoenix should have an original Polaroid of President Kennedy. I thought maybe there was some kind of interesting angle. Some warm, human, woman-who-met-the-President story. But Skellett sure jolted me out of *that*."

"Tell me," said Daniel. "Come on—if you can't trust the guy who runs Daniel's Downhome Diner in Apache Junction, Arizona, you can't trust *anybody*."

"Well," shrugged Kathy, "maybe I can't. But when I took the Polaroid home, the night after I'd found it, I got to thinking. Why did Margot Schneider have this picture among her private possessions? You can't read it here, on the Xerox, but it says on the photograph *"To N, special memories, from P."* I thought P could have been President, and maybe N could have been Norma Jean."

"I guess that makes sense."

"Surely . . . but what was Margot *Schneider's* reason for having this picture? She didn't *collect* pictures of President Kennedy, or anything like that . . . this was the only one. It didn't seem like she collected movie memorabilia, either. There were a few reviews of *The Misfits* along with the picture, but not much else. It could have been a one-of-a-kind souvenir; something she found; something she bought at one of those stores that sell old political campaign buttons. Photographs come into people's possession in the oddest ways."

Daniel gave her a long, expectant look. He began to realize what she was going to say next, and why she was hesitating. The simplest of all reasons for Margot Schneider owning the Polaroid would suggest that recorded history and political logic had for years been standing on their heads.

Kathy said, with a slight catch in her throat, "Then, of course, I had to consider the most *obvious* reason. Margot Schneider owned the picture because it belonged to her; because it had been given to her by President Kennedy. Maybe she had taken it herself."

"She was supposed to be an Air Force widow, so what had she been doing in Hollywood taking Polaroids of President Kennedy?"

"Exactly. She was supposed to be an Air Force widow, a normal middle-aged lady living on a military pension, leading a routine, unexceptional life. Yet she had no Social Security card that anybody could find; there were no pictures of her anywhere, not even in the files at Luke Air Force Base, where her husband was posted. And for no apparent motive she was murdered by an unknown man or woman in the most gruesome way you can think of. She wasn't raped and she wasn't robbed. Her head was removed so that nobody could identify her; and within twenty-four hours the National Security Agency sent an agent down to remove the rest of her, too—an agent who had *carte-blanche* to kill anybody he liked, just so long as he got the body back.''

''Why didn't the guy who killed her take the body in the first place?'' Daniel wanted to know. ''He could have dumped her in the desert somewhere and nobody would have found her for *years*, if at all.''

''I thought about that, too. But if Margot Schneider had simply disappeared without trace, the police would have started making much more intensive inquiries into her background: where she came from, who her relatives were, that kind of thing, instead of accepting the apparent fact that here was poor Mrs. Margot Schneider and here she was dead.''

Kathy paused, and then she said, ''She was the right age, she had the right kind of physique, and the police found hairs in the bathroom washbasin which corresponded with *her* natural hair color, before she bleached it. There was a circular mark on the back of her right arm, too.''

''You really believe it was possible? I mean, you really believe it was *her?*''

''I'm eighty percent sure. Why else did Skellett react so violently when I asked him if she was connected with Cuba? I couldn't fit the bricks together but I could tell that they all came out of the same kiln. Kennedy—Monroe—Margot Schneider. If Margot Schneider *hadn't* been Marilyn Monroe, why would Skellett have bothered to torture me? He tried to tell me that Margot Schneider was part of a Soviet spy ring or something like that; but he completely failed to explain why the very mention of Cuba in connection with Margot Schneider was enough to make him speed through Phoenix at 90 miles an hour, kill two cops, and then behave like an Inquisition torturer. And I can tell you something—whatever Skellett knows about Margot Schneider, or Marilyn Monroe—it was sufficiently devastating to make it worthwhile blowing one of his own men into tiny little pieces, just to help him get away.''

Daniel said, ''Why *did* you ask him about Cuba?''

"No particular reason. Reporter's nose for trouble, I guess. It was the biggest political storm that was brewing at the time, in 1962. I just took a shot at it. I've been reading through most of the books on Marilyn Monroe's death, and trying to form some opinions about the various theories on why she died, and how; and I couldn't find any idea that was actually solid enough either to justify somebody killing her, or to justify her going into hiding in Arizona for the rest of her life."

"Didn't somebody once say that she was killed by agents of the Communist party because she was threatening to expose Bobby's plans to legalize a whole lot of left wing political organizations?"

Kathy Forbes shook her head. "There are *scores* of theories, most of them crack-pot. Hardly any of them stand up to the simple test of asking yourself, Would Marilyn Monroe really have done that? She wasn't a politically active person, neither was she vengeful. No, it's *my* view that she simply overheard too much from Jack and Bobby; listened to one too many of their political problems. And one day they realized that she knew so much about one *particular* political problem that her life could be in danger. *Their* lives were in danger, too, as we know from what happened in November, 1963, and in June, 1968, and it makes much more sense to me that all three of them—Marilyn, Jack, and Bobby—were under threat from the same people. Skellett's people, whoever they are."

She replaced her sunglasses, and then she said, "Whether Marilyn died in 1962 or not, and I really believe now that she *didn't,* she was killed because of something she knew that was crucially important, and as far as I can see, Cuba was the only crisis big enough. What's more, if Margot Schneider really *was* Marilyn Monroe, the crisis had long-lasting implications—enough to make it worthwhile murdering her after twenty years. I chose Cuba, and Skellett's reaction proved me right."

"Now there's Willy," said Daniel. "Where do you think *he* fits in?"

"I don't know," said Kathy. "I've been swiveling the whole thing around in my mind like a Rubik's cube, ever since you telephoned me this morning."

"I never could solve Rubik's cube."

"Well, I've only done it five times. But let's try some theories out and see if they fit. Or half-fit, at least. The first thing we know for sure is that your friend Willy was killed in a very similar way to Margot Schneider, in the same general locality, within three days. And the method of killing was sufficiently unusual to make it quite likely that he was killed by the same individual. I mean, you don't get too many flexible-saw murderers."

Daniel wiped sweat from his face. "I could use a beer," he said. "Do you think we could continue this discussion down at the saloon?"

"Sure," Kathy nodded. "Do you mind if my friend comes along? He looks tough, but actually he's very harmless."

"That's what they all say," Daniel remarked.

TWENTY-ONE

They sat at a dark corner-table drinking beer by the neck while the local "cowpokes" entertained the tourists with gun-twirling and pretended drunkenness. Kathy's heavyweight bodyguard dragged his chair back a few feet out of earshot, and tossed peanuts into his mouth by the monotonous handful. The buxom girl behind the bar gave him a sassy wink or two, but he remained expressionless, and unmoved.

Kathy said to Daniel, "I have about four main theories why Willy Monahan was killed by the same man who killed Marilyn Monroe. None of them may be completely right. For instance, we have to allow that he may have been disposed of by somebody at Williams AFB who cut his head off in the same way as Marilyn's for no other reason except to throw us off the trail, and the two homicides might be completely unconnected. But my feeling is that if the murderer wanted people to *think* that both murders were committed by the same individual, then he or she wouldn't have kept Willy's death such a secret—unless they were devious enough to make it all *seem* like a mystery, so that anyone who had actually suspected what was going on, like you and Ronald Kinishba, would be flushed out into the open. Maybe that's *too* devious. I don't know."

"It wasn't difficult for me to get *into* the air base mortuary," said Daniel. "Getting *out* was the tough part."

"Well, that's something to bear in mind," agreed Kathy. "Now—we have to think what Marilyn Monroe could possibly have known about Cuba that related to what your friend Willy Monahan had learned about the missiles at Williams AFB. Monroe— Kennedy—Cuba—missiles. Nuclear missiles were the principal point of contention in the Cuban crisis of 1962; so maybe what Willy Monahan discovered was something to do with a disarmament agreement that was reached between Kennedy and Khruschev. All we know about the treaty of July 25, 1963 is that it prohibited all nuclear tests except those conducted underground; and that was a direct result of the crisis over Cuba. But maybe there were other agreements, secret agreements which only a few people ever got to hear about."

"You mean those missiles that Willy discovered weren't ever *supposed* to work against Soviet planes? That Kennedy might have agreed with Khruschev that U.S. planes wouldn't be able to shoot down any Soviet aircraft?"

"It's a theory."

"But surely subsequent Presidents would have done something about it. I can't see Marshall Roberts allowing U.S. fighter planes to fly around with useless weapons."

"A couple of years ago, I couldn't see Marshall Roberts agreeing to the RINC talks."

Daniel sat silent for a moment, then took another swallow of cold beer. "It seems incredible."

"That's what I thought. But the more I went over the idea, the more I rearranged it in my mind, the more sense it seemed to make. That could be dangerous, of course. Journalistic theories have a habit of fitting all the known facts, and still remaining preposterously untrue. But if there *had* been a number of secret nuclear agreements between Kennedy and Khruschev; if the price of getting the Russians to take their missiles out of Cuba and back to Russia *had* been much higher than the rest of us poor suckers were led to believe at the time, then Marilyn Monroe's murder would begin to make sense, so would Willy's, and so would Jack and Robert Kennedy's. Skellett's behavior still seems a little peculiar, to say the least. I don't know why he had to make such a three-ring circus out of recovering Marilyn's body when she was already safely dead. All he did was draw everybody's attention to the murder, when it could easily have remained another nasty unsolved mystery, for ever and ever. But maybe we'll find that out later.''

"You don't think we ought to go to the police?'' asked Daniel.

"No, *sir*. If even one half of this bears any relation to the real facts, then we're dealing with some very heavy people indeed; and the fewer people who know what we know, the better. I don't much relish being beheaded, do you?''

"I thought you were going to publish the whole inside story in the *Flag?*''

"All I'm going to publish in the *Flag*, Mr. Korvitz, is 'My Kidnap Ordeal by Kathy Forbes,' with all the salacious details of what they tried to do to me. I haven't told anyone about my Marilyn Monroe theory yet, except you, and Skellett, and that was only because Skellett tortured me. I really think it's too early and it's too damned dangerous. Unless, of course, you're one of Skellett's agents, in which case you're probably going to take me out right now and string me up from the town gallows.''

Daniel finished his beer. "What do you think we can do? Any ideas? Any *sane* ideas? Maybe it's best if we don't do anything. Pretend it never happened. I mean, what possible effect can you and I have on the history of the entire world?''

"Are you kidding?'' asked Kathy. "If Kennedy made a secret disarmament deal with Khruschev that U.S. missiles should be totally ineffective against Soviet airplanes, and if President Roberts is still sticking to the terms of that agreement today—you know what a news story that would be? We'd be famous forever. And rich. You want to run a *diner* all your life?''

"I want to stay *alive* for all my life, that's all.''

Kathy said briskly, "Well, it's up to you. I've got to investigate it, because it's my job. My instinct, too. If you don't want to help me, well, that's it, don't help me. But I'll have to make you promise not to blow the story to any other newspaper. I think after what I've been through I'm entitled to an exclusive, don't you?''

"You're really going to start poking your nose around in this?

You're serious? After the way they've been killing people off, blowing people up, sticking goddamned—*needles* in you?''

"Mr. Korvitz—"

"Please, Daniel."

"Daniel, I have to. It's my vocation. This is the kind of break that every newspaper reporter dreams about."

"So what are you going to do?"

"First of all, I'm going to Los Angeles. I want to talk to as many people as I can who saw Marilyn Monroe in the last few days of her life, and particularly on the night of her alleged death. I want to talk to the mortician who laid her out and everybody who saw her body. If there's even the slightest suggestion that the body they buried at Westwood isn't Marilyn . . . well then, we'll know that we're on to something."

Daniel rubbed his eyes, tiredly. "It would be easier, you know, if it didn't all sound so goddamned far-fetched."

"Mr. Korvitz, Daniel, the whole trouble is that it *isn't* far-fetched. It's actually *less* far-fetched than all the accepted historical explanations about Marilyn Monroe and the Kennedys and the Cuban Missile Crisis. It fits the facts better, and it *could* account for all kinds of apparently inexplicable trends in the way that this country has been governed for the past twenty years."

"If you say so," said Daniel, unconvinced.

"Let me spend some time in Los Angeles, and then get back to you," said Kathy. "Maybe we can talk it over again."

"All right," Daniel agreed. Suddenly it didn't seem so important to find out why Willy had died, or how. Suddenly it seemed more important that Willy should be left to rest in peace, and not have his sleep troubled by distant rumbles of thunder from 1962.

They said goodbye to each other in the dusty parking-lot. Daniel was fairly sure that he would never see her again, this snappy over-enthusiastic lady reporter, although he would probably read her story in the *Arizona Flag,* and follow her investigation into the Cuban Missile Crisis. He shook hands with her politely and went back to his car. He sat down behind the steering-wheel, and sorted through his keys, and wondered why he felt so down.

He was just about to start up the engine when Kathy came across again, and leaned into the open passenger window.

"You know what you're feeling now, don't you?" she asked him.

He didn't answer. He didn't know what to say.

"You're feeling fear, that's what," she told him. "And do you want to know something, I *respect* you for it. It means you've got enough imagination to realize that what I'm saying is true, or could be. I know you've got a little girl, Daniel. I know you're the kind of guy who wants to be left alone. But just remember you had enough guts to break into that air base to find out what had happened to Willy; and you had enough guts to come here and talk to me about it."

Daniel said, "You're the second person today to tell me how gutsy I am. I'm beginning to feel like Audie Murphy."

"I'll be in touch, okay?" said Kathy, and left him. He shrugged to himself, and started up his car. The engine coughed, backfired loudly, and died away with a whine like a broken washing-machine.

Kathy, who had been halfway back to her own car, walked over again and looked in at the passenger window. "You don't happen to need a ride?" she asked him.

As they drove back to Apache Junction, they began to relax with each other. Kathy told Daniel how she had gone to California, and then come back to make her name on the *Flag*. "I thought I was going to win the Pulitzer Prize the first year I was there." Daniel told her about Candii and Susie; and about the attractions of living a simple and uncomplicated life in the shadow of the Superstition Mountains.

"Are you afraid of life? Afraid of success? Or what?" asked Kathy. "I'm not being rude. It's just that you seem to want things out of life that don't actually exist, like women out of country-and-western fantasies, and complete peace and quiet. There isn't any such thing as complete peace and quiet. Life will never leave you alone. And all the women I've ever met who look like country-and-western fantasies are pretty as cotton-candy on the outside and hard as reinforced concrete on the inside."

Daniel said, "I don't lack confidence, I can tell you that. I don't lack determination, either. But I look around me and I begin to wonder what all that confidence and determination is going to bring me. Money? I'm eating okay. Happiness? I've got my daughter, and my occasional girlfriends. Fame? I'm famous with the people who know me. You may think I'm backing off, opting out, but I don't seriously think so. What I want is what I've got, and I think the real strength comes in saying to yourself, that's it, I'm happy.''

"The trouble is," said Kathy, "I don't believe that you *are*."

They drew up in front of Daniel's Downhome Diner. Kathy said, "I noticed this place on the way out here. Do you think you could spare us a cup of coffee, and a muffin maybe? Neither of us had time for lunch."

Daniel hesitated, and Kathy said, "You could send the check to my paper. They'll pay you."

Daniel grinned. "Come on in," he said. "I think I can just about afford to treat you."

But the second that Daniel walked into the place he realized there was something wrong. Pete Burns was in there, and two Highway Patrol officers, and three or four other regular customers, but none of them were eating. Then he saw Cara's legs on the floor, in between the chairlegs, and he felt as if everything was suddenly rushing in to meet him with the velocity of a locomotive, faces, chairs, tables, walls, and Pete Burns was turning to say something with an expression which he knew in that first explosive instant meant bad news.

"There were two guys. They came in here about a half-hour ago. Neil says they asked for you.

"She's not dead, Daniel. Daniel, she's not dead. Okay? She's going to be fine. They hurt her a little, that's all. But the doc put her under a sedative, and she's fine. Listen, will you calm down?

"They asked for you by name. That's what Neil says. Jimmy here heard them too. They said, where's Daniel Korvitz; and when Cara said you were out, and she didn't know where, they started pushing her around, you know? One of them hit her with something; nobody saw what it was, but it lacerated her face and her shoulder. Maybe a broken bottle. The ambulance is coming, anyway. The thing is, Daniel —"

Daniel stared at them blurrily. Somebody jostled against him and he turned around; but then Pete Burns said, "The thing is, Daniel, Susie was coming home from school right then—"

"Susie?"

"Well, it was pretty bad luck. A couple of minutes later and she would've missed them completely. But they were just leaving and the school bus turned up, and when she came into the diner and said, you know, where's my daddy—

"Don't know what the hell they hit her with. Will you look at those cuts?"

"Pete, what happened? Where's Susie?"

Charlie McEvers said, in his gravely gold-prospector's voice, "She's kidnapped, Daniel. That's the meat of it. They just picked her up and carried her out and there wasn't a darned thing that any of us could do about it."

Daniel looked around. By the door, Kathy Forbes was watching him with sympathy and pain. *"There isn't any such thing as complete peace and quiet. Life will never leave you alone."*

Somebody brought Daniel a chair and he sat down. He kept saying to Pete Burns, "You've got to find her, you understand? I want her found. And, by God, if anybody touches one hair on her head, I'm going to kill him. I warn you now, Pete. I'm going to kill him stone dead."

"Sure, Daniel. Nobody blames you."

The ambulance arrived outside, its siren moaning in the afternoon heat. The medics lifted Cara on to a stretcher, and carried her past Daniel as if she were just another victim of the disaster he called his life. She was deeply sedated, her eyes closed, her mouth open. But Daniel could clearly see the rows of parallel lash-marks that lacerated her cheek and her collar bone. She looked almost as if she had been clawed by a tiger.

Pete Burns said to Daniel, "How about some coffee? A shot of brandy, maybe?"

Daniel shook his head.

"You don't know what these guys *wanted,* do you?" asked Pete. "What would they want from *you?*"

"I don't know," said Daniel. "I don't have any idea. I sure don't have any money worth speaking of."

"You haven't been threatened recently? Sometimes somebody's Sicilian brother wants to open a liquor store or a restaurant, and then everybody around gets leaned on, just to make sure that nobody objects.''

"Nothing like that,"—said Daniel.

Kathy came up and laid her hand on his shoulder. "Are you okay?" she asked him. "Is there anything I can do?"

One of the customers was saying, "Kind of skinny guy, one of them, but the other was big. Real gorilla, with a red birthmark."

Daniel raised his eyes and looked at Kathy with angry intensity.

"Skellett," she whispered, and Daniel nodded, and for the first time in his life he felt like killing.

TWENTY-TWO

She met Ikon in his private dining-room on the sixth floor. He rarely went out these days; even though he still harbored a longing for the *sole fouree tzarine* at the Montpellier restaurant on 15th and M. He had grown old in a particularly Russian way, as if all the gravity to which his thickset body had been subjected in the eighty-two years of his life had cumulatively dragged him down, pouching his eyes and jowling his chin, and spreading his stomach until it pressed against the rim of his antique dining-table. He spoke thickly, and took frequent sips of the rare Tokaj wine which was specially imported for him from Hungary. In the dark, densely-carpeted room, with the drapes drawn so closely that only a tall two-dimensional triangle of summer sunlight could penetrate, he looked like one of the decaying provincial gentry from Mikhail Saltykov's novel *The Golovlev Family*.

"You look tired," she told him, as she squeezed lemon on her Sevruga caviar.

"Well," said Ikon, "I *am* tired. Those who have to struggle will always have to pay the price."

"As long as you can carry on for two or three months; long enough for Marshall Roberts to get the RINC talks restarted."

Ikon shrugged heavily, and reached for one of the small buckwheat pancakes which were always served to him with his caviar. He spread the sturgeons' eggs as thick as a child would spread peanut-butter, and then ladled sour cream on top, and took a quick and unexpectedly avaricious mouthful.

"Marshall had better act soon; otherwise he may very well sink both of us."

"He's doing his best. But you can understand what a difficult situation he's in."

"Of course," said Ikon, wiping his mouth with his napkin. "But he is the President, *nyet?* And the President should be capable of dealing with any problem which confronts him. That is what Presidents are *for.*"

"Your English improves every day," smiled Nadine.

"Hmmmph," said Ikon. "I never get out as much as I should. I should go to parties, and receptions. I am beginning to speak like an American television anchorman. I even understand 'what's coming down' means. Now, there's a colloquial rarity for you, 'what's coming down.' In Russia, we would say 'what is it that flows this way.' "

"Did you see the doctor?" asked Nadine.

Ikon looked at her with unconcealed fondness. In all the years he had been in Washington, in all the days and nights he had lived in this building, he had never come across anyone so alive and so determined as Nadine. He had never come across a woman who combined so successfully the values of Leninism with the enthusiasm of the modern age. If only he were forty years younger. She was such a vibrant, sexual woman. Tall, and proud, and intelligent. The sort of woman who could look any man commandingly in the eye.

"The doctor?" he said. "The doctor is as pessimistic as ever. I believe that all doctors are born pessimists; or perhaps all pessimists become doctors. In any case, my leukemia is as virulent as ever, and I shall be lucky to see next May Day."

"Nikolai Nekrasov," said Nadine, and reached out her hand. Ikon touched her fingers with his, and then withdrew them.

"You must eat, enjoy yourself," he told her. "*Your* problems will come next. And there will be many."

"My problems have already started. Titus has warned Marshall that if he persists with RINC II, then all this business with Colleen Petley will be made public immediately. He's given

Marshall a little time to think it over. First he gave him only an hour, now he's agreed to give him a day. But that day will be over in an hour or so. And, believe me, Titus is serious.''

"That was always Titus' trouble, wasn't it?" remarked Ikon, spreading more caviar. "So *serious*. It will lead to his downfall, you know."

Nadine put down her knife. "I'm waiting for your instructions. You know that, don't you?"

"Well," said Ikon. "It seems as if there is only one course open to us. The RINC talks must continue; otherwise everything we have been working for will collapse. I know that gradualism is tedious; I know how much the young administrators champ at their bits for progress. But only gradualism will lead the American people towards an eventual understanding of their true situation without bloodshed, or riot, or civic resistance. Can you imagine what would happen if you told them *now?* The country would burn from end to end. There would be fighting, barricades, organized resistance. Thousands of people would die. And this is in the 1980s, when people are supposed to have become far more liberal and understanding. You can just picture what would have happened if they had known about it in 1962.''

Nadine said, "What do you want me to do?"

Ikon stared into his glass. His shaggy eyebrows reminded Nadine of a thoughtful bear. He said, "Colleen Petley will have to go, that is all. Can you arrange for it? And the chambermaid at the Futura Hotel . . . she will have to go, too."

"You want *me* to—"

"Nobody else can get close enough without arousing suspicion. Besides I have the ideal method."

Nadine laid her caviar spoon on to her serving-plate. "You're quite sure? You want me to *kill* her?"

Ikon placed a finger over his lips and said, "Ssh. We don't usually mention such subjects here. Not . . . disposal. Not in such terms."

"How do you expect me to do it?"

"It will be very easy. You will simply tell Miss Petley that she has to have an injection against influenza so that there is no risk of her being unwell when the Congressional hearing is convened. The medicine will look like this—" Ikon held up a small glass vial of straw-colored fluid, and then laid it carefully in the vine-leaf ashtray. "It is a mixture of water, simple sugars, and a single drop of hydrocyanic acid. Death will be almost instantaneous—a seizure of the heart."

Nadine stared at the old, Slavic mask of his face. He could have been made of latex rubber. He had asked her to perform many strange and disagreeable tasks in the past; out of all of them, courting and marrying Titus Alexander had probably been the most complex and the most self-sacrificing. But he had never required her to *kill* anyone before; and it was particularly unnerving that he should have asked her to kill Colleen Petley, the first woman in years with whom she had formed a warm and immediate sexual relationship. She had dreamed of Colleen when she had been making love with Titus.

Now, he was asking her to kill Colleen stone-cold, with the most lethal poison known to man.

"I can see that I have disturbed you," said Ikon.

Nadine pushed back her plate of caviar, and stood up. She walked to the window, and looked out through the inch-wide gap in the drapes, her face unnaturally illuminated by the single shaft of sunlight which fell through it into the room.

"You shrink from the thought of killing for your country?" asked Ikon. He took another mouthful of pancake and sour cream. "Soldiers are required to do it as a matter of course; yet nobody thinks that what soldiers have to do is disturbing, or exceptional."

"Colleen Petley is . . . well, Colleen Petley is different," said Nadine. "It's difficult for me to think of her as an enemy."

"She *is* an enemy, nevertheless. She is worse than an enemy. She could have remained neutral, and yet she was prepared to sell her information for money."

"That, Nikolai Nekrasov, is what a girl like Colleen Petley would call 'turning an honest buck.' "

"You're *refusing?*" asked Ikon, and there was a rumble of displeasure in his voice.

Nadine turned back towards him. Today she wore a soft black watered-silk blouse with wide sleeves and a narrow tailored waist, and a canary-yellow taffeta skirt; and for a moment Ikon would have forgiven her anything, absolved her from any kind of duty or duress. But, the times were too threatening. Everybody had to be used to keep the *Peredoviki* from taking over once Ikon himself had gone; everything had to be sacrificed to keep the world in political balance for at least a generation longer, even love, and self-indulgence, and kindness itself. "You are kind," he had read, in the works of the American poet Gregory Corso, "because you lead a kind life." Ikon knew that he had never led a kind life.

"There was a time," said Ikon, without waiting for Nadine to reply, "there was a time when I, too, was in love with a member of my own sex. It was in 1937, when I was working for Goelro, the State Commission for the Electrification of Russia. We were building a new power-station at Saratov, in the Privolskaja Vozvysennost. We were shockworkers, you understand, young men who backed their belief in Communism with intensively hard work, seven days a week, twelve or thirteen hours a day. We could build in a month a factory that, these days, it would take a year to complete. Well, there was a fellow there, a bricklayer; and for some reason I fell in love with him. He was devastatingly handsome, muscular, and yet innocent, too. What he could have done in Hollywood! One day, after we had finished a record day of building, we went to bed together almost completely exhausted, he and I, and made love. Yes, sodomized each other; but with pride and fellowship, and the genuine affection of two men who have worked side-by-side for the same political and industrial ideal."

Ikon was silent for a little while, and drummed his fingertips on the white damask tablecloth. Then he said, "I understand, you see, what you may be feeling about Colleen Petley."

"You don't know anything about me and Colleen Petley."

"I don't, no," Ikon admitted. "But I have known for some years about the affair you had in school, and I recognize the look. You have the look of being infatuated. Not in love, maybe, but infatuated, and I know for sure that it cannot be Titus."

"You've grown far too American," Nadine complained. "Do you know that? You're so American I can't believe it."

"You will still do what I ask, with Colleen Petley."

"You mean, murder her?"

Ikon raised his finger to his lips again; a reminder that here, in the hushest and darkest of the rooms of power, such words as death and killing and disposal were never spoken out loud. It was an indulgence that Nadine should even be allowed to eat here; and to speak to Ikon in person. It was a special favor that she should be allowed to address him by his name, Nikolai Nekrasov; the first four letters of which had been twisted around to form his code-name, Ikon. Everybody else in the building had to call him "Premier Ikon."

It was a typically ironic Russian joke that the foremost representative of Communism in the Western hemisphere should be named after a symbol of religious veneration; and that a man of such stout three dimensions should be associated with works of art which were traditionally executed in the flat.

Nadine said, "Has it occurred to you that you might be asking too much of me?"

"I am dying," Ikon told her. "I can ask as much as I like of anybody. Do you want to see the *Peredoviki* tear down everything for which I have worked? Do you want to see bloodshed, and chaos? I was not sent here to preside over the wholesale destruction of the United States. I was sent here to maintain the balance. To keep the world intact. One life, even if it happens to be the life of the woman you love, is never going to be worth as much as that."

"Did you hear what happened in Arizona?" Nadine asked him.

"Oh, yes," nodded Ikon. "And have no fear that I have already spoken to Kama about it. Kama, of course, was polite. 'I was only doing what I thought fit, Comrade Ikon. I was only acting expediently, Comrade Ikon.' But we should have no illusions about Kama, and what he is trying to do. He is trying his very best to bring the whole Supervisory Committee into the open, in such a way that he is not personally blamed for the revelation. He is trying his very best to dig up old corpses, and turn the world into a charnel-house! But, we have kept him at bay for seven years; and we can continue to keep him at bay until RINC II is ratified. This is—if you agree to support me, and do what you have to do with Colleen Petley."

Nadine sat down on the far side of the room, on a walnut side-chair. She kept her head lowered, as if she were thinking, or praying. Ikon watched her, occasionally reaching for his wine, or spreading more Sevruga caviar on his pancakes, his breathing harsh and unpleasant, rattling in the fluid-filled recesses of his lungs.

"If I don't agree to get rid of her, I suppose that you'll ask somebody else to do it?"

"Of course."

"Then I think that I'd prefer to do it myself. At least I'll be facing up to myself, and what I am, and what I've done to her."

"Well, I knew that you would say yes. Why don't you sit down and finish your caviar? Do you know how much it costs these days, in America? The best Sevruga?"

Nadine sat down at the dining-table with a rustle of yellow taffeta. "You know something, Nikolai Nekrasov, the strange thing about you is that you're not a bad man at all. I think history may see you as a saint."

Ikon wobbled his jowls in disagreement. "Moderates are never canonized. You have to be an extremist to be a saint. You have to poke your own eyes out, or set yourself alight. You know from experience that I am not that kind of a man. A fruitcake, the Americans say. I prefer to live, and eat, and survive, and make sure that all around me do the same. Men such as me are never remembered; but we do the most good."

They finished their meal in complete silence; eating, drinking, and thinking. Then they went into the conservatory that overlooked Pennsylvania Avenue, and one of the staff put Prokofiev's *The Love For Three Oranges* on the stereo. "Beautiful music," said Ikon, one hand thrust into the pocket of his enormous pants, the other holding a glass of strawberry vodka. "It makes me cry, sometimes, because the world cannot be ordered like an opera. Life cannot be scripted, or scored."

"Are you afraid of Kama?" asked Nadine.

"You always have a knack of asking the most direct questions."

"I have to know. You may be dead by next May; but I won't."

"Kama was one of Brezhnev's protégés. He has always supported Brezhnev's doctrine on polycentrism. But where Brezhnev was prepared to let the situation in the United States take an apparently natural course—not pushing too quickly, nor too fast—Kama believes that we ought to announce the 16th Soviet Socialist Republic overnight. A thunder-and-lightning man, Kama. Sweep away the old, sweep in the new! Damn the consequences! Unfortunately, he made sure that he took control of all the executive agencies which would give him the power to enact such measures. The National Security Agency, the Council of Economic Advisers, the Office of Administration. You cannot underestimate him, my dear Nadine. He is the second most powerful administrator after me; and even though I am superior to him, I cannot possibly keep him in check.''

"So he *wanted* that woman's body to be identified."

"Of course. He must be deeply chagrined that the media have been so slow to understand what his agents were doing. All these stories of 'Cadaver Kidnapping' and 'Fanatics Torture Girl Reporter.' The American press never looks further than the first pair of breasts. No wonder Marilyn Monroe was such a heroine. Personally, I thought she was a plump little cow. Fit for milking, not much else.''

The evening began to wind down. They drank more strawberry vodka, and Ikon told her about his boyhood in Zarajsk, on the Os'otr River, in the days of the Tsar; and how he had picked cherries and lain back on the haycarts as they trundled home through the long warm evenings of August, seventy-two years ago.

At seven o'clock, Nadine said, "I have to go now. We have a party at the British Embassy. Sir Leonard Grosvenor.''

"Very well," said Ikon. He made no attempt to rise from his chair.

Nadine collected her wrap, and her pocketbook, and the staff saw her out to the elevator. Ikon waited for five minutes before he eventually eased himself up, and walked with a slightly dragging step into the dining-room. He went across to the table, and peered into the vine-leaf ashtray, where earlier that evening he had lain the capsule of hydrocyanic acid.

To his satisfaction, he saw that it was empty.

TWENTY-THREE

Titus, that evening, was in a wolfishly ebullient mood. As a rule, he hated going to the British Embassy. "The British speak like they're carrying their rolled-up cricket socks in their cheeks." But he grasped Sir Leonard Grosvenor's hand as if he were greeting a long-lost buddy from the Class of '38, and he bussed Lady Grosvenor on the cheek with unusual enthusiasm.

Nadine could guess what was responsible. During the afternoon, shortly after three o'clock, Marshall Roberts had phoned Titus at the State Department and reluctantly agreed to postpone RINC II "certainly for the time being, if not indefinitely." No announcement had yet been made to the media, but Titus had insisted that the President should quickly make his acquiescence public. The White House press department was working on a statement which would satisfy both Marshall and Titus; and which wouldn't appear too sudden and too bizarre when announced to the media.

The British Embassy party was alcoholic and fatuous. There was jingoistic talk about the Falklands; and heaps of fatty roast beef; and two young British actresses with breasts like half-set blancmanges sat on the laps of as many long-suffering middle-aged diplomats as they could, and giggled endlessly. At the end of the evening, there was an hour-long demonstration of Morris dancing, which Titus watched with the glazed expression of a man who suddenly wishes that he was at home in bed.

On the way back to Georgetown, in the sudden frigidity of their air-conditioned Cadillac, Nadine said, "You've heard from Marshall, haven't you?"

Titus, who had been rubbing his eyes, suddenly stared at her. "Yes. As a matter of fact I have. How did you know?"

"Titus, my dear, you can't fool me. Up until they started that ridiculous folk-dancing, you were as chipper as fifteen beavers. And only *one* thing that I can think of could make you feel like that."

"You're right," said Titus. "Marshall called me mid-afternoon, and conceded. RINC II is dead as a doughnut."

There was a long silence, and then Nadine said, "Titus, I have to talk to you."

"Sure. Go ahead."

"Serious talk, Titus. Professional talk."

"All right. Serious talk. Tell me. What is it, your children are leaving home? That can't be true. God wouldn't smile on me twice in one day."

"Titus, I want you to call Marshall Roberts tonight, tell him it was all a mistake. You know, an error of judgment."

"You want me to what?"

"I want you to call Marshall Roberts tonight, and—"

"You want me to *what*???"

"Titus, it's vital."

"You bet your *ass* it's vital. Marshall was just about to concede every last strategic defense we ever had in the European theater. No neutron bombs, no ALCMs, no third-generation missiles of any kind. Have you *read* what he wants to do? The guy's crazy! He wants to open us up like a fucking oyster, all ready for the Soviets to swallow us down!"

"Titus," said Nadine, with extraordinary calmness. Her hair shone intermittently in the light from the passing street-lamps. "What would you say if we'd *already* been swallowed?"

Titus sniffed, and harrumphed, and stared at her. "What are you talking about? What do you mean, *already* been swallowed?"

"Just that. Supposing we had?"

"But by *what*? By *whom*? Damn it, Nadine, what the hell are you talking about?"

"I'm sorry, Titus. You're drunk. I didn't mean you to be drunk when I told you."

"What the hell do you mean, I'm drunk? All right, I'm drunk, but I still want to know what you're talking about."

"Titus, wait until we get home. Look, we'll be home in ten minutes."

"No, goddamn it, we'll talk about it here. *Swallowed*, what the hell are you talking about, *swallowed*? John, stop this goddamn car. Here! That's right, here! Anywhere! What the hell."

The chauffeur pulled the car into the curb on Constitution Avenue, just across the road from the lake in Constitution Gardens. It was a warm, well-lit night, one of those odd summer nights when sleep seems almost unnecessary, except at dawn, and even though it was nearly twelve o'clock, people were still promenading along the sidewalks, or trying to photograph the floodlit Lincoln Memorial, or walking their dogs, or smoking and talking as easily as if it were daylight.

Titus and Nadine walked down to the lake, and stood beside the wind-rippled waters, two or three feet apart, Titus in his tuxedo and black tie, Nadine in a long pleated evening gown of turquoise crêpe.

Nadine said, "I knew that I was going to have to tell you this one day. Well—you would have found out anyway, if you were ever elected President. But things have changed. Events are becoming critical. It's partly your fault, of course, although you weren't to know. If you hadn't blackmailed Roberts into postponing his disarmament talks . . . well, perhaps we could have carried it off. But there doesn't seem to be very much hope of that now, not unless you agree to back down."

"Nadine," said Titus, in a phlegmy, uncontrolled voice, "I want to know what the *hell* you're talking about."

"I'm trying to tell you. I'm *trying*, Titus. But it's important for you to understand, as well as listen. Everything you ever imagined to be solid, irrefutable truth; every political and constitutional guideline by which you've worked; everything, Titus, that you've believed to be real . . . well, it just *isn't*. The world is a completely different place from the one in which you think you've been living."

Titus glanced behind him. His Secret Service men had parked their car close behind his limousine, and were now standing fifteen or twenty feet away, their heads raised as if they were sniffing the air for snipers or explosives, their hands nervously perched inside their coats.

"Nadine," Titus said, more soberly now, more gently, "did anybody give you anything to *snort* at that party?"

Nadine brushed back her hair with her hand. "You think I'm high? Is that what you think?"

"I think you're talking like you're so spaced out you're not going to come down till Thanksgiving."

"Titus," she said, "it's absolutely *vital* that Marshall continues his RINC talks."

"Do you want to tell me why?"

"You want it straight from the shoulder? The reality?"

"Shoot. I'm not standing beside this fucking lake all night."

"The truth is, Titus, that the United States has been administered for the past twenty years not by Congress, nor by any of its Presidents, but by a committee of Soviet caretakers."

She waited to see how Titus would react, but Titus said nothing, just stared at her narrowly with one eye slightly closed, as if he were trying to focus on some very distant landmark.

"In Moscow, the United States of America is actually known as the ACOA, the Autonomous Capitalist Oblast of America. The caretaking committee is made up of thirty senior Communist party officials. You actually know quite a few of them already. Yevgeni Saratov, from the United Nations delegation? Anton Sviridov from the Russian Arts Council? And the chairman of the committee is a one-time friend of Leonid Brezhnev, a man whom the Russians code-name Ikon."

Again, Nadine hesitated. Titus was giving no indication either that he understood her, or that he believed her. But he said, "Go on," in a flat, toneless voice, and waited for her to continue.

"Ikon has been governing America for the past twenty years," said Nadine. "Every President, on the evening of his Inauguration Day, has been told exactly what I'm telling you now. He's been told that the general style of his administration must remain true to his own character, but that everything he does . . . politically, economically and militarily . . . must conform to Ikon's overall plan.''

"Yes?'' said Titus.

Nadine crossed her arms over her breasts, as if she were cold. Quietly, she said, "Ikon, whatever you think of his Marxist beliefs, is a wise and sensitive man. He's been doing his utmost to convert America *gradually* towards complete social democracy, without sacrificing any of the spirit of self-determination that made America what it is. Or, what it *was*, before Ikon took power.

"One thing that Ikon's always argued against is a sudden public revelation that America is a conquered nation. He argued against announcing it in 1962 and he's still arguing against it. His idea is that America should be allowed to prosper and grow in her own way; and that the *appearance* of international conflict between East and West should be kept up. That's all part of his fundamental thirty-year plan. He's a socialist, you see; but he's also a social realist, and a humanitarian. 'You must never take the struggle out of people's lives,' that's what he says. 'Once you take away the necessity to struggle, you take away the reason to live.' "

Titus turned towards the lake, and studied it raptly, as if he were facing an ocean, rather than an ornamental pond.

Nadine said, "Everything you believe about the cause-and-effect of U.S. policy over the whole of the past two decades, in every area of government, is wrong. Ikon controls it all. And every policy that Ikon implements is aimed towards the gradual acceptance by the American people that they are world citizens, that the Soviet people are their friends and their comrades, and that Communism is the *only* way in which men can be free. *All* men, not just a grotesquely wealthy elite.''

"I see,'' said Titus, with preternatural self-control. "And how has Ikon been working this social and political miracle?''

"Through the U.S. economy, mostly,'' said Nadine. "Ikon's been using Russia's influence on the Middle-Eastern oil-producing countries, as well as Russia's leverage in the world banking system, to force the economy of the United States into a false decline. His aim has been to eat away the power-base of the capitalist system; and to encourage the American working-man to start turning towards new political alternatives. A man can sometimes only accept the truth when he needs to."

"And where does RINC come in?"

"RINC is one of the last of Ikon's long-term measures to go for nuclear disarmament. He drafted all of the SALT agreements but RINC was his special pride, especially since it won the support of so many of Europe's politicians and military men— even General Rogers, the Supreme Allied Commander for Europe. RINC, when it's ratified, will mean the end of what NATO calls the 'flexible response,' the notion that the West might strike with nuclear weapons first. It will also mark the beginning of unopposed Soviet superiority in Europe. And peace, too, in time."

"I can't believe I'm hearing any of this," said Titus.

"I know it's difficult," said Nadine. "But you have to listen and you have to make an effort to understand, because it's crucial. You made it more crucial yourself, by your own belligerence. Ikon is old now, and very ill. He may not survive six months. At least two other committee members want to see him ousted, and most of the committee already believe that America should be openly declared a subject nation of the USSR. Ikon wanted to preserve the United States, to keep her traditions and her folklore and her color, not to mention her sanity. But Kama in particular, the Commissar in charge of National Security, is hungry to see the Red Flag flying over Washington, and all the trappings of capitalism swept away in a tide of scarlet. Kama's the leader of the *Peredoviki*, the innovators, the revolutionaries."

Nadine went on. "If RINC succeeds, the American public may gradually be brought to believe that true mutual disarmament is not only possible but imminent. Can you imagine the feeling of relief, after thirty years of cold war? The *hope* that people will feel, if they realize that all nuclear weapons are at last going to be dismantled? Moscow has been impatient with Ikon on more than one occasion. They've pushed him to assert an overt Communist rule over the United States at almost twice the historic speed at which he first planned it. He's managed by the skin of his teeth to keep control; he's managed to assure the Kremlin that RINC I and RINC II *can* be ratified, and that along

with all his other measures, America can be safely Sovietized
within the next decade.''

"But?" demanded Titus.

"But, if RINC fails, the *Peredoviki* will almost certainly take
control. Kama and Ilyushkin will force Marshall Roberts to
announce that America is an administrative *oblast* directly an-
swerable to the Communist Party of the Soviet Union. And then,
all hell will break out. I promise you, Titus, all hell. We will see
the H-bombs dropped yet. America will certainly melt.''

Titus hunkered down on the grass and stared for a very long
time at the wavering reflections of the passing promenaders, and
the Lincoln Memorial. One of his security men came a little
closer, not too close, and called politely, "Whenever you're
ready to leave, Mr. Secretary. We're kind of nervous about the
security around here.''

Titus stood up again, and cocked his head towards Nadine.
Then he said, "We're leaving now. Directly. Come along,
Nadine. Let's finish this little discussion at home.''

They drove back to Georgetown in silence. Titus drummed his
fingers on the gray hide of the Cadillac's interior, and coughed
from time to time, sharp, barking coughs, but he didn't look
once at Nadine, and wouldn't respond to her even when she said,
"Titus? Are you okay?''

In the living-room, Carl and Samantha had spread their record
albums all over the floor, and were playing the soundtrack from
Fame at a volume which made the Waterford-crystal chandeliers
jingle in horror. Titus stalked into the room and said, "Turn off
that goddamned noise and get the hell out of here.''

"I'm sorry, Tight, I can't hear you too good," said Carl.
"This music's too loud.''

Titus skirted around the coffee-table at remarkable speed. He
went to the turn-table, and there was a ripping blurt of noise as
the stylus slid sideways across the record. Then Titus wrenched
out the wires which connected it to the amplifier, and hurled it
clear across the room. It struck the marble mantlepiece, knocking the head off a Staffordshire shepherdess and smashing part of
the gilded mirror behind it.

"Now get out of here," quaked Titus, his eyes protuberant
with anger. "Get out of here before I do the same to you.''

Carl and Samantha gathered up their records, and left the room in unparalleled swiftness and silence.

Nadine said, "I'm going to bed. I'm not going to put up with your ridiculous bursts of temper. I've risked my life tonight to tell you the truth, and all you can do is rant and rave like a petty-minded drill sergeant."

"You're not going anywhere," snapped Titus. He went to the liquor cabinet, slammed open the doors, and found the bottle of ten-year-old Glenmorangie malt whiskey.

"If you're going to start drinking—"

"*Don't*—!" roared Titus, jabbing his finger at her, "—lecture to me!"

"Very well," said Nadine. "Since you're there, you can pour me a Campari-soda."

"You're sure you don't want a Stolichnaya?"

"I *am* Russian, if that's what you're trying to suggest."

"Oh, you're *Russian*, are you? And I suppose Carl and Samantha are Russian, and the dogs are Russian, and the servants are Russian, and all this time I've never suspected it. Nadine, for Christ's sake, I'm the Secretary of State. I'm the goddamned Secretary of *State*."

He sat down heavily in his favorite chintz armchair, crossed his legs, and took two or three furious swallows of whiskey. "Jesus Christ," he kept saying.

Nadine sat on the rug opposite him, her hands in her lap. Her expression when she looked at him was very sorrowful.

"I didn't know what else to do," she told him. "I couldn't see any other way out of it."

"You couldn't see any other way out of *what*?"

"Titus, I had a choice. Either I told you everything, and convinced you to withdraw your opposition to the RINC talks, or else I killed Colleen Petley."

"Now I *know* you're bananas," said Titus.

"Titus, please, you have to understand that I—"

"I understand already! I understand perfectly! I understand that my loyal, supportive wife is prepared to use some obscene and unpatriotic bullshit just to try and make me feel guilty about stopping Marshall Roberts and those disarmament discussions! Come on, Nadine, I'm not utterly stupid. I know an allegory when I hear one. An allegory, that's what it was, wasn't it? An Aesop's fable, about America. A story to make me feel that I was selling out on tomorrow's hope of a bomb-free world."

Nadine was aghast, no color in her cheeks at all. Titus jabbed his finger at her again, and said, "Let me tell you something, my lady. You're a very beautiful woman. You've got everything it's ever going to take. But when you start snorting coke at embassy parties, and when you start trying to get at my moral conscience by making up crappy bad-taste un-American stories like that— that's when you and I are going to fall out. And when you and I fall out—boy, I can tell you, you're going to know about it."

"Titus," she whispered. "For God's sake. Don't you *realize*?"

"I realize that I married a princess with the brain of a witch, that's what I realize. But do you know what you're going to do? Well, I'll tell you what. This princess is going to take off all of her clothes, and this princess is going to grovel on the floor and kiss my feet, and tell me she's sorry, and that she apologizes abjectly not only to *me*, but to the United States of America, and the proud heritage which made this nation great."

"Titus, you're incredibly drunk."

"Oh, no, Nadine. Not drunk. Poisoned by everything you've told me. But not drunk. Not any more. No man could stay drunk, not with you around. You're the most sobering influence since death."

"Titus—"

"Fuck you, lady!" roared Titus, and smashed his glass of whiskey against the fireplace. Then with two savage wrenches, he pulled open the front of Nadine's evening-gown, baring her breasts, and stripped it right down to her waist.

"How dare you tell me such shit," he trembled. "I've fought for this country and sweated for this country all of my adult life. I've seen my friends disemboweled; I've seen my family go crazy with grief. I've given everything and anything for that flag of stars and stripes, and for the American Constitution."

He stood up. He was so drunk that he had to grab for the arm of his chair to steady himself. Then he began to sing, in a loud, flat voice, the last verse of *The Star-Spangled Banner*.

"Oh! thus be it ever, when freemen shall stand

Between their loved home and the war's desolation!
Blest with victory and peace, may the heav'n rescued land
Praise the Power that hath made and preserved us a nation."

Nadine clung at his sleeve, and said, "Titus, please." But Titus slapped her away, and stood in the center of the room, his eyes crimson and swollen with alcohol, and sang at the top of his lungs,

"Then conquer we must, when our cause is just,
And this be our motto: 'In God is our trust.'
And the star-spangled banner in triumph shall wave
O'er the land of the free and the home of the brave."

Nadine said, "Titus, please. You have to listen."

"I've listened enough, damn it! I've known ever since I've married you how much of a goddamned pacifist you are. I couldn't have failed to, really, the way you've always taunted me. Nuclear imbalance, you said, like it was some kind of joke. And now all this. The American Capitalist Oblast. You think that's funny? You damn well think that's *funny*?"

"Titus!" screamed Nadine. "It's true! But I don't want to have to kill Colleen! Please! Listen! If you don't listen, I'll have to kill Colleen! Titus! *Titus*! Damn you, Titus! God curse you, Titus, I love her!"

Titus swung around and punched Nadine with his closed fist, right in the jaw. She fell back and Titus fell down beside her, on his knees, and ripped apart her gown until she was almost naked, except for her stockings and her silk panties.

"Jesus, you're a bitch," he snarled at her. She opened her eyes, concussed, and stared at him as if she didn't know who he was. "Titus?" she whispered.

He dragged down her panties as he jostled himself out of his own clothes, leaving his shirt with its starched collar awry; and then he clambered on top of her. She didn't resist, couldn't. He was too heavy, too powerful, too enraged, too insistent, too drunk. His penis was a weapon; masculine, thrusting, but somehow inanimate. He jammed it into her again and again and again, raping her, because she didn't participate and she didn't

consent; and then he turned her over and jammed it into her
again, and her hands gripped the thick pile of the Persian rug and
tore it out in agonized handfuls. He shuddered, and came deep
inside her tightest place, and she closed her eyes and tried to
hope that this would be her ultimate sacrifice to everything she
had been born and trained to believe in. She couldn't give any
more, except for her life.

Titus stood up, swayed, and tried to focus on her, triumphant
and lewd. "You're *nothing*, you know that? A Washington
whore. A political groupie. You know that? You make me
sick." Then, with an inaccurate gait, he made for the door.

Nadine sat up amongst the rags of her torn evening-gown.
There were vivid red fingermarks on her breasts, and on her
stomach. Her head ached with a sharp, shrill, endless pain. She
lowered her head in sexual defeat, and felt a trickle of fluid
escape from her battered openings. Titus had invaded her and her
privacy, both erotically and politically, without care, without any
feeling at all; as if she were there to be used, and nothing else.
He had denied her where Colleen had aroused her and accepted
her; he had given her coldness and cruelty where Colleen had
given her kisses and understanding. And yet the irony was that it
was Colleen whom Ikon had asked her to kill; and Titus whom
Ikon had asked her to care for.

Titus came back into the room, pushing the door open so hard
that it banged against one of the occasional tables.

"Are you coming to bed?" he demanded.

"No," she said. Then, "Yes."

"Listen," he enunciated. Then, more softly, "Listen. I'm sorry
I hit you. Sorry I hurt you. You just—made me lose my temper."

He looked down and saw her naked among the shreds of her
gown and the flicker in his eyes told her that he was aroused
again. Titus was a soldier, after all. His success had always been
measured by the pain inflicted on other people. That was what
soldiers were for. He had hurt her; badly; and yet he felt
triumphant.

Later, he whispered in her ear, "That stuff about Russia."

"Yes?" She could imagine her voice rising to the high molded
ceiling like an airship filled with chilled helium.

"Well, that was bullshit, wasn't it?"

"If that's what you want to think."

"The American Capitalist Oblast? I mean, that's a joke, right? A sharp, intellectual joke. A little too sharp for a regular patriotic guy like me."

"You're still drunk."

"No, I'm not. There wasn't one single officer in Nam who could drink me under the table. Not one. And in those days we were drinking Chivas Regal with Singha Beer chasers. You know Singha Beer? Comes from Thailand. Two—just *two* of those—would wipe your average American beer drinker out completely."

"Titus, it's true. Ikon is true. The American Oblast exists; and has for twenty years."

Titus squeezed his eyes shut. "Nadine," he said. "You and I are going to talk about this in the morning. You got me? And another thing we're going to talk about is your fucking children, all right? Got that? Meanwhile I'm going to go crash out on the library couch."

"Thank God for that," she told him. The bitterness in her voice was like lemon juice on a cut.

He stood and watched her as she got up painfully from the floor, gathered her torn clothes, and limped towards the stairs. He couldn't even begin to understand at that moment the agony she felt; not just physically, from what he had done to her, but mentally. There was no alternative left to her now but to poison Colleen Petley; no hope but to destroy the one person in whom she had felt able to invest her romantic trust.

"Oblast, for Christ's sake," said Titus, as she passed him.

It was only at five o'clock that morning, when Titus awoke to find his cheek pressed against the shiny brown leather of the library couch, bathed in the dribble coming out of the side of his mouth, that he thought for the very first time that Nadine might not have been joking; and that Ikon's administration might for twenty years have been a hideous reality. He sat up: the library clock chimed five. He thought: Jesus H. Christ.

Upstairs, Nadine's bed was empty, cold, and unslept-in. Titus stared at it for almost five minutes. Then he picked up the telephone and dialed Joe Jasper.

TWENTY-FOUR

It had taken furious arguments, slammed doors, and moments of silent pain, but at last Kathy Forbes persuaded Daniel to come with her to Los Angeles. It had taken two days without a telephone call, two days without a ransom note, two days without anything but knots in his stomach and two nights without sleep.

And always, that remembered rhyme,

"My daddy is dead, but I can't tell you how;
He left me six horses to follow the plow:
With my whim-wham waddle-ho!"

Against Kathy's direct advice, Pete Burns had put out a Missing Child poster, with a black-and-white photograph of Susie from Thanksgiving Day.

Pete Burns, as a matter of course, had passed on the details of the case to Lieutenant Berridge in Phoenix. Under "Possible Suspects" was the name "Skellett."

Daniel had left a forwarding address; and on the last Thursday in August they had flown out of Sky Harbor, eastwards at first, and then curving around to the southwest so that he could see the whole criss-cross landscape of Phoenix spreading out towards the New River Mountains.

He had thought of Cara. She was still in hospital, with 26 stitches and three fractured ribs. Then he had glanced at Kathy, sitting next to him, and she had smiled sympathetically and he had felt at least that he was not alone.

Now he and Kathy were installed in a quiet rented cottage just off Sunset Boulevard, and were spending most of their time trying to talk to anyone who could remember Marilyn Monroe. Some agents and actors ate the lunches they bought at the expense of the *Arizona Flag*, and told them apocryphal stories about the night that Marilyn died, or about imaginary arguments between Marilyn and a variety of people, or anything that came into their heads. But most of the Hollywood professionals just shrugged, and averted their eyes, as if Marilyn's going was still a personal embarrassment, as if all of them were individually responsible for that week when she had failed to turn up on the set of *Something's Got to Give*. As if all of them had gathered together and crammed Nembutals down her throat, to extinguish that bleached-blond *angst* forever, and give them, who knows, some kind of haunted peace from the sexual spirit of the late 1950s.

Every one of them said, "She'd be 56 years old now, if she were still alive, you know that? Fifty-six years old. She would have *hated* it."

And most of them said, "You want to know about Marilyn? What for? It's all over. It's all dead and buried."

Then, by chance, they met Rollo Sekulovich.

It was on the morning of the third day. They were eating breakfast at the counter of the Sunset Hyatt, and Daniel had just come back from the pay phone, checking with Pete Burns to find out if there was any news of Susie. The restaurant smelled of burned coffee and bacon; and there was that jangled conversation of businessmen who have just woken up; wives who are just about to go out shopping; waitresses who refuse to serve anything that isn't written on the menu.

Kathy asked, "Any news?"

Daniel shook his head. "Nothing. Not even a ransom note."

"That isn't a bad sign."

"It isn't a *good* sign, either."

"I know. I'm not going to pretend that everything's fine and dandy. It's not my style."

Daniel sat down, and stared at his plate of Canadian bacon and eggs. "You think they've killed her?" he asked.

"No," said Kathy. "Everything points away from it. I mean, why would they kill her? If they want money, they'll keep her alive; if they want a hostage they'll keep her alive. If they want *you*, they'll keep her alive."

"Why would they want me?"

"Maybe a little Air Force bird told them that you'd been snooping around the morgue at Williams Air Force Base. Maybe that's the whole reason they kidnapped her."

"If they want me, why don't they contact me? It's this damned *silence*. I don't know if she's dead or alive. I don't know where she is, or what they might have done to her. And she's *mine*, you know? My daughter. My responsibility."

Kathy reached across the table and touched his hand. "You've got to stop blaming yourself. It wasn't your fault."

"Nobody else was responsible. Not even her mother."

"Have you gotten in touch with her mother?"

"Candii? What for? She wouldn't care. Too busy whooping it up somewhere with some poor man's Howard Keel."

It was then that a man in a loud purple blazer sat down next to them, and said, "Okay if I join you people?"

"Go ahead," said Daniel. Then, to Kathy, "Who have we got on the list today? Did you manage to get in touch with MGM? Isn't there anybody else who might have known what Marilyn did on that last night? The police, maybe, or doctors?"

"Excuse me," said the man in the purple blazer, "are you talking about Marilyn Monroe?"

Daniel and Kathy looked at each other, and then Daniel said guardedly, "That's right. We're, uh, journalists. Writing a book on famous scandals in Hollywood."

"Well, there's always plenty of material," the man grinned. He reminded Daniel of Ed Koch, only shorter. "But when you talk about Marilyn, then you're talking. That was a scandal, all right. You talk about Marilyn and half the people in Hollywood start shitting their pants, even today, if you'll excuse my Hebrew. I knew Marilyn. Sure, you don't have to look surprised. I knew Marilyn just about as well as my cousin Fruma. And, to tell you the truth, there wasn't much in it, except Fruma has a bigger chest.''

Kathy said, ''You saw Marilyn the night she died? Or that week?''

The man said, ''Better than that. Or more *interesting* than that. But listen, I should introduce myself. Rollo Sekulovich, I'm an agent. Most people call me R.S. You've heard of Christy Welcome? She's one of my girls. Girls, I handle mainly. New girls, giving them some kind of movie work without the necessity to screw producers, excuse me. Call me a one-man social mission, if you like. But Christy Welcome didn't have to sleep with Don Oppenheim to get that lead part in *Triple Murder*; and Jean Prisnik didn't have to sleep with Jim Martin, although she did. Well, she liked him, he's a nice guy.''

Kathy forked up the last slice of her tropical-fruit salad. ''You want to tell us about Marilyn?''

''Marilyn, sure. It's an interesting story. Maybe you won't believe it, who knows? But you can always check. Maybe the Brentwood police know somebody who remembers that night, one of their officers. It was twenty years ago, right? But I can remember it like today. You want to know why? I had a new girl called Vera Rutledge. What a name, you know? Vera Rutledge. Sometimes I think people become actors just to get rid of their crappy names, excuse me.''

''What about Vera Rutledge?'' Kathy persisted.

''She was terrific,'' said Rollo Sekulovich. ''She was blond, natural blond, and she looked exactly like Marilyn. Marilyn had a nose-job, you know that, but Vera didn't need anything like that. She looked like Marilyn *should* have looked like, only her big disadvantage was that Marilyn happened to have looked like that *first*. Ten years earlier, I could have made her a big-name star. She had that luminous look about her skin, you know, like Marilyn had; and that kind of innocent-sexy come-hither look in her eyes. Vera Rutledge, one of the great names that never was.''

''What happened to her?'' asked Daniel.

''This is the point,'' said Rollo Sekulovich. ''Vera Rutledge was invited to a party the same night that Marilyn died . . . a party that Marilyn was expected to go to as well. I tipped off my

friends on the *Times* that there was going to be a good look-alike
picture if they could get Vera and Marilyn together—you know
the kind of thing I'm talking about—'Marilyn meets Marilyn,' or
'The Twin Monroes,' or something like that. Well—about midnight I'm still working on a new contract for one of my latest
girls—Darlene Hughes, I think it was—and this guy Rick Montez
calls me from the *Times* and says neither Vera nor Marilyn
showed up at this party, and of course he's pissed about it,
excuse me."

"It's a matter of history where Marilyn was," said Kathy.
"So what are you telling me that's new? A starlet called Vera
Rutledge didn't show up to the same party twenty years ago that
Marilyn Monroe didn't show up to?"

"No, listen to me," said Rollo Sekulovich. "Neither of them
was ever seen alive again. Marilyn Monroe was said to have
taken an overdose of sleeping-pills, Vera Rutledge disappeared
without a trace. I hired two private detectives to look for her,
Vera; but they had to give up after six months. They found some
strays, all right, and how many corpses of young girls, you'd be
amazed. Two murderers were prosecuted as a result of that
investigation, and one of them went to prison for life. But I
never found Vera. She just vanished, piff, the same night that
Marilyn died, just like she was a ghost or something; just like
she and Marilyn were part of the same person."

Kathy said, "Where did Vera live, Mr. Sekulovich? In Los
Angeles?"

"She lived with her mother in Van Nuys. Not far from where
Marilyn used to live with Jim Dougherty, when she was first
married. Her mother always used to say that the Rutledge family
were friends with the Doughertys, but I believe that was just a
story. Her mother lives there still."

Daniel finished his breakfast and pushed away his plate. "Mr.
Sekulovich," he said, "why did you tell us all this?"

Rollo Sekulovich made a silly, sentimental face. "You want
to know the truth? That Vera Rutledge was always a fantasy to
me. I never took her to bed. I was true to my wife, God rest her
soul. I always thought I had principles. But Vera Rutledge was
special; much more special to me than Marilyn ever was. If you
could have made Marilyn perfect, and bright, then that's what

Vera was. And I sent her off to that party that night. 'It'll be good for your career,' I told her. 'Just go.' And so she went, and I never saw her again. Never.''

Daniel thought of Susie, that he might never see Susie again for all he knew. Vera Rutledge and Marilyn Monroe and Susie Korvitz, fellow wanderers in a mysterious dimension.

That afternoon, they drove out to Brentwood. Before they went to Mandeville Canyon Road, where Lieutenant Lindblad lived, they took a left off Sunset Boulevard and drove slowly past the rows of exclusive cul-de-sacs called Helena Drives. There are twenty-five Helena Drives, eighteen of them south of Sunset; and on Fifth Helena Drive, Marilyn Monroe used to live, and was supposed to have died.

They stopped. It was a hot, smoggy afternoon; the sun was screened by mid-day pollution. The engine of their rented Monaco burbled and whistled, but on Fifth Helena Drive that was the only sound, apart from a distant radio playing, with almost absurd irony, *Candle in the Wind*. It occurred to Daniel that it could actually have been possible for Elton John to have known Norma Jean; if only anyone had realized that she was hiding in Phoenix in fear of her life, under the assumed name of Margot Schneider.

Kathy said, ''That's the Monroe house. Not much, is it?''

''It doesn't look like anything at all. A cement-brick hacienda.''

Kathy said, ''Please have courage. I'm sure Susie's all right.''

''Courage? What the hell does courage have to do with it?''

''I'm not sure. But it'll help.''

''If you say so.''

Lieutenant Lindblad lived in a small white combed-stucco bungalow with red Mexican tiles on the roof and a wrought-iron sign on the wall announcing that this was La Casita Mia. He was sprinkling the lawn when they drew up, a thin sixty-seven-year-old in a white short-sleeved shirt and light gray slacks, the kind of man from whom all the flesh seems to have shrunk, leaving nothing beneath his darkly-tanned skin but sinews and bones and arteries. His clip-on sunglasses were raised, revealing eyes that were faded by years of sun and years of detective work. He raised his hand in greeting as they approached, and Daniel could see his loose ropes of muscle rolling around on top of his arm. A walking anatomy lesson.

"You folks care for some guacamole? My wife made some fresh. Makes the best guacamole in Greater Los Angeles, I can tell you. Rosa, come out and say hi."

A pretty, plump Mexican woman came out of the house, her hair stuck up in combs, and smiled and shook hands and said, "hi," and "hi," and that was about all. She wore a bright crimson-and-yellow frock that just about managed to contain her enormous breasts and her huge haunches, and she jiggled back into the bungalow as if every part of her body was dancing to a different maracas-player.

"She's a terrific woman, Rosa," said Lieutenant Lindblad. "My second wife. Just the sort of woman I always wanted. My first wife was thin and mean and sour as hell. I wanted a woman I could get hold of. You know what I mean? Never had so much damned fun in my whole life."

They sat inside, in the cool, around a glass table with black wrought-iron legs, and ate guacamole with fresh-baked taco chips and drank Budweiser. "I came from Wisconsin originally, did my training in Milwaukee. Can't touch this Western beer, not for nothing."

Daniel said, "They told us round at the police station that you were concerned with the Vera Rutledge disappearance. Well, they checked it in the files."

Lieutenant Lindblad steadily ground up a taco chip between his dentures. He took a swallow of Bud. Then he said, "Vera Rutledge, huh? I thought you said you were writing a book on famous Hollywood scandals."

"Wasn't Vera Rutledge a scandal?"

"Vera Rutledge was a disappearance, that was all."

"Routine, yes? Nothing special about it?"

"Not that I remember."

"I'm surprised you remember it at all," said Kathy. "It was more than twenty years ago, after all. Just one case in a hundred thousand."

"She disappeared the night Monroe died, that's all. That's why I remember it."

"And she looked like Monroe?"

"I guess so. That was one description."

There was a very long silence. Lieutenant Lindblad looked from Daniel to Kathy and then back again. "Is that all you want to know?" he asked them.

"It depends whether that's all you're going to tell us," said Kathy.

"What's to tell? I was on duty that night; I was given a report that some blond young starlet was missing. Then it came over the radio that we were supposed to go round to Fifth Helena, because Marilyn Monroe was suffering from some kind of an overdose. That's all. That's all I remember. We put out the usual searches for Vera Rutledge. We found quite a few bodies, quite a few stray starlets, but then you always do when you comb Hollywood real thorough. You could do it today and you'd find the same. But we never found Vera Rutledge."

"What time was Vera Rutledge reported missing?"

"Ten o'clock maybe. I don't exactly remember."

"And what time was Marilyn reported to have O.D.'d?"

"Listen," said Lieutenant Lindblad, sharply. His dentures made a loud clicking noise. "You want history, you go to the history books. Don't bother me about it. I was only doing my job."

"The history books are full of lies and discrepancies," Kathy insisted. "You know they are, because you were actually there, and you know what happened."

"What are you trying to say, that something happened different?"

"I *know* something happened different."

"Well, there's no use in asking me. I don't remember too much about it. It was one of those nights, you know? Pretty confused. Lots of publicity, lots of confusion. And everybody lying their asses off to protect their reputations."

Daniel said, "We know that Marilyn Monroe didn't die that night."

Lieutenant Lindblad stared at him. "Are you crazy?"

Daniel shook his head. His heart was bouncing like a dolphin at Sea World, but he was determined to stick to his story. "Marilyn Monroe didn't die that night, but somebody did. Some girl who hadn't eaten supper, like Marilyn had. Marilyn ate supper that night with Bobby Kennedy and Peter Lawford, as well as Pat Newcomb, and her housekeeper Mrs. Murray. But the autopsy on the girl's body showed that her stomach and her intestines were completely empty. Only her blood was thick with barbiturates.''

Kathy said, in her gentlest voice, ''On the same night in 1962, Marilyn Monroe was supposed to have died in mysterious circumstances; and a girl who looked almost exactly like her disappeared without a trace. Twenty years later, in Phoenix, Arizona, a woman was murdered; a woman who in all probability is Norma Jean Baker, aged 57. So what kind of a conclusion can you draw now?''

Lieutenant Lindblad said, ''What are you trying to suggest? Why don't you say it straight?''

''You want me to?'' said Kathy.

Lieutenant Lindblad sucked thoughtfully and anxiously at his dentures. Then he said, ''I don't know why you want to dig all of this up. It's all dead and buried, twenty years ago. It doesn't make no difference, not now. If that woman who was murdered was Norma Jean; well, what of it? What difference does it make? They're both dead now; and so are Jack and Bobby, and that's the end of it.''

''Lieutenant, that isn't the end of it. That's just the very beginning. Marilyn Monroe was hustled out of Brentwood in 1962 because she knew something she shouldn't have known. And maybe Bobby Kennedy was trying to protect her. But he couldn't protect her after he was dead; and after twenty years someone found her and killed her. And if what she knew was important enough for someone to look for her for twenty years, then believe me it must have been damned important. I don't know *how* important, I'll admit that. But people don't get sacrificed for nothing, not even by Kennedys.''

Lieutenant Lindblad put down his beer, stood up, and went to the door. His wife Rosa was cheerily cooking in the kitchen. He gave her a little finger-wave and then closed the door. Then he went to the window and looked up and down the street. ''You don't have no microphone, do you?'' he asked Kathy. ''I don't want no record of this; not in my own voice.''

Kathy raised her hands to show that she was clean. Daniel did the same.

"How much is this worth?" asked Lieutenant Lindblad.

"What's the bottom line?" Kathy wanted to know.

"Two thousand, cash."

"Fifteen hundred, that's all I've got."

"Okay, then," said Lieutenant Lindblad. "Money first."

Kathy opened her purse, took out the large roll of bills which the *Flag* had given her for buying street information in Los Angeles, and stripped off $1,500. It left her with nothing more than two $20s, and a $5. Lieutenant Lindblad took the money and pushed it into his back pants pocket without a murmur.

He poured out three more beers, and then settled down in his armchair.

"I'm going to say this once only, okay, and I'm not going to repeat myself. You don't take notes, got it, and you don't make no recordings; and if you ever ask me again if this is what I've said, then I'll deny it. I'll deny that I've even seen you, and so will Rosa. So don't try to get funny. I've still got plenty of friends on the force, and I still carry my own gun, I'm entitled. So don't try to get funny."

"I promise you that neither of us will try to get funny," said Daniel.

Lieutenant Lindblad gave him a wary look. But Daniel managed to keep his face deadly serious; and at last Lieutenant Lindblad said, "Right. This is the way it happened. Way back in August, 1962 . . . this is the way it really happened."

TWENTY-FIVE

Joe Jasper carefully hung up the phone and ran his hand through his hair. On the other side of the room, on a makeshift cot, Crack Nielsen was still swaddled in a pink blanket, his mouth gaping open, snoring his way through sixty cords of good dreamland lumber. Joe looked at him for a while, pursing his lips, then got up from his own bed and went through to the living-room and opened the drapes.

Colleen was already up, although it was only a minute or two past seven o'clock. She was wearing a pale-green baby-doll nightie in flounces of transparent nylon, through which her nipples showed with unremitting prominence. Joe ignored her. He was not a sexual creature in the conventional sense; he was not aroused by America's naked big-breasted babies, or by women in general.

Joe Jasper was aroused only by humiliation; and by hurt. If he had any credo in life, it was probably that the obedient and the masochistic will eventually inherit the earth.

"You're up early," he told Colleen.

"I haven't been to bed yet."

"What time did you get in?"

"Four."

"Crack was with you?"

"Most of the time."

"You realize you're running a risk, going out so much?"

"Fuck it, Joe, Nadine said I could. Besides, I'm not *The Prisoner of Zenda*."

"I didn't say you were. But you've known all along that you'd have to do this someday. Stay inside, keep yourself safe. That's valuable evidence you've got there."

"Don't you keep reminding me. It was me who had to do what Marshall Roberts wanted. Not you. Or maybe you would have liked to."

"What was the difference between Marshall Roberts and any other man? You do it all the time."

"I do it when I feel like it for money. That's all. With Marshall Roberts, I got paid."

"Such a hardship."

"Asshole."

Joe Jasper went to the drinks cabinet and poured himself a large DOM liqueur. It was dry and strong and if you were going to drink first thing in the morning in the company of transparently-clad whores, it was probably the best drink going. Colleen watched him, and said, "I don't even know what the hell this is all about."

"You're not supposed to. Nobody is supposed to. Not even *I* know what it's all about. Not completely."

"Well, that shows what a cretin *you* are."

Joe took a mouthful of liquor, and closed his eyes. In actual fact, he was desperately worried, although he was trying his utmost not to show it to Colleen. If Titus believed for one moment that Nadine was right, and that the United States really *had* become the American Capitalist Oblast in the summer of 1962; then there was a strong possibility that Titus would allow Marshall Roberts to go ahead with RINC II, and seriously threaten Kama's chances of taking over from Ikon as chairman of the Oblast committee. Titus was a hawk; and he hated Marshall Roberts for giving so much away to the Russians in the RINC talks. But Titus was also a patriot, fierce and dogged; and if he was brought to perceive that RINC was the lesser of two threats to what was left of the American nation; if he actually understood that RINC would mean only a gradual decline in

American influence, while Kama wanted an immediate takeover on all levels, then Titus would withdraw his opposition at once, and leave Joe holding the tar-baby.

On the phone this morning, Titus had said that he was "anxious, to say the least" about the things that Nadine had told him. Joe had denied any knowledge of an American Oblast. In fact, he had laughed out loud. Was Nadine serious? How could the United States possibly be run by a Soviet committee? It was just a gag; a way of making Titus feel uncomfortable about putting such an immediate stop to the RINC talks. They both knew how strongly Nadine felt about nuclear disarmament. She was a liberal, wasn't she? That was the kind of thing you had to expect from liberals.

But all the time, Joe had detected in Titus' voice a lack of sureness; a suspicion that Nadine would never have told him such a preposterous story if something about it hadn't been true. I mean, the *Russians* running the United States for twenty years? Did she really expect a hardnosed soldier like Titus to swallow anything so patently stupid? You only had to look at America, didn't you? Free, prosperous, and as nutty as ever. Would the Russians allow Times Square sleaze; or whores in hotpants on Hollywood Boulevard? Would the Russians allow drugs, and booze, and profiteering? America hadn't changed, or had it? Look at all the money we've been spending on defense. What was the point of *that*, if Russia was in charge? Would the Russians finance MX, or B-1 bombers, or cruise missiles that were targeted straight towards the heart of Moscow?

Except, of course, if the Russians had theorized that the United States was too large and too hostile to be conquered in the usual way in which nations are conquered; that perhaps the easiest way of taking over a prosperous and opinionated continent of 220 million people would be simply to reach out and grasp the reins of finance and power, and leave the body of the nation to continue to grow in its own characteristic way, at least for the time being.

And further, except if the Russians had theorized that a balance of armed conflict was necessary for global stability; and in particular for stability within the Soviet Union itself, and its satellites. For who within the Soviet bloc would knuckle down to the Communist regime if there was no threat from the West? Who would tolerate a life of repression and deprivation, of lines and boredom and no fresh meat, if there was no corrupt capitalist ogre at the gates, waving his nuclear club?

Joe knew Titus well enough to guess that thoughts like these must at least have flickered through Titus' mind; and that Kama's succession to the committee could immediately and substantially be threatened. Joe had been tempted to argue with Titus, but he had managed to control himself sufficiently to say nothing more than, "Well, sir . . . it all seems pretty far-fetched to me. I mean, I haven't seen anybody on Constitution Avenue with snow on their boots."

Colleen said, "I'm hungry. Is anybody going to fix breakfast?"

"What do you want?" Joe asked her, with considerable self-control.

"I don't know. Eggs, maybe. Bacon."

"Why don't you fix it yourself?"

Colleen looked up at him. There was nothing in her eyes at all, no sympathy, no friendship, nothing. She was a whore and she knew her value. She knew when she was needed and she knew when she wasn't needed, and exactly how much. Right now, Joe Jasper needed her badly. She didn't understand what it was all about, but she could smell his fear.

"Okay," said Joe. "I'll see what I can rustle up. You want muffins with it? Juice?"

Colleen didn't answer, and after a moment or two, Joe Jasper turned around and marched himself stiffly in to the kitchenette. Fuck it, he thought, as he tied on a vinyl apron. Fuck all women to hell. He opened up the Tupperware box in the refrigerator and took out a pack of bacon. If he didn't need that woman so badly, he'd slice her from cunt to chin, and feed her to the State Department dogs.

There was a chime at the front door. He wiped his hands and went to answer it, but Colleen had reached the lobby first. To Joe's horror, it was Nadine, in a severe white linen suit, with a smart white-feathered hat, with a net veil.

"Joe," Nadine nodded. "I like your apron."

Joe looked at himself. It was one of those aprons with a woman's curvaceous body printed on it, complete with heavy-duty bra and garter-black frilly belt. Colleen laughed, and her breasts jounced up and down beneath the garishly-green nylon of her nightie.

"How do you do, Mrs. Alexander," said Joe, trying to twist his mouth into something like a smile of welcome. "The Secretary was on the phone a little earlier; asking about you."

"I left the house early, before he woke up," said Nadine, and stalked confidently into the center of the living-room, where she rolled off her white net gloves. "Are you making breakfast? I'd adore some coffee."

"How do you like it?" asked Joe, with humiliated wrath.

Nadine handed him her gloves, in a small white snowball, and then her hat. "Impenetrably black," she said, in an exaggeratedly husky voice.

While Joe began to grill the bacon and perk the coffee, Nadine and Colleen went through to the bedroom. Colleen was erotic and immediate: she tugged her baby-doll nightie over her head, so that she was naked, and then came up and held Nadine close, and kissed her full on the mouth.

"I've missed you," she whispered. She pressed her bare breasts against Nadine's immaculately-tailored white suit. She kissed her again, and then touched her mouth with her fingertips, as if she could scarcely believe that her kisses were real.

"You've been out," said Nadine. "A friend of mine saw you last night at Ulvaro's."

"You can't keep me in prison," said Colleen.

"I think that from now on I'm going to have to. The situation is getting very dangerous."

Colleen kissed her again, and again, so fiercely that she smudged her lipstick. Nadine tried to pull away, but Colleen gripped her arms and held her tight. "Make love to me," she insisted.

"Now? What about Joe?"

"That's what you came for, isn't it, to make love to me?"

"I came—" Nadine hesitated. She turned her head away, and looked down at the white kid purse in her hand; the purse which contained the poison which Ikon had given her. She had almost let it slip out, completely and frankly, "I came to kill you." She had been thinking of nothing else all night and somehow it seemed quite natural; to blurt it out. That was why she hadn't slept. "Yes, I came to make love to you."

"My darling," smiled Colleen. Her eyes darted from side to side as they took in the pleasure of Nadine's face. "My famous, elegant, sophisticated darling."

Colleen lay back on the rumpled quilt of the bed as if she were diving backwards in slow-motion into a swimming-pool. The quilt was eau-de-nil, silk, and could have been shimmering water. She parted both her lips and her thighs as she fell back, her lips licked and moist, her sex open and slippery as a morning flower. Perhaps she had made love to a man last night; perhaps her slipperiness was simply the result of heated dreams. Whatever it was, Nadine knelt at the end of the bed and pressed her face deeply into it as if it were a fleshy oxygen mask, as if she needed to breathe it as well as taste it.

"Nadine," Colleen gasped. Then, "*Nadine . . .*"

She lifted her legs high so that Nadine could explore every crevice of her; and it was then that Nadine reached across with one blind hand until she found her purse, and twisted it open, and took out of it the syringe of cyanide which Ikon had given her.

Colleen was panting, tugging at Nadine's hair, pulling Nadine's face as close as she could, writhing, tossing her head from side to side, feeling Nadine's endlessly lapping tongue against her peaked-up clitoris.

"Nadine, what you do to me . . ."

Nadine held the hypodermic in her right hand like a dagger. It only needed one stab; one single drop would be enough. She drew back her arm and closed her eyes and prepared herself to dig the needle deep into Colleen's upraised thigh.

It was then that the door racketed wide open and a high-pitched voice screamed, "Freeze! Freeze! You touch her with that needle and I'll blow your goddamned head off!"

Nadine lifted her head with a breathless gasp; her cheeks flushed and her mouth glistening with Colleen's fluids. At that instant, Colleen rolled away across the bed.

Joe Jasper was standing in the doorway with a huge .357 Magnum held in both hands, pointed straight at Nadine's neck. His eyes were wide and his mouth was contorted into an Eduard

Munch grimace. The revolver was so heavy that he could scarcely keep it still. Colleen reached for her bathwrap and struggled into it, tying the belt tight around her waist, glancing from Joe to Nadine and back again in confused terror.

"All right, Mrs. Alexander, you drop the needle, you understand me? You drop it. Right there, on the rug. That's it. Now, get up, please, and back off right to the wall."

Nadine brushed straight her skirt as she stepped back against the bedroom wall. She left the hypodermic on the thick white rug, glistening in the morning sunlight. Joe Jasper came forward and picked it up.

"What's this? Strychnine? Cyanide?"

Nadine didn't answer. Joe held the hypodermic up towards Colleen, and said, "This is how much your precious Mrs. Alexander has been looking after you. Making love to you with one hand, and getting ready to murder you with the other. So what do you think about that?"

"That's *poison*?" asked Colleen, in shock.

"It's just a sedative," said Nadine. "All I wanted to do was to make sure you stayed in the house today."

"A sedative?" asked Joe, disbelievingly. "All right, if it's a sedative, why don't you show us yourself? Here . . . inject this into your own arm. Then we'll see just what kind of a sedative it is."

Nadine said, "Don't be ridiculous. I'm only trying to keep Colleen from going out. Titus wanted to make sure that she was around today."

"Mr. Alexander called me this morning before you got here," said Joe. "That wasn't the story *he* told me. Mr. Alexander was worried you might be thinking of doing something stupid."

"That's a sedative, nothing else. A solution of chloral hydrate."

"Then prove it."

"I don't have to."

"Oh yes, you do. Crack! Get out of that cot and give me some help! Crack! Do you hear me?"

It was a little while before Crack Neilsen appeared in the doorway, in undervest and jockey-shorts, rubbing his face as if it were made out of the same heavy silicon syrup as a Stretch

Hulk. "What's going on here? Oh, hi, Mrs. Alexander. Hi, Colleen. What's the matter, Joe?"

Joe waved the Magnum towards Nadine. "Mrs. Alexander here wants some help with an injection. Here's the syringe. All you have to do is make sure that she jabs it right into herself. That's it. Right into a vein."

Crack frowned at Joe and then at Nadine. "Have you people had some kind of an argument?"

"Stop asking questions, Crack, for Christ's sake, and just take the syringe and make sure that Mrs. Alexander gets her injection."

Crack hesitated, and then shrugged. "Whatever you say, Joe." He took the syringe and held it up between one stubby finger and one stubby thumb. "What is it, anyway? Dope, or something?"

"Nothing like that. Just a little sleeping potion. That's what Mrs. Alexander says, anyway."

Crack came up to Nadine and lifted up her arm. Nadine stared at Joe with an expression that was cold as Barre granite, and just as unreadable. In response, and maybe in fear, Joe raised the muzzle of the Magnum a little higher. If the hypodermic really contained poison, she would die almost instantly. But if it didn't, he would be faced with the prospect of having to kill her. It wasn't an easy choice to have to contemplate: apart from the repercussions from police and security services, and from Titus himself, he would have to explain himself to Kama. Besides, a .357 Magnum was a completely unsuitable weapon for killing a woman in a white-carpeted bedroom. The whole room would have to be redecorated, ceiling and all.

Crack Nielsen turned to Joe, and asked, "Now?" and in the instant Crack turned, *Jesus*, Joe could see it happening, he could see it taking place right in front of his eyes but Crack was too close to Nadine for him to think of pulling the trigger, apart from all the reservations already inside him. But Nadine seized Crack's wrist, the wrist of the hand which held the hypodermic, and thrust it upwards into Crack's face, so that the needle stuck right up into the fleshy underside of his nose, right up to the chromium hilt, and then she pressed the plunger halfway in before Crack even had time to react.

Crack said, "Shit," and tugged the hypodermic out, and

threw it across the room. Then he lifted his eyes and realized that everybody was staring at him. Joe, Nadine, and Colleen.

"Well," he demanded, "what's so fucking fascinating?"

Joe said to Nadine, "If he dies, I warn you. I'm going to kill you right where you stand."

Colleen moved around the bed, but Joe waved the revolver in her direction, too, and said, "You stay back, lady, or the same thing's going to happen to you."

"If he dies?" Crack demanded. His face looked suddenly and remarkably blue. "What are you talking about, if he dies? What do you mean, *if he dies*?"

The hydrocyanic acid was diffused through Crack's nervous system with frightening speed. He suddenly choked, and tried to reach up to feel his face, but dropped heavily on to his knees. Then, before anybody could touch him or help him, he twisted and fell flat on his back, and lay there shuddering and twitching, and then died.

They knew he was dead. His eyes glassed over, and a bright turquoise tongue slid out from between his parted lips as if it were some disgusting parasitic worm making an unsuccessful attempt to escape from its expired host.

Joe Jasper raised the Magnum again, but Nadine knew now that he wasn't going to shoot her. Not straight away, at least. Not here. Not unless she did something too quick and too foolish.

"They taught you well, didn't they?" he asked her. "But let me tell you here and now, you're not going to get away with it."

"I always had a suspicion that you were one of the *Peredoviki*," Nadine replied. "You were always much too subservient, much too helpful. Nobody could treat anyone like that unless they believed that, ultimately, they were going to be able to rub it all back in their face."

Joe didn't answer, but said to Colleen, loudly, "You see what she really is, Colleen? A traitor. Look at poor Nielsen there. That's what she meant to do to you. Cyanide. You would have been dead by now, like he is."

Colleen stepped back, well away from both Joe and Nadine, her bathwrap clutched around her as if she had been physically chilled by what she had seen, one breast bare, her hair awry.

"Nadine Alexander," Joe told her, loudly, waving the gun with a flourish. "In reality, Nadiana Katia Voroshilova, one of the finest sleeping agents of modern times. Said to have been born as the illegitimate daughter of Kliment Voroshilov, who was the titular head of Russia after Stalin's death; and who is still a symbolic hero from the revolutionary past. Brought to the United States at the age of 17, and planted in the Mayhew family, of Back Bay, Boston, as their adopted daughter. First married to the young, energetic president of Sparling Aeronautics; feeding back to the Soviet Union the complete details of some of America's latest advances in missile guidance. Then, after a discreet affair with General Titus Alexander, and an even more discreet divorce, married to the leading military officer in the U.S. Army and later, of course, to the Secretary of State. Perhaps, next year, to the President. An impressive career. And a very elegant lady. If somewhat dangerous."

Nadine said, "What are you going to do now? I presume that you've decided not to kill me."

"That particular option is still open to me, Mrs. Alexander," said Joe. His face was white and glossy with sweat. "But, right now, I'd prefer to keep you alive. For one thing, I don't want any trouble with the police. And, for another, I want you to go back and tell the Secretary that everything is fine; and well under control; and that everything you told him about Ikon was nothing more than a little bit of left-wing feminist fantasy. Just a way of making him feel bad about stopping the RINC talks."

"You don't seriously think that I'm going to do that, do you?" asked Nadine.

Joe lowered the gun. He looked at it, gently released the hammer, and then laid it on the bedroom side-table.

"Mrs. Alexander," he said, taking out his handkerchief, unfolding it, and carefully dabbing the sweat away from his face, "this room is fitted with a two-way mirror. Everything you've been doing in here with Ms. Petley, and I mean *everything*, has been photographed and recorded."

Nadine looked quickly at Colleen, but Colleen did nothing but shrug in apparent mystification.

"It was always your weakness, wasn't it?" smiled Joe. "It was your weakness at school; and later, of course, when you first moved to Boston. That's right, we have records of what you did at school.''

Nadine pressed her hands together in front of her mouth, as if she were thinking deeply, or praying.

Joe said, "I don't really have to threaten you with a gun, do I? If any of this gets out, Titus' chances of becoming President will evaporate instantly; and any influence *you* ever had in Washington will evaporate, too. It will have to be the biggest female gay scandal since Billie Jean King. Worse. You won't get invited to Girl Scout cookouts any more, let alone White House banquets.''

Nadine turned her face away. She should have realized that Joe Jasper had always been too good, or too slimy, to be true. But the Soviet infiltration of American politics was so complex that often it was impossible to tell if you were talking to an infiltrated Russian or not.

Self-mockingly using the title which had once been given to aristocratic administrators both military and civil in the days before Peter the Great, the infiltrators called themselves *boyars*; and their administration the *boyars' duma*. Percy F. Nash, the Comptroller of the Currency, was a *boyar*. So was the Chairman of the Board of Immigration Appeals, Frank Runcie. The Ikon administration had spread across the entire breadth of the United States on many different levels; in twenty years it had penetrated thousands of political and bureaucratic offices like an undetected cancer. Often, the head of a government or local department would be "straight," a genuine American, unaware of Ikon's control; while his subordinates would all be *boyars*. With particular exceptions, Ikon's policy had been to extend his influence through the executive stratum, and it had all been achieved in almost complete secrecy.

Nadine said, "I suppose I should be grateful that you didn't shoot me straight away; and that your simian friend here didn't manage to inject me.''

"I doubt if Ikon will be pleased," grinned Joe. "Come to that, I don't suppose Kama will be very well pleased, either.''

"What should I do now?" asked Nadine.

"Go home, that's all. Apologize to Titus for being so hysterical. Explain that it was all a mistake. Then call me, and tell me that it all went well.''

"You're quite a rat, you know," said Nadine.

Joe raised his hands, as if in surrender. "It's the part I play the best. They trained me for four years at Severo-Zadonsk, where Lee Harvey Oswald was trained. You probably would have liked me before."

"I doubt it," said Nadine, frostily. "As you so rightly point out, my real weakness is for other women."

"Those pictures would fetch a fortune on 42nd Street," Joe mocked her. "*The Lady and the Tramp.*"

It was only when Joe moved towards her that Nadine realized how Colleen Petley had been edging her way around the bedroom behind him; and how Colleen was now only a foot away from the table where the revolver was lying. She stared at Colleen and her eyes widened; but Colleen gave her a stare in return which defied her to say anything, defied her to do anything but stay where she was. She looked back at Joe, and Joe was just opening up his handkerchief again, his face slightly contorted in preparation for blowing his nose, and every split-second seemed like eternity.

Colleen lifted the Magnum off the table, and raised it up in both hands, cocking back the hammer as she did so. She took up the stance of an educated shootist, ignoring the way that her bathwrap fell away and revealed her naked body. Nadine half-lifted her hand; Joe flicked up his eyes and saw the expression on her face; and then the Magnum went off with a bang like a jet airplane breaking the sound barrier, and Joe's pants exploded in a spray of blood and nylon locknit.

Still clutching his handkerchief, shocked, goggle-eyed, Joe looked down at his shattered crotch. What remained of his genitals was a crisis of blood and muscle. He said, "Wha—" and then Colleen fired again, and this time the bullet entered the back of his head, expanding his face for one fraction of a moment as if it were a balloon. Then everything blew apart, and he toppled around sideways, leaving a mist of blood in the air, and bounced dead onto the bed, and then on to the floor.

Colleen threw the gun down beside him. She made no attempt to fasten her wrap. Nadine stared down at the body; then across at Crack Nielsen; then back at Colleen.

"It seems as if *you're* not everything you've been pretending to be, either," said Nadine.

"Not all Americans are innocent," said Colleen. She gave a wry, quick smile. "We've known about Ikon for years."

"Who *are* you?"

"I'm Colleen Petley, that's all you have to know. I should kill you, too, except that I have specific instructions to make sure that you're safe. Compromised, but safe."

"Supposing *I* tried to kill *you*? I did, after all, didn't I?"

"Yes," said Colleen. She ran her hand through her hair, the gesture of somebody who hates what has happened, but has to be resigned to it. "Yes, I could be dead by now. So could you. But I suppose that both of us are used to taking risks, in our own particular way."

"You belong to some kind of resistance movement? Is that it?" asked Nadine.

"You could say that."

"Well, we've always felt that there might be some kind of organized opposition. I mean, it's difficult to tell, this country being so *naturally* violent. But those bombs that were found in Greenwich Village last year—we seriously suspected that *they* were going to be used against Soviet targets."

Colleen walked around Joe Jasper's body and stood silent for a moment. Then she said, "We started off as rebels against America. You know that, don't you? Black Panthers, the Weather Underground, the Symbionese Army. We wanted to see an end to capitalism and the absolute death of prejudice. Then we realized that this country we were fighting against wasn't the country we believed it to be. Our Presidents were puppets; our whole way of life was a carefully-preserved sham. And nobody seemed to understand—or if they did understand, to *care*! None of us knows how it happened, or when exactly; but we guess that it was sometime in the '60s. Something happened then, and it was like national shock; the same sort of shock that a human body suffers when you shoot a bullet into it. An alien intrusion, you know? Something that sends shudders to every quarter of your body, down to your toes. That intrusion was Ikon. And as soon as we found out what it was all about, we amalgamated ourselves together, Black Panthers and Weather Underground and all, and we made up our minds that you bastards weren't going to get away with it, not easily, anyhow; and that if nobody else was going to carry the torch for liberty, then we would. We call ourselves Free Columbia. You know?"

"You're a terrorist," said Nadine.

"Of a kind. This is the first time I've ever killed anybody."

"But all this blackmail business with Marshall Roberts . . . you don't mean to tell me that it was all planned by *you* . . . by whatever you call yourselves, Free Columbia?"

"We were almost duped ourselves," said Colleen. She sat down on the end of the bed, well away from Joe's twisted body. "We had girls going to bed with as many candidates as we possibly could at the last election; and all of their sessions were filmed. The idea was that we would try to blackmail whichever candidate was elected President, and see what kind of response we got; see what defense mechanisms we could flush out into the open; see if any heads popped up that we could shoot at."

She was silent for what seemed like whole minutes. Then she said, "I had to set myself up as a real Las Vegas hooker. Can you imagine that? I had to invent a background, find myself a pimp, and *be* a hooker. I think it probably wiped me out as far as men are concerned. I think *forever*. That was why I made love with you . . . well, not totally. I did want to put you into a position where you'd be forced to let me go out now and again, so that I could rendezvous with other people from Free Columbia."

She paused again, and then she said, "We didn't realize that there was such an internal struggle within the Soviet administration. We didn't know anything about Kama, or the *Peredoviki*. We simply thought that Joe Jasper wanted to get hold of our video-tapes and photographs and destroy them, to protect the President. That's what he *said* he wanted to do. We thought we'd be doing nothing more than flushing out a few Soviet infiltrators, so that we could waste them."

Another pause. Then, "Kama would be worse than Ikon, wouldn't he? Kama would rip this country apart from top to bottom."

"That's right," said Nadine. "Kama would be hell. Back to the days of the Terror."

Colleen looked at her questioningly. "What are you going to do now? Are you going to try to persuade Titus to let RINC continue?"

"I doubt if he'll listen. I've told him far more than I should have."

"But surely he'll take notice of what you're saying if you tell him about the *Peredoviki*?"

"I don't think so."

Colleen suddenly realized that she had left the gun lying on the carpet, right beside Joe Jasper's body. And she also realized that if Nadine was so deeply pessimistic about her chances of persuading Titus to let RINC go ahead, there was only one positive way left to her to release Titus' grip on Marshall Roberts, and make sure that the disarmament talks went ahead. To kill Titus' principal witness—her. And after all, hadn't Nadine come here this morning with the intention of killing her anyway?

There was a flash of recognition between the two women that was almost electrical, like the crackling current of a generator. Both of them dived towards the gun at the same time; Nadine snatching the grip, but Colleen slapping it out of her hand so that it tumbled heavily across the room.

They wrestled fiercely on the floor, Nadine twisting Colleen's hair and forcing her head back. But as Nadine tried to reach out again for the gun, Colleen grabbed at her white skirt, and wrenched it, and there was a tearing of cotton and silk lining as Colleen rolled her over and pushed her violently against the bed. Colleen scrabbled for the gun now, but Nadine threw herself on top of her, and for minutes on end the two women struggled and scratched and tore at each other. They didn't scream, like women fighting out of jealousy or anger. They both knew that only one of them was going to survive.

Abruptly, Colleen banged her head against the bridge of Nadine's nose. Nadine jerked back in pain, and that moment was all that Colleen needed. She wriggled out from under Nadine and grasped the gun.

Nadine held on to Colleen's wrist with both hands, keeping the gun in the air. Colleen fired once, and the bullet hit the ceiling and showered them both in stucco. They fought and rolled onto Joe Jasper's body, smothering their arms in his blood; then rolled back again across the white carpet, leaving gory tracks. Gasping, Nadine pressed her head close to Colleen's breasts, gritting her teeth and trying to summon up her last particle of energy.

But gradually, in a series of gasping jerks, Colleen brought the gun down so that the muzzle was pointing less than an inch away from Nadine's head. Nadine grunted with strain, but the muzzle was so close now that she could smell the burned gunpowder. She was flooded with the terrifying understanding that she was about to die.

She did the only thing she could think of. She pushed back against Colleen's gun-wrist as forcefully as possible, and buried her teeth deep into Colleen's breast. She tasted blood as Colleen screamed and there was a brief, bloody wrestle. Nadine wrenched the gun out of Colleen's hand, staggered back from her, and pointed it directly at her head.

Colleen's face was a mask. She said something like, "Whatever you do—" and then Nadine pulled the trigger and Colleen's head dissolved in an explosion.

Slowly, stiffly, Nadine stood up. She weaved in place for a while, shivering. Then she walked with dragging feet into the living-room, and sat down on the sofa. Apart from the chambermaid in Nevada, Titus' attempts to blackmail Marshall Roberts were finished; and it was unlikely that the chambermaid's testimony would satisfy a Congressional committee. The videotapes were all here, in the house, in a floor safe which Joe Jasper had arranged to be installed at the same time as Colleen's hot tub.

She reached for the phone beside the sofa, and dialed Ikon's action number. A calm woman's voice answered her, and said, *"How can I help you?"*

"This is V. A matter of utmost urgency. Do you understand? There's been an incident at the Rockville house. Three down with severe headaches. I need clean-up people, also a locksmith. And the first priority is to call our contacts at the Rockville police to keep them away. Somebody must have heard the firecrackers."

"Is that all?" asked the woman's voice, unruffled.

Nadine looked down at her blood-smeared hand, and her torn skirt.

"That's all," she said.

She put down the phone. She sat with her head bent while the clock ticked loudly over the fireplace. Then, she began to weep; silent tears at first, followed by deep, agonized sobs.

TWENTY-SIX

Ikon met Kama at the Smithsonian Institution, in front of the black-painted X-15 aircraft; and they solemnly shook hands. Neither man was alone: there were two dark-suited young body-guards following Ikon at a discreet but watchful distance; and a man in a gray houndstooth jacket following Kama. Ikon wore a camelhair overcoat, even in the summer heat, and looked heavy and unwell. Kama was leaner, taller, and younger, although his head was completely bald and he wore magnifying spectacles which enlarged his bright blue eyes.

It was the first time that Ikon had been out for a month, and he was already coughing and laboring for breath. But there was an understanding now that he and Kama could only meet on neutral territory; the rift in the supervisory committee was too wide and too intricately stratified for Ikon to be able to assert his authority across it. He had long ago begun to lose his strongest supporters in the Kremlin; either through death, or old age, or political unpopularity; or through desertion. Kama, after all, was the younger and the stronger man. Kama had powerful contacts in the international KGB and the Central Committee. And, what was more, Kama was ferociously dedicated to the idea of pub-licly announcing that the United States had been overthrown by Russia, almost to the point of obsession. "The American Capitalist Oblast is *ours*," he used to repeat. "It has been ours for twenty years. We should treat it as ours."

Ikon thrust his hands into his coat pockets and contemplated the black slender shape of the X-15. "America's first thrust into space," he said. "Even before we took over. You have to admire their technology."

Kama gave a noncommittal nod. Ikon was still the titular head of the committee; and Kama wasn't rash enough to disagree with him outright. Kama's whole political career had nearly collapsed in 1961 when he had expressed out loud his support for Khruschev's isolation of China. Even Khruschev had refused to support him; and it was only his friendship with Leonid Brezhnev that had saved him from permanent exile.

The two men walked side by side through the echoing museum. In the next hall, a party of black schoolchildren were giggling and shuffling as their teacher tried to show them around. The light that filtered through the windows had a strangely wintry quality, as if they were back in Moscow.

Kama said, "It was good of you to come out and meet me here. I thought it more discreet."

"Occasionally, I can benefit from the exercise," said Ikon.

Kama gave a tepid smile. "You're thinking of retiring soon, of course."

"As soon as I'm convinced that the American Oblast is in capable hands. And as soon as I'm sure that RINC II is near completion."

Kama said, "You'll have to forgive me, Nikolai Nekrasov, but I do think that these RINC talks are an unnecessary pretense. I may be naive, of course. You're so much wiser and more experienced. But what *is* the use of them, when no American nuclear warhead is capable of being fired? America is already disarmed. Why make such trouble over nuclear reduction talks?"

Ikon raised one bushy, bear-like eyebrow. "You have a great deal to learn about social psychology, Comrade Kama. A whole nation cannot be dragged kicking and screaming into a new philosophical age, not without grave repercussions that can last for decades afterwards. The Soviet Union is a classic example. We have *still* to recover from the October revolution morally, politically, and economically. It will take a hundred years before we do.''

"That sounds remarkably like heresy," smiled Kama.

"Heresy is usually nothing more than the simple truth," Ikon retorted.

They jousted and prodded at each other for another ten minutes; and then Ikon suggested they leave the Institution and take a walk outside. He felt trapped, and suffocated, as much by Kama's relentless opportunism as he did by the Smithsonian. They crossed Jefferson Drive and then walked across the grass of The Mall, towards the Washington Monument, while red and white kites flew around them, and traffic nudged and beeped and growled on either side like a herd of impatient cattle.

Kama said, "You've heard, of course, that Marshall Roberts has decided to *postpone* the RINC talks?"

Ikon checked his watch. Colleen Petley should be dead by now. He had no guarantee of it, of course. Nadine may have run into difficulties with Joe Jasper. But she was an efficient, elegant woman, an extraordinary agent, the very cream of the KGB. There hadn't been a female agent to touch her since Maria Denisova, who had used her sexual abilities to turn the tables against both Churchill and Roosevelt at Yalta, and had later supplied Moscow with some of the most important details of the hydrogen bomb.

Ikon said, "I believe that the President had some temporary difficulty, yes."

"Temporary? If RINC II fails to go ahead, the Sovietization of America could be put back for ten years."

"You exaggerate," said Ikon. "Perhaps five."

"Nikolai Nekrasov, it is essential that the Soviet Union asserts her authority over America *now*. America is still too much of a corrupting influence; American culture is like rabies, driving everybody mad. The whole world will be mad until America is revealed to be subordinate to Moscow—until everybody realizes that political sanity has at last prevailed."

"You want a national massacre?" asked Ikon.

"Of course not, although a certain amount of spilled blood will be unavoidable. America is full of lunatics who say that they would rather die than let the Soviet Union take over. Better dead than Red. But once most of them perceive the conquest as a *fait accompli* . . . well, I truly don't believe that we will experience half the trouble you seem to think we will. The Americans are a tired nation, Nikolai Nekrasov; the fire has gone out of their veins, and has been replaced by cholesterol. Now they want to do nothing else but sit down in front of their television sets and be left alone."

Ikon paused. Out of the corner of his eye, he had seen one of his bodyguards begin to walk diagonally towards him across the grass. The man turned away when he was still fifteen or twenty paces distant; and went with exaggerated thoroughness to peer into a pale blue Chrysler which somebody had parked nearby on a red line.

"An American car enthusiast, huh?" asked Kama, sarcastically. "Or perhaps he's concerned that somebody might be trying to do to *you* what *you* tried to do to Titus Alexander."

"An American car enthusiast," Ikon asserted, without any expression in his voice at all. He didn't tell Kama that the bodyguard's walk towards him was a pre-arranged signal which meant that the bodyguard had received direct news on his walkie-talkie from Rockville. A turn to the left would have meant bad news. A turn to the right had meant that everything was satisfactory, and under control.

Nadine must have been able to kill Colleen Petley. Now the horse was answering to a different driver. Ikon turned to Kama, and he was unable to suppress a grandfatherly smile.

Kama said, "I came here to suggest that we could come to some arrangement, you and I. The ideological differences between us seem to grow wider every day. But they needn't. You are old, Nikolai Nekrasov, you have to admit your years. And while I am always respectful of age, and the wisdom that comes with it, I believe that you have been neglecting the natural progress of America towards her inevitable acceptance of what she really is: a Soviet possession."

"Well?" asked Ikon. "What is your suggestion?"

"I suggest your resignation," Kama told him. "You have achieved tremendous things; but it must be time for you to go. The failure of RINC II shows that gradualism is no longer the answer. But, if you agree to resign, I believe that you should be allowed to stay in the American Capitalist Oblast as a figurehead, as a grand old man to whom the American people can turn in their hour of disillusionment and surprise. We can announce you as the man who has personally taken care of the American republic for over twenty years; the man who took onto his shoulders the enormous burden of preparing America for the day when she would have to be told that the Soviet Union has been in effective control of her government since August 6, 1962. Red Monday.''

Ikon carefully cleared his throat. "Is that all?" he asked. "Is that the sum-total of your suggestion? Is that why I got myself dressed this afternoon, and came out to the Smithsonian, instead of taking my usual rest?"

"Nikolai Nekrasov," said Kama, more sharply now, "you have no hope of staying in control of the Supervisory Committee once Moscow becomes aware that RINC II has utterly failed. Even the moderates will ask for faster results; and your failure will feed added fuel to those in the Kremlin who have always opposed your chairmanship and who have always opposed gradualism.''

"And that is your offer? That I should let you take over complete control of the Autonomous Capitalist Oblast of America, and become nothing more than a national grandparent? A kind of Socialist Father Christmas?"

Kama grimaced. He had little sense of humor, and no time at all for the trappings of Christianity and other such superstitions. In his youth, he had worked doggedly against the continuing presence in Russia of Roman Catholicism and the Russian Orthodox Church in the conviction that any worship of so-called spiritual beings was a direct denial of the reality of the State.

"Well," said Ikon, "I am not sure that I want such a job. I am not sure that I am adequately benign."

"*Somebody* has to explain what happened," Kama insisted. "*Somebody* has to explain how President Kennedy saw that America was defenseless against the missiles on Cuba. *Somebody* has to tell the American people that he had no choice at all but to surrender."

"You are talking of destroying some powerful national myths," warned Ikon.

"There isn't any *alternative*," said Kama. "And besides, I believe that the American people will almost be relieved when they understand how many of their national myths were not myths or mysteries at all; but explicable fact. How long have they fretted over Kennedy's assassination? For twenty years! And after twenty years you will simply be able to tell them the truth: that he tried to go back on his promise of surrender, that he tried to organize a national resistance movement, and that he had to be eliminated to preserve a Socialist peace. The same for his brother, and all those witnesses and other malcontents who knew what had actually happened. Nikolai Nekrasov, you can tell them why they had to go to war in Viet Nam: that it was essential for China's belief in the hostility between America and the Soviet Union. And you can tell them why they lost, and had to withdraw, because it was always intended that they should. You can explain about Nixon . . . how Nixon was the only President ever to try to rebel against the Supervisory Committee, and how Watergate was engineered by the KGB to have him disgraced and ousted. The American people will see you as a great leader, as a great demystifier of everything that has confused and worried them in the past twenty years. Why did President Carter cancel the B-1 bomber? Why did Marshall Roberts fight so hard for the RINC talks?"

Ikon listened to Kama with studied politeness. Then he pointed towards a public bench, and said, "I think I'd like to sit down. Your offer has almost overwhelmed me."

Kama hesitated, and looked around him. It was a nervousness born of years of political brinkmanship. He sat down, though, and Ikon sat beside him, two men on a seat in the sunlight of a Washington lunchtime; two men who could have been anybody at all; a lawyer and his clerk; a father and his wayward son; an advertising executive and his brightest young copywriter.

The truth was, though, that they were the two most powerful men in the entire Western hemisphere. Between them, they could control the lives and the destinies of nearly a thousand million people.

Ikon took out a Dristan nasal spray and squirted it vigorously up each nostril. "I have to be careful, ever since they started poisoning Tylenol and God knows what else. It might give somebody on the Supervisory Committee a bright idea.''

"You know that's not the way I want this to be," said Kama. "The old techniques, the killings, that's not the way to run an Oblast like America."

"We found Marilyn Monroe, you know," said Ikon, with some satisfaction. "Twenty years we've been looking for her. Twenty years! And all the time she was living in Arizona."

"Kolpasev told me. Impressive. That was Henry Friend, wasn't it?"

"Henry Friend, yes. Well, you know it was. You called him back straight away to blow up that unfortunate police chief for you. I sent you a critical memorandum about that. Did you read it?"

"I only used him because he was the best available."

"Still, it wasn't wise. I considered recommending to Moscow that you shouldn't be permitted to sanction any kind of termination at all."

"He was the best; and it was essential that her body was taken away as quickly as possible. Friend should have had instructions to remove it before."

"You really think so?" asked Ikon. His tone was altogether too bland for Kama's liking. He sounded as if he were discussing a rather dull dinner party, instead of violent assassinations and power struggles, and the fate of the entire Oblast of America.

"Of course I think so," said Kama. "Supposing the autopsy had revealed that she was Marilyn Monroe?"

"It wouldn't have. Well, the chances that it would were very slim. It was necessary to remove the head, of course. Dental identification: and the risk that somebody might have recognized her picture if it were published in the newspapers. But all of this cowboys-and-Indians business to snatch her body from the Phoenix morgue . . ."

"I have the authority," said Kama, coldly.

"Of course. But you also have the *responsibility*. And in my view you deliberately and irresponsibly instructed your agents to run amok in Phoenix in order to stir up trouble. It's a pity for you that the American media are so resolutely dense. Not one single newspaper asked the questions you wanted them to ask:

was this police chief's death a conspiracy? If so, who were the conspirators? That was your aim, wasn't it, as it's always been? To have the conquest of America discovered by the media, so that you don't have to explain to Moscow why you personally decided to announce it?''

Ikon adjusted his horn-rimmed spectacles, and looked upwards. An American Airlines jet was turning noisily over the city, its silver body sparkling in the sunlight.

"You have consistently over-reached yourself, Comrade Kama," said Ikon. "You have tried again and again to usurp my authority; and again and again to trigger a revelation in the press that America may not be the democratic country that its inhabitants believe it to be. I have to say that I don't like you at all and that I like your henchmen on the Supervisory Committee almost as little. As for the human rodents your agencies employ to carry out your verminous missions . . . I think the less I say about them, the better. I was given a full report on that bombing in Phoenix, and also on what happened afterwards, when a girl reporter was kidnapped. Those were your men, weren't they? Rats, from the National Security Agency. More fuss, more trouble; more cowboys-and-Indians. Well, Comrade Kama, that is not the way in which a great Oblast can be run. An Oblast is a province of the Union of Soviet Socialist Republics; and in time this Oblast will take its place as one of those Republics. Not as a conglomeration of greedy and misguided capitalists, run by brutal and criminal socialist gangsters; no, not even with me as a figurehead. But as a proud and productive member of a worldwide socialist community; a community which at last can drop all vestiges of war and antagonism, real and pretended, and live in genuine global peace.''

Kama said, "You're not addressing the Central Committee, Comrade Nekrasov.''

"No," said Ikon, with some dignity, "I'm not. I'm addressing *you*.''

Kama stood up, and buttoned his coat. " A fine speech. You could save some of it for your valedictory address.''

"I'm not resigning," said Ikon, hoarsely—so hoarsely that Kama scarcely caught what he said.

Kama said, "What?''

"I said, I'm not resigning. Only death will force me to give up the chairmanship. Certainly not you."

"Nikolai Nekrasov, RINC II is dead; and that means that *you're* dead."

Ikon shook his head, so that his jowls wobbled. "The only person who is dead, Comrade Kama, is Colleen Petley."

Kama stared at him. "You'd better be joking, Nikolai Nekrasov."

Ikon shook his head again. "No jokes, Comrade Kama. Colleen Petley is dead."

"There are tapes. Videotapes."

"I have all of them."

"Nadiana Voroshilova," said Kama.

"Well, you could be right," agreed Ikon.

"Nadiana Voroshilova," Kama repeated, with such hysterical annoyance that he was almost laughing. "Nadiana Voroshilova!"

"It was your gamble, Comrade Kama. You wanted to twist Nadiana into your little blackmail too, I suppose? Well, you took the gamble, and you lost. Nadiana is no amateur. Neither am I. I'm sorry for you. Sorrow is a good Russian emotion. Here, take my hand if you want to. Sob on my shoulder. But whatever you do, believe me, RINC II will go ahead. And after RINC II is completed, there will be trade agreements, and increasing détente, and in time, a great socialist amalgamation."

"Nadiana Voroshilova," whispered Kama.

Ikon coughed, and coughed again. "I have to get back to Pennsylvania Avenue," he said. "I like a little fresh air . . . but not too much."

Kama ignored him, and pressed his hand to his forehead. He was doing his best to keep himself under control, to suppress his anger. Tonight, he would go back to his apartment in Arlington and drink himself into a blind stupor with Polish Pure Spirit. Then he would probably break something; a vase, a table, a set of glasses. Not hysterically, but with all the frigid calculated fury of a man who cannot bear to be bested. His maid would sweep up.

He closed his eyes; and when he opened them again, Ikon had gone.

TWENTY-SEVEN

Lieutenant Lindblad said, "Somebody called me August 1, 1962, that was the Wednesday previous to the Sunday that Marilyn was supposed to have died. They said they represented the White House and they required some local assistance in a difficult situation."

"Did you believe them?" asked Kathy.

"I don't know. I guess I *half*-believed them. The Kennedys had been buzzing in and out of Los Angeles quite a lot in those days, so it wasn't a total surprise."

"Why did they call *you*, in particular? Surely there were plenty of superior officers who could have helped them better."

"I never really found out. I was young then, newly promoted; and I'd had my picture in the papers a couple of times. I guess the Kennedys just thought that I was their style. They were anxious they didn't make too many waves, too, and I guess that a superior officer would have felt himself obliged to report the matter higher up, to the Commissioner, or the Mayor. That was the last thing they wanted."

Daniel stayed by the window while Lieutenant Lindblad talked. The smog that had blurred Los Angeles for most of the day had thickened again. There was a strange sense of doom about the landscape: tacky Spanish-style houses, forested with TV antennae,

275

under a William Blake sky. Children played in the surrounding yards, and their cries of laughter could just as easily have been cries of desperation.

Lieutenant Lindblad drank more beer and continued. "They told me that it was essential that I should meet their representative at The Brown Derby on Thursday night. I said that wasn't a particularly clever place to meet, because by 1962 The Brown Derby wasn't a fashionable place to eat anymore, and the chances were that me and this representative would be the only people there. So in the end they agreed on Dino's, on Sunset. At least it was dark."

He caught sight of his wife in the doorway, and gave her another little wave, and cooed, "It's okay, sugar. I won't be long." Then he turned back to Kathy, and said, "You can imagine what I felt when this representative turned out to be Bobby Kennedy himself. There was one other guy there, but he didn't look too smart, and I guessed he was just a bodyguard. He didn't say anything, anyway."

"What did Bobby Kennedy say to you? Did he seem worried?"

"Worried? The guy was jumping all over the place. He couldn't sit still for a second. He said that *a certain lady movie star*, who was a friend of his, was having some trouble. Her life was in danger, he said, and it was vital that she disappear."

"I said, well, that wouldn't be too hard to arrange, but then Bobby Kennedy said that one of his aides had noticed in one of the movie magazines a girl who looked exactly like this certain lady movie star, and asked if it wouldn't be possible for the two of them to switch rôles. He said the idea was that the certain lady movie star would be spirited away, and settled someplace out of town: while the look-alike girl would be spirited into the certain lady movie star's house, given a slight overdose of barbiturate drugs, and then rescued in a blaze of publicity which would establish that the certain lady movie star was still around, and still in town, but which would also give her an excuse to go into a clinic, maybe the Payne-Whitney, where she would be guarded well enough, you understand, but where she would keep any hostile attention away from the certain lady movie star herself.

"All the time, I knew he was talking about Monroe. Well, that wasn't no secret. But, I let him say 'certain lady movie star' all through the conversation and I didn't argue. Well, for Christ's sake, he *was* the Attorney General. But I did ask what kind of justification he might have for exposing an innocent young girl to the sort of danger he was so anxious that his certain lady movie star shouldn't be exposed to. And he said, it was a difficult decision, but in the end it all came down to a question of national security. In the larger view, that's what he said, the whole of America was at risk."

Daniel asked, "Did he say any more? Did he explain what he meant by that?"

"No, sir," said Lieutenant Lindblad. "He took one more drink and then he left."

"How much did he agree to pay you?"

"I didn't ask for money."

"What did you ask for?"

"This house, that's all. A nice house in Brentwood. And I asked him to fix it so that people would believe I was willed it. An old uncle of mine. That was the story."

"You found the girl?" asked Kathy.

"Sure. Vera Rutledge. I'd seen her myself, in *Fotoplay*, something like that. Very pretty girl. Prettier than Monroe, if you ask me. Fresher. Didn't look like she'd been living on Nembutals."

Kathy took off her spectacles and folded them up. "Did you have any inkling at all that Vera Rutledge might be killed? There had to be a risk, after all, if they were going to give her an overdose."

Lieutenant Lindblad gave a noncommittal shrug of his shoulders. "I wasn't particularly *impressed* by what they were trying to do. It seemed kind of amateurish, to tell you the truth. But, like I said, he *was* the Attorney General, and I did believe that he knew what he was doing. If you want my opinion, I still think he knew what he was doing, even when Vera Rutledge died. They told me that the girl would be ready for rescuing round about four o'clock in the morning, without any danger at all. But they made sure that plenty of other people got around there first; people who would be independent witnesses. Mrs. Murray was round there at three in the morning; then Dr. Greenson; then Dr.

Engelberg. By the time the police arrived it was all over. She was long dead.''

Kathy said carefully, ''Marilyn Monroe made some telephone calls on her last night alive . . . I mean on Vera Rutledge's last night alive. But not many people ever admitted receiving them, and the FBI removed the taped record of calls from the Santa Monica telephone company. Have you any explanation for that?''

Lieutenant Lindblad said, ''I know for sure that the arrangement was for the real Marilyn Monroe to telephone a few people she knew, and act like she was fuzzy and sick, and going over the line from too many pills. But of course she wasn't actually calling from Brentwood, she was calling long-distance from San Diego, which is the first place they sent her to; and the telephone company's tape would have shown that no calls came from the Brentwood number. That's why the FBI had to collar the tape as quickly as they could, before some smartass reporter got to it.''

''Didn't anybody—ambulancemen, or doctors, anybody like that—didn't anybody recognize that this girl *wasn't* Marilyn? She was quite a few years younger, after all.''

''The whole thing was rushed, on purpose, so that nobody got more than a glimpse. As far as the autopsy was concerned . . . I really don't know. My guess is that the medical examiners were looking for cause of death, in the belief that the body had already been satisfactorily identified. I really don't know for sure. Once it was out of my hands, it was out of my hands.''

They left Lieutenant Lindblad's house twenty minutes later, and drove westwards, looping around by the Will Rogers State Historical Park, and at last reaching the ocean. Daniel parked the Monaco by the side of the highway, and they took off their shoes and walked along the gray sandy beach for a while, with the Pacific seething beside them, and the unearthly twilight of a smoggy Los Angeles summer all around.

''What do you think?'' asked Daniel.

''I don't know,'' said Kathy. ''I guess it reinforces my Cuban theory in one way. I mean, I think it's obvious now that Bobby Kennedy really did have Marilyn Monroe smuggled out of Hollywood to save her life; and if she was prepared to agree to give up her whole career and everything, just for the sake of survival, then whoever was threatening her must have been pretty damned threatening. Well—they ended up cutting her head off, didn't they? But there still aren't any facts about Cuba or the Kennedys to get my teeth into."

"I would have thought Skellett's behavior was enough."

"Skellett might be nothing more than a lone crackpot. I don't think that he actually *is*, but he could be; and we don't have any way of proving that he isn't."

"Did you have any more luck with the National Security Agency?" asked Daniel.

"Unh-hunh. Wall of silence time. 'We regret that in the interests of national security we are unable to respond to your enquiries at this time.' "

Daniel stood by the shoreline, his bare toes dimpling the sand, his hands thrust into the pockets of his khaki slacks. "What do we do now? Who else do we talk to? Or do we just give up, and throw in the towel, and go back home?"

"Is that what you want to do?"

He turned and looked at her, and then shook his head. "Home isn't home without Susie."

"How about Cara?"

"Cara came like all the rest of them. Pretty, footloose, sweet and kind. She went the same way. I called the hospital this morning and they said she'd discharged herself. No forwarding address."

"I'm sorry," said Kathy. "You didn't tell me."

"There wasn't any need, was there, really? They come and they go. Susie's mother was just like that. It doesn't stop you liking them; it doesn't stop you loving them sometimes. But it stops you crying over them, when they're gone."

They walked back to the car. A few yards further along the Pacific Coast Highway, sitting on a large backpack, was a suntanned young man of about twenty-seven, good-looking in a way that Daniel could only think of as prematurely battered, drinking a can of Tab. He wore *lederhosen*, with a halter front, and a green check short-sleeved shirt, and large grubby sneakers.

"Hey, sir!" he called, as Daniel opened the door of the car. "Pardon me, sir!"

Daniel paused, and looked at him over the roof of the car. The young man hopped to his feet, disentangling his sneakers from the strap of his backpack, and said, "You don't happen to be heading towards Hollywood? Well, I know you're pointing south, but the way you walked on the beach, I wondered if you were heading back east."

"You're on a north-south highway and you want a ride *east*?"

The young man sheepishly rubbed at the back of his neck. "Actually, I was trying to thumb a ride north, to Santa Barbara. I had a row with my girl this afternoon, and she sort of threw me out. I was going back home to see my parents. Now I've been sitting here for two hours without getting a ride and I've kind of cooled towards it, you know? I was thinking of going back to Hollywood and looking up this other girl I know."

"Indecisive, huh?" asked Kathy.

The young man nodded. "I guess you could say that. Mind you, it doesn't take a lot to change my mind about going home to see my folks."

Daniel reached into the car and pressed the trunk-release button. "Get in," he told the young man. "We can take you as far as Doheny."

On the way back along Sunset, the young man leaned forward and folded his arms on the front seats and told them all about his girlfriend. "She's from weird, you know? I guess most Holly-wood ladies are. Very beautiful. But really from weird. Ever since she found out that Halley's Comet was on the way back, she's started getting these *feelings*. She thinks the comet's going to fly past the Earth just to investigate *her*."

"Maybe she's right," said Daniel. "You mustn't underesti-mate the importance of the individual."

"Hey," frowned the young man. "*You're* not into that stuff too, are you?"

"I'm beginning to feel that I might be."

The young man looked towards Kathy, and said, "Is your husband feeling okay, ma'am?"

"He's not my husband. But, sure, yes, he's feeling all right."

The young man suddenly stuck out his hand. "I didn't intro-duce myself. What an airhead. My name's Rick Terroni. You've seen me a hundred times before, on the movies. And television. Pratfaller Extraordinaire, that's how I advertise myself. That's a specialist kind of a stuntman, like I make my living falling on my ass. Somebody gets pushed over, hit by a car, kicked by a horse, sits on a collapsing deckchair, slips on a squashed tomato, that's what I do. You ever see that movie where Ryan O'Neal walks up those steps and then slides on all of those marbles? That was me, doing the sliding. Let's face it, Ryan O'Neal doesn't want to walk around for the rest of the week with a multi-colored ass."

"Pleased to know you," said Daniel.

They drove in silence for a while, past the gates of Bel Air, and then Rick Terroni said, "You guys seem kind of down. Is there a loss in your family? You're coming back from a funeral?"

Daniel said, "It's nothing, okay?"

"If you say so. It's just that I've got a nose for misery."

"A nose for misery?" asked Kathy. "What kind of a self-commendation is that?"

"Did I say it was a self-commendation?"

Daniel pulled up at Doheny, with an unnecessarily violent jerk on the brakes. "That's it, then," he said. "You're back in Hollywood."

Rick peered out of the Monaco's window. "Hm," he said. "Doheny Drive."

"That's where I told you, Doheny."

"You can't take me any further?"

"Unh-hunh. This is it."

Rick took a breath. "Listen," he said, "the real truth is that I don't have anyplace to go."

"You want a home, as well as a ride?" asked Daniel.

"I didn't say that," Rick protested. "If you want me to get out, I'll get out."

"Daniel," said Kathy, "he's not a *bum*. Come on, we can give him one square meal and floorspace for tonight. The *Flag* will pay for it. Hell, the *Flag*'s paying for this car, *and* for you. So you and he are just about equals, when you think about it. Two bums together."

Daniel turned around to Rick with a smile that would have soured cream. "You'll have to excuse my wife," he said, as he pulled out into the traffic of Sunset Boulevard again. At the moment, he didn't particularly care, one way or the other. He didn't even know why he was here. He should be in Arizona, taking care of the diner and waiting for news of Susie. Two days ago, following Kathy Forbes to Hollywood had seemed like the only positive thing he could do. But now he was beginning to feel that it was a terrible dead end, a news story that never was, the tearful parent interviewed on the evening news bulletin, "If I'd know what those animals were doing to my daughter . . ."

He made a squealing left into Sunset Plaza, narrowly avoiding an oncoming truck, and pulled up beside their rented house. Karhy touched his arm, and said, "Are you all right?"

He stared at her. He felt as if his eyelids would never close again. "Yes, sure, I'm all right. A little tired, maybe."

Rick Terroni said, "Listen, if you guys are into something that's none of my business . . . I mean, I feel like I'm interfering or something like that . . . I can easily find someplace to sleep . . ."

Kathy said, "Do your parents really live in Santa Barbara?"

"Sure they do."

"When was the last time you worked? In movies, I mean, or in television?"

"Couple of months ago. I doubled for Keiller Pierce in *Nightmare II*. He had to fall off a balcony. He looked over that balcony, you know, down at the ground where he was supposed to fall, and he said, 'If you think I'm going to jump down there, you've got to be fucking joking.' And the director said, 'Keiller, it's easy,' and gave him a shove, and Keiller toppled right off that balcony and broke both of his ankles, and the picture was held up for seven months while he learned how to walk all over again. So that's why, when it came to the balcony scene, they made *me* do it."

"And that was the last job you had?"

"I'm shortlisted for a new TV detective series."

Kathy shook her head, and smiled at him. "Come on," she said, "Daniel will fix you some of his special fried shrimp. Daniel runs a restaurant, you know. He's a genius when it comes to cooking."

"Cooking is a substitute for oral sex, didn't you know that?" asked Daniel perversely.

"I thought it was the other way around," said Rick. "I thought oral sex was a substitute for cooking."

They went into the house, Rick carrying his backpack slung over his shoulder. It was a typical rented Hollywood house: with a Spanish-style living-room with dark polished floor tiles, a fitted kitchen, and off-white bedroom rugs that had probably been white when they were new.

"It's not the Beverly Wilshire," said Daniel.

"Who cares? As long as it's not the Y."

Kathy said, "*Daniel.*" There was a warning in her voice which immediately made Daniel freeze.

"What is it?"

"Someone's been in here. Look. The garden door's been broken open. I left it locked."

Daniel felt a chill sensation of sudden alarm. He moved quickly and quietly past Kathy, and checked the bedroom; then the bathroom, kicking the door open with his foot. The house was empty, but there was no question that during the afternoon someone had intruded here. Rick stayed where he was, in the hallway, his pack by his feet, looking puzzled and anxious.

"Are you sure you guys really want me around? I don't mind leaving if I'm getting in your way."

"It's all right," said Daniel. "At least, I *think* it's all right."

"There couldn't be a bomb anywhere, could there?" asked Kathy.

"A *bomb*?" asked Rick. "Jesus, I think I'm beginning to wish I was back on the Pacific Coast Highway."

"Have a beer and settle down," said Daniel. "They're in the icebox."

Rick opened the icebox and took out a six-pack of Coors.

"At least the icebox isn't booby-trapped," said Kathy.

Rick stared at her. "*Supposing it had been*?"

Daniel shrugged.

They found the letter in the living-room, on the table beside the sofa. It was neatly addressed to *D. Korvitz*, in green fiber-tipped pen. Kathy said, "You think you should touch it? Maybe it's got fingerprints on it." Daniel ignored her, and tore it open.

In the same green handwriting, the letter said simply, "Dear Mr. Korvitz, We are now in Los Angeles, and we have your daughter with us. We have some serious business to discuss with you, and we would like to meet you personally. If you come to the multi-story parking lot on Santa Monica Boulevard at Wilcox at 9:15 a.m. tomorrow morning, we will return your daughter and take you with us to a suitable locale for more extensive talks.''

Daniel's hand was shaking as he read the letter. When he had finished, he handed it to Kathy without a word.

"You know what they meant by wanting to discuss *business* with me, don't you?" he asked.

Kathy folded up the letter, and laid a hand on his arm. "They want to kill you, Daniel, I'm sure of it. You can't possibly go."

"And Susie?"

"I don't know. I don't know what to say. Maybe it's time we called the police."

"They probably *are* the police, if what you're saying about Cuba has any truth in it."

"So what are you going to do?" Kathy demanded. "Give yourself up like a cow going to the cannery? What's the point of Susie going free if they kill you? Who's going to look after her?"

"She's got a mother."

"Oh, stop trying to be so ridiculously heroic."

Daniel snatched the letter away from her. "Damn it, it's nothing to do with heroism, Kathy. She's my little girl. I've brought her up day by day from the time she was tiny. She's seven years old, and God knows what those bastards have been doing to her. Think what they did to you. Besides, they probably don't want to kill me. Just frighten me off."

"Daniel," Kathy retorted, "if you were them, and you knew that somebody had discovered everything about the murders you'd committed, and your motives, what the hell would you do?"

"I'm still going," Daniel insisted. His fear and anger about Susie were almost overwhelming. He felt like shouting at Kathy, except that none of it was Kathy's fault. By God, if those animals had so much as laid one finger on Susie . . . But all he could think of was Susie's face, bruised from repeated beatings; and Susie's body, raped by foul-smelling men.

"Daniel," said Kathy. Then, when he turned away, "Daniel. There has to be some other kind of answer."

"I can't think of one, can you? What's the choice? Either Susie dies or else I take my chances. Come on, Kathy, I'm older than Susie. At least I've got the strength and the experience to protect myself. She's just a seven-year-old kid who's never known anything but friendly smiling people."

"Daniel—"

"You can't change my mind! Don't try!"

Kathy rubbed her eyes in tension and fatigue. Daniel screwed off the cap of a bottle of Coors, and poured it out, too quickly, so that the glass was filled to the brim with foam. "Shit," he said, but drank it all the same.

Rick said, "I honestly feel like I'm intruding or something."

"You're not intruding," said Daniel. "Just shut up and find yourself someplace to crash down."

"I don't mean to be presumptuous or anything," said Rick, "but it seems like you've got some kind of real gnarly problem going on here. Maybe I could help."

"Have you ever seen anybody killed?" asked Daniel.

"Only by accident. One stuntman I knew, got smashed up in a car crash."

Daniel finished his foamy beer, and poured himself some more. Rick watched him expectantly. "Let me tell you something," said Daniel. "Tomorrow morning at a quarter after nine I'm supposed to go to a multi-level parking-lot on Santa Monica Boulevard and surrender myself to one or more known killers in exchange for my seven-year-old daughter Susie, who was kidnapped in Arizona last week. The possibility is that the killers will seek to widen their expertise by killing me, too."

"Are you kidding?" asked Rick. "Is this *Candid Camera* or something?"

"It doesn't matter to you whether I'm kidding or not," Daniel told him. "You don't have to be there. You don't have to worry about any of us. So why don't you just unpack your bag, make yourself comfortable, and keep your mouth shut. What you don't know won't hurt you."

Rick pushed his hands into the tight pockets of his *lederhosen*. "Is that the parking lot at Seward, or the parking lot at Wilcox?"

"Wilcox. Why?"

"Well . . . this is only a thought . . . but a friend of mine got spaced out one day when he was driving into the Wilcox parking-lot, and he drove right through the railings on Level 3 and he ended up parked on the roof next door.''

"What the hell does that have to do with anything?'' asked Daniel.

"Well, just hold up a minute; what my friend said was that anybody who might have had a mind to could have driven clear across the roof, and clear across the roof of the next building, as far as Cole.''

Kathy said tautly, "I still don't understand what you're saying.''

"Well, is this real, what you're telling me, or are you making a movie?'' asked Rick. He bit his lip, and his eyes flicked from Daniel to Kathy, and back to Daniel. "I mean, is it *real*?''

"Supposing it were?'' asked Kathy.

"Well, if it's real . . . if you've really got to come face-to-face with some killers in the Wilcox Avenue parking lot, then you've got to plan it like a movie stunt, you know? Plan it first. I'm always looking for good stunt locations, and this place is one of them. I mean, you could snatch your daughter back, right, and then drive up the ramp instead of out of the parking lot—the way they wouldn't expect you to go—and right through the railings and over the next-door rooftops. Then you could leap out of the car and get away while these killers are still fooling around wondering which level you're on.''

"You're nuts,'' said Kathy.

"But it's what people do in the movies, for Christ's sake. And if they can do it in the movies, why can't you do it for real?''

Daniel set down his glass, and looked at Rick thoughtfully. At last, he said, "Let's go down to Wilcox, and see what this parking lot looks like. Maybe you're right. Maybe we do have a chance. You said, drive across the rooftops?''

"That's right. You might knock over a couple of ventilation stacks, but nothing worse than that. You see what I'm trying to say to you, don't you? You could snatch your daughter back and get away yourself, if you planned it properly. I can tell you something, all of the stunts we do for the movies are planned like clockwork. We could be in and out of that place in six seconds flat, and nobody would scarcely know we'd been there.''

"We?''

"You don't think you're going to leave me out of this, do you? Besides, I don't have anyplace else to stay."

Daniel looked down at his empty glass. "*Melech Ham'lochim*," he said, under his breath.

TWENTY-EIGHT

The same afternoon, Titus left the State Department and drove in his own Porsche down to Bolling Air Force Base in Virginia, wearing dark sunglasses and a white fishing hat in the hope that nobody would recognize him. The sentry outside Bolling had already been alerted to let him through without stopping him, and he was waved by a white-gloved MP towards the outer perimeter road, past rows of giant C-141 Starlifters, and all the organized confusion of Jeeps and ammunition boxes and half-tracked vehicles that were the hallmark of a Military Airlift Command base.

General Caulfield's shiny black Lincoln was parked under the shade of a large Virginia oak, not far from the perimeter fence. General Caulfield himself was standing nearby with his hands on his hips, watching a C-5A transport taxi around to the main runway in preparation for take-off. The noise and the heat came in waves.

"How are you keeping, Pierce?" asked Titus, as he slammed the door of his car and came walking across with his white fishing hat held in his hands.

"I'm well," said General Caulfield. He had a relentlessly short military haircut which gave him the appearance of a 55-

year-old boy of 11. "I haven't had too much time for fishing lately; but I guess we all have our crosses to bear."

"Fishing is the least of my worries right now," said Titus.

"Well, I guess. It shook me, when I was first told about it. I couldn't believe my own ears. It depressed me, I can tell you. It does, when you first understand that everything you ever fought for, everything you ever believed in, your flag, your country, it's all been taken away from you and you never knew."

"Then it's true," said Titus. He looked at Pierce Caulfield narrowly, his head slightly angled to one side, as if he were challenging the general to deny everything; to admit that Ikon was all an impossible joke.

Pierce Caulfield turned to Titus, and said, crisply, "Yes, it's true. The United States has been administered by the Soviet Union since the summer of 1962. And one of the very first things the Soviets did was to ensure that the American forces could no longer effectively threaten the Soviet Union."

"But why didn't they simply dismantle the U.S. forces? Surely that would have been easier than all this elaborate pretense?"

— "They weren't stupid," said Pierce. "They knew that in spite of the nuclear edge they had managed to win over us, it would still be touch and go if they tried to take us over by brute force. I don't know all of the details; I wasn't privy to what was going on at the time. In fact, I personally wasn't told until 1974, nearly twelve years later. But, as far as I can gather, they decided to convert us to Communism over a very long period of time; to break us down, socially and morally, politically and economically, until at last we would consider that Communism was the only option left open to us, and we would consider that amalgamating with the Soviet Union was the only sensible answer."

"You have to be kidding," said Titus.

Pierce shook his head. "I think that they were far too optimistic about the time that it would take for the American people to be converted to international socialism. I believe that Ikon's been having some trouble over that with the Kremlin. But the deliberate destruction of the U.S. economy seems to have gone according to plan; and there's no question that it's brought with it all the social disillusionment that Russia expected."

Titus stood with his head lowered while Pierce Caulfield

shaded his eyes and followed the flight-path of the C-5A as it turned around and headed west. "That's a magnificent airplane, you know that? An amazing technical achievement. Do you know how much that airplane weighs? Over 325,000 lbs, empty. They had some difficulty with wing fatigue, but they've solved it now. That's one of the reasons the Soviets didn't want to tamper too much with America as she was. They recognized our technical expertise, they recognized our educational advancement, they saw us as leaders in almost every field of sophisticated life. It would have been absurd and wasteful of them to throw our space program away; or take our armed forces to pieces. What was the point, when they could infiltrate enough of their own officers into U.S. military ranks to ensure that our key defenses were useless; and that none of our major weapons would ever work? All that our Distant Early Warning stations do these days is to monitor air traffic, for the express benefit of Aeroflot and the Soviet forces. There's no threat from the Soviet Union any more, there hasn't been for twenty years. It's no good fearing the coming conflict; it's all over, and all of us here in America are nothing more than prisoners of war."

"But our missiles—" said Titus. "Our troops, our airplanes . . . We've just ordered a new *tank*, damn it!"

"I know," said Pierce, with great calmness. "I know how you must be feeling. I wondered when *I* first found out if I ought to kill myself; I even considered launching a one-man suicide mission against the Kremlin. But, in the end, it was strangely reassuring to know that everything that had happened in American life over the past twenty years was *planned*, that America's recent moral decay was not our fault. The sexual revolution was planned; the widespread introduction of addictive and hallucinogenic drugs was planned; so was large-scale birth control in order to keep the American population under control. Every major national trend from student uprisings to est to jogging to conservative chic was a part of a carefully-devised socio-psychological scheme to make Americans more uncertain of their future, more critical of their past. Thus, when Ikon considers that the time is right, the new golden age of socialism will be announced. A full détente between America and the Soviet Union will form the basis for a proletarian amalgamation. In five or ten years' time, we'll all be drinking vodka and singing *The Red Flag*."

"But how did they do it? How did they do it without anybody finding *out*?" demanded Titus.

"A great many people *did* find out. Some have been killed. Others have decided that it is probably safer to keep quiet. Like me. They summoned me up to the Pentagon one September morning and said that they were going to tell me something I wouldn't much like; but that if I didn't help them, my sons and daughters and wife would all be murdered. So you can see that I didn't really have very much choice, did I? I was personally to ensure that all Minutemen missiles were safe, by which they meant that not one of them was to carry a warhead that actually worked. The delivery systems are still functional; and Boeing is still carrying out research on new warheads. But they will never be used against the Soviet Union. If they are ever re-activated and used against anybody at all, it will be the Chinese. We have to be quite clear on this, Titus. Ever since Khruschev called up Kennedy and said that there were dozens of long-range nuclear missiles on Cuba, all aimed toward the American heartland, Kennedy didn't have any choice. Kennedy surrendered, and then to keep the world on an even political keel, he and Khruschev decided between them to make it appear that Khruschev had stood down, and agreed to withdraw the missiles. I guess it was surprising that nobody realized what had actually happened at the time. I suppose we were all too relieved. But that was the *only* occasion on which Khruschev ever appeared to back down. Backing down just wasn't in his character. Here, come into the car, let me show you something. I expect you could use a drink, too."

The two old friends sat in the back of the Lincoln limousine, and closed the doors. Pierce let down the walnut cocktail table, and poured them each a large glassful of Wild Turkey. Then he produced a brown envelope, with a HIGHLY SECRET label on it, and shook out two or three old but still-glossy photographs.

"These are the pictures we *didn't* release to the media, the day that the Russians supposedly started shipping their missiles back to the Soviet Union."

Titus picked them up, and frowned at them quickly. "What

am I looking at?" he wanted to know. "They look just the same as any other picture to me. Missile tubes on the decks of Russian freighters."

"Ah, but you look here. The airplane taking the picture has flown quite low. *Too* low, as it turns out. You can see quite clearly that the nearest missile container, on the port side of the deck, is *hollow*. The sun's shining through it. You see here, where the sun falls on the bulkhead? These missile tubes are nothing but shams. Cuba is still bristling with strategic nuclear missiles and always will be."

Titus sipped his whiskey, and then sat back in his seat and looked at Pierce with an expression that was half-defeat, half-resentment.

"Why didn't you tell me, Pierce? All these years, and I never even guessed. Jesus, Pierce, I was in *charge* of most of those weapons. It never once occurred to me that there was anything wrong with them. Blind faith, I suppose. Blind stupidity."

"You weren't to know, Titus. It wasn't the ordinary kind of sabotage. It was a massive and systematic program of secret disarmament, carried out by experts who weren't afraid to use maximum force. I know for a fact that at least a hundred servicemen have been killed over the years for trying to disclose secret information to the media. And quite a few of the media people have found themselves being blackmailed or threatened. One reporter who was working on a nuclear disarmament story for the *Reader's Digest* was found in his car at the bottom of Chincoteague Bay. It's quite possible that if anyone finds out what I've been saying to you, then *I'll* be at serious risk, too. But when you called me this morning, I couldn't very well fob you off. It's time you knew. I just hope that you'll be able to face up to the implications of it."

"It means I'm a captive," said Titus, in a throaty voice. "It means I'm not free any more."

"You haven't been free for twenty years."

"But, damn it, Pierce, now I *know* it! Last week I was the happy idiot who didn't realize that he was locked up in a cage; now I can feel the bars."

Pierce laid a hand on his arm. "I don't want you to rush off and do anything rash, Titus. You'll be putting a whole lot of people at risk, including me and my family. Just go home tonight and think about it, and then decide what you're going to do. That's if you're going to do anything at all. Meet me tomorrow if you can; around the same time; on the shoreline at Windmill Point."

Titus finished the rest of his whiskey with one grimacing swallow. Then he climbed out of the Lincoln and walked back towards his Porsche, tugging his fishing hat on to his head as he did so.

"Remember what Kennedy once said," Pierce called after him. "The basic problems facing the world today are not susceptible to a military solution."

Titus stopped, and turned around. "That was after the option of a military solution was no longer available to him," he snapped. "That was after he had already sold us out."

Pierce said something in reply, but his voice was drowned by the enormous thunder of another C-5A Galaxy, coming in to land from the west. Its shadow passed over them both like the shadow of history; a history which filled them both with fear, and which neither of them would ever be able to influence again.

TWENTY-NINE

Lieutenant Berridge was out jogging with his wife Stella on the banks of the Arizona Canal. It was just six o'clock in the morning; still cool; and the slowly-rippling waters of the Indian-built canal reflected the freshly-risen sun and the overhanging leaves of the willows. They crossed the canal by the bridge which leads into the Biltmore Hotel, and turned west through the groves of orange trees, their professional running-shoes slapping on the blacktop, their Lacoste jogging suits stained down the back with sweat.

"This kidnap case isn't doing anything for my running," protested Lieutenant Berridge. "I'm exhausted."

"I'm not surprised," said Stella. Her blonde hair bounced as she ran. "That's two nights straight without any sleep. Can't you leave it to Mulligan?"

"Not yet. Not until I find out what the hell it's all about."

"Supposing you never do? They could have taken the girl and killed her and buried her in the desert; and who would ever know?"

"*I* would know. *Me*. I have an instinct for abductions like that. But I think this girl is still alive. What's more, I think that the father knows something that we don't. You know? I think he's holding something back. Because why else would he fly off to LA with that Kathy Forbes girl from the *Flag*?"

"Maybe they're in love," said Stella.

"In love? Nobody would go for that type."

"Oh, no? I thought she looked quite pretty in her photograph."

"She's average, that's all."

Stella dug at his ribs with her elbow. "Whenever you say that a girl is 'average, that's all,' that means that you want her like all hell. Wolfman Berridge is on the prowl again. Thank God she's gone off to the Coast."

They had almost reached 24th Street, although they were still screened from the main road by a right-hand curve and a thicket of orange trees. Without any warning, a pale-blue Thunderbird came rolling out of a side-turning and stopped just in front of them, wallowing on its suspension. Lieutenant Berridge broke his jogging rhythm and slowed down, catching at Stella's arm to slow her down, too. The Thunderbird stayed where it was, right on the corner, its engine running and its driver silhouetted in the shadowy interior.

"Something wrong?" Stella asked Lieutenant Berridge.

"I don't think so," said Lieutenant Berridge cautiously, but slowed right down to a walk. He circled around the front of the Thunderbird and approached the driver's window. With the whine of a tired electric motor, the window was lowered. The numbered sticker on the car's windshield informed Lieutenant Berridge at once that this was a rental car; and the first thing he saw as the window opened was the plastic Avis tag on the ignition keys.

The driver was a man in late middle-age, wearing a poisonous brown sport shirt and sunglasses. He smiled at Lieutenant Berridge, and said, "Can I help you?"

"I'm a police officer. You're causing a potential obstruction here. Would you mind moving on?"

"You're a *police* officer?" asked the man, looking Lieutenant Berridge up and down.

"Even police officers get time off," Lieutenant Berridge told him. "But I'd appreciate it if you'd move along now, please."

The man took off his sunglasses. His eyes were as dead as stones, and surrounded by wrinkles. The eyes of a man who has spent years searching distant horizons: years peering through smoky bars; years looking for one thing and one thing only, and has found it; and is enjoying his triumph.

"You must be Lieutenant Berridge," the man said.

Lieutenant Berridge backed off a little; and then glanced behind him at Stella. Strangers who called him by name always alarmed him. He had been on the beat with a cop called O'Manion once, back in his rookie days, and one night on Indian School Road, just as they were climbing into their car, someone had yelled out, "O'Manion!" and a shotgun blast had hit O'Manion full in the back.

"Don't be frightened, lieutenant," the man said. "I'm not going to cause any trouble unless I have to. But don't try to be a hero, either. I'm holding an Ingram machine-gun in my lap, and it's pointing at you through the door, and one incautious move will result in severe damage to this automobile's bodywork, and you."

Lieutenant Berridge reached one hand behind him, and tried to wave at Stella to back away. But Stella came a few steps closer, and said, "Come *on*, honey. I'm losing my adrenalin."

"Don't say a word," the man cautioned Lieutenant Berridge. "I've come here to warn you, not to hurt you. You're dealing with the kidnapping of Susie Korvitz, right? And that little bit of business at Tempe."

"That's right." Lieutenant Berridge's face was stiff. "What does that have to do with you?"

"You don't need to know. All you have to do is fail to find any useful evidence: decline to follow up any cock-and-bull leads; and eventually let both cases sink with silence and dignity into the files."

"And what if I tell you to go fuck yourself?"

"Then I'll kill you. You remember poor Chief Ruse?"

"You killed Chief Ruse?"

"That's right. And I'll kill you too, if you don't behave yourself. Well—I have to make threats like that, you understand. They're part of my orders."

Lieutenant Berridge said to Stella, in a clear voice, "Back away, baby, you understand me?"

Stella said, "What? What did you say?"

"I said back away! I said—*take cover!*"

The man in the car suddenly lifted from his lap a small blackpainted gun. Lieutenant Berridge recognized it at once, and felt a freezing surge of fear. For one chip of one second he couldn't decide what to do: but then he ran straight towards the car, straight towards the man with the gun, jumped up and over him, and hurled himself with a clumbering bang on to the Thunderbird's roof.

His unorthodox action probably saved his life, for as he jumped, the man opened fire, and Lieutenant Berridge heard that brisk and terrifying burp that characterized the Ingram 11's high-speed fire. The very first burst of 30 bullets took one-and-a-half seconds, and tore into Stella's legs as she stood in front of the car in total surprise and confusion.

Both her legs were completely severed at mid-thigh, in a horrifying splatter of blood and bone. She had time to look down at her legs with an expression of baffled hurt. She even had time to look up again, her eyes wide, searching for Lieutenant Berridge. Then her body literally fell off her legs, and she hit the ground with a hideous thump. Her scream was so high-pitched that Lieutenant Berridge could scarcely hear it. It was the kind of scream that could wake dogs at night; the kind of scream that would come to you for year after year in hideous dreams.

The man in the car wrestled to change magazines. Lieutenant Berridge slithered forward across the vinyl roof, and hooked his left arm down into the open window, grappling at the man's shoulder, and then at his neck. The man struck at him with the machine-gun, chipping flesh from his knuckles, but Lieutenant Berridge hung on to his throat and swung himself down from the car's roof. Now he could seize the man with both hands; and he did so, directly, and slammed the man's head forward so that he broke his nose against the car's window-shelf. There was a vivid splash of blood, and the man gargled and tried to wrench himself away.

"Out!" shrieked Lieutenant Berridge, hysterical. "Out of the fucking car!" He tore open the door and dragged the man on to the road, punching him again and again in the face. The machine-gun clattered on to the blacktop and skidded underneath the car.

The man tried to stand up, but Lieutenant Berridge gave him a karate chop to the side of his throat that snapped one of the bones in his right hand. Then, as the man collapsed, Lieutenant Berridge delivered a piledriving kick in the balls, and felt a testicle smash. The man dragged himself a few feet towards the side of the road, and then collapsed, whimpering and groaning.

Lieutenant Berridge knelt down beside Stella. Her face under her suntan was the color of ashes, as if she had suddenly become a very old woman. The blood was pumping out of her severed thighs undammed, and unstoppable, and the shock had already numbed her senses so deeply that she could only stare at him, and reach out for his arm. She was dying very quickly. To her, perhaps Lieutenant Berridge was already a dim reminder of her lost lifetime, and the world which she was entering was already more real.

"Stella," whispered Lieutenant Berridge. He knew that she couldn't hear him. He was sickeningly conscious that her left leg was lying at an odd angle within his field of vision. He said again, "Stella," and she died in his arms, and he thanked God in a way that she had. He knelt beside her for two or three minutes, not speaking, not thinking, wishing that this was nothing more than a hideous illusion, and knowing all the time that it was real.

He heard a metallic clicking sound behind him, and he stiffened. Slowly, he turned his head around; and there he was. Bloody-faced, eyes bulging with agony, leaning up against the front of the Thunderbird with the Ingram upraised, and a fresh magazine already inserted.

Lieutenant Berridge stood up. "Drop the weapon," he said. "You're under arrest. Homicide in the first degree."

The man fired, a half-second batch of bullets that blew off the side of Lieutenant Berridge's head. But with the fixed concentration of a man who no longer cares if he lives or dies, Lieutenant Berridge walked right up to the killer, and laid his hand on his shoulder.

"I said, you're under arrest," he repeated. The man stared at him and didn't fire again. Lieutenant Berridge could see the man's face in front of him, swollen and blurred, and a dark triangle of red which must have been the man's broken nose. He shivered with bone chilling cold, but kept his grip on the man's shoulder, and said, "arrest," and then, in a halting voice, "a . . . rest."

He fell in the road. He was not quite dead. He could see the road surface close to his face. A little further away was a fallen orange. The last thing he heard was a car engine coughing into life, and the sound of a door slamming.

The man backed up the Thunderbird, then slammed it into drive, and ran over Lieutenant Berridge, crushing his chest and finishing the job. The man then drove to the intersection with 24th Street and made a left against a red light, provoking an outraged chorus of horns. He shouted at the top of his voice, "Suck off, you bastards!" even though nobody could hear him. The pain from his broken nose was more than he could actually bear: he could feel the bone grating under the skin. And his right testicle was a fiery throb of agony. It felt as if it were eight times its normal size, and quivering.

He reached the safe house in Tempe in twenty minutes, railing all the time against the slowness of the traffic, the stop-lights, and the monumental pain in his genitals. He parked outside, and hobbled up the front steps, gasping and sweating. He fumbled for the key, and at last managed to let himself in. Then, with a terrible cry, he collapsed face-first on to the rug, and lay there shuddering and shaking and feeling as if the whole world were nothing more than two cubic inches of utter pain.

It was almost noon when the telephone rang. He managed to reach out and drag it onto the floor. "Yes?" he asked, in a clotted, nasal voice.

The call was long-distance. There was a faint singing of electronics, the blurping of other people's dialing. A man's voice said, "We just heard about Berridge. Good work. Nice and messy."

"I'm hurt."

"We'll be staying in Los Angeles for a week or so. Why don't you come back for good? We've got two more jobs for you; then you can retire forever."

"You said Ruse was the last one. Then you said that Berridge was the last one. Come on, Skellett, I'm hurt. I don't want any more. I'm finished."

"How can you be finished? You're the best."

"I spent twenty years looking for that one woman. I'm finished. No work for twenty years and now this. Three in one week. I can't take it any more, Mr. Skellett. I'm through. And, besides,

I'm not sure that everybody in Washington is going to be as pleased with these jobs as you are. Some people don't like to make a fuss, that's what I've heard. Especially these days, with those nuclear talks coming up.''

"Henry," replied Skellett, and his tone was like chilled vinegar, strained through a pot-scourer, "Henry, nuclear talks are none of your business. You're a man for hire, that's all."

"I'm a man for hire and right now I quit. My nose is broken. Can't you hear my nose is broken? And that goddamned Lieutenant Berridge kicked me straight between the legs. I need a doctor, goddamn it, not more work. Send me a goddamned doctor."

There was a silence. Then Skellett said, "Can you make the LA flight this afternoon? Western has one at 1:40."

"I'll try. I don't know."

"Well, try. Okay? I'll book you a room at the Welford Clinic. But I want you here. You're still the best, as far as I'm concerned, broken nose or not. You're a man after my own heart."

"I didn't know you had one."

Skellett laughed, jarringly. "Make sure you catch the 1:40," he said. "I'll have a car waiting for you at LAX."

"So long as you never send me back to Phoenix."

Skellett laughed again; and then just as abruptly hung up.

THIRTY

They drew up outside the multi-story parking-lot on Santa Monica and Wilcox, and sat staring at it like apprehensive knights considering the uncertain prospects of entering some evil wizard's castle. They were driving their rented Monaco still, but Rick had spent a couple of hours last night tuning its engine, with a flashlight clenched between his teeth and a ring spanner in each hand, and although the Monaco wasn't exactly a Shelby Cobra, it did run with a reasonably satisfying burble, and gave kicky little surges of power whenever Rick put his foot down. Under the circumstances, Rick had promoted himself to driver.

"My guess is that they've arrived already," said Daniel. "They've probably deployed themselves around the parking-lot in case we try anything funny."

Rick said, "What do you want to do?"

Daniel checked his watch. "Drive straight in, I guess, and take it as it comes. But for God's sake be careful. These guys are really dangerous. I mean, they're wild beasts."

Rick revved the engine, and cleared his throat. "You ever done anything like this before?"

Daniel shook his head.

"Me neither." Then he paused. Then he said, "Fucking scary, isn't it?"

302   *Graham Masterton*

They turned cautiously into the parking-lot ramp, and Rick collected the ticket from the gate. Up went the barrier, and they drove into the darkness with tires squealing loudly on the polished concrete floor.

"They didn't say what level?" asked Rick.

"They didn't even say that they'd actually be inside."

"Well, we're just going to have to make this up as we go along."

They reached the end of the first level, and drove through a sudden burst of sunlight up the ramp to the second level. The muffled throb of their engine echoed against the walls; and with the long drawn-out shrieking of their tires, the noise made the parking-lot seem more like an evil wizard's domain than ever.

Kathy whispered, "We should have brought guns."

"We should have brought the National Guard," said Rick.

Daniel, thinking tensely about Susie, could say nothing at all. His fists were clenched tight and his muscles were so rigid that he felt as if they might lock.

They reached the end of the second level, and turned up the ramp to the third. Rick said, "This is the one. Look along to the end there, where the railings are. Nothing but rows of flat rooftops. We can drive straight through the railings, right out across the tops of those buildings, as far as that water-tank there. Then we can get out and climb down the fire-escape."

Daniel looked dubiously out over the tar-papered rooftops. There seemed to be heaps of trash out there, as well as several awkwardly-protruding ventilation stacks and chimneys. "What happens if the railings don't give way?" he wanted to know. "And supposing we collide with one of those chimneys?"

"And supposing your killers aren't even here at all?" Rick retorted. "We sure as hell haven't seen them *yet*; and we're up to the third level already."

But as they turned up the ramp to the fourth level, they heard the growl of another engine; and when they reached the top of the ramp, and turned again, the reception committee was there, waiting for them at the very end of the level, five of them, flanked by two gray Cadillac limousines, their headlights shining and their engines running.

"Skellett," said Kathy, breathlessly, recognizing at once the thin man standing in the center of the group in his pale blue sharkskin suit and bolus tie and wide-brimmed Western hat. Next to Skellett was the man called Walsh, with the crimson strawberry-mark on his face; and a little way behind him stood three Los Angeles Hell's Angels, hard-looking men in sleeveless denim jerkins and high-heeled boots, all tattooes and earrings and studs. Presumably Skellett had paid cash for a little supportive muscle.

Daniel said to Rick, "Stop the car. Don't get too close."

Rick drew the car to a halt, its engine warbling, and pushed on the parking-brake. But then he leaned over to Daniel, and said in a mock-British accent, "I think we have a slight flaw in the jolly old plan here."

"What's that? What are you talking about?"

"Well, hate to say it, old chap; but we're up here on the fourth level, unable to turn around so that our vehicle is facing the other way because of our hostile friends here; and yet our only route of escape is *behind* us."

Daniel said, uncomfortably, "What does that mean?"

"That means that when we hightail it out of here, old chum, we're going to have to do it in reverse."

Daniel peered out through the back window at the sloping concrete ramp which led down to the third level again. It was almost obscured by the Monaco's trunk. He certainly wouldn't have liked to have tried backing down there himself, even slowly.

He stared at Rick for a long time, while fifty feet away the men who had tortured Kathy and kidnapped Susie stood silent and impassive, half-obscured in front of the dazzling headlights of their parked cars, waiting like men who had all morning to kill.

"Do you think you can do it?" asked Daniel. "If you can't, we might just as well back off now. I don't mind trading myself for Susie, if that's what the deal has to be; but I don't intend to be killed right here in front of her."

"You don't even know that they've brought her here," said Kathy. "We haven't seen her yet."

Rick lifted himself up in the driver's seat and took a good long look behind him. Then he smiled ingenuously at Daniel, and said, "I'm a stuntman, remember. I can do these things."

"Can you back down that ramp at high speed? And then back all the way along the third level, and across those rooftops?"

"Piece of shit," smiled Rick. Daniel shot a look at Kathy, as if to suggest that Rick may not be as good as he boasted. But Rick caught the look, and gave Daniel a friendly punch on the upper arm, and said, "You know what you are? A Doubting Daniel. If I came up there *forwards*, I can go down there *backwards*."

One of the Hell's Angels came striding forward, and tapped on the Monaco's window with the tip of a baseball bat. Daniel put down the window, and said, "What is it?"

"You're Korvitz, right?"

"That's correct."

"Mr. Skellett wants you should step out of the car."

"Tell Mr. Skellett I don't do anything until I see my daughter safe and well."

The Hell's Angel thought about this for a while, and then turned around to Skellett and yelled, "Guy says he wants to see the girl."

Skellett didn't appear at first to have heard this raucously-broadcast message; but eventually he turned around, and beckoned to Walsh to follow him. The two men retreated to one of the gray Cadillac limousines, and opened up the back door. Her arms tied, blindfolded, Susie was helped out of the car, and pushed forward so that her father could see her.

"Susie?" called Daniel. His voice echoed.

"Susie?" he called again.

Susie said suddenly, "Daddy," in a voice of utter despair and anguish, and it took all the self-control he could squeeze out of himself for Daniel not to run forward and hold her protectively in his arms. His own little girl; Candii's girl. He thought to himself: that's the first time I've ever considered Susie to be Candii's daughter. Properly, I mean. The permanent fruit of Candii's fickle and transient affections. It gave him strength, somehow; a feeling that he would never really be alone.

"Skellett!" he called.

"Yes, Mr. Korvitz. I hear you."

"Skellett, I want you to let Susie go."

"That's what we're here for, Mr. Korvitz. But first, we want to hear that you're prepared to tell us what you know."

"I don't know anything, Skellett. Nothing at all. Just let Susie go, and you won't hear anything more about anything."

"Promises, Mr. Korvitz, promises. Assurances and promises. There isn't an assurance or a promise in this whole damn world you could go out and buy yourself lunch with. Promises and assurances are so much crap. Now, get out of the car, come over here, and we'll let your daughter go."

Daniel shifted around in his seat to look at Kathy. "Listen," he said, quickly, "it strikes me that their weakest moment is going to be when they let Susie go. Susie can't physically fight back at them; but *I* can, and I intend to. So the second that Susie is back at the car, tug her in, and I'll start hitting out. I may get away. I may not. But the first thing you have to do is drive directly towards me, so that I can have one good try at breaking free."

"They're armed, for Christ's sake," protested Rick.

"Sure they're armed. But we've got the benefit of knowing what's going to happen, and they haven't. So use the surprise."

"You're being very masterful all of a sudden," said Kathy.

Daniel opened the car door. "That's my daughter out there, with one of the most sadistic people I've ever heard of. You think I care about anything else?"

"*Bonne chance*," said Kathy.

Daniel stood beside the Monaco, using the open passenger door to shield the lower part of his body. He felt chilled, but very determined. He wanted Susie back, he wanted Susie safe. If there was anything at all that he had ever done in his entire life which was worth preserving, it was Susie. He wanted her alive, and that was all.

"Skellett!" he called. Then, quieter, "I'm coming across. I want you to let the girl go."

"We'll let the girl go when you're halfway, Mr. Korvitz. No point in taking risks. But I warn you—any ridiculous tricks and you're both dead meat."

"I'm coming, Mr. Skellett."

Daniel left the car and began to walk the twenty echoing paces towards Skellett and his entourage. Free of the blindfold, Susie's eyes widened as he came nearer, but she didn't cry out any more. Skellett at last gave her a gentle push and said, "Start walking, Susie. Walk towards the blue car. Don't stop to talk to Daddy. You'll be seeing him later."

Warily, unsteadily, like a fresh-born foal, Susie began walking towards Daniel. She stared at him intently all the time, as if she was desperately hoping for some kind of signal that everything was all right, that this entire pantomime of Skellett's was a bad adult joke; and that soon they would be back at the Downhome Diner, frying bacon and boiling grits and waiting for the first grumpy customers of another Apache Junction day.

As they passed each other, Daniel paused, and Susie instinctively paused, too. Skellett called, "Come on, Korvitz. Let's move it."

With extraordinary unpractised grace, Daniel rolled over sideways, snatching Susie as he did so, and rolled over again and again and again. For a long perceptible moment, nobody spoke, nobody reacted; but then two things happened at once. Rick gunned the Monaco's engine, and Walsh reached inside his sport coat for his gun. There was a scuffling blurt of echoes as Skellett and his three Hell's Angel bodyguards started running towards Daniel, and Daniel staggered, fell, got on to his feet, and grasped the Monaco's door-handle just as Rick skidded to a halt beside him.

Walsh fired twice: two light automatic bullets which ricocheted off the car's hood and roof, and snapped away across the parking-lot. Then Daniel had bundled Susie into the front seat of the car, and heaved himself in beside her, knocking his head against the half-open door, and Rick had thrown the Monaco into reverse and started to back up, with blue smoke screeching out from the tires.

Walsh fired again, and the windshield turned to milk. "Thank Christ we're going backwards!" yelled Rick, his backside half-lifted in his seat, one hand on the steering-wheel, his eyes fixed on the rear window as they skidded at 30 mph in reverse along the whole length of level four.

But at the corner his stuntman's judgment failed him: he collided heavily with a car that was parked right by the top of the ramp, and there was a smash of impacted metal. He thrust the gearshift into drive, then reverse again, and swung the Monaco wider this time, backing wildly down the concrete ramp and saying a prayer that nobody would be trying to come up the ramp in search of a parking-place.

As they swerved backwards into level three, Daniel realized with horror that Skellett had been running after them; and that he had caught up with them. Skellett thrust his gun into the open window and pointed it directly at Rick's head and screamed, "Stop! Stop this goddamned car or I'll kill you!"

Daniel seized Skellett's wrist and twisted it around so hard that the tendons burst. The gun fired once, inside the car: a sooty hot blast of flame and smoke that tore the ceiling lining to shreds, and left them all deafened. Daniel almost let go of Skellett's arm, but Rick yelled, "Hold on to the bastard! Daniel! Hold on to the bastard, you hear me?"

Lifting himself up in his seat again, Rick jammed his left foot against the gas pedal, and the Monaco roared backwards along the entire length of level three. Skellett, his arm twisted in Daniel's grip, was dragged along with it, his shoes bouncing and jarring on the concrete, his face contorted with surprise and pain. He shrieked, "Let me go! *Let me go!*" but Daniel held on to his arm so tightly that he succeded only in turning himself over on to his back, and wrenching his arm muscles. He let out a long, desperate, "*Yaaaaaahhhhhh!*"

The Monaco reached the end of level three just as a small family ranch wagon appeared at the crest of the ramp. The driver of the ranch wagon jammed on his brakes and stared pop-eyed as the Monaco hurtled towards him in reverse, and then smashed through the railings at the end of level three with a noise like a derailed locomotive, and bounced out into the sunshine on to the roof of the building next door. Skellett, his legs flying in the air, was still being dragged along with them. Daniel wasn't going to release him for anything or anybody, except the Lord Himself.

"*Jesus!*" cried Skellett, in total fear. "*Jesus Christ, let me go!*"

Walsh, at the far end of level three, crouched down and opened fire with his small automatic. One bullet penetrated the

Monaco's radiator, and there was a sudden hiss of released pressure. Another slapped into a tire, but didn't deflate it.

"Go!" shouted Daniel, and Rick swerved the car backwards in between the ventilation stacks and the garbage and the brick chimneys, and four buildings away they slithered to a halt beside a wide vehicle ramp, leading downwards.

"Get that bastard into the car!" said Rick. "Quick, move!"

Daniel released Skellett's arm, then opened his door, and opened the back door, and heaved Skellett on to the back seat, next to Kathy. Kathy stared at Skellett in fright and distaste, but Skellett was too bruised and concussed even to notice her. He groaned, and sank down on to the seat, and hunched there with bloody dribble hanging down on to the lapel of his powder-blue suit.

"Where does that ramp lead?" asked Kathy.

"It looks like a car showroom," said Daniel. "That means that we should be able to drive all the way out to the street."

"Daddy!" shouted Susie. "Daddy, they're coming!"

Daniel stuck his head quickly out of the Monaco's side window, and saw that Skellett's assistants must have run back to their limousines, and were speeding towards them along level three, headlights blazing. Rick wrapped his shirt-tail around his wrist and punched out the milk-white windshield; then gunned the engine again, and drove the Monaco straight down the vehicle ramp into the dark depths of the building at nearly 40 mph.

They collided against the left-hand wall as the ramp spiraled tightly downwards, losing hubcaps and doorhandles and ribbons of chrome trim. They passed a bodyshop floor, where mechanics were working on cars with acetylene torches and hammers; then they passed an upper showroom floor, crowded with sparkling new cars. Then they suddenly found themselves zooming into a first-floor showroom, with bright lights and brand new Toyotas on turntables, and customers walking between the cars, peering into the windows and browsing through brochures.

"Oh, God!" gasped Rick. He didn't have to tell them that he couldn't stop. The Monaco careened across the showroom floor at full speed, its tires howling on the polished marble, colliding with patted palm trees, desks, cardboard displays, light fixtures, and chairs. It rear-ended a brand-new bright-red Toyota estate car, crushing the back end and sending it nose-first into a concrete pillar. Then, when Rick frantically tried to back up, the Monaco's rear bumper caught another new Toyota's bumper, and tore off half the front grille.

"Daddy, they're here!" cried Susie; and with a throaty scream of engines and a scraping of metal, Skellett's two gray Cadillacs came barreling out of the service ramp like huge hungry wolves, lights full on, horns blaring.

"Here goes!" Rick shouted, and banged his foot down onto the gas pedal.

The Monaco burst straight through the car showroom's front window into the street, with glittering glass exploding everywhere, and tumbling in the morning sunlight. There were fragments like diamonds, fragments like swords, and all the time his ears were filled with a sound like breaking glaciers, creaking and crackling and tinkling and pattering.

The first of Skellett's Cadillac limousines skidded around sideways in a vain attempt to chase them. Its long rear-end slammed against the red Toyota station wagon which Rick had already wrecked. Its wheels spun on the polished floor. The second Cadillac collided with it, denting its nearside door, and then tried to drive around the side of the showroom and chase the Monaco by heading towards another window. But it skidded, struck a concrete pillar, and came to an abrupt stop.

There was a huge explosion as the Cadillac's gas tank blew. A rolling mushroom of orange fire incinerated the car, and everything living or mechanical within twenty feet. Then the first Cadillac's tank blew, too, and the showroom was turned into a furnace. The showroom blazed with a hungry rumbling sound, and all that anybody could do was stand and watch, and thank God that they hadn't been inside.

THIRTY-ONE

They stripped Skellett naked, tied him with cord, and locked him into the bathroom, which was the only room without a window. Rick and Daniel and Kathy went into the sitting-room and awarded themselves a large whiskey each, and sat there staring at each other in delayed shock and overwhelming relief. It was extraordinary to Daniel that the sun was still shining through the patterned net curtains, and that it wasn't even lunchtime. They still had plenty of time to go to Butterfield's for a salad and a glass of wine; or to the Cock'n'Bull for ribs. Not that any of them had the stomach for eating.

Susie had seemed unmarked, and unhurt, although her hair was filthy and she hadn't changed her clothes since she had been kidnapped. Daniel had gently bathed her, and given her milk to drink, and a child's sedative, and tucked her into his own bed. She had fallen asleep within minutes, a child's immediate and innocent reaction to being safe.

Rick yawned, loudly. "I'm sorry," he said. "I always yawn when the tension's over."

Daniel glanced over at Kathy, and wondered if she were thinking the same things that he was.

Rick said, "Those guys are madmen, right? I mean, they're really crazies. Just like you said."

Daniel nodded, and sipped his whiskey.

Kathy said, "I couldn't believe the way we went right through that showroom. I'm going to have nightmares about that tonight."

"Pretty fancy piece of driving," said Daniel.

"Why, thank you," Rick acknowledged.

"Pretty fancy piece of lying, too," said Daniel.

Rick swallowed whiskey, and then sat up straight in his chair, pointing at his own chest. "You mean me? Is that *me* you're talking about?"

"That's right. Rick Terroni, the happy-go-lucky stuntman and fortunate hitch-hiker. Let's say rather *too* fortunate hitch-hiker. The hitch-hiker who doesn't quite know where he's going, and doesn't quite know where he's been. The hitch-hiker who's got friends all over town and no place to stay. The hitch-hiker who will happily spend half the night tuning a car for a dangerous and crazy expedition with total strangers, and never complain once."

"I think you've got me wrong, Daniel," frowned Rick. "I think you've got me completely mixed-up."

Daniel shook his head. "One thing gave you away more than anything else. Why did you insist that I hold onto Skellett, and why did you make sure that I dragged him into the car? If you were nothing more than a hitch-hiker, you wouldn't care what happened to Skellett; in fact, you'd probably be delighted to see the back of him. You certainly wouldn't insist that we take him along with us, or take such obvious relish in tying him up and locking him into the john. You're not what you say you are, Rick. I don't quite understand what you really might be, or what interest you could possibly have in any of this. But you *do* have an interest, and I'd like for you to explain it to me."

Rick grinned, and finished his whiskey, and gave both of them a cheerful smile. "You're not satisfied you got the little girl back?"

"I'm more than satisfied. I'll never be able to repay you for what you did today. I mean that. But I still believe that you're lying."

"Well, there are lies and lies."

"Which particular kind of lies do you tell?"

"I tell the patriotic kind of lies."

"Can there *be* such a thing?" asked Kathy, caustically.

"Of course. Any lie that you use in defense of the American people and their right to be free: that's a patriotic lie, you get me? And therefore forgivable at all times."

"Rick," said Daniel, gently, "I want to thank you with everything I possibly can for saving Susie today. For saving all of us. That was a wild and risky plan, but as it turned out, it worked. *You* made it work, with that stunt driving of yours. But there's something you have to know. We're not just dealing with hoodlums and kidnappers here. We're dealing with political conspiracy; something far greater and far more frightening than anything this nation had to face before. Leastways, that's what we believe it to be."

"Well," said Rick, "that's what I *know* it to be."

"You *know* about this?" asked Kathy, in disbelief. "You know about Cuba and Kennedy, and Marilyn Monroe?"

"I don't know about Marilyn Monroe; what about Marilyn Monroe?"

"She was killed because she was involved in all this, whatever it is. But not in 1962 . . . this month, only a week ago."

Rick said, "Listen, I'll have to come clean with you people. I intended to anyway, but our meeting out there on the Pacific Coast Highway wasn't an accident. I'd been following your car for two days, seeing what you were up to. When you stopped by the beach, my friend left me by the side of the highway there, and I asked you for a ride. If you'd turned me down, well, my friend would have picked me up straight away and we would have followed you again. But we reckoned that you looked like the kind of people who might give a guy a ride—and that hitching would be one of the best ways of getting to know you."

"Who are you?" Kathy asked him. "Are you some kind of detective, or what? You're obviously not in cahoots with *those* people." She nodded towards the bathroom where Skellett was locked up.

"No, I'm not," said Rick. He tugged his fingers through his hair, and stretched himself out, relaxing. "I'm the chapter chief of Free Columbia. You've heard of Free Columbia?"

Daniel shook his head, but Kathy said, "I've heard some rumors about it. It's supposed to be an amalgamation of all the subversive groups of the 1960s, isn't it? The Panthers, the

Weathermen, the Yippies. Some people even say ex-Mansonites, the Dune Buggy Attack Battalion.''

''Whatever you've read about it, or heard about it, is bullshit,'' said Rick. ''Free Columbia was a get-together of all these groups to liberate America from one thing and one thing only: the Soviets. Of course, the propaganda you get in the media makes us out to be a bunch of irresponsible terrorists. And anybody who attempts to stand up and tell the truth gets pretty quickly wasted. But it's true. Ever since 1962, the United States has been controlled by a Soviet committee, chaired by an old-time Bolshevik politician they call Ikon.''

''Are you high or something?'' Daniel demanded.

''I wish I was,'' Rick told him. ''But I'm not, and it's true. Kennedy didn't succeed in facing down Khruschev over the Cuban missiles at all. By the time the 'Cuban missile crisis' was supposed to be coming to a head, the Russians were already in charge, and infiltrating the government and the armed forces. As far as any of us have been able to find out, the missile crisis was simply a way of concealing the shift in government, and giving the American public a feeling of false security. It also made the fake 'disarmament' talks of 1963 seem justified. You know, we've licked the Russians, let's be magnanimous.''

Daniel said, ''You're trying to tell me that the Soviet Union is in charge of America? That's what you're saying?''

''Don't worry,'' Rick reassured him. ''Everybody reacts the same way when they first find out. A couple of people I know have even committed suicide. You know, suddenly they discover that the life they've been living for the past twenty years was something altogether different. The world is someplace alien and strange.''

''But how can it possibly have been kept a secret for so long? When so many people must know?''

''How did Hitler keep the concentration camps secret? How did Stalin conceal the deaths of thousands of Russians? A secret doesn't have to be too much of a secret if you can enforce its secrecy with terror. You say they killed Marilyn Monroe, recently. Well, I believe you. That's exactly the way they do things. They never let you escape. They hunt you down and hunt you down until they find you, and then they kill you and there's no mercy.

I mean that. We lost eight Panthers in April. Did you hear about eight black guys dying in a blazing bus in Georgia? Not the kind of news story you'd remember, is it? But that bus was bombed by Ikon's people. Look at you—you're afraid to go to the police. You don't know who's going to be a Soviet stool-pigeon and who isn't; and believe me, if you open your mouth to the wrong person, you're dead.''

He reached over and poured himself some more whiskey. ''I don't know how many members Free Columbia has altogether. It could be as few as thirty thousand, or as many as a million. We're trying all the time to raise the public's awareness to the Soviet take-over, but do you know how *difficult* it is to get a message like that across? One of our members used to work for a print union, and he managed to run a story in *The New York Times*, foot of page one, announcing that the United States was under the control of the Soviet Union and that we should all rise up and overthrow them. That was July 17, 1964. And do you know what happened? Two people called up *The New York Times* and asked if it were true. Two people. And of course that brought the story to the attention of the sub-editors, and they knocked it out and replaced it with a story about a British mail strike. A week later the guy who had sneaked the story into print was found drowned.''

Kathy said, ''I don't understand why the Soviets haven't put the country under more overt Russian rule.''

''They don't need to. They can exploit us economically and politically without having to turn us all into Communists—although we've always believed that this is their eventual aim. That's what all these disarmament talks are all about: they want gradually to educate the American public into thinking that there's no more prospect of nuclear war, and that it's time the U.S.A. and the U.S.S.R. were all buddies. That's what this economic recession is all about, too. The Soviets are manipulating American banks and funds so that huge amounts of investment money simply isn't reaching American industry. The recession isn't real at all. We're simply the victims of the greatest siege in global history. Outside of our borders, in Japan and Switzerland and the Soviet Union, there's enough American money stashed away to end the recession overnight: and I mean *overnight*. But the

Soviets aren't going to let us get our hands on it until we've turned to international socialism, and Leninism: and it's only *then* they're going to release their grip on the world economy, so that we believe that Communism has brought us instant prosperity.''

They sat in silence while the sunshine blew through the net curtains, and the sounds of Sunset Strip came faintly across the flowering back yard. Daniel felt as if he were dreaming; as if he would wake up in a minute or two and find that he was back in his bed in Apache Junction. Kathy finished her drink, and then said, "I'm stunned. I don't know what to think about it. I mean, the whole of my world has turned out to be something I didn't imagine it ever could be, and I don't know how to work it out in my mind any more. There's nothing to relate to any more.''

"There *is* one thing," said Rick, "and if you ever thought you'd hear a one-time card-carrying member of the Weather Underground say this . . . well, I wouldn't believe you. But the one thing you *can* relate to is the American Constitution. What it says in the Constitution is what we're fighting for now. And everything you learned in school. John Paul Jones, Sam Houston, Benjamin Franklin, George Washington. The spirit lives on; and always will do. They still have their own heroes in Poland, remember. They still remember Imre Nagy in Hungary.''

Softly, Kathy said, "What are we going to do?''

"There's nothing we *can* do, except go on fighting. If you want to join in, you're welcome.''

Daniel said, "The risk—''

"Is very high," Rick interrupted. "You saw for yourself today what Ikon's hit-men can do. It was only by plain old California luck that we managed to get away.''

"Why were you so keen on capturing Skellett?''

"He's a leading agent of theirs, that's why. And he has a reputation for being one of the most vicious. We'll take him out to the Mojave Movie Ranch, where we usually take any Soviet infiltrators we capture. We'll interrogate him; and then I guess we'll probably kill him.''

"That's murder.''

"You think so? There are dozens of agents like Skellett, and they're all as cold-blooded as anybody can be. They've got Siberian ice-water in their veins.''

"Are they Russian?"

"Some of them are, not him. The Soviets have a program of recruitment from most of the major American penitentiaries. They pick the real hard nuts and train them in weapons and unarmed combat to make them even harder. Some of them are kind of weird, you know, head-cases. That's why you get the occasional well-publicized mass-murder, or shoot-out. And we've believed for about a year now that there's something of a power struggle going on inside the Soviet committee, and that some of Ikon's agents have become polarized to another leader. Ikon is obviously ruthless; but there's some evidence now that one or two agents are acting even more violently and even more openly than Ikon's men usually do. It could be that one of the Soviet leaders is trying to show Ikon up; or threaten him in some way. We don't know, and that's why I want to interrogate Skellett.''

"Do you think he'll tell you anything?"

"I don't know. Some of them do. We've captured maybe six in the past three years. But some of the new agents are like kamikaze pilots; completely indoctrinated to the point where they'll shoot themselves just to annoy you.''

"I saw one like that," said Kathy. "A young man in Arizona, who packed his own intestines with explosives and blew himself up, simply to give Skellett time to escape.''

"Some way to go, huh?" nodded Rick.

Later, Daniel went into Susie's room and watched her sleeping. Her hair was spread on the pillow, one hand was clutching the sheet, as if to prevent herself from falling into some dark and unwanted dream. Daniel wondered how he would ever be able to explain to her that America was no longer free: that within her lifetime she may be a slave to Communism; that the land he had hoped to give her as her birthright had been forfeited before she had even been born.

"My daddy is dead, but I can't tell you how;
He left me six horses to follow the plow:
I sold my six horses to buy me a cow;
And wasn't that a pretty thing to follow the plow?

I sold my cow to buy me a cat,
To sit down before the fire to warm her little back.
I sold my cat to buy me a mouse,
But she took fire in her tail and burn'd down my house.
With my whim-wham waddle-ho!"

Susie stirred. Daniel closed the bedroom door, but he stood outside for a long time, listening, keeping guard.

THIRTY-TWO

Nadine came back to the house at midnight that night to find that Titus was still up, sitting by himself in the library, drinking the bottle of 1924 brandy which had been given him by President Giscard d'Estaing of France, and which he had always sworn he would never open. He raised his head in some surprise as she came through the door, and stood there in her smart gray-flecked dress, her gloves upraised in one hand, her hat at an angle so that the brim shadowed her face.

"Well," he said gruffly, "you've got a goddamned nerve. I'm surprised they let you in."

"Don't worry. They've probably called the FBI already."

Titus said, "You killed those people, all of them. You actually killed them."

"You won't find any proof. Nor will you ever find your precious videos again."

"God damn it, Nadine, I know you killed those people."

"What you know and what you can prove are two very different things. Now, since you've opened up your precious bottle of 1924 brandy, aren't you going to offer any to me?"

A security guard arrived breathlessly in the hallway outside, and knocked on the paneling.

"Mr. Secretary? Are you okay?"

"It's just as well that I am," growled Titus. "If she'd had any intention of killing me, I would have been well dead by now."

"Yes, sir. I'm sorry, sir."

"You're sorry? Get back to your station."

Titus poured Nadine a small measure of brandy and held it out to her, without getting up from his chair. Nadine came forward with an arch smile and took it.

"I'm sorry it had to happen this way," she said. "You didn't leave me with any alternative."

"I've been hearing a lot of people saying that lately."

"You seem angry."

"I am angry. I'm also sick, confused, bewildered, frightened, disoriented, upset, and tired."

"That's quite a list."

Titus swallowed the remaining liquor in his glass, stared at the bottle, and then poured himself another one, much larger this time. "What the hell, it's only brandy."

Nadine sniffed it. "It's very fine."

Titus said, "Yesterday afternoon I went down to Bolling Air Force Base and spoke to my old friend Pierce Caulfield."

"General Caufield? I know him."

"You should. He's one of your stooges. He's known about Ikon since 1974 and he's never once breathed a word about it. Never once! God damn it all, I've been to dinner with that man, gone fishing with him, attended his stupid daughter's wedding, and all the time he knew about Ikon and he never told me!"

Nadine sat down on the floor, and rested one hand on Titus' knee. "I'm sorry," she said. "You've been a remarkable husband; even if we have argued all the time. An unparalleled lover. And you're the best Secretary of State that America ever had."

"America?" asked Titus, bitterly. "The Autonomous Capitalist Oblast of Sod-all."

Nadine said, "Joe was one of ours too, you know."

Titus stared at her; and then said, "Really?" and then "Mmh," as if he didn't care at all. He had already suffered the greatest disenchantment; a few minor betrayals didn't seem to make very much difference.

"I wasn't going to leave you, you know," said Nadine.

"I think I'd prefer it if you did."

"I want you to come and meet Ikon."

"You want what?"

"Tomorrow morning, I want you to come and meet Ikon. I want you to see what he's like, talk to him, and understand his problems. Ikon needs all the help he can get right now; and whatever you think about the Autonomous Capitalist Oblast of America, Ikon is the lesser of two evils. I think you have a duty to help him survive."

"I'll tear his goddamned Commie neck off."

"Titus, please. I'm trying to help."

"How can you help?" Titus shouted at her. "How can you possibly help? My entire life was flushed down some sneaky historical toilet when I wasn't looking; and for twenty years I've been marching forward with my head in the air and my pants round my goddamned ankles. How the hell can you *help*?"

"Titus—"

"Leave me alone, Nadine, for the love of God. I've got a bottle of brandy to finish."

"Titus, please."

Titus shook his head, again and again and again, until his jowls wobbled. Then he stamped both feet on the floor and roared, "No! No! No! No! No!"

Nadine put down her drink, stood up quietly, and left him. On the way out, the security guard said, "Everything all right, Mrs. Alexander?"

"Everything's fine, thank you. Oh—and could you do something for me? Could you arrange for Mr. Alexander's car to be waiting outside for us at ten o' clock tomorrow morning? We have an appointment on Pennsylvania Avenue."

The security guard glanced into the library, where Titus was glowering at the floor as if he could make the rug catch fire by the heat of his vision alone. "Sure thing, Mrs. Alexander," he said, in a cautious voice. "Ten o'clock sharp."

THIRTY-THREE

Two other incidents occurred at midnight that night, although in Las Vegas, Nevada, in the Pacific Time Zone, midnight came three hours later. A chambermaid from the Las Vegas Futura Hotel left the hotel's service entrance and walked north-eastwards along the alleyway which led out on to Bonanza Road, where she intended to catch a cab to take her home. Her cleaning shift had finished at 11:15 p.m., but she had spent three-quarters of an hour in the hotel kitchen, talking to a friend who had recently divorced her husband and eating a supper of cold ham, cheese, and salad.

She was halfway along the alleyway when a voice called out, "Anna!" She turned around to say, "I'm not Anna," when there was a deafening shotgun blast, then another. The shots were fired at such close range that she was completely eviscerated, and she died before she fell to the ground. The Chinese night-chef, who had heard the shots, came running out to the alleyway to find it plastered spectacularly in blood. But there was no sign of the chambermaid's killer; only an inquisitive cat which had jumped away when the gun first went off, and had now returned to sniff the warm scent of death.

At home, on the scrubby edge of the Nevada desert, the chambermaid's husband lay awake, waiting for the familiar sound of the cab bringing his wife back from town. The radio beside his bed was turned down low, so that it wouldn't wake up the children. It played *Stand By Your Man*, by Tammy Wynette, and he whistled along with it, under his breath.

He had never known that two years ago his wife had caught a glimpse of Senator Marshall Roberts leaving Room 1198 of the Futura Hotel with a high-class hooker known as Rita Haze. He never would know. But, in about twenty minutes' time, he would hear the warble of a police siren as a patrol-car sped out along the desert road to bring him the news that his wife was dead. He would see the red light flashing across his bedroom ceiling and know, before they told him, that something had gone terribly wrong.

Also at midnight, the President of the United States, Marshall Roberts, was undressing for bed when there was a ring on his private telephone. He called to his wife, "It's all right, dear, I'll get it," and walked across the white-carpeted bedroom, unbuttoning his cuffs as he went. He picked up the Louis Quinze-style telephone, and said, "Marshall Roberts."

"Good evening, Mr. President," said a thick voice. "This is Nikolai. Please forgive me for calling you so late."

"Not at all," said Marshall, although without much patience. "What can I do for you, Nikolai?"

"I couldn't sleep, Mr. President."

"Is that unusual?"

"Well, I have my tablets. But it is not the pain . . . I have a feeling of fear, Mr. President. I feel like Caesar before the Ides of March."

"Is it Kama you're worried about?"

"I'm not sure. I've never felt like this before, not in my entire career. Mr. President, do you think perhaps that tonight is the night when I am going to die?"

"Don't talk nonsense. You're probably over-tired."

"Perhaps." There was a breathy pause. Then Ikon said, "You know that the RINC talks may now proceed. All opposition has been completely eliminated."

"The chambermaid?"

"Later tonight. But there won't be any slip-ups."

"I see. Well, I'll start drafting the announcement tomorrow."

There was another, longer pause. Marshall Roberts said, "Is that all, Nikolai? I'm quite tired. I'd like to get some sleep now."

"I'm afraid, Mr. President. Don't you think that's strange?"

"Not in your position, not at your time of life."

"But I'm afraid."

"Have a drink. Some of that cherry vodka of yours. Then count sheep. Or blessings."

"What blessings do *I* have, Mr. President?"

"You're still alive, Nikolai. That's a blessing. And the world hasn't yet been incinerated by nuclear weapons. That's another blessing. And, if you like, I'll stop by at Pennsylvania Avenue tomorrow afternoon and share a drink with you."

"Very well," said Ikon, with audible uncertainty. Then, "Very well, I will try to sleep. But this feeling I have . . . of death. It makes me cold!"

"Try an electric blanket," suggested Marshall Roberts, and hung up.

THIRTY-FOUR

That night, as Daniel lay in bed, he heard the door creak open. He froze, and reached across for the three-foot-long section of angle-iron which he had left beside his bed-head. The room was utterly dark, except for a single yellow wedge of light, the size of a piece of cheese, on the opposite side of the ceiling.

"Who's there?" Daniel whispered. His nose had been feeling slightly blocked up, which was one reason he had been finding it difficult to sleep; but now his sinuses emptied instantly. His balls tightened, and there was a flicker of nerves in his stomach.

"It's *me*," came the whispered reply. "Kathy. Can I come in?"

Daniel let out a breath, and relaxed. "For God's sake, I could have killed you. What do you want?"

She glided across the room and leaned over him. He dimly saw the shape of her breasts, and realized that she was naked. She smelled of Cie. "I can't get to sleep in that room, right next to the bathroom. Skellett keeps banging his head against the wall and making terrible groaning noises."

"Well, jump in here, then."

She lifted the cover and bounced in beside him, taking him immediately into her arms. She was warm and rounded and soft, but ner nipples were as stiff and sweet and wrinkled as California raisins. She thrust one leg in between Daniel's, so that she was straddling his thigh; and the message of that move was obvious when he felt the night-cooled stickiness of her pubic hair against his bare skin. He said, "Kathy?" But questions were unnecessary. His cock rose against her stomach until it was pushing against her navel; and he took her face in her hands and kissed her, deeply and urgently.

She gasped. "Please don't wait."

He twisted around in the bedsheets, and climbed on top of her. She reached down and held his erection in her hand, and guided it up between her legs. He hesitated for a second, and then pushed slowly forward so that he slid deep into her slippery warmth, until it was impossible for him to push any deeper.

"Fuck me," she demanded, digging her fingernails into the muscles at the small of his back. "I don't want to *think*, I don't want to be afraid. I just want to fuck."

They made love for nearly an hour, strenuously and sometimes furiously. She cursed him and cooed at him, stroked him and bit him. She forced her hips up against him whenever he began to falter, and coaxed him into one erection after another. Then the moment came when she was straddling him, pushing herself up and down on him so quickly that with each upward stroke she almost lost the tip of his penis. And in that moment she seemed to collapse like a dark warm wind drawing in on itself; and she trembled and shook and cried out to him, "Daniel, save me! Daniel!"

They lay for a long time side by side in silence. Kathy said, after a while, "You're thinking what a whore I am."

"A whore? No? Exactly the opposite. Whores do it for money. You did it because you wanted to."

"And you?"

"I did it because I like you, and because I think you're very pretty, and very attractive, and because you're exactly my type."

"I thought country-and-western heroines were your type."

"Isn't a man allowed to change his type?"

"A man's allowed to do anything he wants to. But then so is a woman."

Daniel reached across her and switched on the bedside lamp.

"Do you want a drink or anything? I don't think I'm going to be able to sleep tonight. I keep thinking about Ikon."

She kissed his shoulder. "You know something . . . when I went out to report on Margot Schneider's murder . . . I never dreamed it would lead to anything like this."

"Neither did Willy Monahan. God, if only he'd known."

"Poor Willy."

"Yes," said Daniel. "Poor Willy."

Kathy stroked the inside of his upraised arm. "You know something?" she said, "I liked the look of you the moment I first met you. Did anyone tell you how attractive you are, as a man? You look sensitive, but you look strong, too."

He leaned forward and kissed her. "I'm not always strong. I haven't been particularly strong over the past few years."

"But why not? You have a charm about you; did you know that? A real sexual grace. And yet you don't have the confidence that ought to go with it."

"Well, I guess it's partly because Candii walked out on me. She was kind of my dream girl. That was before I changed my type, I hasten to add."

Kathy laughed. "You don't have to change your type, just for me."

"The way you raped me just then, I think it's the least I can do."

"I raped you? I didn't notice you protesting."

"I was afraid you might hurt me if I did."

Kathy held herself close to him, her breasts pressed against his chest, her hand possessively cupping his soft penis. She said, very quietly, "I can hear your heart beating. That frightens me, sometimes, to hear somebody's heart beating. I keep thinking that it's going to stop."

Daniel said nothing, but stroked her hair. In spite of Kathy's company, in spite of her closeness, he felt peculiarly lonesome. Perhaps it was the cold knowledge that America was no longer free; and that the future was no longer certain. How long before the Soviets would openly reveal their ownership of the United States, and begin to suppress free speech? How long before nobody would be allowed to say or write anything against the State and the everyday grumbles at the Downhome Diner would be censored by fear? How long before the late-night television news would report nothing more than official party information, and all the silliness and eccentricity and childish greed of American television was lost forever? He thought of the Joni Mitchell song which had warned "You don't miss what you've got 'till it's gone," and already, in Kathy's arms, he began to miss America.

Kathy said, "I don't know what to think about Kennedy any more. I used to adore him. He was my hero, when I was fourteen years old. And Jackie!"

"It probably wasn't his fault," said Daniel. "God Almighty— what would *you* have done if somebody had told you that fifty 10-megaton missiles were aimed at New York, and St. Louis, and Chicago, and Denver, and that they were so close that you had no possible chance of stopping them? Do you know how long it would take a missile to get from Cuba to Houston? Well, I don't know either, but it can't be more than a couple of minutes. Willy would have known."

"I'll have that drink now," she told Daniel, gently. "A vodka, if there's any left. I guess I might as well get used to drinking the stuff."

Daniel climbed over her, and out of bed. He bent over and kissed her, and said, "You don't want a midnight hamburger, do you? I'm beginning to feel like cooking again. There's plenty of ground beef in the icebox; and onions."

"What are you trying to do, turn me into a San Francisco sideshow? The Fattest Female Reporter in the West?"

"I'm beginning to miss cooking, that's all."

"Well, don't start acting your culinary obsessions out on me."

Daniel raised both of his hands in surrender. "Okay, I promise I won't cook you a hamburger. But don't start complaining when you see mine."

"Daniel," she said, as he put his hand on the doorhandle.

He looked at her, his smile only just beginning to fade. Sitting up in bed, she looked pretty and short-sighted, vulnerable and almost childish. One breast was bare, soft and curved and pink-nippled.

"What we did tonight, don't read any special meanings into

it," she said. "It was just that I was tired, and frightened, and I wanted you. But don't expect anything out of it tomorrow."

"Tomorrow?" asked Daniel. "I never look that far ahead. Tell me about tomorrow when it's tomorrow."

He opened the door, and there was Skellett. Not only Skellett, but Walsh, and both of them were armed.

"Back into the room," said Skellett. Daniel hesitated; and Skellett shrieked at him, "*Back into the room, dummy!*"

Daniel backed away, holding up his hands. Both Skellett and Walsh were carrying .45 automatics, powerful enough to blow off the average human head. Daniel stepped back as far as the bedroom wall, and stood there stock still, his hands still held high, saying nothing.

Skellett said, tartly, "Mr. Walsh and the Los Angeles Police Department wish to thank you for your consideration in leaving your car parked right outside the house where you happen to be staying; and for checking in with the house-rental agency under your real names. You couldn't have made it easier for them to locate you if you'd fired signal rockets off from the roof."

"How did you get away?" Kathy asked Skellett. "I thought you were tied up naked in the bathroom."

"I was, lady, I was, and believe me I won't forget it. But Mr. Walsh here has an incomparable way with locked doors, don't you, Mr. Walsh? He tears them off their hinges. And damned lucky for you that you didn't throw away my clothes; that sharkskin suit cost $450, and that was without the vest."

"Where's Rick?" asked Daniel. "Rick Terroni, the other guy who was here?"

"Oh, Rick *Terroni*. That's it! Rick Terroni, Pratfaller Extraordinaire. Well, he's comfortably tied up in his room right now, courtesy of Mr. Walsh, and there isn't much chance that he's going to be able to get away. The simple reason is, we've nailed his hands to the floor."

"God, you're a savage bastard," said Kathy.

Skellett stalked across to the bed, raised his hand, and slapped Kathy right across the cheek, a cracking slap that broke the skin, and left the clear imprint of a man's hand on her face.

"You got away from me once, lady. You should have *kept* away."

Daniel lowered his hands, his blood thundering through his veins like boiling mercury; but Skellett did nothing more than swing his .45 around to point directly at Daniel's face. "As for you, *schmuck*, you should have stayed out of it, too. You and your nosey Air Force friend."

"You hit her again—" warned Daniel.

Skellett stalked up to him, and pointed the automatic right between his eyes. "Yes?" he demanded. "I hit her again, and *what*? What are you going to do about it?"

Daniel lowered his head. "Just do what you've got to do," he said, in a humiliated mutter. "Just do it, all right?"

Skellett stared at Daniel with eyes like pebbles. "If it was up to me, friend, I'd kill you here and now. Four of our people, dead, because of what you did yesterday morning, at the Wilcox Street parking-lot. Four trained agents, three of them spent years infiltrating the California Hell's Angels. You know what you threw away yesterday, with those stunts of yours? Years of patient work. *Years*."

"Skellett—"

"Don't annoy me, do you understand? Just don't annoy me. I'm taking all of you to Washington. I don't want to, I'd rather blow your fucking heads off, personally. Right here, kill the whole damn lot of you, Susie included. But it seems like you know much more than you ought to; and the *boyars* in Washington want to know exactly *how* much. They want to put you through the mill, you get me?"

Skellett said to Kathy, "Get dressed. We have a plane leaving from Burbank at three o'clock."

Kathy hesitantly held the sheets up against her naked body.

"Get dressed!" snapped Skellett. "We've seen it all before!"

But both he and Walsh watched her pruriently as she wrapped the sheet around herself and trailed through the door to her own bedroom.

"Keep an eye on her, Walsh," said Skellett. "Korvitz—you get dressed, too. Come on, let's get going. I've had it up to here with this dump of a house."

Daniel quickly pulled on his jeans and his Arizona sweatshirt, and then went into Susie's room to get her dressed, too. When she saw Skellett standing in the doorway, her face went rigid with fright; but Daniel sat down beside her and said, "It's okay. You understand? We're all together this time. Nothing's going to happen."

Skellett cleared his throat loudly and nastily, but didn't make any comments.

They came across Rick in the hallway, stretched out on his stomach like a man crucified, with a dishcloth forced into his mouth. He was very white, and he was trembling with unstoppable quakes like an epileptic. His hands had been pierced by kitchen knives, the points of which had been stuck deeply into the polished wooden floor. Skellett stood over him for a while, watching him with distant satisfaction, and then said, "All right, Walsh. Release him. He's coming with us."

Walsh plucked out the knives, one after the other, and tossed them across the hallway. Rick stayed where he was, shaking, white as death. Walsh kicked him in the ribs; and then turned him over with his foot.

"Get up, okay?" he demanded. "You want me to jump on your guts?"

Shivering, wild-eyed, Rick managed to sit up. Walsh cuffed him, hard enough to send him sprawling, and then kicked him again. "I told you to get up, didn't I? What's the matter with you? Get up!"

Rick at last managed to pull himself up on to his feet. He stared at Daniel as if he didn't recognize him. Daniel said nothing, but kept his arm around Susie, and prayed again and again that Skellett wasn't going to kill them. Not now, oh Lord. Please not now.

THIRTY-FIVE

Ikon was still asleep at ten o'clock the following morning; even though two important parties were arriving almost simultaneously at the large gray-stone building on Pennsylvania Avenue. At the front entrance, with its six semi-circular steps, and its uniformed doorman, a long dark-gray Cadillac Fleetwood was drawing up, with Titus and Nadine Alexander.

At the back entrance, in a plain brown panel van, Skellett was arriving with Daniel, Kathy, Rick, and Susie. They had been flown in a Gulfstream III from Burbank to College Park Airport, just north-east of Washington, and then been driven into the city along Highway 1. Skellett had ordered them not to speak to each other, and so for hours they had remained in anxious silence. Susie had only just recovered from her first kidnap by Skellett and Walsh and now she was being abducted again; her face was as drawn and haggard as the face of an old woman. Daniel kept his arm tightly around her—that was all he could do.

"Okay, *out*," said Skellett, as the doors of the panel-van were opened up. "And don't try anything stupid. There's nothing that you can possibly do here that's worth dying for. You understand me? Just do what you're told, keep quiet, and you may survive."

They were ushered quickly along a peeling green-painted corridor until they reached a service elevator. Skellett pushed the

331

call-button, and while they waited, he stood there smiling at them as if they were school-children, and he was taking them to see the head teacher. There was that particularly wolfish look on his face: You wait until you see what we've got in store for *you*. The door opened and he ushered them in.

The service elevator rose with a jarring shudder to the tenth floor, and then Skellett drew back the gates and said, "Out. Walk straight ahead of you. Keep on going until you reach the end of the corridor. Then make a left."

They walked along the fluorescent-lit corridor in silence. The only sound was the squeak and clatter of their shoes. At the end of the corridor, they were met by two men who looked like security guards, dressed in gray uniforms with badges on their shoulders that Daniel had never seen before, but whose meaning he immediately grasped. They showed an eagle, perched on a sickle. The motif of the Autonomous Capitalist Oblast of America. Kathy glanced across at Daniel for the first time since they had been herded into the building, and he knew what she was thinking. There wouldn't be guards with these badges if Ikon didn't exist, if everything that Rick had said about a Soviet takeover of the United States hadn't been a reality.

Skellett said, "This way. You can wait in here." Then he said something in Russian to the two security guards, who briskly answered him back, and saluted.

The four of them were pushed into a plain, green-painted room with a morning-misted view of the Internal Revenue Service building. There was no furniture, no drapes, no carpet. The door was slammed shut behind them and locked.

They went to the window and looked down ten dizzying stories at Pennsylvania Avenue. Rick tentatively tried the window-catch, wincing with the pain in his wounded hands, and said, "It's not locked. We could all just about squeeze out of here." The window was hinged at the top so that when it was open they could peer straight down at Pennsylvania Avenue.

"Three hundred feet in the air?" said Daniel. "You have to be joking."

Rick opened the window wider. "There's a ledge below us, as a matter of fact. We could climb out on to the ledge."

"Forget it, Rick. We're not stuntmen, like you. We're just

ordinary people who don't feel like climbing all over high-rise buildings. Besides, if we got out on that ledge, where could we possibly go?''

Kathy said seriously, "Do you think they're going to—well, do you think they're going to torture us? I'm not sure I could take any more of what Skellett did to me in Phoenix."

Daniel reached out and held her arm. The chances were that they would all be tortured, all of them except Susie, who didn't know anything at all; and she would be tortured enough by the pain that her father would have to bear. Susie would be tortured beyond endurance if Daniel were to die.

Rick said, "Listen, will you listen? We could climb out on to the ledge, and then we could climb upwards."

"What are you talking about?" Daniel demanded. "We're ten stories up in the air. We're supposed to climb out of a window and then climb *higher*?"

"We can do it, God damn it," said Rick. "The ledges only start on the ninth floor, but then there's all this decorative molding that goes right up to the roof. If we climb out on to the ledge below this window, and make out way along to the corner of the building, there's a whole lot of concrete acanthus leaves; and we could climb up on those to the roof."

"Rick, I've got a seven-year-old girl here."

"What's wrong with that? A seven-year-old girl could climb up there better than you can, probably."

"But Jesus, Rick, *it's three hundred feet to the ground.*"

Rick stood up straight, and spread his arms. "Daniel, we're not *going* to the ground. We're going to the roof."

Daniel stared at Rick with an expression that could have bored holes in solid concrete, but when Rick refused to flinch he knew that Rick was sure that they could make it—or at least that their chances of surviving outside on the ledge were higher than their chances of surviving at the hands of Skellett and Walsh, and whatever other torturers Ikon could call upon. He turned away, and looked at Kathy, and Susie, and all he could feel was fear. Fear for them, because he knew that they were weaker, and that if anybody was going to fall from the ledge, it was going to be one of them. Fear for himself, too: for what he was going to have to do, and for the responsibility of looking after all these lives.

There was a sharp rapping at the door. A voice said, "Ten minutes, then you see Ikon! Make smart!"

"You hear that?" asked Rick. "We've got ten minutes to make our minds up. Less than that. We've got two minutes to make up our minds up, and eight minutes to climb out of that goddamned window."

Daniel closed his eyes for a moment.

"You praying again?" asked Rick.

Daniel opened his eyes again.

"I was just trying to work out what I would say to God on the way down to the sidewalk. 'Forgive me, Lord, for I lost my footing?' "

Kathy took Daniel's arm. "Come on, Daniel. Calm down. We don't have to do it, any of us, if we really don't want to."

"Are you going to do it?"

"I'm going to try."

Rick opened the window as far as it would go. Although it was such a still, misty morning, the wind blew in through the foot-wide aperture with a sound like howling demons. "I think I'd better go first, then I can show you the best way to climb. The rule is, don't hurry, don't make a step unless you're sure where your foot's going to land, and stay confident. We're all going to make it. Nobody's going to fall, and that's all there is to it."

He lifted himself up on to the window-sill, and then lowered himself feet-first down through the open casement until his feet had reached the ledge. "It's okay," he said. "The ledge is pretty wide. Three inches, at least. Let's have Susie next, then Kathy. Daniel, you can bring up the rear. Catch anybody if they look like they're dropping off."

"Are you kidding?" asked Daniel.

"Who's kidding?"

Daniel leaned over beside Susie, and said quietly, "We're going to try to get away by climbing out of this window and up on to the roof. It's going to be scary, okay? But Kathy and I are going to be right behind you all the time, and all I want you to do is hold on tight and do everything that Rick tells you to do."

Susie nodded. There was a sparkle in her eyes that looked

suspiciously like tears. Daniel hugged her close, then lifted her up, and helped her to scramble over the window-sill, down through the open window, and on to the narrow ledge. Rick held her close to him, and showed her how to hold on.

"You don't have to look down if you don't want to," said Rick. "But if you do, just think of it as Toytown. Nothing to get alarmed about."

Kathy climbed out next, then Daniel. Now they were standing in a line, their heads, with the exception of Susie's, still up inside the open window. They would have to edge their way sideways to the left, ducking their heads under the metal supporting arm which kept the window open, and then cross three feet of open space before they reached the decorative concrete moldings on the corner.

The wind gusted and moaned, and Daniel felt as if it were going to suck him off the side of the building. He had only glanced down once, at the beetling traffic and the crowds of tiny pedestrians, and in that one downward glance, he had felt as if his entire psyche had dropped three hundred feet to the sidewalk and vanished through the concrete into a strange purgatory of sewers and conduits and cables.

Rick shouted at them, "Take one sideways step at a time. Move one foot and then slide the other foot along to join it. Don't try to move both feet at once. You get me? Okay, let's go."

Rick ducked under the window-bar, and started making his way to the corner. Susie looked back at Daniel, her eyes wide, but Daniel managed to grin at her and say, "Go on. You're going to be fine."

Kathy, under her breath, said something that sounded like a private prayer. But then she turned around to Daniel, and kissed him quickly, and said, "Let's go. Who's afraid of a little height?"

It took them almost five minutes to edge their way to the acanthus leaves on the corner. It was windier here: unexpected blasts of chilly air kept moaning around the building from the north-west front, and they all had to grip the concrete tightly.

Rick arched his head back and looked up towards the building's roof. "It's only two stories. If you had to climb this molding from ground-level upwards, you'd be able to go running up there like a monkey up a coconut tree. Come on, let's get going before they find out where we've gone."

Inch by inch, gingerly clutching at each concrete leaf, Rick climbed up the corner of the building to the level of the next story. Susie came carefully up behind him. Kathy was more hesitant, but occasionally Rick would look down and tell her, "Put your hand there, on that leaf there. That's right. Now your foot there. And up. That's terrific."

Another ten minutes went by before Rick finally managed to reach the curled-over leaves of the top parapet. He edged himself up, and at last managed to swing himself over the parapet on to the building's roof. "Be careful of that corner molding. I felt it shift a little. It's probably safe, but don't risk putting your full weight on it."

He reached down and helped Susie to climb up the last two feet, then held out his hand for Kathy. As Kathy was climbing up, she suddenly lost her foothold, and her feet scrabbled desperately at the building's concrete face. She gasped, and then drew her breath in with a sound like a bellows. She was too frightened to scream. Daniel reached up and managed to hold her left foot. "Stop kicking!" he shouted. "Kathy, *stop kicking*! There's a foothold here!"

She jabbed her foot towards the top of one of the concrete leaves, and at last found somewhere to lodge her toe. Then she managed to climb up the last three feet to the roof, shaking violently.

Daniel glanced down again. The sidewalk seemed even further away than twelve stories. He felt as if he were on top of a dizzying mountain, and that the world had shrunk so far away that it had completely lost any reality. He grasped the last corner molding, and pulled himself up; but as he did so, there was a grating noise, and a shower of mortar, and suddenly the molding toppled off the side of the building and fell towards the ground.

Daniel almost went with it. But Rick had snatched his sleeve to steady him; and with a last panting scramble, Daniel swung himself up and over the parapet. He looked down and saw the concrete molding dwindle and dwindle and dwindle, and at last hit the sidewalk below like a bomb. Pedestrians scattered in all directions, and several cars swerved, but nobody was hit.

"We'd better move," said Rick. "It won't be long before somebody starts asking where that lump of stone came from."

"But how are we going to get out of here?" asked Kathy. "They're bound to search the building when they find out we're gone; and all the entrances are guarded."

"We *don't* get out," said Daniel.

"You got an idea?" asked Rick.

"The first thing they'll be expecting us to do is make a run for it; and of course they'll be waiting for us. So what we have to do is stay in the building. The best place is probably the basement. There'll be plenty of places to hide down there, and we won't be too far from the exits when we feel we're ready to make our break."

"Sounds like some sort of sense to me," said Kathy.

"It doesn't sound very *heroic*," said Rick.

"You want heroic, you make a dash for the entrance and see how far you get," said Daniel.

"Okay," said Rick, dubiously. "We'd better find ourselves an elevator. Let's just hope the door to the roof isn't locked."

They heard sirens in the street below: the Washington Fire Department, investigating the falling molding. Kathy said, "Let's move it. *Anywhere's* got to be safer than here."

THIRTY-SIX

Kama had intended that morning to fly to New York to talk to Serge Gaponenko at the United Nations. But Gaponenko had been called back to Moscow for an important briefing, and so Kama had decided instead to call on Nikolai Nekrasov at Pennsylvania Avenue, to see if it wasn't time for him to beard the mangy old lion in his den.

Kama was still furious that Ikon had outwitted him; he had badly underestimated the old man's ruthlessness. His ears still went hot when he thought about how he had offered Ikon the job of a harmless "figurehead" when all the time Ikon had already destroyed all the evidence that would have halted the RINC talks. How Ikon must have been laughing at him!

Now, to cap everything, his limousine was stuck in a gridlock traffic-jam on E Street, and the car's air-conditioning was faltering. He sweated and ground his teeth, and every now and then he punched one hand into the palm of the other as if he were relishing the prospect of hitting that complacent Nikolai Nekrasov right where it would hurt him the most.

In his darkened room on Pennsylvania Avenue, however, Nikolai Nekrasov was enjoying his breakfast. Swathed in a silk smoking-robe patterned with dragons which had been given to him by Chai Zemin, the Chinese Ambassador to the Autonomous

Capitalist Oblast of America, he was spreading Mexican honey
on to thick slices of whole wheat bread, and drinking lemon tea
from a Russian glass.

Titus sat on the opposite side of the room, stiff as a tailor's
dummy. Nadine sat a little way away from him, as chic as ever,
her hair drawn back, watching this first encounter between the
two most important men in her life with a mixture of pride and
deep apprehension. They were both fierce-willed, both uncompromising; and while Nikolai Nekrasov felt that his administration of America was both rightful and historic, Titus saw him
as a usurper, and a bitter enemy. More so because Nikolai
Nekrasov had secretly controlled Titus' life and his destiny for
more than twenty years, and Titus had only just found out about
it.

"This honey is very good," said Ikon. "Are you sure you
won't join me for breakfast?"

Titus didn't answer.

"I have always believed in eating a slow and satisfying
breakfast," Ikon went on, unperturbed. "After that, there is
nothing that the day can bring that cannot be dealt with calmly
and effectively."

"You know that I wasn't particularly anxious to meet you,"
said Titus. His voice was tight and chill.

"Well, that is only natural," said Ikon. "It must have been
greatly disturbing for you to discover that so much of what you
have been accomplishing was for other ends entirely."

"I don't know how the hell you managed to get away with
this for so long."

Ikon raised his shaggy eyebrows, and smiled. "It was a
question of preserving that valuable ideal known as 'the American Way.' In the Kremlin, very few of my colleagues actually
understand what 'the American Way' means, and how strongly it
motivates the American people. But, I took pains to understand
it, and to keep it as the central core of my administration.
Slowly, over the years, I have tried to alter your national concept
of 'the American Way,' so that in a comparatively short time
from now, international socialism and 'the American Way' will
be seen to be almost indistinguishable."

Titus was silent for a very long moment. Then he said, "I see it as nothing more than treachery, subversion, betrayal, and criminal activity."

Ikon nodded. "I thought you would."

THIRTY-SEVEN

At that second, Daniel, Susie, Rick and Kathy had reached the basement. The door to the roof had been locked from inside with a single bolt, but between them Daniel and Rick had been able to kick it free: then they had quickly run down two flights of stairs to the eleventh-floor elevator. They had been obliged to wait while it climbed slowly up to them from 5, stopping at almost every floor, but at last it had arrived and it had been empty. They had pressed the button for LG, and prayed that it wouldn't stop on the way down.

Down on the basement level, there was a corridor of white-washed brick with three doors in it. The first door led to the boiler-room; the second to the broom cupboard. The third door was fastened with a padlock.

"What do we do now?" asked Kathy.

Rick smiled. "It's very easy. All padlocks are susceptible to being picked, and that's another small talent of mine. I used to work for a locksmith on Pico Boulevard: keys cut, cars broken into, ladies rescued from lavatories. All part of a day's work."

In the broom cupboard, Rick found a cardboard box of rubbish, which included paper-clips from the upstairs offices. Gingerly favoring his cut hands, he twisted one of the paper-clips around, and inserted it into the padlock. They watched and waited in tense silence while he attempted to release the levers.

"I don't think this particular padlock is going to prove susceptible," said Kathy.

"Patience," Rick told her.

They waited five more minutes. Rick's forehead was crowned in sweat, and his tongue was jammed between his teeth in concentration. Still the padlock refused to open.

"The elevator's coming down again," said Susie. "Look, the light's gone green."

"I think you'd better get that door open," said Kathy.

"*Patience*, for Christ's sake," said Rick.

Daniel said, "Here, let me try it."

"What do *you* know about picking locks?"

"Will you let me do it? I couldn't do any worse than you."

Rick stood up straight, and then handed the paper-clip to Daniel. "A paper-clip isn't strong enough. I need a sharp metal lock-pick, or something like it."

Daniel took the padlock in his hand. It was warm and sweaty from Rick's attempts to open it. He thrust the paper-clip straight into the keyhole, jiggled it violently, and said, "Open up, will you. Just for God's sake, open up."

Rick said, "He's *talking* to it, would you believe this?"

There was a sharp springing noise and the padlock opened. Daniel unhooked it from the hasp, and threw it at Rick with an expression of mock-professional nonchalance, and then laughed.

"You did it, you bastard!"

Daniel put his hand over his mouth, and then let out a breath. "I never did that before in my life, do you know that?"

They could hear the elevator descending towards the basement. The cables were rattling inside the shaft. Quickly, they opened the basement door, stepped inside, and found themselves in a huge darkened storage-room.

"The light, for God's sake," said Daniel.

Rick found the switch and turned it on. Kathy quietly closed the door behind them, and then ushered Susie off to the side.

The storage-room smelled very dry and cool, as if it was being kept at a regulated temperature. There was another smell, too: a faintly nutty odor which reminded Daniel of something he couldn't quite place. One wall of the room was stacked high with small wooden crates, each bearing a stencil of the eagle-and-sickle symbol, and a legend in Russian, including the code RPG7V. Rick immediately walked across to the crates, and sniffed at them. Then he scouted around the basement until he found a screwdriver.

"If these boxes contain what I think they do . . ." he said, and started prizing off one of the lids. There was a splintering sound, and a pop of nails, and the lid came up, and dropped to the floor. There was sawdust packing inside, and nestling in the sawdust packing were six four-inch high-explosive rockets.

"Are those *bombs*?" asked Kathy.

Rick picked one up and turned it over. "Rocket bombs. Presumably they keep them here as siege supplies, in case anything goes wrong, and the building gets attacked. Most of the major embassies have arsenals of one kind or another, even if it's only a couple of machine-guns."

"Well, for God's sake be careful with it," said Kathy.

"It won't go off until it's triggered," Rick told her, putting it back in the crate. "It has an electric fuse which detonates it automatically after it's been fired. It's usually launched from an RPG7, that's a kind of one-man rocket gun. The Russians used to dish them out to guerrilla organizations, like the PLO, and the IRA. They even sent some to the Weathermen, but I think they were seized by the U.S. Coastguard."

"There must be at least a couple of *thousand* of them here," said Daniel. "There isn't any way to trigger them without a launcher, is there?"

"Well, sure, you could—" Rick started but then he raised his hands in warning. "Oh, no. You're not thinking what I *think* you're thinking, are you? You mean you want to—"

"Why not? We could bring down the whole headquarters of the Autonomous Capitalist Oblast of America, all at once. And presumably Ikon's here, too."

Rick looked at Kathy. "You understand what this man's saying?"

"Sure, I understand."

Rick looked back at Daniel. "You know something?" he said. "You're crazier than I thought. If we set this little stack of goodies off, what are *we* going to do? How the hell are *we* going to get out of here?''

"You fix a way of setting it all off; I'll think about how we escape," said Daniel.

Rick wiped his hands on his jeans. The blood from his two knife-wounds had dried into black stigmata. "All right," he said, resignedly. "I'll do my best."

It took Rick nearly an hour to set up a timing-device. He used Daniel's wristwatch, and connected it to a second light-switch at the far end of the store-room, so that when the hands of the watch reached a pre-selected time, the full 120-volt main current would run into the electric timing device of one of the RPG7 rocket bombs. He was proud of his handiwork when he was finished, although he was sweating from concentration and starry-eyed from connecting tiny pieces of wire from the watch to the light-switch.

"I hope you've thought of a way to get out of here," he said, wiping his forehead on his sleeve. "I don't intend to stay around when this lot goes up in the air."

Daniel said, "I think the riskiest way is going to be the best. I think we should set the timing-device for no more than three minutes, then simply take the elevator to the lobby, and attempt to walk straight out of the front door. When these bombs go off, nobody will worry what we're doing."

"You hope," said Rick.

"I can *hope*, can't I?" retorted Daniel.

Kathy ventured, "If we're going to do it, we might as well do it. Rick—you set the timing device. We'll call the elevator and make sure we keep it here until it's time to leave."

Cautiously, they opened the storage-room door again, and emerged into the whitewashed corridor. Susie pressed the button for the elevator, and they heard it clank and whine and start on its journey downwards.

"Are you ready yet?" Daniel called to Rick. "The elevator's almost here."

"I'm coming! We've got three minutes dead!"

Rick came running out of the storage-room just as the elevator doors opened. To their mutual surprise, there was a Soviet security guard standing inside.

"I want your hands up!" he demanded, unbuttoning his holster. But Rick was too quick for him. With a flying drop-kick that he had learned for his stunt parts in *Kung-Fu*, he belted the guard under the chin with his sneakers, and both of them crashed to the floor of the elevator in a tangled heap.

Daniel dragged the stunned security guard out into the corridor, and then all of them crowded into the elevator and pressed the button for G. The elevator doors closed, hesitated, opened again, and then eventually closed again. They stood staring at each other in total silence as the elevator rose to the first floor, and then opened.

The lobby was busy with security-guards and diplomats and messengers. It was a high-vaulted room, clad in mottled gray marble, with a huge chandelier suspended from the center of the ceiling in the grandiose style of the Hotel Moscow. Telephones rang, feet clattered, and there was a buzz of conversation.

"Come on," said Daniel. "All we have to do is look natural."

"*Natural?*" queried Rick, looking around at all the Soviet diplomats and office-workers in their tight dark suits and their polished black shoes.

They crossed the lobby without being challenged, and pushed their way through the revolving-doors. Now they were out on the steps that led down to the sidewalk, and sunshine, and freedom. Susie gave a little childish whimper of tension.

"We've made it," said Rick. "Would you believe it—we've made it."

At that moment, two uniformed security guards stepped out in front of them. Out here on the street, they wore no badges, and carried their guns under their coats, but from the Cossack stolidity of their faces, and the way in which their hands were held in their pockets, it was obvious that they would have no compunction about shooting to kill.

"You will please return to the building," said one of the guards.

They stopped where they were. Rick started to raise his hands.

"You will not put up your hands. You will do nothing more than turn around and re-enter the building."

Daniel reached out and held Susie's hand. "Mister," he said,

"I've got a little girl here. She's only seven. Have a heart, will you, let her go? She's not going to do *you* any harm."

Rick glanced at Daniel and all over his face was written the muscle-tightening message: *Supposing the timing-device hasn't worked. Supposing the rockets don't explode.*

One of the guards said to the other, "Call Comrade Skellett. These are the prisoners who escaped from the 10th floor. Tell him to come down here urgently."

Then the guard turned to Daniel, and said, "The girl must remain here until your business with Comrade Skellett is completely settled. Those are my instructions."

"What did you say?" asked Daniel.

The guard came up one step nearer, his coat held out threateningly. "I said—"

But his words were totally obliterated in the most colossal explosion that Daniel had ever heard. The marble-clad steps beneath their feet jumped into the air two or three feet, and threw all of them out across the sidewalk like tenpins, scratched and bruised and breathless and tumbling over and over as if they would never stop.

There was a second explosion, then a third. Daniel, dazed, picked himself out of the roadway, and looked around for Susie. To his relief, she was only a few yards away, being helped out of the gutter by an elderly man. Kathy too was safe, and so was Rick, although Rick's face was badly gashed.

A fourth explosion shook Pennsylvania Avenue, and huge chunks of masonry began to tumble from the Ikon building as if it was an erupting volcano. Showers of glass and twisted aluminum window-frames clattered and sparkled down on all sides. Daniel picked up Susie in his arms and ran across the street, through the halted traffic, and as far away from the building as he could.

What happened next was spectacular: the public fall of a secret empire.

The first floor of the building collapsed into the basement, in a rolling billow of dust and smoke. Then, floor by floor, the entire building dropped in on itself, with a rending, thundering, tearing noise that made any kind of conversation inaudible, any kind of sensible thought impossible. Massive steel girders clanged down like the bells of doom, one on top of the other, and all the time there was a steady drumroll of breaking concrete, collapsing floors, tearing pipework, falling staircases. Soon it was impossible to see where the building had been: there was nothing but a cloud of dust, rising hundreds of feet into the misty morning sky, and a persistent drizzle of grit.

It took the building more than ten minutes to fall, although most of its collapse was obscured from sight by dust. By the time the roof had fallen in, and the last showers of glass had come down, the emergency services had already arrived, and Pennsylvania Avenue was crowded with fire-trucks, ambulances, and police cars. Most of them were parked on the grass opposite the Post Office Department, some were parked on the sidewalks by the Internal Revenue Service building.

Skellett had died on his way down to the lobby in the elevator. He had reached the fifth floor when the rockets exploded, and the building started to collapse. The elevator shaft had gradually been compressed between two main structural beams, squashing the elevator sideways, and squashing Skellett with it. He had felt a hideous pressure on his ribcage, and on his skull, an intolerable compression that had made him want to scream out loud, if there had been any way of drawing breath to scream.

Ikon had died even before the ceiling came down, of a massive coronary. He had cried out, *"No!"* just as Titus had cried out in denial of Nadine's truth the previous night, and then he had fallen across his breakfast table, his hand resting on a thickly-honeyed piece of bread.

Titus and Nadine, terrified, had gotten up from their seats. Nadine had said. "My God, it's an earthquake! The building's coming down!"

But Titus had turned back to her almost gleefully, and shouted, "Earthquake, nothing! Some son-of-a-bitch has blown the whole damn thing up!"

Then the ceiling came down, tons of masonry and steel and concrete, and both Titus and Nadine had been consumed. They were found later by firemen—crushed but still holding hands.

Kama was saved by the traffic jam on E Street. His limousine reached the intersection of E Street and 14th Street just as the Ikon building blew up, and he immediately ordered his driver to turn around. Through the tinted rear window, he saw dust and debris rising into the air, and knew that it had to be the headquarters of the Autonomous Capitalist Oblast of America.

If Ikon had been there when the building blew up, then the strong possibility was that ACOA would soon be his.

"Where to, sir?" his driver asked him.

"Nowhere in particular. Don't worry. Tomorrow, we'll decide where to go next."

THIRTY-EIGHT

Daniel opened his eyes and looked up at the ceiling. It was six-thirty in the morning, and the Arizona sun was already in bright bands through the drapes. He yawned, and rubbed his face, and then sat up.

Cara was still dreaming. He looked at her russet curls, at her pale bare back, at the flared curve of her bottom. He knew she was dreaming because she was murmuring to herself. He couldn't guess what she was dreaming about, though. She was one of those ladies with secrets.

He climbed out of bed. It was four days since he and Susie had returned to Apache Junction; and they were settled now. Daniel was cooking up bacon and eggs as usual, Susie was back in school.

The pleasantest surprise had been to find that Cara was waiting for him when he returned; that she had hitch-hiked as far west as Havasu City, and then decided to turn around and come back. "Don't call it love," she had told him. "But I do want to stay."

Kathy Forbes had gone back to the *Flag* to begin work on a multi-part exposé of what she had learned and experienced; a feature which her editor would eventually kill. "Nobody's going to believe this," he would tell her, kindly. "If it's true, and

Ikon's dead, then it doesn't matter. If it *isn't* true, it doesn't matter, either. People don't want to hear about this kind of thing. I'm in the business of selling newspapers, not scaring people half to death.''

Rick Terroni had returned to Hollywood, and to the half-world of Free Columbia. He would die a year later in a traffic accident on the Ventura Freeway. The death would be reported in *Variety* in a scant two lines.

Daniel picked his jeans up off the floor and wrestled his way into them. He thought of Willy Monahan, and what Willy would have said if he had ever found out what had happened. Perhaps Willy knew anyway, somewhere in Nirvana. Daniel had tried calling Williams AFB for news of Willy's funeral, but he had repeatedly been met with a courteous "Sorry, that's family information. We're not permitted to release it.''

He looked out of the window as he buttoned up his plaid Western shirt. He thought: at least America's free again. A country that never even knew it was conquered. He tucked in his shirt, turned around, and went down to the kitchen to start breakfast.

What he had failed to see when he looked out across Apache Junction was the dark-blue rented Pontiac with the Texas plates parked next to Feeley's Drugs. Inside it, listening to the radio with the patience of a man who has waited for hours, for days, for whole years for what he is after, even just clean-up tasks, sat Henry Friend.

The announcer said, "Good morning, folks. It's going to be another hot one today.''